Beyond That, the Sea

BEYOND THAT, THE SEA

LAURA SPENCE-ASH

THORNDIKE PRESS
A part of Gale, a Cengage Company

Copyright © 2023 by Laura Spence-Ash.
Thorndike Press, a part of Gale, a Cengage Company.

ALL RIGHTS RESERVED

Thorndike Press® Large Print Core.
The text of this Large Print edition is unabridged.
Other aspects of the book may vary from the original edition.
Set in 16 pt. Plantin.

LIBRARY OF CONGRESS CIP DATA ON FILE.
CATALOGUING IN PUBLICATION FOR THIS BOOK
IS AVAILABLE FROM THE LIBRARY OF CONGRESS.

ISBN-13: 979-8-88578-712-3 (hardcover alk. paper).

Published in 2023 by arrangement with Celadon Books.

Printed in Mexico
Print Number: 1   Print Year: 2023

For M and D

The present's hardly there; the future doesn't exist. Only love matters in the bits and pieces of a person's life.

— WILLIAM TREVOR, *Two Lives*

In the beginning, there was the nursery, with windows opening on to a garden, and beyond that the sea.

— VIRGINIA WOOLF, *The Waves*

CONTENTS

CONTENTS

■ ■ ■ ■

PROLOGUE:
OCTOBER 1963

■ ■ ■ ■

BEATRIX

Back then, Beatrix liked to sit next to Mr. G when he rowed them all to the mainland. She would watch the town come into focus, the buildings growing larger, the white steeple in relief against the bluest sky. This was in Maine, where the family went each summer, and it was during the war, although that was hard to remember when they were there. Mrs. G often wore a pink or yellow sundress, her pearls tight round her neck, and she squawked about getting wet as William and Gerald splashed each other with water. Mr. G would roll his eyes and half-heartedly tell the boys to stop, his glasses spotted with sea salt, his tanned arms moving the oars forward and back in a smooth rhythm. When they got close, he would hand Beatrix an oar, and they would row, together, to shore.

Once a year, they ate at the small restaurant in town that was located at the end of the dock. They sat at the same table every year, a corner table with five seats facing the water. This way, Mrs. G said, they could all watch the sunset sky change over the island, their island, the sharp spikes of the evergreens set off by the pink and orange streaks, before the trees lost their edges as the sky grew dark. Not once, in the years that Beatrix was there, did the weather on this night disappoint. She was struck, whenever she saw the island from the mainland, by how different it was when seen from afar. It was beautiful, a blurry patch of green, caught up between the ocean and the sky. It was also so small that she could hold it in the palm of her hand. When they were on the island, though, she was the one who was small; it was her whole world. It was as though nowhere else existed.

They ordered clam chowder and corn on the cob and lobster. Baked potatoes still in their tinfoil wrappers, the heat escaping from a vertical slice across the top. The first summer Beatrix was there, the boys started to crack open the hard, red shells as soon as the plates were in front of them. Gerald was so excited that he was standing rather than sitting, and William was the first to find some meat, tipping his head back to catch the drips of butter. Beatrix slowly tied her bib, watching, and then took a swallow of water. Mr. G nodded at Mrs. G, who was seated next to her, and she patted her on the leg before she set to work on her lobster, pausing to let her see exactly what she was doing, so that she could do the same.

But that was all in the past. Tonight, alone in this seaside restaurant, Beatrix orders the lobster as the waitress lights the votive candle on the table. When the lobster arrives, she ties the bib around her neck, watching her reflection in the dark window. In August, she turned thirty-four. Twenty years have gone by. She often finds it hard to reconcile the girl she was then with the adult she is now. They seem like two separate people. For so many years she has tried to forget. She smells the cuff of her jacket; the ocean has nestled into her clothes. She can hear the waves crashing onto the shore. This place — a town on the Firth of Forth, just outside Edinburgh — is flat, the wind rough. Islands and rocky outcroppings are scattered offshore. There's a wildness to it that reminds her of Maine. If she closes her eyes, it's almost as though she's there.

She'd come back from her trip to America in early September and thrown herself into work. The new school year started in a blur, someone always needing something from her, days when she might as well have slept in her office she spent so little time in her flat. In October, when she could finally slow down, she realized she felt adrift. Unmoored. Seeing the Gregorys in America, standing with them in the graveyard, had brought everything back — the five years that she spent there, the family she called her own for that briefest of moments. The grief at losing them. The grief she had worked so hard to bury. There she was, back in that familiar house, in that kitchen that smelled of lemon and cinnamon and butter, feeling Mrs. G's arms wrapped around her neck, her whispers in her ear. Once again she hadn't wanted to leave, and once again she had. She had lost them all over again.

Mum was the one who suggested that she might take a little holiday, to break up her routine, to try something new. Maybe that would help. She recommended this town because she had come here often as a small girl, and she'd loved it. She said something about the beaches and the birds, the relaxing train ride from London. It was fine, Beatrix supposed, although probably not the quaint Victorian town that her mother had known. She wondered whether her mother would have even seen the connection to Maine. She'd never been, after all. Beatrix

16

wouldn't have thought of it herself.

She eats some lobster but it turns out that most of the fun was in doing it together. She feels a fool, wrestling with it alone, in this tired and empty dining room. It makes her feel worse. She pushes the plate away and orders a coffee. The beam from the lighthouse is now visible, sweeping regularly across the black sea. There were nights when she and Gerald and William would sleep in tents in the woods, never far from the house, but they felt completely on their own, as though they were stranded on an island, the only ones to survive. The darkness was almost solid. They'd use their flashlights to walk down to the water and sit on one of the big rocks, shining the beams this way and that, then turn off the lights to absorb the black night, the whole world of stars shining down on the sea. She was happiest when she sat in the middle, when she could feel them on either side.

Dinner in town was always capped off by a chocolate layer cake, made by Mrs. G and brought over earlier in the day, with cold scoops of peppermint ice cream. Three fat candles to be blown out: one for William, one for Gerald, and one for Beatrix. Their names in fanciful blue script on the vanilla icing. *My August birthday children,* Mrs. G said. *Another year gone by.* The whole restaurant would sing "Happy Birthday" when the lit cake was carried out of the kitchen. The three of them stood and bent toward the cake in the center of the table, Mrs. G holding Beatrix's hair back from the flames. The restaurant was dark by then, the sun having set, and their faces were lit by the candlelight. Gerald, with his red hair and freckles, his infectious smile. William, his curly hair bleached blond by the sun, his smile hidden from his face. What did they see when they looked at her? She doesn't know, except that she imagines her face must have reflected the joy she felt. When she thinks of the three of them, together, she remembers this, the moment before the candles were blown out, as they all drew in their breaths, deciding what to wish for, and caught one another's eyes.

That final summer, her wish was to stay. To be with them all, forever. She leans forward now, blows out the flame in the votive, and closes her eyes.

■ ■ ■ ■

PART ONE:
1940–1945

■ ■ ■ ■

REGINALD

That night, Reginald tells the fellows in the local pub how proud he is. He recounts the story of Beatrix leaving to everyone who comes in, telling the story again and again. They ask questions, they want to know the details. The ones whose children left before know this story, or a version of this story, already. How the morning was hot and sticky. How they stood in the ballroom at the Grosvenor Hotel and how he'd knelt on one knee when it had been time to go. How Beatrix had nodded at his last words, her face tilted to his, her chest held high. How she had been resolute and hadn't cried, even though he could see the tears forming.

But a day later, he cannot quite remember what he said to her while he was kneeling on the floor. He worries, privately, that he forgot to say what was most important. But he tells everyone in the pub that night what a trooper she'd been. My brave eleven-year-old girl. He makes up the words that they said to each other. And he doesn't explain that while he and Millie held it together for as long as possible, they turned away from Beatrix and moved through the crowds before he was truly ready to do so. He doesn't imagine that he would ever be ready to leave.

In the dream he has again and again, he walks into the ocean, fully dressed, the wet fabric a weight. He pushes the waves aside as he goes deeper and finds himself back in that ballroom, leaving as others are arriving, his shoulders brushing against them, trying not to stare at the faces of the incoming parents, knowing that his eyes must mirror theirs, shocked to find themselves in this place, having made this decision, to send their children far away. Alone, across the sea. Only outside, on the street by the Grosvenor, the air thick, the gray clouds pushing down, did Millie begin to cry, pleading with him to go back and get their girl. He'd held her hand and pulled her away. In the dream he holds out his hands, reaching, wishing he could pick up the ship she's now on and turn it around. Wishing he could reverse its course. He extends his arms again, trying to touch the land where she will now live.

But the story that he tells the boys is only

half the truth. Beatrix was crying, holding on to him, her arms wrapped around his waist. She blamed Millie for sending her away, and she refused to say goodbye to her, was angry with her for the twenty-four hours between the time they told her and the moment she left. Reginald, in fact, was the one to insist she leave, knowing that the bombs were coming closer and closer, that there was no possible way to keep her, or any of them, safe. His older brother fought in the last war, and so he knew what was coming. That war cast a long shadow over his childhood. It was how he had learned the edges of fear. He and Millie were faced with an impossible choice. Better that she go to America, he thought, where the fingers of war were less likely to touch her. But he never told her that he'd forced Millie's hand. He let her believe it was Millie's choice.

MILLIE

Millie can't rid herself of the fury. There was Beatrix's anger at her, for forcing her to go, and Millie's own at Reg, for not wavering when she pleaded. *Let me go with her,* she said. And then, later, in the middle of the night, neither of them sleeping, nor touching, staring up at the dark ceiling: *Let's just keep her here. We've got the shelter and the Underground. We can go to my parents in the country. I can keep her safe,* she whispered again and again. *I will keep her safe.* But Reg's mind was made up.

She has never thought of herself as an angry person. Emotional, yes. Stubborn, absolutely. But now she is overflowing with sorrow and rage. She can't imagine a time when she will forgive Reg. She knows she will never forgive herself. Over and over she revisits the ballroom, the final moments, the warmth of her daughter's cheek.

She pinned the label the man handed her

onto Beatrix's chest. It was a hot day but Millie's hands were icy cold and so she rubbed them together, again and again, before tucking one inside the top of Beatrix's dress to guide the pin in and out. The label had a long number on it, in addition to the name, and Millie memorized the number, thinking she would need to know it forever. She thought that it might be the only way she could locate her girl. On the way home from the ballroom, she became frantic when she could no longer be sure whether the final number was a three or a six.

The night before, Millie had washed and cut Beatrix's hair in the small kitchen, a towel underfoot. Beatrix was in her underwear. Millie brushed the wet hair out before cutting, marveling that the thick strands almost reached Beatrix's waist. It was then, when Millie turned Beatrix around to comb out the front, that she realized that her breasts were beginning to bud and that when she saw her again, she would have changed. She would no longer be a girl. And there was that fury again, but it was in her hands now, so without thinking, she chopped off her daughter's hair, cutting it just below the chin, locks of hair falling to the floor, the scissors slicing, the white towel turning brown, Beatrix crying. She cut the thick, dark bangs in a severe line across the middle of her forehead. It was the haircut she had given her, every three weeks, when she was a little girl.

Now she can no longer sleep. She lies in Beatrix's bed, curling her body into a ball. She tries to imagine where her girl is, in the middle of the Atlantic. Is she hungry? Is she alone? How frightened she must be by the deep water that wraps itself around the ship. The rocking waves. That vast sea. Millie smells a curl of the hair, tucked into a small glassine envelope, hidden in the middle of her book.

BEATRIX

Beatrix hates her new haircut. She looks like a child. She reaches for her hair only to find her neck. All the girls in the cabin share a small handheld mirror that one of the girls brought in her trunk. Beatrix pushes her bangs off her forehead, using water and spit, and curses her mother out loud, to the delight of the youngest girls.

The days are full. They dress, helping one another to fasten the cork life preservers, and go to breakfast, where they're allowed to eat chocolate ice cream. They run, in a pack, from one end of the ship to the other, Beatrix always holding tight to the rails, staying to the inside when possible. The ship rarely follows a straight course, weaving its way through the silver icebergs that glitter in the sun. There's also a pack of boys, but they're wilder than the girls, and Beatrix mostly avoids them. There are sugar cookies bigger than their hands for tea. The vomiting isn't as much now. Those first days, they were all throwing up in the small sinks, in the garbage, in coffee cans. Sometimes at night when Beatrix can't sleep, when the littlest one is sniffling in the bed beneath her, she goes to the deck to look at the stars. She wraps herself in her blanket and lies down on a deck chair, far from the edge. It is cold and dark and yet perhaps it is one of the most beautiful things she has ever seen. She could not imagine a sky so full, so alive. Never before had she realized the depth of the sky. The air is clean. She wonders whether they will ever get to America. They feel suspended here, even as the ship moves forward. They ask one another what will happen if the war ends while they're at sea. Will they turn around and go back? How will their parents know?

At the beginning, Beatrix had been scared. The darkened train filled with children. The escort singing "There'll Always Be an England" as she waved a small British flag. The rows of cots in the fish warehouse in Liverpool. The enormous ship covered by a black tarp. The gangway swaying with every step. They were all quiet and frightened, not sure whom to trust. Almost all the girls were crying. Beatrix refused. Dad had said she must be strong.

It has only been days, but when Beatrix thinks back to the leaving, she already only has shards. She sees herself sitting cross-legged on the floor of her bedroom, refusing to help, watching as her mother packs her small brown suitcase. Dresses folded in thirds, socks rolled into balls, and a fluttery, flowery scarf laid on top, a gift for the woman in America. Beatrix sees her father's hands, his wedding band loose on his finger, as he tucks a handful of photographs into a side pocket, as he pulls the straps to tighten around the case. The pink-and-blue floral hooked rug that was at her bedside forever, a stain on the corner that looked like a dog's head. The unfamiliar smell of pancakes, the sugar borrowed from the neighbors to make the last breakfast special.

One month before that, her mother had come home to find her, alone in the flat, sitting on the floor of the living room, playing solitaire, the gas mask covering her face. She'd begun wearing it whenever she was left alone. She hated the way it felt and the way it smelled, like tar on a summer road. The boys at school would wear them at recess, chasing one another round the playground, their oinking sounds muffled by the mask. But Beatrix knew that it could save her life. Her uncle had been burned in

29

the first war, rivers of darker pink flesh running up his arms. Her mother had dropped the groceries when she saw her, a precious egg cracking and breaking on the wood floor. She knows it was this moment that made her mother decide that Beatrix could not stay.

Already her memories of the ballroom are fading. There are only snippets, late at night. The large letters of the alphabet posted around the room. A dark balcony full of adults peering down and waving. A woman sobbing. Strange American accents.

The backs of her parents, walking away. Her father's hand on her mother's shoulder. A run in her mother's stocking.

BEATRIX

On the dock in Boston, Beatrix is alone. Everyone else has been picked up. It is already hot, even though it's early in the day, the moon etched in chalk on the pale blue sky. Beatrix is wearing her favorite dress, red wool with a white collar and piping at the cuffs. She picked it out carefully, remembering that her mother told her to look her best, but it is the wrong dress for the day, and sweat drips down her neck and back.

The woman who paired up the other children with their host families keeps checking her watch and looking at her clipboard. *The Gregorys,* she says again and again, her voice getting sharper each time. *That's the family name, is that right?* Beatrix nods. The sun moves higher, tucks behind a cloud, and Beatrix shifts her weight from one foot to the other. She touches the label that she has repinned every morning since she left London. The edges are beginning to fray.

Beatrix feels as though she left home years ago, as though the girl she was there is separate from the girl standing here. So much has transpired, although it has only been two weeks, and yet it seems like something out of a book, like it all must have happened to someone else. Docking in Canada and saying goodbye to most of her new friends. Another train and then a small ferry, rolling through the rough waves. Finally, calm water as they entered Boston Harbor. On a small island, three barefoot children on a dock, holding fishing rods, waving as the ferry passed. Welcome to America, Beatrix thought.

She looks down, making sure that her suitcase and gas mask are still at her side, and when she looks up, a boy is standing in front of her. It is almost as though she willed him to exist. He's taller than she is, with curly blond hair so long it's practically at his collar. He raises his arm to block the sun out of his eyes with his hand. This is William, she thinks, she knows. They'd had a letter, describing the house and the family, and Beatrix read it every night on the ship. She memorized sections. Gerald is the younger boy, just turned nine, and William is thirteen. *He's too smart for his own good,* Mrs. Gregory wrote. *Wants to be a baseball player when he grows up.* Beatrix thought he'd have brown hair. She didn't think he'd be so tall or that his eyes would be green. But, still, this must be him.

Beatrix, he says, and his voice is lower than she anticipated. He is almost smiling. She nods and then another boy runs up, his face flushed, his crooked smile wide, his red-gold hair shining in the sun. This is most certainly Gerald. *You're Beatrix, aren't you,* he says. *You must be, I just know it.* Yes, she says, smiling, at last, because his accent is funny and his freckles are everywhere and he's a wide-open American boy.

NANCY

After the dishes are done, Nancy prepares the batter for the morning muffins, combining the sugar and butter until they are one. The house is slowly quieting down. Ethan has retired to his study. William is in his room. Even Gerald, who's already had his bath and been put to bed but has run downstairs three times since then, seems to have settled. This is usually her favorite time of the day, when everything is peaceful, when she can be by herself, to bake, to read, to have a cup of tea. To breathe.

It's the girl's turn for a bath, though. At the dock, Nancy had been shocked by the look of her, with her skin so pale, dirty white socks disappearing into heavy boots, eyes black and watchful. What on earth had they signed on for? What must this be like for her? To be sent away from home, by yourself? Nancy wonders what kind of a parent could make this choice, although she knows she has no idea what it's like to live through a war. She doesn't think she could do it, though; she can't imagine putting William or Gerald on a ship by himself. And, Lord, what will happen if the United States enters this war. She prays each night that it won't happen or, if it does, that her boys will still be too young.

The batter ready for the morning, Nancy pulls out the box she'd stored in the back hall closet. She'd brought it over from her sister's house last week when they'd returned from Maine, and it's full of girl things: dolls, books, tea sets. Some of the items had belonged to Nancy as a child; others, like these fancy china dolls, had been her nieces'. Beatrix doesn't seem like a doll girl; Nancy hadn't been one, either. Nancy pulls each item out and sets it on the kitchen table. Her mother's miniature dolls, with their Victorian dresses. A cracked teacup that Nancy remembers as once being part of a set. The Katy Did books, which had been her favorites. They're old and worn, though, with pages no longer attached to the binding, and Nancy isn't sure they would appeal to Beatrix. Although, really, she has no idea what the girl is like. She packs up the box again and pushes it back into the closet. It all seems so childish for a person who has lived in war. Nancy has been haunted by the first letter from the parents: *In her room, we found a stash of newspaper articles about nerve gas. She had circled this line: "Victims will die within two minutes of exposure."*

Nancy walks noiselessly down the upstairs hall. The door to the spare room is opened a crack. The girl sits in the corner, her knees pulled up to her chest, talking to a framed photograph. *Dad,* she says, *I made it. I'm here.* Nancy backs against the wall, wiping her face with her apron.

BEATRIX

The claw-foot bathtub is set into an alcove, with three windows above, all of them facing the garden. It's night now, though, so it's dark and there's nothing to see, and Mrs. Gregory pulls the white shades down one at a time. The water pours into the tub, and she keeps putting her hand in the stream and adjusting the knobs. She picks up a towel and undoes it, shaking it out, then folds it in half, running her hand along the softness. Her large sapphire ring catches the light. Her lipstick is bright red and her teeth white as she bites down on her lower lip.

She is nothing like Beatrix's mother, who is tall and dark and slender. This woman is wide and smells of lemon. At the dock, she had run up after the boys and wrapped her arms around Beatrix, kissing her on one cheek and then the other. Beatrix had stood still as the woman had hugged her. She had unpinned the label and tucked it into her purse. *You don't need this anymore, dear,* she had said. *You're part of us now.*

Beatrix, she says, her hand in the warm water, *I don't know what to do here.* She looks at Beatrix, her eyes drawn together, and Beatrix can see Gerald's smile and William's frown. *Do you want me to help you, or would you prefer to do this on your own?* The lines on her face deepen and then she tucks Beatrix's hair back behind her ear, resting the weight of her thick hand on her shoulder. *You'll have to teach me how to be with a girl,* she says with a laugh and a sigh. *I've been surrounded by all these boys for so long.* She pauses and waits.

Beatrix doesn't respond. She doesn't really understand what the woman is asking, all she knows is that she doesn't want her to leave so she sheds her clothes until she is naked, standing in front of this strange woman, feeling the soft rug beneath her feet, a bit of a breeze coming in through the windows, the shades knocking against the frames. She climbs up on the footstool and steps into the hot water carefully, then, as she gets used to the temperature, she sits and lies down, everything but her head underwater. It feels marvelous. Mrs. Gregory lathers up a washcloth and lifts Beatrix's arm, gently scrubbing. Beatrix closes her eyes and almost falls asleep. She lifts her legs so they float.

Later, in the bed so high off the floor that she has to climb onto yet another footstool, Beatrix smells the lemon soap on each of her fingers.

BEATRIX

The stairs wrap around in a half circle as they descend, an entrance hall with a floor of white and black marble squares below. Beatrix descends slowly, her hand on the mahogany banister, her shoes quiet on the oriental runners that cover the stairs. Enormous oil portraits in gold frames line the walls of the stairs. This must be what Princess Margaret feels like each morning when she comes down for breakfast, Beatrix thinks. She almost laughs out loud. The house is awash in light. On the table in the entrance hall, a grand crystal vase is overflowing with pink and yellow flowers.

Beatrix can hear voices — it sounds like Mrs. Gregory and Gerald — but for this moment she stands alone in the entrance hall. The living room is down a few stairs to her right, and she feels quite sure that their entire flat could fit within that one room. Last night, Gerald had shown her a secret set of circular stairs hidden behind a bookcase that was filled with fake books. There's an entire third floor she hasn't even seen yet. She looks out at the garden. King, their German shepherd, is asleep on the patio, his head resting on his large paw. There are flower beds close to the house, a vegetable garden beyond, and then a green lawn that stretches out toward a row of pine trees in the far distance. Everything here is enormous. How far is it, she wonders, to the sea? Which direction is home?

ETHAN

Ethan sits in his study down the hall from the kitchen, the door almost shut, trying to prepare lesson plans for the first few days of school but listening instead to the noise coming from the kitchen. The girl has come downstairs for breakfast. He can hear the excitement in Nancy's voice, the way her pitch rises, and he knows she's filling a plate too full with eggs and bacon. Gerald is bouncing a rubber ball, over and over, and Ethan forces himself not to yell.

He hadn't wanted to take this girl in. There's the cost, for one thing. Nancy had dismissed his concerns with a wave of her hand. *What's one more small mouth to feed,* she said. *Honestly, Ethan. We all need to be doing our part.* But his other concern is almost as pressing: he doesn't know much about girls. He'd grown up — here, in this house — with no siblings. His father had chaired the math department at the Boys

School and, after Harvard, he'd returned here to work under his father and then, later, to take his place. He thinks about boys all day: how best to teach them; how to bring them up to be decent young men; how to reprimand them when they stray over the line. He has felt, since becoming a father, strangely less sure of himself. He had thought he would be the lead parent, the one who always knew what to do, the one the children would follow. But strategies that work in the classroom don't work at home. What works with Gerald doesn't seem to work with William. And they both gravitate toward Nancy, whose touch is often too gentle. It's messier at home, he's less in control, and more and more, he retreats to the comfort and solitude of his study. Still, he feels comfortable with boys, knows how to get them at ease, knows what to talk to them about. Except for Nancy and Mother and a cousin or two, his life has been filled with boys and men.

But he knows that Nancy sees this as her way of finally getting a girl. She'd been disappointed when William was born and then again with Gerald. They'd tried repeatedly but after the third miscarriage, the doctor had told her no more. She's never said anything — about the disappointment with having one boy and then another, about the miscarriages, about the doctor's orders — as she's always unfailingly positive. About everything, really. And that's what he had seen in her at the start. He'd hoped that her willingness to see the good would help draw him out of himself, help him become a better version of who he thinks he truly is.

There's a quiet knock on the door. *Yes,* he says, forcing his voice to be soft, knowing it's not Nancy or either of the boys. The girl pushes the door open but stands in the narrow hall. *Hello,* she says. *Sorry to bother you, sir.* She barely catches his eye before they both look away. *Mrs. Gregory asked if you could please come into the kitchen for breakfast.* Ethan nods, shuffling his papers. He should ask whether she slept all right, or whether there's anything she needs, but by the time he looks up, she has disappeared.

MILLIE

The telegram is tucked under the door, and Millie steps on it as she walks into the flat. BEATRIX ARRIVED SAFELY STOP A LOVELY GIRL STOP SETTLING IN NICELY STOP. She hasn't cried since the night Beatrix left but now, holding the telegram in her hand, Millie collapses onto the wood floor and lies on her side, tucking her knees up to her chin. The tears run down her face and pool onto the floor. There is relief but there is mostly regret. She should have told Beatrix that she wanted her to stay. She should have forced Reg to change his mind. The room darkens before she stands, to change out of her work clothes, to start dinner. Reg will be home soon. Every day he has asked, upon entering the flat in the evening, whether a telegram had arrived.

Tonight, though, he doesn't ask, even as she watches his hands thumb through the mail on the hall table. And so she doesn't

45

tell him, not yet. She hides the telegram, folded softly in quarters, in the zipped pocket of her handbag.

A week goes by and she reads the telegram again and again on her way to work and back home. The corners begin to tear. Newsprint from her fingers dirties the yellow paper. The block letters begin to fade. She's not sure, now, that she can show it to Reg. He'll suspect that she had it all along.

NANCY

On the first day of school, the sky blooms blue and wide. Nancy has made the children their lunch, packed into brown paper bags: hard-boiled eggs, tomato sandwiches, oatmeal raisin cookies. She takes their photo, on the back porch, before kissing William and Gerald on their foreheads and squeezing Beatrix on the shoulder. She knows she doesn't always like to be touched, but she can't help herself and wraps her arms around the girl's skinny body. Beatrix stiffens but then Nancy feels — to her surprise — a kiss brush across her cheek.

In the two weeks since Beatrix's been here, her face has filled out a bit but her eyes still watch in fear. She's unfailingly polite — always responding to a question or inquiry, helping out in the kitchen, keeping her room tidy — although she is never the first to talk. But she laughs at Gerald's antics and seems comfortable around Wil-

47

liam. Nancy's proud of her boys, at the way in which they've taken to the girl. *Have a good day,* Beatrix says. *Thank you for making my lunch.* Nancy boxes Gerald on the arm. *You could learn a thing or two from Beatrix's lovely manners,* she says. *Now off with you all.* She's anxious for them to leave, but she knows she will spend all day waiting for them to return.

GERALD

We'll all walk together to school, Mum, Gerald says, jumping off the porch steps onto the ground below. He loves imitating the way Beatrix talks. She sounds so smart all the time. So he calls Mother Mum, enters the room saying cheerio, and last night at dinner he claimed Father was making a bit of a kerfuffle over nothing. He knows it annoys William — another good reason to do it — but it also brings a shadow of a smile to Beatrix's face. *Don't you cross the street until she's inside,* Mother says again, and William nods, then gestures at Bea with his chin. So like Father, William is, that's what they all say. Gerald knows that means he's not.

The three of them walk along the path that cuts through the field behind the school. A desire line, Father calls it. Their very best way of getting from here to there. William is in front, leading the way, and

49

Gerald takes up the rear. The hair that had reached both of their collars is gone now, a visit to the barber the day before revealing pink, scratchy necks and glistening scalps. Gerald likes running his hand over the bristles. The sun is already warm. None of the leaves have begun to turn, and the field is an explosion of wildflowers. Gerald snaps a yellow flower off and then another and then a third, holding the flowers behind his back. At the door to the Lower School, they all stop, standing in a circle. Gerald gives Beatrix a quick hug around the waist. How thin she is. He can feel her ribs. *Top of the morning to ya,* he says, grinning, and he shoves the bouquet into her hands before he disappears through the heavy door. *Idiot,* Gerald hears William say. When he's sure they've continued on their way, he steps back out the door. He sees them stop by the Girls School, both looking at the ground, and then Beatrix enters the building, his flowers still clutched in her hand. Gerald watches William cross the street toward the Boys School. Once on the other side, right before he enters the building, William turns back just slightly, and Gerald knows he's checking to make sure that she made it inside. Gerald waves at him but William turns and walks inside.

Each student in Gerald's class is asked to write a letter to the teacher detailing the most exciting thing that happened to them over the summer. *Dear Mr. Thatcher,* Gerald writes, *Beatrix joined us from London to escape the bombs.* When he puts his pencil down, he notices that his palms are stained yellow from the pollen.

BEATRIX

The letters arrive, not predictably, but clustered. There are days when Beatrix arrives home from school to find two or three waiting for her on the kitchen table. Then there can be weeks with nothing. She never reads the letters there, in the kitchen, but she rubs the thin paper between her thumb and forefinger while she's eating her snack, amazed that she is touching something that her parents touched not so long ago. That it has somehow made it from there to here. In her room, later, with the door almost shut, Beatrix reads each letter again and again. The format is always the same: Mummy writes first, and Dad second, his words often crammed into smaller and smaller spaces, sometimes cascading up and down the sides, one word at a time. Dad's handwriting is hard to decipher; Mummy's is all curves. They tell her about the neighbors, about her grandparents, what they ate for dinner. Dad tells knock-knock jokes. Beatrix tries to hear their voices as she reads.

After she's finished with each letter, she carefully rips off the stamp for Gerald, then places the letter in the pile with the others, tucked into the drawer of her desk. Sometimes at night she reads them all. The more she reads them, the more she thinks about what's left out. She doesn't know whether they're spending each night in the shelter. She's not sure how often the bombs are falling. She wonders whether they've left her chair at the kitchen table.

Beatrix writes back every week, after church and Sunday dinner, sitting at the little desk in her room that overlooks the garden. She wants to tell them about the colors here: the way the yellow leaves cover the ground under the trees; the tiny purple flowers on the wallpaper on her bedroom wall; the golden raspberries from the garden that ooze out of the breakfast muffins. But she can never find the words. Or the words are there but it feels wrong to share them. She imagines the two of them sitting on the couch in the dark flat, her father worrying the hole in the arm, his fingers pulling at the white innards. Or she sees them heading to the shelter beneath their building, to their spot a few feet from the unsteady pine steps. The smell of urine and the skittering of the rats. Everything there feels muted, shades of gray and brown. So, instead, she tells them funny stories about Gerald. How she's doing well in Latin. That William got in trouble for cheating on a history exam. About her new friend who's invited her to the symphony in Boston.

She doesn't tell them that every Saturday morning Mr. Gregory wraps a worn, berry-stained apron around his waist and makes pancakes. That Mrs. Gregory gives her a bath and tucks her in each night. That Sunday afternoons are her favorite time, when she and the Gregorys all sit in the library and listen to the New York Philharmonic on the radio. That some nights she can no longer remember what they look like. On those nights, she turns the light back on and stares at their photo, trying to memorize the details. Those are the nights they enter her dreams.

WILLIAM

Beatrix is not like any other girl William knows. She's smart, for one thing, and serious, except when she laughs at Gerald's stupid jokes. But as much as she shouldn't be encouraging Gerald, William looks forward to those moments because something seems to lift off her, a bird taking flight. Her face relaxes and almost seems to bloom. She's not pretty, not like Lucy Emery or Marian Smith, with their blond curls and bright eyes. Beatrix's eyes and hair are dark and when she's worried, her eyes turn almost black. There's no seeing through to her thoughts. She rubs her thumb under her nose or rolls her hair between her fingers when she's feeling particularly anxious.

William thinks that he would rather like being sent away, across an ocean, to live with another family. He wonders what Beatrix thinks about her "adventure," as his mother calls it. She never talks about it to the family — he wonders what she says to her new girlfriends. She answers questions from Mother and Father but she never elaborates, never tells them more than they ask. He knows that she finds everything here different and that's what he wishes he knew more about. How is it different? What was it like to live in London with the bombs arriving each night?

He tries to imagine her apartment in London. He sees long floor-to-ceiling windows and candles on a mantel. Paintings in hues of blues and purples on the walls. Dark velvet curtains. He studies the photo of her parents next to her bed when she's not at home. He likes the look of her dad; he seems like he would always get the joke, unlike his father, who rarely has a sense of humor. Her mom seems a bit cold, a bit more removed. And yet the look on her face — not a smile, not a frown — is one that he often catches on Beatrix's face when she's somewhere else, before she gets snapped back to the present. Before she remembers where she is.

The week before Thanksgiving, Mother sets them all to work after school, cleaning up the yard and the patio, making pies and cakes, tidying up the house. They rotate

Thanksgiving among Mother and the three aunts, and this year it's their turn. William feels a bubble of excitement that he tries hard not to show. Gerald is bursting at the seams. *It's so much fun,* he tells Beatrix as they sweep the back patio. *So much food.* *Sounds wonderful,* Beatrix says, nodding, although William knows she's heard this all before. She rakes another pile of leaves onto the black tarp. He had to show her how to use a rake. Gerald throws himself onto the pile of leaves. *I can't wait,* he yells to the brilliant blue sky. *I love Thanksgiving.*

Beatrix shakes her head at him, then turns to William. *What about you,* she asks. *Do you love it, too?* When she asks questions like this, she tilts her head to the side and she wants to know the real answer, what he really thinks. He's not sure there's anyone else in his life who asks questions without an answer in mind. *It's okay,* he says, raking the leaves out of the flower beds and tossing them onto Gerald. *What's your favorite part,* she asks. *The cousins? The food? The thanks?* The thanks. He'd never thought of it like that. The thanks part of the holiday. It was a day, a nice day, to get together with everyone. A day when Father was too distracted to be annoyed with him. But he wasn't sure his family felt thankful. Mother's

57

family has been here forever, with ancestors dating back to the *Mayflower*. Probably some of them were at that first Thanksgiving. Should they feel more grateful than they do? He's never really thought about it before. But now, with Beatrix, he wonders. Maybe his image of her apartment is all wrong.

Yes, he says. *The whole thing. You know, the breaking away from the British thing. The thanks that we have our own country.* He grins at her, and she rolls her eyes. *Can't wait to see what happens on July Fourth*, she says. *I'll probably be tarred and feathered and thrown in the harbor. Oh, we're planning on it*, William says, covering a squirming Gerald with more dirt and leaves.

Mother calls out the back door for Gerald to get up and stop horsing around and for Beatrix to come help with setting the large tables, and Beatrix hands her rake to William but not before throwing a handful of leaves on top of Gerald. When she runs past William, she throws him a rare smile, and he catches a whiff of her. Her cheeks are bright red.

BEATRIX

On the kitchen table, after school, lie two hand-delivered invitations. Crisp ivory stationery with Beatrix's name on one and William's on the other in fancy lettering. Mrs. G smiles as Beatrix opens hers, careful not to rip the envelope. She's never seen anything so elegant with her name on it. Gerald watches from the other side of the table, his chin on his hands. A Christmas party at Lucy Emery's, the Saturday before Christmas. *We must get you a dress, child,* Mrs. G says. *We'll go into town this weekend.* Beatrix frowns. *But I have my red dress,* she says, *it's my favorite.* There's a pause and then Mrs. G turns around. *No, dear,* she says, her voice soft. *The Emerys are a fancy lot. You'll want a proper party dress.*

On Saturday, Beatrix and Mrs. G go to Downtown Crossing. The streets are filled with shoppers, and Mrs. G pushes through the crowd in front of the store, holding tight to Beatrix's mittened hand. *You must see this,* she says. In the windows of Jordan Marsh, a family celebrates Christmas. The father is in a tartan robe, reading the paper by the fire. The mother, in a matching sky-blue robe and nightgown, is clapping her hands, again and again, as the three children — two boys and one girl — open their gifts. The floor is covered with toys and wrapping paper. The outdoor speakers are blaring Christmas carols. Beatrix can't stop looking. She's never seen such a thing. It's just like our family, she thinks, with the father reading and the mother engaged and the two boys and one girl. She feels Mrs. G looking at her, the way she does when she wants to hug her but feels that she shouldn't.

As they enter the brightly lit and bustling store, Mrs. G keeps her hand on Beatrix's back as she steers her toward the elevators. Once on the third floor, jewel-toned dresses line the walls. *Oh, this is such fun,* Mrs. G says, her voice full of joy as she fingers the silk and satin. *It's been years since I've been able to fit into a dress I love. But with your figure? You can wear anything that catches your eye.* Beatrix nods. She's already seen the dress. It's a blue satin with a tulle underskirt in a lighter shade of blue, and she points at it, shyly. Princess Margaret wore something like this last year. Mrs. G motions to a salesgirl and then the dressing room is filled with dresses; Beatrix tries on one after another, alone in the room, stepping out into the narrow hall to have Mrs. G zip her up and fasten the hooks and eyes. She walks back and forth toward the long mirror, learning to swish when she turns, making that glorious sound, the skirts brushing up against her legs and the walls. She spins and each dress billows out and flares.

Beatrix loves the blue dress the best, even though Mrs. G prefers the emerald-green one. *It works with your coloring, dear, and it's just so Christmasy. But I want you to be happy and love the dress you're wearing, so we'll get the blue one, yes?* Beatrix nods, worried she will cry if she speaks. She has never worn anything as elegant as this. *And,* Mrs. G continues, speaking to the salesgirl, *we'll need matching gloves and shoes. Don't worry about the jewelry, dear,* she says to Beatrix, *I've got a perfect set of pearls that will be just the right length for that neckline.*

As they make their way out of the store, boxes in hand, Beatrix sees legs that look like her mother's moving through the crowd, the seam running perfectly up the back of the slender calf, and at first she thinks that it must be her, and she gestures with something like a moan, certainly not a word, her hands reaching to try to touch her mother's sleeve. *What is it, dear,* asks Mrs. G, concerned, and the woman turns around and it's not her mother at all. Of course it's not. Beatrix shakes her head and she can feel the blush rising into her cheeks as bodies push past them, past the makeup and perfume counters, past the handbags and jewelry, heading to the front doors. *I'm sorry,* she mumbles. *I thought I saw something. I was wrong. I'm sorry.* She realizes that she hasn't thought of Mummy once during this shopping trip. What would she have thought of this? Would she have approved of the dress? Should she offer to pay, even though she has no money? Perhaps Dad could send some. Mrs. G bustles along beside her. *Oh, Bea,* she says, and Beatrix can see the bit of worry creeping into her face, the way she gets when Beatrix pulls away, *they have the most delicious blueberry muffins here. Shall we have a treat, then, before we leave?* Beatrix shakes her head again, suddenly furious at this woman who seems to have everything and want for nothing. She can tell that she has hurt her feelings but she has no way to explain what she is thinking. Then Mrs. G's face slides back to her usual calm self, a protection of sorts, Beatrix knows. She's learned that everyone wears a mask. *Let's get to the car, then, dear. It's been a long day.*

On the way home, Beatrix stares out the side window. It snowed two days earlier and now even beautiful Boston is gray and cold and dirty. She wonders whether there's snow at home. How can there even be a war on? So often it seems as though she's living in a fairy tale, a land where you buy fancy dresses and go to parties and eat blueberry muffins. The girl in the tale is different from the girl at home. It's a facade, she tells herself, soon she will go back to her real home, and this will all become something that once happened to her in a dream. How stupid of her to think the family in the window was hers, how ridiculous to ever believe that she belonged here. She looks at her watch, which she keeps to London time. It is eight in the evening at home. Her parents are sitting in the dark, the candles dripping down to almost nothing before they blow themselves out.

REGINALD

On Christmas, Reginald arranges for a phone call, using the phone at the factory. He paces in his supervisor's chilly, darkened office, waiting for the phone to ring; Millie sits right next to the phone. *They've forgotten,* Millie says when five minutes have passed. *Nonsense,* Reginald replies, *something's up with the connection, that's all. Lots of people calling home today. We should have been the ones to call,* Millie says, and Reginald closes his eyes. There's no point in responding.

When the phone rings, though, it startles them both and Reg looks at Millie, almost in surprise. She picks up the receiver before it rings a second time. *Sweetheart,* she says, *my sweetheart.* Reg watches her face reharden in the dark. *Yes, hello, Nancy,* she says. *And the same to you.* Millie sounds like her mother, that chilly, formal voice. They chat for a few minutes, Reg hardly listening, he's so anxious to hear his girl's voice. Then he hears Millie's voice lighten. *Sweetheart,* she says, *my love.* And then she's crying so much that she can't talk and Reg takes the receiver out of her hand and holds it so they both can hear. *Beatrix,* he says, *talk to us.* And she does. Her dear voice rising from the darkness, moments of scratchy silence in between the words.

On the way home, the familiar streets strange in their darkness, Millie is silent, removed, her hands in her pockets, her mouth set.

Reg knows that Beatrix sounded different, but he's finding it difficult to pinpoint what it is. The accent, for sure. *Oh, gosh,* she'd said at one point. She had prattled on about a party that she'd gone to with William, or was it with Gerald, he struggles to remember which is which, and then when he had talked to Ethan, he had called her Bea. There was a familiarity there that should have settled Reginald's mind, should have made him feel she was safe and sound, but instead it has lodged in his stomach, where it worries at him.

Happy Christmas, Millie says later, holding her glass aloft in the dark flat, only candle nubs lighting the room. Reginald

raises his glass but can't seem to find the
words to respond.

GERALD

The snow started falling before bedtime last night and when Gerald wakes, he is thrilled to find his windowpanes covered with icicles that look like branches from the fir tree. No two snowflakes are alike. Gerald marvels at the possibilities. The snow is still coming down, blowing about, and the world has gone quiet. No one else is yet awake. When Gerald lets King out the back door, the dog disappears behind a snowdrift and then jumps with all four paws, leaping to his next spot on the snow-covered lawn.

Gerald covers the glass on the door with his warm breath and then writes his initials with his index finger: GG, Age 9. He has no interest in going outside. The joy of a day like this isn't missing school. He rather likes school, although he's learned to never say that out loud. But on a day like this he can stay at home and muddle about. He can work on his stamp collection or help Mother in the kitchen or play a board game with Bea. Willie will want to go out, to go sledding with his friends, to hitch a bumper ride down the hill.

He turns when he hears footsteps on the stairs. Bea, coming quietly down as always, and, also as always, dressed for the day. He's never seen her in her nightgown. Does she wear a nightgown like Mother? Perhaps she wears pajamas like he does. *Morning, G,* she says, her face open, her eyes wide. *I've never seen so much snow.* She comes and stands next to him at the window, and they stand there, without talking, their shoulders touching, watching King leap and pounce. *Look,* she says, pointing. *Whose tracks are those, do you think?*

Rabbit, probably. Maybe cat. Bea nods. *Winter's different in the city,* she says finally. *And our flat was on the fourth floor, so I've never woken up to see such an all-white world.* Gerald stays quiet. He's learned that the best way to get her to open up is not to ask too many questions, although he's always burning to, the questions knocking up against one another in his head.

He likes having her here. It was exciting, at the beginning, but now she just fits into the household, taking up a space that he

68

hadn't realized was empty until she filled it. He adores Willie but he knows that Willie's no longer interested in him; he only tolerates him, at best, and Gerald can feel him moving farther and farther away. And that's where Bea fits. He loves that she calls him G. He wants more than anything to hold her hand or to wrap his arm around her shoulder or kiss her cheek as they stand there but he knows he mustn't so he makes do by feeling her so close by. Beatrix exhales onto the glass and in the white mist, right above his initials, she writes BT, Age 11. They stand there, together, until King reappears, his snout covered in wet snow, begging to be let back in.

MILLIE

There comes a day that spring when Millie empties Beatrix's closet. Everything must be too small by now, she figures, and it doesn't seem as if she'll be coming home soon. What was she thinking keeping all these clothes? Her unspoken hope that she would be back before a year is up is dwindling by the day. She probably wouldn't want any of these clothes, anyway. She's become so posh. A photo came a while back, taken at Christmas, Beatrix standing in front of an enormous tree decorated to the nines. The angel on the top of the tree touched the high ceiling. Real candles lit up the branches, with glass ornaments reflecting their light. Her hair was brushing her shoulders, curling up at the ends, and the bangs were gone, or at least held back by a headband. Millie didn't recognize the dress, it was so fancy, and she thought it seemed a little too grown-up, a little too form-fitting through the chest, the neckline dipping down. And what were those pearls?

Should we be sending them money for clothes, do you think? Millie asked Reg then. *We never discussed that.* Reg shrugged. *Honestly, Mil, I think they're happy to buy her things.* But pearls? she asked. *They're buying her pearls?* Reg shook his head. *If they want, what's the harm. There seems to be plenty of money.*

That is what's worrying Millie. How small life would seem when Beatrix got back. There would be no fancy parties or baseball game outings or trips to the symphony. She's happy, of course, that she seems so well cared for. She seems to have a nice group of friends. But that will make the return more difficult. She will no longer be a little girl. She no longer is a little girl. They sent her away so she could have a childhood. They hadn't realized, though, that their decision meant that her childhood would, instead, be taken away from them. Millie feels as though something has been stolen from her, never to be returned.

So, one beautiful Saturday morning, when she should have gone outside as winter has finally lifted, the streets and parks full of people, a sense of freedom in the air, Millie stays at home. Reg goes out to meet friends for a picnic. The bombs have lessened lately, and everyone is happy to forget they are at war, if only for a few hours. Millie fills garbage bag after garbage bag for charity, putting aside a few things for the neighbors.

She finds Beatrix's favorite stuffed dog from when she was little tucked into the back corner of the closet. A Steiff dog, one ear worn down to almost nothing. Beatrix had loved the eyes, rubbing her thumb over one and then the other, a soothing technique that helped to calm her down. Millie throws the dog out — because, honestly, what would an almost-grown girl want with a worn stuffed animal — but then, on their way back up from the shelter after the all clear, she goes out to the trash bins, opens the bag, and feels her way through the darkness to the small matted dog.

Millie puts the dog on top of her dresser but she finds the dog's gaze unforgiving. Reg complains, too. *There are bound to be bugs in that thing, Mil. Plus, it's German. I don't want it in the house.* When he's out, she tucks the dog into the back of the drawer of her bedside table, where she now keeps the envelope with Beatrix's hair and that first telegram.

Beatrix's closet is empty. Millie sweeps it out, even dusts the top shelf.

REGINALD

Reginald is getting ready to head home from the pub when the bombs begin to fall just after eleven. Everyone in the pub rushes out to the Anderson shelter in the back garden and crowds inside, men sitting on each other's laps, pints still in hand. The laughter quiets as they realize that this will not be a normal night. One blast follows another with no space in between. The noise is deafening. Fire trucks go screaming by. Horses are neighing. Brian, one of Reg's buddies from work, grows agitated. *We need to get out there and help, boys. Full moon tonight. The Krauts can see the whole city, lit up like a show on the West End.*

Reginald says he should be getting home, but then he realizes Millie's most likely already in the building shelter. Better for him to stay and help. So, he and Brian and a few other men head out and jump aboard pump trucks heading north. *Not a lot of water,* one of the firemen says to Reg. *Low tide. We can't handle this volume.* The truck stops, and all the men tumble out. Reg hears a scream for help and heads to the nearest bombed-out house, the fire lashing the upper windows, to help a woman pull her young son out from under the rubble. *Still alive, thank the Lord,* the woman says. *Jesus, I thought this terror was over.*

All night Reg helps out, doing whatever is necessary. He goes into a burning house to retrieve a wedding album. He lifts a desk off a woman's leg. He sits down on the curb to take a breath, and a boy offers him a biscuit. *You from here,* Reg asks, and the boy nods. *Our house got bombed a few months ago,* he says. *I'm living with my aunt down the way. Your parents,* Reg says, but as he does he knows the answer. *Gone,* the boy responds. *But my aunt, she takes good care.* Reg nods, unable to speak. He often feels guilty that Beatrix is far away and safe. A woman runs by, heading for a burning house. *My ration book,* she cries, *I forgot to take it to work today. What will we do?*

By the time the night is over, the entire city is on fire. Later, they hear that German bombers flew over 550 missions, with some crews returning two and three times. When

Reginald is finally on his way home, to see what's happened to Millie, he looks toward the city center. At first he thinks the sun is rising behind the thick smoke and is relieved that the night, this horrible night, is over. Then he realizes that the orange glow is coming from the Houses of Parliament, flames rising all around.

Bea

Every summer, once school is out at the start of June, the family heads up to Maine, staying until the end of August. Going to the island, that's what they say. It took Bea months to understand that the island is theirs and theirs alone. The house was built by Mrs. G's father and now it belongs to Mr. and Mrs. G and one day it will belong to William and Gerald. They already argue about how they will split the summer months when they're older, when they have families of their own. They both want July so they can set off fireworks and have a big party.

They love the island and while Bea wants to share their excitement, all she can think about is the water. The boys talk incessantly about swimming out to the dock, swimming around the island — *I did it in under an hour last year,* William crows — and swimming to town. Bea doesn't know how to swim but she can't figure out how to tell them that. They all seem as comfortable in the water as on land. It seems like something she should know how to do. Maybe it's not that hard, she thinks, maybe I can just pretend. But she finds her chest seizing as she thinks that.

Finally, the night before they are due to leave, she tells Mrs. G as she sits in the bathtub, Mrs. G lathering up her back. *The thing is,* she says tentatively, apropos of nothing, wrapping her arms around her knees, *I don't know how to swim.* She begins to cry, a real cry, gasping for air. She feels a fool. *Oh, my dear, my sweetheart,* Mrs. G says, wrapping her dry arms around Bea's wet body. *It's nothing to cry about. We just take it for granted, that's all. I never would have thought to ask.* She pauses and bites her lip. Bea is reminded of that first bath, all those months earlier, and knows that Mrs. G is once again judging her, in some small way. It's never malicious, she knows that, but there is a kind of looking down that Bea reads between her words, in the lines around her mouth. *But it makes sense, of course, you growing up in London and all. Don't you worry, now. We'll have you swimming in no time.*

Bea isn't so sure about that. On the drive

up, once they cross into New Hampshire, the ocean seems to be in constant view on their right. *There,* Gerald shouts when they get to town, *there's the island,* his finger pointing at a green bit of land in the harbor. A friend, a man from town with a large motorboat, meets them at the dock and ferries them and the trunks and the groceries and the dog all over. Bea is the only one to don a life jacket. She sits down next to King, his ears pinned back, his eyes wide, and she imagines she must look like him. Mr. G gives her a hand out of the rocking boat, and she struggles to go to sleep that first night, the waves a persistent rhythm on the rocks below.

The boys can't wait and right away, after breakfast the next morning, they swim out to the floating dock, Beatrix watching them from the rocky shore. She bends down to run her fingers through the ice-cold water. It is the boys' favorite place, and she realizes that it's such a rarity that they both like the same thing. They race out to the dock and back three times, William winning each time, the dog swimming along beside them. Bea can hear them chattering away as they swim, and as they lie, spent, on the sunny dock, surrounded by the flashing, blue-green sea. She desperately wants to be there, too. She feels like an outsider, something she hasn't felt for a long time.

The second morning, she comes downstairs to find Mr. G at the kitchen table. *Today's the day,* he says, and he smiles at her. *Okay,* she says, drawing herself up tall, *the day for what?* She likes him, even as she's scared of him, often preferring his company to that of Mrs. G, who always means well but whose energy can be exhausting. *We're going swimming,* he says. *Just you and me.* After breakfast, they set out for the far side of the island, following a trail that cuts through a forest of fir trees, the soft needles blanketing the forest floor. *The water's a little warmer over here,* he says, and then he takes off his shoes and, wearing his swim trunks and a T-shirt, wades in up to his stomach, holding tight to her hand.

He fastens a bathing cap under her chin before he teaches her to put her face in the water and to blow bubbles as she moves her face from right to left. He shows her how the salt in the water will help her to float. She laughs, almost, as pockets of warm water surprise her. He brings her farther and farther out, away from the island, always supporting her, always by her side.

They do this every morning for the first week they are there, Bea rising earlier each day, finding Mr. G at the kitchen table, waiting. It's cold, but she gets used to it, almost gets to a place where she welcomes the little intake of breath as the cold water surprises her. By the end of the week, he is no longer supporting her.

From her bedroom window, she can see the mainland. They have a bunch of little rowboats — a "fleet," William calls it with a cynical eye roll, and Gerald does, too, but without any irony — so they can row over whenever they want. Town has a grocery, a restaurant, the post office, and a few small shops; it also has tennis courts and friends, other families who live either on the mainland or on other islands. Before the summer is over, Bea tells herself, she will swim to town.

REGINALD

Reginald joins the Home Guard, explaining to Millie that he needs to be involved. *What I do at the factory makes a difference, I suppose,* he tells her, *but I need to do more. There's no point in sitting around in the evenings and on the weekends. I might as well be out in the streets, helping.*

The truth is, Reg will do almost anything to get out of the flat. He often has a pint after work to delay coming home, unsure of what waits for him on the other side of the door. Some days it's fine, and he is reminded of the girl he fell in love with all those years ago. But other days she's angry at everything. He can do nothing right. He knows it's too simplistic to think that life has divided into Beatrix and After Beatrix. It's this damn war, these damn bombs. It's changed everything.

He wishes now that he had joined up, back at the start, back in '39. But he had been a year older than the conscription age, and his brother's time in the first war had made him wary, even as he wanted to fight for the cause. Relief had flooded through him that he didn't have to sign up. He hadn't wanted to be separated from Beatrix and Millie, and yet here he is: his daughter across the Atlantic, his wife wrapped up in her worries.

Millie's not the only one. All the fellows at work complain about their wives, about how they're obsessed with what's happening to the children who were sent away. But no one else they know sent their children to America. Reg still thinks this was the right choice. It does seem increasingly likely that America will enter this war. Still, it's safer there. If she was in the country, where many of the children are, he would constantly be on edge. He likes the fact that he no longer has to worry. She's eating well, she's excelling in school, she's with a family who cares.

He comes home from a Saturday of training to find Millie on the couch, waving a letter at him. *A new one,* she says, smiling. *Shall I read it aloud to you?* But her voice is sharp, and Reg can smell the liquor before he sees the bottle. It's often this way on Saturdays. *Go ahead,* he says, collapsing into his chair, untying and kicking off his boots. Training is more difficult than he'd imagined it would be, but he likes that his mind and body are occupied for hours at a stretch. It's difficult to think about anything else.

Dear Mummy and Dad, Millie reads, *Today I caught a bluefish! We went out in one of the neighbor's big boats. I caught it myself and then Mrs. G cooked it up with lemon and butter. It was delicious.* Millie stops reading and looks at the ceiling, a crack from a blast early in the war running from east to west. *I've never had bluefish,* she says, pronouncing *bluefish* with an American accent and drawing the word out into multiple syllables. *I wonder what it tastes like.*

Reg pours himself a drink from the bottle on the coffee table. *Fishy, probably,* he says, and Millie laughs. *You got it,* she says. *Fishy, indeed.* Her laugh is grating. She continues reading the letter, which is full of the stuff of summer life in America: food and hikes and tennis and sunsets. Reg loves to hear the details; they allow him to see her in this unknown place. The dog injured his paw. Beatrix beat Gerald in a swimming race. She taught the boys how to make paper boats, just like Reg had taught her. *Do you think,* Millie says, *these people even know there's a war on? That people are dying every day?*

Jesus Christ, Reg sighs, *she's happy. Isn't that what we wanted? I wanted to keep her here,* Millie says. Reg is tired of this conversation. *Stop rehashing the past, Mil. She's getting to be a child.* He feels the drink starting to take hold, he feels drawn into the fight. *Let me tell you what I heard the other day. In the country, children are being made to sleep in barns. A boy was beaten for breaking a dish.* Reg stops then and wonders whether he should tell her the worst of it. Yes, he decides, she needs to know. *I heard that a girl, just Beatrix's age, was raped by the father in her home.*

Millie doesn't seem shocked. She's probably heard this through her own grapevines. *And how do we know those things aren't happening to our girl?* she asks. *We don't know that man. Those two boys. Don't you ever think that could be happening under and behind and within this idyllic life? These beautiful words?* She shakes the letter in his face. *We have no idea. She's presenting a world to us, one that she wants us to see. We do the same to her. She has no idea how much we fight, how miserable I am. No one knows what's really happening*

84

behind closed doors.

Reginald slumps in his chair and closes his eyes. He guesses she doesn't really believe what she is saying. She's only drunk and trying to provoke him. He knows, in his heart, that Beatrix is safe. He believes the stories she tells. They give him joy. He can see her, climbing out of the water onto the dock, a grin on her face, her wet hair streaming down her back. He smiles at the thought of it.

You, Millie hisses. *Cozying up to those Americans. They're just as nasty as we are.*

NANCY

Lying on her stomach on the lawn, pretending to read a book, Nancy wonders whether they should go to town for dinner this weekend. It's Bea's one-year anniversary with the family. She feels sure the girl is aware of the date, and she's also confident that her oblivious boys have no idea. Nancy flips over and covers her eyes with her hand as she watches the three children out on the floating dock.

Gerald has been teaching Bea to dive. At the start of the summer, she couldn't even swim. What a shock that was to them all. She knew Bea grew up in London and all, but honestly, teaching your child to swim is a necessity. How could they put her on that ship without her knowing how to swim? Ethan worked with her every day for over a week and then they had a grand presentation, where Bea and King swam out to the floating dock together, William swimming ahead and Gerald bringing up the rear. Ethan was puffed up with pride as they waved to the children from the shore. When William wanted to teach her to dive, she refused, content to slip into the dark water from the dock feetfirst. But her stroke has gotten strong and Nancy knows that she wants to learn to dive in order to race William. She won't win, of course, but she'll do well. Better, Nancy suspects, than William thinks she can.

Now William is lying on his back on the floating dock, and Bea is diving over and over, Gerald holding up a kickboard for her to dive over. Nancy wouldn't want William to teach her to do anything either; Gerald is the one who has the patience. Nancy can't hear what they're saying to each other but she can hear occasional bursts of laughter.

What a difference this girl has made in their lives. Especially on the island. Before, William and Gerald would have been at each other's throats by this moment in the summer, sick of each other's company. They couldn't have raised two more different boys. She always tells Ethan that if they could just put the two of them together, they would have one perfect child. A strength for one is a weakness of the other. Back when they were little, they got along well, although William easily tired of Gerald's boundless energy and good humor. As they've grown, Nancy has sadly watched them gravitate away from each other, as William has moved more into the world. It's not what she had hoped. She suspects — no, she knows, she has asked — that Gerald struggles to find friends at school. He is awkward around other children and too sensitive, she imagines. Such little space between his head and his heart. William, though, is always at the middle of a gaggle of boys, far preferring their company to anyone in the family. He often seems restless now, rarely content with where he is. His temper can flare up over anything. The secondary school years — which will start when they get back in just a few weeks — are worrying her.

But Bea has shaken things up, quite without her knowing. It's as though her presence has changed the family equilibrium. Even Ethan has taken a shine to her. Nancy wasn't sure, at the start, that he would ever come around. Yesterday, after dinner, Bea stood next to him on the porch, watching the sunset. They didn't say a word to each other but simply stood there, without moving, until the color began to drain from the sky.

Yes, dinner at the restaurant on Saturday, she thinks. To celebrate not just the anniversary but also all three of the children's August birthdays. Hard to believe they're turning ten, twelve, and fourteen. Lobster and corn on the cob and a lovely chocolate cake with perhaps some peppermint ice cream for a treat.

BEA

Bea wishes summer could last forever. They've been in Maine for almost three months now, and she's dreading leaving the day after tomorrow. The boys' hair is long and wild. Bedtime is abolished. Meals feel less like an extension of school — Mr. G's lessons tend to spill over into the dinner hour at home — and more of a free-for-all. Bea wears overalls every day — hand-me-downs from William — slipped on over her bathing suit. Every day is a new adventure, even if they are doing things they've done before and before and before.

How easily the days unfold and unspool. One thing leads simply into the next. A hike through the woods might end with William and Gerald doing cannonballs off the high rocks. Or filling mouths and buckets with wild berries could mean an afternoon of baking — muffins or pies — the kitchen awash in flour and eggs and sugar. They col-

90

lect things to display indoors: pine cones, shells, bird feathers. Even rainy days are sublime. The house is lined with books. Bea likes to read on the faded green couch in the living room, putting her book down every once in a while to watch the mist reaching up out of the water to touch and then to blend into the white sky.

The Gregorys are relaxed, too. Mrs. G works in her gardens, braves the cold water every day before lunch, and sits out in the sun in the afternoons, pulling her bathing suit straps off her freckled shoulders. Even Mr. G is different here. It isn't just at dinner. He taught Bea to swim, but he also taught her how to row a boat, how to make popovers, how to skip rocks. He often disappears for half the day — to catch bluefish on his boat, to hike in the forest, or to paint watercolors outside the old barn — and when he returns, he sits on the front porch, a whiskey in one hand, his pipe in the other, and watches the pinking of the sky.

Today, Bea is swimming to town. She's made it round the island twice, which is a farther distance than the swim into town, although easier because the land is always at her side. On the way to town, there might be boats and whitecaps and tide. The boys will be in a boat, behind her, and Mr. and

Mrs. G will have headed into town ahead of time, so they'll be there with towels and dry clothes. William's told her it takes him forty-five minutes, so she's expecting that it will take her closer to an hour.

Before the Gs leave for town, Mr. G pulls her aside. *You can do this,* he says. *I know you can. You're a strong swimmer, and I'm awfully proud of you. Never would have thought we'd see this, given where you started at the beginning of the summer.* Bea twists her hair as she nods and looks back at him. *But if you do start to get into trouble, just tread water until the boys get there. Promise me that, will you?*

He gives her a quick hug and she's not sure that he's ever done that before. *I'll tread water if I need to,* she says, meeting his gaze. *But I won't need to. I can do this.* He winks back at her. *That's my girl,* he says.

The water is calm today, a sheet of blue that stretches between the island and town. She can make out the steeple of the church, where they go each Sunday morning, and the smaller tower of the library, where she's spent hours curled up on the floor, reading. She waves at the boys, standing by their boat, and she fastens her bathing cap under her chin, before she walks into the water as though she's walking to town, the cold rising up her body as she strides. She loses touch with the rocky bottom, kicks her legs up behind, and begins her slow, steady stroke, breathing and blowing bubbles as Mr. G had taught her, feeling her body slowly warm up as she moves forward. Occasionally she looks ahead to make sure she's heading in the right direction, but mostly she concentrates on her breathing and on her stroke, reminding herself occasionally to keep kicking. Bea knows the boys are behind her and the Gs are in town, a line connecting them all, with Bea in the middle.

She takes a break by rolling over on her back and when she does, she raises her head and waves at the boys. Gerald stands and waves frantically back, almost losing his balance in the boat. William salutes her, then yanks Gerald down. She almost laughs at the two of them, how predictable they are, how much she feels sandwiched between them, how safe they make her feel. Rolling over again, she does the breaststroke for a bit and then returns to the crawl.

What would Mummy say if she saw this? Dad would be proud, she thinks, but Mummy, she's not so sure. This ocean that she's swimming in right now, the ocean that separates her from them, has grown wider over the past year. That life, that girl has begun to evaporate. She still writes home each Sunday but now she struggles to fill a sheet with words. Their letters, too, seem shorter and less connected. As though they don't know what to write to her about. They ask a lot of questions. Dad no longer tells jokes. She was glad to learn, in their last letter, that the bombings in London have almost stopped. Hitler has moved on. But it's still not safe: Dad said, right from the start, that she wouldn't return home until the war was over.

When she next lifts her head, her arms and legs feel heavy. Each stroke seems harder than the last. But she's close now. Mr. and Mrs. G took the blue rowboat, and she can see it, moored by the dock, and she knows they must be close by. She begins to pass the boats anchored farther out, and on the larger boats, some people come out and wave. *Almost there,* one man shouts. *Won't be long now!* She had worried about passing the boats and the people, but she rather likes the attention, waving at them when she can. And then she sees Mrs. G, jumping up and down on the dock, and she realizes, not for the first time, that Gerald and Mrs. G are carbon copies of each other. She can't see the boys, but she imagines that

Gerald is doing the same thing.

Finally, she feels the plants growing up from the bottom and, after a few tries, her feet find the soft seaweed. She stops swimming to walk the rest of the way. The Gs come to meet her on the beach, and Mrs. G wraps a big yellow towel around her before kissing her on the cheek, over and over. *You did it, I knew you would,* she says. Mr. G smiles. *My girl,* he says again, and she wishes he would hug her again, but mostly she wishes she could hear her father say those words. Before they all leave the beach, she turns from the Gregorys and faces east, back toward the island, and beyond that, the sea.

MILLIE

This separation, Millie has come to understand, is rather like surviving grief. The sorrow comes and goes in waves, but now that it's been over a year, the lows come less frequently. On some level it is as though Beatrix is gone for good. Millie has heard that some mothers have visited their children abroad but she knows this is not possible for her. Reg has been clear about that, especially after they heard about that boat with all the children on it that was torpedoed. The next time she sees Beatrix will be when she is back in London, when the war is over. Somehow, knowing that is what has allowed her to move forward. There are moments now when it feels so long ago, as though being a mother was something that happened to someone else. This American woman seems to be doing a fine job. Every once in a while, though, she allows envy to creep in. Perhaps Nancy is a better mother than she ever was. It seems clear that Beatrix is often happier there than she was here, and Millie can never dwell on this for long. It's best when she can stop thinking about it altogether. There are now longer stretches of time when that happens.

How different London seems now that the raids have stopped. Millie feels as though she can breathe once again. That constant dread of the night is gone. The blackout is still enforced, but they stay in the flat. Or, she stays in the flat. Often Reg is out with his unit. There are so many older men in the Guard that Reg is considered one of the strongest and most fit. He's risen to the top, of course, and so he's on duty more and more.

Millie, too, is busy. During the weekdays, she's now doing the bookkeeping for several local shops. She also volunteers as an ambulance driver and spends her weekends and an occasional evening driving around London. She is one of only a few women on the force, having learned to drive on her grandparents' farm. In London, it's mostly the upper-class women who know how to drive. So she's found herself with a new crowd, women who grew up on Eaton Square, spent summers in the south of France.

One night, on duty, she's paired with Julia Ainsley, and in the dark of the car she tells her about Beatrix and where she lives in Massachusetts. *Oh, it's lovely in Boston,* Julia says. *I'm sure she's being dreadfully well taken care of.* Yes, Millie responds. *I'm sure you're right. But it must be hard,* Julia says, *to have her so far away. My fiancé is somewhere in France. There are nights when I wake up because I hear his voice. Does that happen to you? No,* Millie says. *It did at the beginning. But I don't know what she sounds like anymore.* She pauses and looks out the window but sees only her reflection. It's easy to talk to a stranger. She rarely says such things to Reg. She lights a cigarette and rolls the window down to blow the smoke out. *It's not just not knowing her voice,* she continues, but then can't go on. Her biggest fear is that she won't recognize her when she comes home. She's heard about these mothers whose children walk right past them when they return. What kind of a mother, she wonders, would not know her own child. She crushes the cigarette in the ashtray. *Enough,* she says to Julia. *Let's talk about something else.*

REGINALD

Most nights during the week, Reg stays at the factory. On the days he's on duty, as soon as his shift is over, he changes into his uniform and patrols the grounds. As he marches, he practices the little German he knows, the German they were taught in case they were ever to apprehend a soldier. But he also stays at the factory when he's not on duty, telling Millie he has duty almost every night.

On those nights, he goes to the pub with the boys and then returns to the barracks. He likes sleeping on the upper bunk, and he often writes letters to Beatrix when he returns, a little tipsy and relaxed. *Beatrix, my dear,* he writes. *How I long to see you. How I wish to know the girl you've become. Do you remember when I would read you stories and tuck you into bed? I suppose you're too big for that now.* He cannot imagine what it will be like when she comes home. He was worried about how she would adjust to America. Now he's sure that she'll never fit back in with them.

He doesn't mail the letters. In the morning light, over a cup of coffee, he rereads them and he sees a weak version of himself portrayed on the pages. A shadow of who he used to be. He doesn't want Beatrix to know that man exists. So he lights the letters on fire, grinding the ashes into the concrete. One morning, emboldened, angry at the world, he writes to Ethan Gregory, asking him to reply to the address at the factory. He tells the man that Millie is worried about Beatrix. He recounts some of the stories they've heard about the children in the country. *We are saving money to pay back any extra expenses you may have incurred,* he writes, even though it's not true. They have no money in savings at all. He half expects the man to never respond.

Instead, a letter comes far sooner than he would have thought possible. He hasn't had much of a sense of this fellow, really. The weekly letters are written by Nancy and they are cheerful missives, full of exclamation points and an occasional heart or flower. Ethan, he sees now, is a more serious chap. Impossible to know, of course, but he seems like an upstanding fellow, not someone who would yell or beat or, God forbid, abuse his little girl. They begin to write back and forth, about Beatrix, of course, but also about Churchill and Roosevelt, about the steady push of the Germans, about Japan. Ethan tells him not to worry about the cost, although he lets Reg know that the Gregorys, also, are not wealthy. *We're house-rich,* he writes, *and dollar-poor. Nancy's the one who came from money.*

Ethan mentions running the chess club at school and how he'd failed to interest Beatrix in the game. *No one in my house plays,* he writes. *Nancy's too distractible. Gerald's like her — they rarely think three steps ahead. William would be an excellent player if he wanted to spend time with his old man.* Reg hasn't played since he was a child, but he writes back right away: *I'm up for a match, if you like.* They begin playing postal chess, sending the card back and forth across the Atlantic. When the card is not in his possession, Reg checks his postbox every day at work. Finding the card in the mail brings him joy; it's as though playing with Ethan brings him that much closer to Beatrix.

He never tells Millie about writing to Ethan or playing chess. Once, Nancy mentions in a letter that she's so happy the men have found a common interest. *After this conflict ends,* she writes, *we'll need to get together. You simply must come up to the island.* Reg worries that Millie will zero in on that line about the common interest. But, instead, she focuses on the island. *I suppose she's just being nice but, honestly. We won't be traveling to America when Beatrix gets back. When this war is over, Beatrix is coming home for good.* Reg knows he should tell her about the chess, about the letters from this man. But he doesn't want to. He wants to keep it all for himself.

GERALD

Gerald has convinced Bea to play a game of Monopoly. She loves playing the game, he knows, but she hates how it drags on for hours. It's the Gregory version, which Mother made for Christmas one year, with the house on Hillside Avenue and the Boys School and the island and the floating dock. And besides, Willie's off with his friends, so it won't be a competitive game. It will just be fun. The last time the three of them played, Willie turned over the board and sent money and little houses flying. He was sent to bed without any supper.

Three hours in and Bea is draped on the couch, moaning. *For goodness' sake, G,* she says. *Can't we just end this thing. You win.* He smiles at her. Neither of them care much about winning. Mother brings in a tray with oatmeal cookies and mugs of cocoa. *It's a miserable day out there,* she says. *This ought to warm you up.* She turns up the wireless to hear the music. Father listens to the same program in his study, down the hall. *Stereo,* Willie always says, rolling his eyes, and then, pretending to be an adult, using an affected voice, saying, *Aren't we the modern family.* Once Gerald had snuck into the kitchen on a Sunday afternoon and turned on that radio, too. *Hey, Willie,* he shouted. *What's it called when there are three speakers?*

The music abruptly stops, and Mother's hands freeze, the knitting needles in an X. *Oh, Lord,* she says. *Is it today?* Her face is stricken. What is she talking about? Gerald wonders. *Ethan,* she calls, her voice rising. A man's voice comes on the radio and says, with no introduction: *The Japanese have attacked Pearl Harbor, Hawaii, by air, President Roosevelt has just announced. Oh, Lord,* Mother says again and then Father is in the doorway and they're staring at each other and the man is talking more and Beatrix is sitting up straight and her face is bone white.

BEA

The popular girls huddle around Bea at lunch. They ask her questions about taping windows, about rations, about living without meat. Bea tries to answer their questions, the best she can, but as always now, the way things felt in London and the girl she was there seem very far away.

She has longed for these girls to bring her into their circle. The girls who've befriended her up until now have been the quiet girls, the nice girls, not really the group she wants to be with, although, she suspects, that's where she belongs. These girls are the exciting girls, the ones who laugh loud and exchange glances that mean something. The girls who include her only when they need to understand the Latin homework or when they want to know something about William. One day Lucy Emery sidled up to her after lunch. *Is your room next to William's*, she asked. *Do you ever see him in his skiv-*

vies? Bea didn't know how to respond. *Down the hall,* she said, feeling dull. *His room is down the hall.* That is true, but the two rooms share a wall. Sometimes she puts her hand on that wall, knowing he is just on the other side, before she gets into bed.

Everyone's focus has turned toward the war. The school builds a hastily constructed viewing platform on top of the chapel, which is on a bit of a rise, and sets up a schedule for the faculty and the older boys to take shifts looking for enemy aircraft. To Bea's surprise, William is one of the first to volunteer, and he even signs up for the six-thirty shift, before classes begin.

Every morning, Bea listens to him getting ready in the room next door and then crashing down the stairs. Moments later, she hears the back door swing open and his footsteps as he runs toward the chapel. For two weeks she lies in bed each morning, and then, one morning in January, she is dressed and down in the kitchen at six fifteen. He bursts into the kitchen, wrapping a scarf around his neck. *What are you doing,* he asks, grabbing a muffin and an apple. *I'm going with you,* she says. *No,* he replies. *No, you're not.* Bea shrugs. *Why not? No girls allowed,* he says. *Well, that's stupid,* she says. *I've lived through more war than you have. Why can't I be there, too?*

William shakes his head and runs out the door. *I'm going to be late,* he calls back, and she follows him down the path, knowing that he can hear her footsteps, but he doesn't look back. He's faster than she is, but not by much, and he's still taking out the gear from the storage box when she emerges onto the roof from the narrow circular stairs.

I'll get in trouble, he says, not looking at her, sticking a pen behind his ear, and with clipboard in hand, he begins to scan the sky. *William Gregory,* she says, laughing, *when have you ever cared about getting in trouble. You just don't want me here. I don't care if you're here,* he replies, *but don't get in my way. This is important work.*

A month earlier, she would have laughed in his face. He, too, would have mocked someone who said this. *Important work,* he would have said with a sneer. But William has changed. Bea knows this shift. She saw it in her father in '39, although she was too young to understand it then. But she gets it now. It's fear, made real. Before the declaration of war, it looms over everything, a heavy weight, a constant worry. But once your country is at war, it's a concrete thing that bores its way in, that never leaves. There will be consequences. People you know and love will die. She'd heard her parents arguing the night before she left London. *I don't want her to grow up so fast,* Dad said. *I want her to be a child as long as she can.* She rolled under her covers, blocking her ears with her fists. I stopped being a child on the day war was declared, she wanted to scream. And you both disappeared even as you stayed by my side.

She sits down next to William and scans the dark gray sky just as he's doing, remembering how the sky looked from the ship so long ago. *Hard to see anything, isn't it,* she says. *Right now,* he says, and nods. *But sunrise will be in* — he checks his watch — *eleven minutes. Then it'll be beautiful.* She nods back. *What are we looking for?* she asks. He explains and shows her how to fill out the form.

Later, on their way down the stairs, he stops at the bottom and faces her. He's taller, suddenly, his face more angular. *Don't tell anyone you were here, okay?* Bea shrugs. She won't agree to anything, although she's happy to keep this between them. *I don't mind you being here,* he says, and she knows how hard it is for him to say something like that. She touches his arm in thanks. They run down the side of the hill, and she peels off, heading for the Girls School. *See you, William,* she calls. She feels happier than she has felt since war was declared.

MILLIE

It occurs to Millie, sitting in church on Easter Sunday, that Beatrix could come home now. The bombs have stopped. America is at war. Is she really any safer there? As she mulls this over, smelling the old wood and the prayer books and singing the familiar words to the hymns, she wonders why she hasn't thought about this until now. Why hasn't she brought it up with Reg? They never considered the possibility that London might become safer than America.

She closes her eyes during the sermon and remembers an Easter from before the war. Not this church. The church that was bombed early in the war. The church where Beatrix was baptized. Beatrix was wearing the sweetest dress, with smocking on the top and a little Peter Pan collar. As a special treat, they'd bought coordinating shoes, Millie telling Beatrix that she mustn't ever tell her father that they spent so much money on dress shoes. How lovely she looked. The shoes had lavender-blue ribbons as laces, and the color perfectly matched the dress. They walked into church with Beatrix between them, each of them holding a hand, and she heard a lady sigh. *Oh, how adorable,* the woman whispered. *Just look at that little one.*

The three of them walked the long way home after the service, as it was a rare beautiful day in London, with the bluest sky over it all. They ate a proper Easter luncheon, with roast beef and Yorkshire pudding and a lemon tart for dessert. It was just the three of them, in the small kitchen, but she dressed up the table with a lace tablecloth from her mother, and she put new candles in the crystal holders Reg's parents gave them for a wedding gift. Candles were special then. Now those same holders have layers of wax dripped on them after years of daily use.

Why is she remembering this particular Easter? She supposes it's many things: the day, the dress, the pudding that rose just so. The way life was then, when those little moments of joy could be focused on, could be paid proper attention. Before fear was in every breath.

But it was also when she and Beatrix were

close. A year or two later, when Beatrix turned nine, she began to move more toward Reg, asking him to read to her before bedtime, to play cards. It was a quiet and subtle shift, one that she almost didn't notice until the turn was complete. She knew he was more fun. Beatrix had always confided in her, though, told her what was happening at school, would rush to her when she picked her up at the schoolyard to wrap her arms around her waist, to tell her about her day. All of a sudden, it seemed, there was a formality between them. And that break, that space seemed to widen. So of course Beatrix believed that Millie was the one to insist that she leave.

On the way home from church, the streets crowded, she glances at Reg's face. *Don't you think,* she begins, *that it would be a good idea to bring Beatrix home? No,* Reg says flatly, his eyes refusing to meet hers, staring straight ahead down the pavement. *The war's still going on. That was our original agreement.* She grabs his hand. *Not here,* she says, knowing that she's pleading. *It's infinitely safer now. You read her recent letter. She's doing air patrols with the older boy. Seems like it's more likely for bombs to fall there than here. No,* Reg says again. *She's not coming home now. Not until there's a declaration of peace. Safer for her to stay.* Why, she wonders, does he get to make all the rules? Why did he get to decide she would leave and now he gets to decide she can stay?

In a box in the hall closet, Millie finds that Easter dress, with the smocking and the Peter Pan collar. The shoes are long gone. She donates the dress, along with other items, to the church.

WILLIAM

William brings up his plan at the dinner table, after the plates have been served, but before Mother has picked up her fork. *So, he says, fiddling with his napkin, more nervous than he thought he'd be, I want to stay here this summer. Bobby Nelson and I are going to run a lawn-mowing business. That way I can keep on with my air shifts, even pick up a few more hours each day.* He doesn't dare look up or meet anyone's eyes, so he keeps his head down, his eyes fixed on his mashed potatoes.

Willie, Gerald says, *what are you talking about? You're coming to Maine. Like always.* William looks across the table and glares at him. He knew Gerald would react first. The others are taking it in, deciding how to respond. He wonders what Bea thinks. *Oh, no,* Mother says, and William looks at her just enough to see her looking steadily at Father, *you can't stay here for the summer.*

She reaches over and pats his hand. *Honestly, William, what are you thinking? We go to Maine as a family. It's our vacation. Our family vacation.* He steals another look at her, and she's still looking at Father. *Ethan,* she says, *say something. Talk some sense into this boy of yours.*

William looks from his mother to his father. Father takes off his glasses and cleans them with his napkin, first one lens and then the other. The room is as silent as it's ever been. Father seems intent on getting his glasses as clean as possible before speaking. He dips his napkin into his water glass and scrubs at an invisible spot. *Father,* Gerald says, *tell William he can't stay here. We've already talked about sleeping most nights in the tents in the forest. Right, Bea? Back me up!* Beatrix shakes her head but says nothing. She's looking down into her lap.

Still Father works on his glasses. Still he says nothing. William clears his throat. *Bobby talked to his parents already,* he says. *David's room is empty since he left for Europe. They'd be happy to have me.*

Father looks down the table first at Mother and then turns his gaze to William, looking over the top of his glasses. *No,* he says quietly. *This is not an option.* But Father, William replies, his voice higher than he

115

would like it to be. *I want to make money this summer. I want to keep working for the war effort. Going to Maine is just, it's just, I don't know, frivolous. Oh, honestly,* Mother says. *You're just a boy. Stop trying to grow up so quickly. I'm not a boy anymore, Mother. I'm turning fifteen this summer. In three years I can enlist. Going to Maine is frivolous,* he repeats. *It's a waste of time.* He stands up and pushes his chair back. *You don't understand,* he says. *You never understand.* He tries not to cry. *I'm not hungry. May I be excused, please.*

Mother looks at him, and he can see the exhaustion in her eyes as he pushes his chair in. *Yes,* she says. *No,* Father says. *Sit down at the table and finish your dinner. Let him go,* Mother says. *Leave him be.* There's an edge to her voice, a hardness, that William's rarely heard before. Out of the corner of his eye, he can see Father shaking his head but saying nothing more. Gerald is quiet for once. Bea finally looks up at him and he can't read the expression on her face. Is it disappointment? William walks out of the dining room and heads up to his room.

Later, Mother brings him his dinner on the blue wooden tray with the legs that fold out. The tray that she's always used when they've been sick in bed. *Oh, my dear,* she says, sitting on the spare bed. *I wish you were more content to just let things be. Enjoy what you have.* But, Mother, he says. *What will I do all summer in Maine? You can mow lawns there,* she replies. *Plenty of folks in town. And I can find chores for you to do that I'll pay you for.* He nods, subdued. *I bet you there are things you can do up there to help with the war effort, too. Lots of things to do near the ocean, after all.* She kisses the top of his head as she stands to leave. He sees the tears in her eyes.

She's almost at the door when he says, without even thinking, *Why does Father always say no to whatever I suggest. Why does he always come down so hard on me?* She turns and shrugs. *It's the way he is, William,* she says. *You need to remember all the ways you two are alike. It's what causes you to butt up against each other, of course, but try, sometimes, to see things his way. He'd love to help you with your homework. He'd love to play chess.* William almost rolls his eyes. Never, he thinks. *I know,* he says. *Thanks for bringing up dinner.* She shuts the door quietly behind her.

BEA

Bea sits on her bed, her English homework open in her lap, but trying to hear the conversation next door. Dinner was awful. There's rarely confrontation in this family. She has realized, in comparison, that her parents argued a good bit. Sometimes they tried to hide it from her, but the flat was so small that she could hear everything. She has often wondered whether Mr. and Mrs. G ever fight. She's never heard them. Once she asked Gerald: *Don't your parents ever yell? Don't they disagree about anything? No,* Gerald had said, surprised. *They pretty much always get along. It's me and William who fight.*

For the first year or so she was here, she thought they were perfect. But then she began to notice the little things, the way they ignore each other or the way they look at each other from time to time. Like at dinner tonight when Mrs. G excused William from the table. There was a fury in that look that she gave Mr. G that reminded Bea of her own mother, but she's rarely seen Mrs. G like that. And Mr. G didn't respond. If her mother looked at her father like that, he would have exploded.

William should have told her about his plan. She could have told him the best way to handle it, even though she knows that Mr. and Mrs. G would never let him stay. What was he thinking, bringing a big thing like that up at dinner, with all of them there? It's not that he's selfish, exactly, but he rarely thinks things through. No wonder everyone responded as they did. He should know that nothing good could ever come from making a big announcement at the dinner table. Dinner is Mr. G's domain. He likes to control the dinner conversation, to hear about everyone's day, to make plans. She's relieved that they won't let him stay here, though. What would Maine be like without him? Gerald is fine and all, full of ideas and always a comfort, but William's the one at the center. He's the one who makes things happen.

Bea hears Mrs. G leave William's room. She waits five minutes and then knocks on his wall in the code Gerald developed in Maine. Three sets of double knocks to ask whether she could come in. A pause and then an answer: one knock. She pushes open the door to his room, where he's sitting on his bed, eating his dinner. *I know,* he says. *Don't say it. It was a stupid idea. No,* she replies, sitting in his desk chair, twirling round and round, *it's not a stupid idea. But you should have never brought it up in that way. And besides, I thought you loved Maine. I do,* he says. *But don't you ever feel, Bea —* and here he sits up and leans toward her and she stops spinning to listen to him — *that we're wasting time? That we're just waiting for something to happen? I want to do something important, something that matters. Swimming to town, fishing, picking blueberries. Doesn't it seem wrong when there's a war on?*

Bea nods and looks down. She loves that William confides in her. But she's the one who ought to be doing more, the one who shouldn't be enjoying herself. A day can pass now without her thinking about her parents. She feels sick when she remembers where they are, what they are doing. Even with the rations, the war feels so far away. *Why didn't you tell me?* she asks, twirling again, refusing to meet his gaze, looking instead at the pictures of Bobby Doerr and Ted Williams plastered on his walls. They're all going to Opening Day next week. *Why didn't you let me know you were even thinking about this?* He shrugs. *It was just a thing Nelson and I came up with the other day at his house. Right after we figured out the number of days until we can enlist. I've got —* he checks a piece of paper on his bedside table — *1,198 days. He's got 193 fewer: 1,005 days.*

Bea looks at him. His cheeks are flushed and he looks distraught. She can never stay angry for long. *That's forever, William,* she says. *Really. You need to find something else to think about, something that you can do now. Let's make some plans for the summer. I heard your mother talking to you about mowing lawns in town. I can help you with that, we can do it together. No way,* he says, throwing his pillow at her. *You're a girl.* And finally he's almost smiling. She loves that look, the look that reminds her of the day they met.

ETHAN

The night before they leave for Maine, the house is buzzing. It's as though Nancy has parceled out her nervous energy to each of the children. The back hall and pantry are piled full of bags and boxes; Ethan knows that some things will have to be left behind. They've just enough fuel for the trip, and he doesn't want any extra weight. Packing the car in the morning is his task, of course, but it is sure to end in tears from Gerald or frustration from William. Bea tends not to bring as much as the boys, although he wonders this year. She's different now, more one of them than he ever would have thought possible.

He's in his study, drinking a cup of tea and reading the evening paper, when Nancy pushes open the door, her arms full of towels. *I can't find the children's bathing suits anywhere,* she says. *Where must they be? Could we have left them up there last sum-*

mer? Ethan doesn't reply. There's no reason to, really. She'll talk herself into one solution or another and the suits will be there or they won't and then there will be a whole other to-do. He nods at her, as though he's listening, and returns to the paper. When she takes a breath, he tells her, without lifting his eyes, that he wants to be on the road by eight in the morning. *That means starting to pack the car at six thirty,* he says. *So tell the children everything needs to be downstairs tonight before they go to bed.*

Yes, yes, yes, Nancy replies, turning to leave the room. *Still have so much to do. And I've got to give Gerald and Bea their baths. No,* Ethan says, and he can't believe that he's starting this tonight but here he goes. *You don't need to give them baths. This summer, they're turning eleven and thirteen. You don't need to give them baths anymore.*

Nancy stands still, her back to him, and he can see the anger running up into her neck. He knew this would stop her in her tracks. But it's been bothering him for weeks, months even. He began fussing over whether it was right for her to be with Gerald in that way. Certainly she had stopped giving baths to William before he was ten, even. And then he started to think about Bea.

He's hesitated to say anything because he knows it's a time they both enjoy. Sometimes, when he's walking down the hall to the bedroom, he can hear them in there, murmuring. He can smell the soap and once, laying his hand gently upon the door, he felt the steam. He knows it brings comfort for both. And, certainly, at the start, anything they could do to make Bea feel comfortable was important. But he never thought that the evening baths would continue. There's something downright odd about a woman giving a bath to an older child. And not even her own child. That's a big part of it, he supposes.

His other concern, though, is whether Bea would like them to stop but doesn't know how to say so. She's become bolder, speaking up for herself, taking a stand here and there. He can see, though, how this might be a difficult terrain for her to navigate. It's been eating at him, and while he didn't plan to do this tonight, on this frantic evening before they leave, here he is.

Nancy turns around, her face even redder than usual. She pushes her curls away from her sweaty forehead. *Don't tell me how to raise my children,* she says, her voice low. *You, you who sit here, drinking your tea and reading the paper while Rome burns.* He meets her furious gaze and responds slowly, his voice low to match hers. *It's not right, Nan. She's getting too old. She's not your child. What do you think Reginald and Millie would think about this? Do you think it would be okay with them?* She places the towels down on the empty armchair and paces back and forth, picking up a washcloth and wrapping it around her hand before unwrapping it and waving it in the air. *It's a bath, Ethan, a bath. There's nothing wrong with that. You want me to stop giving Gerald baths? Fine. But I will not stop giving Bea baths. It's our special time together.* She turns and looks at him directly, her voice dropping even lower. *I look forward to it every day.*

Ethan sighs and folds the paper back. *Have you asked Bea,* he says, his voice rising. *Do you know how she might feel about this?* He taps his fingers on the table as he waits for her answer. *I'm sure she's fine with it,* Nancy says, but he sees her hesitation, and he knows that she never considered this. *Just like I am,* she says. *She would say if she wasn't.* Ethan raises his eyebrows. *Not so sure about that,* he says, standing and taking the last sweet swallow of tea. He's ready for this conversation to end. *Bea's a pretty oblig-*

ing sort. She may sense that it's important to you so she doesn't want to disappoint.

Keep your voice down, Nancy says. *Do you want the whole household to hear you?* She walks over to him and stands closer than she has been in ages. *Look at me, Ethan Gregory,* she says. *Look at me.* Ethan gazes down into her tired, familiar face. *I don't tell you how to teach, I don't tell you how to fix the roof, I don't tell you how to pay the bills. So, in return, you don't tell me how to raise the children. This is my job, and being a mother is who I am. It's everything to me.* She folds her arms and stares up into his face, her mouth puckered.

Ethan returns the gaze and then steps back, stumbling over the side table. He picks up the newspaper and heads for the door, turning before leaving the room. *She's not your child, Nan. One day soon she's going to leave and never come back. You need to remember that.* He goes into the backyard, the screen door slamming behind him, and stares out at the darkening trees. What he said was true, of course, all facts, but he knows it was cruel. Still, she has fallen in love with this girl, and that's a mistake. Better, always, to protect one's heart. He thinks of his parents, lying in the cemetery across the street. Nancy has planted bulbs there, orchestrated to bloom throughout the spring. What is the point, he wants to ask but never does. For whom do they flower?

REGINALD

Millie's mother, Gertrude, is insistent. She leans across the tea table toward Reginald and Millie, her hands outstretched. *I, will pay for the transit* she says. *I went to the bank and I withdrew all my savings. There's enough for the ticket there and back.* She looks at Reginald, and he sees what he fears Millie will become. What she already has become at certain moments of the day, certain days of the week. An angry and sad woman disconnected from her life.

Millie looks at her mother, shaking her head. *Mother,* she says, speaking slowly and clearly, *we can't go to America now. It's not safe. She's there because we want her to be safe. It doesn't make sense to put ourselves in danger just to see her. She's fine. She'll be back before you know it. But I have the money,* Gertrude says, her voice escalating. She rushes out to the front room, where her desk is, and comes back with fistfuls of cash.

It's enough, she says, *I checked the current passage rate. You can go, Millie, you can go and see her and make sure everything's okay.* Reg tries to find some sympathy for her. Albert's death, three months earlier, was a shock for them all, lung cancer that was found too late. Millie's been up here, in the country, on and off since then, helping out. She's told him that things are bad, but he hadn't realized the extent.

Gertrude runs her hands through her hair. *You said how worried you are about her. What better thing to do than to go and see if she's all right? She's fine, Mother,* Millie says again. *She's fine. Please stop.* Gertrude begins to count out the money, saying the amounts under her breath. She doesn't respond to Millie, and Millie begins to clear the table. *Let's go for a walk, Mother, we can walk down by the canal. It's beautiful out today, and I want to see the gardens along the way.*

Later, lying in Millie's childhood bed, Millie reaches over and touches Reg's face in the dark. *Thanks for coming up to see us,* she says. *It's not easy, being here with her.* He turns toward her, surprised by her touch, by her words. *I know,* he says. *I didn't really understand.* Millie rolls onto her side, facing him. *It's my own stupid fault,* she says.

I told her how I heard about someone who went to visit their daughter in Maryland.

I'm surprised, Reg says, *that anyone would take that risk. To get on a ship right now. I know,* she says, *but this woman did it. She went over there and, Reg, it was awful. Her daughter was sharing a room with three other girls from London. Two girls to a bed. It wasn't clear whether they were going to school much at all.*

Reg cuts her off. *Now, Millie,* he says, *we know that's not the case with Beatrix. We know all is well. She's excelling in school! I know,* she says, *I wasn't saying that. I'm telling you about this one woman's experience. It made me realize that we're very lucky.* He nods, relieved not to fight. *I just feel very far away from her, that's all. She's turning thirteen next week. She's not a girl anymore.*

Reg wraps his arms around her in the small bed. She tucks her body up against his and sighs. They're silent for a few moments. *I've been daydreaming about it, though,* Millie says. *Going there to see her. Don't you want to see this grand house where she lives? To meet Nancy and Ethan and those boys? To understand what it means when she writes about setting up that business with William?* Reg smiles in the darkness. That had come in the last letter: Beatrix and William have been doing garden work for families in Maine. Each morning they row over to the mainland and spend much of the day mowing lawns and weeding gardens. Sometimes they sell berries and other produce in town. They're donating most of the money they earn to the war effort. They even named their business: WB Landscaping. He's proud of her for this. The girl who left them almost two years ago has changed. Of course she has. She is coming into her own.

Let's paint the picture, he says. They haven't done this in a long time. Back at the beginning, when Beatrix first left, they would imagine her together: on the ship, in her new home. But then it got too difficult for them to see. *We get off the train in Boston,* Reg says now, *and they're waiting for us in the station. Ethan is, what, what do you think he looks like? Oh,* Millie says, *he's a little overweight. That way that men get, their stomach bulging over their belt. Mustache, but no beard. Glasses, definitely. Yes,* Reg says, *agreed, and balding, perhaps. Definitely balding,* Millie replies, running her hand through his curls. *Unlike my handsome husband.* They grin at each other in the dark.

How long has it been since they've talked like this? She hasn't even touched him in months. *And Nancy,* he says, wanting to keep this going as long as possible, *what does she look like? Well, we know she's blond, right?* Millie says, with an edge to her voice. *Beatrix has said that. Bottle blond, though, one of those women who can't face losing their youth. Okay,* he says, laughing, *a little nasty, but okay. And a little overweight, too, I think. All that baking that happens all the time.* Now they're both laughing, and Millie covers her mouth with her hands. *Oh, Reginald,* she says, *we're terrible. We shouldn't be making fun. It's okay,* he says, *we're allowed.*

They imagine both boys and the station and the skyline, neither one of them wanting to truly see Beatrix in that world. They head for the cars — because they had to bring two, given how many of them they all are — and they end up in the car driven by Ethan. Reg sits in the front, and Millie and Beatrix are in the back seat. It is only then that Millie turns to look at Beatrix, to really see her. *She's beautiful,* she tells Reg, *she's such a gorgeous girl, with that glossy dark hair pulled back with combs and her lovely eyes, laughing. Her face is more angular, her*

132

cheekbones more prominent. She's wearing a pink linen dress. She's tan, you know, from spending so much time outside. She has freckles, Reg, on her nose and cheeks. And the best part, the very best part? Millie's crying now, and Reg can feel the tears on his chest. *She looks so very happy.* This, Reg believes, is not a fantasy. It is the truth.

GERALD

It's Bea's second anniversary in America, and Mother is making a feast. Mussels, which Gerald collected early this morning with Father and loves more than almost anything else. He suspects he could eat all of them, if given the chance. Corn on the cob. Blueberry pie, made from the wild blueberries on the hill. Bea spent the entire morning working her way through the field, filling pot after pot. She left Mother with what she needed for two pies and then she rowed over to town with the rest, to set up a stand by the library. Gerald wanted to go, too, but she put him off. *Better to do this myself, G,* she said, smiling at him, as she dipped the oars in the water. *I'll be back before dinner.*

Gerald stands on the shore, watching the rowboat get smaller and smaller. They repainted the fleet earlier this summer, and the white boat picks up the light from the sun, as Bea gets closer and closer to town. This is what this summer has been like. He's been left here, to stay on the island, and Willie and Bea have done all sorts of exciting things together on the mainland. Mowing lawns. Trimming bushes. Selling berries. They've hardly raced out to the floating dock. Willie has promised to race Gerald around the island but they haven't done that yet, either, even though Gerald has asked every day. And they're leaving before the end of the week.

Gerald can hardly see the boat anymore. Willie went over early this morning, to paint a house with his friend Fred. Father drove down to Portland to pick up some fireworks. Mother is busy in the kitchen. *Go,* she said to him, pointing at the screen door with her wooden spoon. *Read a book. Play in the woods. Don't come back until tea.* Gerald picks up a rock and throws it against the others. *Jesus Christ,* he says out loud, looking around to make sure no one can hear him. *This place stinks. I'm eleven now, I ought to be able to go to town.* He throws rock after rock, some of them cracking open, and he runs after them to pick them up, to see what's inside. Every once in a while, he finds one heavy with crystals. Mother has one she uses as a bookend that's purple inside. It's like a secret. The outside is gray and boring, but the inside is rich and beautiful, the crystals catching all the light.

Gerald wanders through the forest, aimlessly. Hours to go before dinner, before everyone returns. Plenty of time, he realizes, to swim around the island. It's not like swimming to town, where you need people watching. The land is always there, on your side. As he slips into the house to change into his trunks, though, he does so as quietly as possible. Mother's in the kitchen, the radio tuned to that swing music that she loves, and he can hear her singing along. He creeps up to his room and just as quietly comes back down, avoiding the creaky third and fifth steps.

He heads through the forest to the beach on the town side. Most afternoons, he waits here for William and Bea to return. He watches the boat as it makes its way toward him, and he can hear them talking and laughing. Bea waves when they get closer and always asks him about his day, but then they charge ahead of him, back to the house, talking about people and jobs and plans for the following day. At supper, he'll catch them glancing at each other and smiling, and he wishes that William had stayed home, that he could have Bea all to himself.

He leaves his towel on the rocks and steps into the water. It's the warmest it's been all summer but it's still cold. He slowly wades in up to his stomach and then begins to swim. He breathes to the town side, opening his eyes occasionally to see the boats, the church steeple, the big house on the point. Soon, though, he rounds the island and when he opens his eyes, he sees nothing but water and sky.

It's a beautiful clear day, and Gerald feels strong. Occasionally, he relaxes with the breaststroke or he turns onto his back and floats. He loves the way the water rises and falls beneath him as the waves move toward shore. He keeps a steady eye on the distance between him and the island, knowing that he doesn't want to veer too far off course.

At the floating dock, halfway around, he climbs onto the dock and lies on his stomach, his body warmed by the sunlit wood. He hopes his mother isn't looking out the kitchen window. But he knows how she gets when she's making a feast. Everything is about the food, setting the table, making everything perfect. She's not looking outside. She won't even take her daily swim today, he guesses, as she'll be so busy getting ready. He looks out the other direction, away from the island. Toward England. Bea taught him this song that she said her father sang all the time when he was doing the dishes. Whenever it comes on the radio, she turns it up, and the two of them sing along.

He likes the final verse:

There'll always be an England
And England shall be free
If England means as much to you
As England means to me.

He begins singing the song, hearing Vera Lynn in his head, and before he knows it, he's standing up on the floating dock, stomping his feet and saluting the land across the sea. He sings the song over and over, trying to make his voice as low as William's, and it's not until he sits down on the dock, his stomping having caused the dock to rock back and forth, that he hears someone screaming his name.

Gerald turns toward the island and sees Mother standing on the shore, waving a dish towel. *Gerald Gregory,* he hears, *you get back from that dock this instant. What on earth are you doing?* He waves at her, then dives into the cold and swims back to shore. It's not until he climbs onto the shore, dripping, that he realizes how angry she is. She rarely gets mad at him. *Gerald Perkins Gregory,* she says. *You know the rules. You may not swim out to the dock alone. I know,* he says, wanting to tell her that he swam halfway around but also relieved that she has no idea. *I was just so bored. I have nothing to do.* He can see her face soften, the way it so often does. *I know,* she says, *I should have had you help me.* He shakes the wet out of his hair. *Can I, please? What can I do? Can I help with the pies? Yes, you* may, she says, swatting him on the arm with the dish towel.

As they walk back to the house, she's silent for a moment. *Not a word of this to your father,* she says, *do you hear me? Yes, Mother,* Gerald says. *Your word is my command.* She rolls her eyes. *I'm serious. We keep this between us, yes?* He nods. One secret to layer on top of another. He can have secrets like the others. He's made it halfway. Now he knows he can do the whole thing. He'll just have to convince Willie and Bea to do it with him before they leave.

MILLIE

In a room somewhere behind Millie, down one hall and then another and then another, Reg lies in a coma. She sits alone in the cold waiting room. The bell of the flat had rung in the middle of the night, over and over and over, and she ran down the stairs in her robe to find a man standing there, in his uniform, his eyes wild. *I'm Brian,* he said, *maybe Reg mentioned me. Oh, my God,* she said, *what's happened. Not a bomb,* he said, *a heart attack.* A heart attack. Of course. Just like his brother. Why hadn't she seen this coming? Why did she even worry about the bombs? *I can give you a lift over to the hospital,* he said, nodding at his motorcycle. So she wrapped her arms around this stranger, his belly soft, this man whom Reg had never once talked about, and they rode through the dark streets, the rain falling, cold and wet.

There's nothing to do but wait, the

nurse said.

She sits here, wanting to be anywhere but here. She wants to be with Beatrix. She wants to be with her mother. She wants to be with Reg but not here. She cannot sit in that room with his still body. She wants to run far away and never come back. How could he leave her alone.

NANCY

The telegram arrives in the middle of the day, the delivery boy with his head down as he hands it to Nancy at the front door. Nancy feels for the boy as he returns to his bike, as she slices open the telegram. How much bad news he must be delivering now, day after day. Even in their little town, so many families have sent their boys off. The Swifts, down the street, have all four of their boys overseas. She reads the telegram, covering her mouth with her hand, not letting a sound escape. It doesn't seem right, she thinks, as she rushes over to Ethan's office, forgetting to take off her apron, that the skies be so blue and the leaves so yellow. *It's Reginald,* she says, bursting in, not waiting for him to answer her knock, *but not what we ever imagined. A heart attack while on guard. He's dead, Ethan, he's gone. How shall we ever tell Bea? Should we get her out of class? How dreadfully awful.*

No, Ethan says. *No.* He takes the telegram she waves in his face and lays it down on his desk, taking off his glasses to read it up close. *Calm down, Nan,* he says finally. He looks again at the telegram. *Sit down, will you?* he snaps. *You're making me nervous.*

Nancy sits in the chair where so many boys have sat over the years. She rarely comes to his office. She feels like one of those boys, waiting for him to speak. Her legs are short enough that they don't quite touch the ground, and she's tempted to swing them back and forth. Ethan cleans his glasses with his handkerchief. His stalling technique. *Sad,* he finally says. *So very unexpected. The poor girl.* His voice trails off.

How should I tell her? Nancy asks. *What is the right way to tell a girl her father has died?* Ethan shakes his head. *No,* he says. He stands and walks to the front of his desk, facing Nancy. *You're not to tell her anything. I'll handle this when I get home. Oh, Ethan, no. I can't spend the afternoon with her and not tell her. You need to come home early then. No,* he says. *I can't. You'll simply have to wait.* She looks at his face and wants to slap him. He treats her like a child. But she knows there's nothing she can do to change

143

his mind. *Very well,* she says, *very well,* and she slams the office door on her way out.

Back at home, she paces in the kitchen, looking at the clock. She can't figure out what to do with the telegram. She folds it in half and then in quarters. She tucks it into the top drawer of her desk, but then worries that Bea might look for stamps there, so she puts it in her apron pocket, where she touches it from time to time as she cleans up the house and begins to make dinner. She can't keep her mind on anything, and she ruins the corn bread for dinner by adding a quarter cup of salt instead of sugar. It feels wrong, not to tell Bea. What will she talk with her about? She knows that Bea will see it on her face.

Before the children get home, she takes out the telegram and reads it again. REG IN HOSPITAL STOP HEART ATTACK STOP DIED 7 THIS MORNING STOP SEND LOVE TO MY GIRL STOP. Nancy heads out to the back patio and lights the telegram on fire with a match. She holds it until the flames come too close to her hand and then she throws it to the ground, stomping on the ashes and pushing them into the dirt.

She always does what Ethan says. Most of the time she agrees with him. But with Bea, they've disagreed. She suspects he's jealous of their relationship. She did stop giving Bea baths last summer, after he asked, and she misses their time together. They've taken, instead, to spending their afternoons in the kitchen, Bea doing homework, Nancy cooking dinner. Ethan was probably right about the baths. But here, today, he's wrong. He should not be the one to tell her that Reg has died. This is not doing as Millie requested. This is not sending love.

When the children come home, Nancy sends the boys to their rooms after their snack. Then she sits at the kitchen table, takes Bea's hands in her own, and tells her the news.

WILLIAM

In the middle of the night, William hears Bea sniffling. She hasn't cried much at all since they learned her father had died. That was a week ago. She's not present, though. It feels to him as though she's somewhere else. It takes her a moment to respond, to engage. It's like it was when she first arrived. There's something behind her eyes, something unreadable, but something he almost understands. Sorrow, loneliness, loss. This is what grief must look like.

He's stayed up late this week, wondering whether she wanted to talk, but he never could get up the nerve to come into her room. Now he knocks on her door, not using their code but just tapping. *Bea,* he whispers as loudly as he dares, *are you awake?* She comes to the door and opens it. She's in a flannel nightgown, her feet pale against the floor. He steps in and shuts the door behind him, as she climbs back into bed and pulls the quilt up around her legs. William stands, awkwardly, between the door and the bed.

You okay, he asks. *I don't know what to say. I don't know how to help.* She sort of smiles at him. *Don't look so miserable,* she says. *There's nothing to do. My father died. My mother is all alone. And I am here, not there. I can't even go to the funeral, William. What kind of daughter doesn't go to her father's funeral?* Then she starts laughing. *I mean, how ridiculous is this? He survives the Blitz, he rescues people out of burning buildings, he stands guard night after night, waiting for the Germans to arrive, and then he dies because his heart stops working? It just doesn't make any sense.*

I know, he says. *What kind of a God would let that happen? A stupid God,* she says, and then wrinkles up her nose and shakes her head. *But don't let your mother hear me say that.* Then she leans toward him. *That's what you could do, though, William. Play interference. I know she means well, but I don't want to talk about this. I don't want to talk about him. I just want everything to go on like before.*

Okay, he says. *That I can do.*

She's silent for a few moments. *I have an idea,* William says. She looks up. *You can't* go there for the funeral, but we could have a funeral for him, right? Just the two of us? How could we do that? she asks. He starts pacing back and forth between the window and the door. *We could do something in the woods. The cemetery. Or maybe the chapel.* He doesn't know what he's saying, he only knows he wants to do something, to help her in some small way. *You know, I showed you that side door that's always unlocked.* He's never been to a funeral. He has little idea of what happens at one. But she seems to like the idea. *Yes,* she says, her eyes meeting his, *that sounds good. Let's do that.*

Later, in his room, he lies on his bed, staring up at the ceiling. It frightens him, sometimes, how he longs for her approval. For her smile.

BEA

Bea decides to ask Gerald to come, too. She pulls him into the pantry after dinner and closes the door. *G,* she says, *William and I are going to the chapel tonight. What for,* he says. *To say goodbye to my father. You want to come? Sure,* he says. She lays a finger on her lips. *Not a word to your parents.* He looks at her with wide eyes. *Promise,* he says. *We leave at eleven thirty. Not a word,* she says again before opening the door. She and William fought about this, William saying that Gerald would ruin it. *He'll tell Mother,* he said. *He tells her everything. I want him to be there,* she said. *I want you both there.*

It's remarkably easy to leave the house in the middle of the night. They stand, huddled together in the field, looking back at the house, and the lights in Mr. and Mrs. G's bedroom stay off. *Nothing,* William says, *they heard nothing.* Gerald stays quiet. Bea knows he wants to ask a million questions

149

but he's here only on her invitation and William will snap at him if he opens his mouth. *Let's go,* she says, and the three of them run in a single file along the path. The moon is half-full, but the sky is clear and the stars bright. It's cold, for mid-November. Bea wishes she'd worn her mittens.

Inside the chapel, they let their eyes adjust to the dark before heading down the center aisle. They argued, too, about candles. Bea wanted to light one, to help them see but also because it felt like the right thing to do. *Somebody'll see the light,* William said, *somebody will be up, walking a dog, coming home late, whatever. We can't risk it. Okay,* she said, knowing he was right.

They stand together at the front of the chapel in a tight circle. *Daddy,* she says, and she can feel both William and Gerald tighten, their heads bowed. She looks up at the large stained-glass window behind the altar. It's beautiful during Sunday services, when the sun hits the glass and the colors dance on the walls. Now it's just dark. She can't see any of the images. She can't remember any of the stories. *Daddy,* she says again, *we're here to say goodbye.*

Later, the three of them climb the stairs to the viewing platform. Bea starts jumping up and down. *I'm so cold,* she whispers. *Who knew it would be this cold in November?* William pulls a bottle out from behind the storage cabinet. *There's this,* he says, *this will warm us up. William,* Gerald says, sounding just like Mrs. G. It's the first time he's talked all night. *What,* William says, not looking at him. *A sip, maybe two, what's the problem. You going to run home and tell Mother? No,* Gerald replies. *Stop treating me like that. Boys,* Bea says, also, she realizes, sounding just like Mrs. G. *Not tonight, please. A little whiskey seems just right, William.* She's never had anything to drink before but the smell, as William twists off the top, is familiar. It smells like Mr. G. It smells like her father.

William offers her the bottle first, and she puts it to her lips and tips her head back. The taste is appalling but the liquid slips down her throat and warms her chest. She shakes her head and squeezes her eyes. *Okay, G,* she says. *Your turn.* Gerald looks at her, his eyes wide. *Isn't it nasty,* he whispers, not looking at William. *Kind of,* she says, *but do it. Okay,* he says, and he takes a swallow before handing the bottle to William.

William holds the bottle in the air before taking a swig. *To your father,* he says, *may he rest in peace.* For a moment, Bea forgot why they were there. *To my father,* she says. *I wish you both had met him.* She puts her hand on top of William's and, after a moment, Gerald rests his hand on top of hers. *To your father,* Gerald repeats. A tear slips down his cheek, and Bea wipes it away with her index finger. Holding the bottle aloft, they all tip their heads back to look at the sky.

MILLIE

Days after the funeral, Brian delivers a bag of Reg's stuff to the flat. *From his locker at work,* he says. *Thought you would want everything.* Millie doesn't even invite him in for a cup of tea. *Thanks so much,* she says, *I appreciate it.* She stashes the bag in the hall closet, behind the cleaning supplies and the winter coats. For months she leaves it in the closet, unopened. She spends Christmas and New Year's in the country with her mother. Back in London, she settles into a routine. She takes on another bookkeeping job and she volunteers for more driving shifts: three nights a week and one full day on the weekend. It's best not to have spare time.

In the days following Reg's death, all she wanted was for Beatrix to come home. She drafted message after message, asking the Gregorys to put her on the next ship. But she couldn't manage to send the telegrams.

She knew that they had agreed she would stay in America until the end and that Reg would be disappointed in her. She also knew that she was in no shape to take care of her. Beatrix is happy there. It hurts to acknowledge that, but it is true. By sticking to the original plan, she honors Reg. It is the right thing to do.

On a Sunday in mid-February, Julia comes over for a drink after their shift. She takes one look around the flat and starts opening closets. *Do you have some empty boxes,* she asks. *We need to clear this stuff out of here.* Millie shakes her head. *No,* she says. *I'll get to it. Later in the spring. No,* Julia says, *we're doing this now. It doesn't help you to have Reg's clothes all over the place. Keep a few things, of course, something for both you and Beatrix to remember him by, but let's get rid of most everything else.* Again, Millie protests. *Millie Thompson,* Julia says. *Do you know how many people need warm clothing? And besides, you need to move along here. I would never have taken you to be someone who wallows in their grief. It's not good for you.* Millie nods. She knows Julia's right. She basically gave the same speech to Julia when her fiancé was shot down over Germany.

They empty out his closet and his dresser,

but not before pouring a drink for each of them. Millie keeps a sweater that she had made him before they were married and a plaid tam that he bought in Edinburgh one fall. She doesn't know what Beatrix might like. Then she finds his tweed jacket with the leather patches on the elbows. She sees him picking Beatrix up and holding her aloft in the park, putting her on his shoulders, spinning her round and round. Millie boxes that up for Beatrix, along with some of his books.

In his top bureau drawer, they find a stack of photos: Beatrix as a baby, as a toddler, as the girl she was before she left. Then photos from America: standing by the Christmas tree with the boys; in her bathing suit on a dock, her arms flexed and her smile wide; in a red wool coat, her arms holding a stack of books. And a collection of photos of Millie, too. *Oh, my goodness,* she says, *I'd forgotten about that dress. That was New Year's, the year before we got married. How gorgeous,* Julia says. *What a stunning couple you were. Seems so very long ago,* Millie replies. *I was a different person then. Weren't we all,* Julia says.

They didn't notice that the sun had set while they were working. Millie flips on some lights and pours each of them another drink. They collapse onto the sofa and kick off their shoes, Millie lighting her cigarette off Julia's. *So much stuff,* Millie says, looking at all the boxes piled on top of one another. *It's all that's left at the end, isn't it?* Julia smiles. *But you still have Beatrix,* she says. *Don't forget that. Think about how wonderful that will be, to see her again.* They talk about work and one of the new girls, who didn't know how to drive and yet signed up anyway, and the man whom Julia's just started dating. Julia falls asleep, and Millie covers her with a blanket and turns off the lamp on the side table.

As she's putting the broom away, she sees the bag that Brian dropped off months earlier. No more, she thinks, I can't handle any more. But then the urge to be done, to be finished with all of this, overtakes her and she grabs the bag and heads to the bedroom. She turns it upside down on the bed and shakes until every item is out of the bag.

His work uniform. His Home Guard uniform, including a Tommy helmet and a worn haversack. A book: *The Ideas Behind the Chess Openings.* A scarf that she doesn't recognize. A pile of letters, tied up with twine. She undoes the knot and finds letter after letter from Ethan. From Ethan! The letters they've received from America, written weekly over the years, are from Nancy, with a line or two added from Ethan. But here are pages and pages of news. Mostly they seem to be about politics and the war. There are lines here and there, though, about how Beatrix did on a test or how helpful she was at some family gathering or another. She reads a few, from start to finish, in somewhat of a stupor, her anger growing as she moves from one to the next. They're all addressed to Reg at work. He kept this from her on purpose. She bites her finger until it bleeds. Why would he do this? Why would he keep such a thing a secret?

She goes into the kitchen and grabs the kitchen scissors. Julia's awake and follows her back into the bedroom. *What's all this,* she asks. *My dear husband,* Millie says, *was sending love letters to another man. What?* Julia says. *What are you talking about?* Millie shakes her head. *Ethan, the man in America, you know, where Beatrix lives. They exchanged letters back and forth for over a year. Over a year, Julia! And not once did he tell me about this. Not once.*

She stands in the middle of the room, wielding the scissors. *I'm going to destroy every last one of these,* she says. *I hate him.*

He made Beatrix go away, he let her think I wanted her to go, and then he up and died. And now I find out that he kept all this from me. Julia takes the scissors out of her hands. *Millie,* she says, *calm down. You're overreacting. Don't destroy them. Hold on to the letters for now. You might want to read them more carefully. Beatrix might want to see them one day.* Millie sighs and sits down on the bed. She knows Julia's right. She's so very tired. *I need another drink,* she says, wiping her eyes.

Later, after Julia has left, as she's putting almost everything back into the bag, she finds a yellow postcard with a chessboard on the front and chess moves on the back. It's from Ethan, and it's dated two weeks before Reg died. She rummages through the bag and pulls out the chess book, tucking the card inside. Millie knows little about chess. Her father played, and he tried to teach her, but she didn't have the patience. She didn't know that Reg knew how to play. Ethan is waiting, though. They were in the middle of a game.

NANCY

For Easter, Nancy decides to take the children to New York. It's been a long, snowy winter. She feels as though they all need a change. William has been sullen and out of sorts for months, wanting nothing more than to leave the house as soon as he comes home, while Gerald never seems to want to leave. And Bea, also, has changed. She's become a different person. Oh, she's always polite and helpful, but it's as though she's taken a step away, as though whatever comfort she had found with Nancy is no longer what she wants. It's the loss of Reg, of course, but it's all bundled up with growing up and becoming more independent. She misses Bea, she misses the little girl. She rarely comes home right after school. Nancy can't remember the last time they sat in the kitchen and talked.

Nancy sits with Bea on the train to Grand Central; the boys sit across the way, sleeping and reading. But Bea is sitting at the window, watching the shore as the train races past. It's a gray day, with rain occasionally splattering the dirty windows. Nancy is not fond of New York but she can feel the excitement in Bea's body. She understands the allure of seeing New York for the first time. It's certainly closer to the way that London feels.

I'll be wanting to spend time with my sister, she says to Bea, patting her arm, *but you all should go out and explore New York. We've already talked about it some,* Bea says, her face lighting up. *Gerald wants to show me the American Museum of Natural History. And William has talked about Central Park and the Upper West Side. All good ideas,* Nancy says. *You must also visit the Metropolitan, which is right down the block from my sister's. A beautiful place to spend an afternoon.*

This feels like the old Bea, a Bea excited by everything around her. Nancy takes the opportunity to suggest a trip to B. Altman. *My favorite store in New York,* she says, *almost as nice as Jordan Marsh. Yes,* Bea says, *I would love that.* She fiddles with a thread on her cuff. *Mrs. G,* she says, *some of the girls.* Her voice fades away and she looks back out the window, then over at the boys.

Mrs. G looks at them as well. William is asleep, his head back, his mouth open. Gerald has a stack of comic books on his lap, and as they watch, he smiles at something in the pages. Thoroughly engaged. *Some of the girls,* Bea says again, dropping her voice. *You know, they've started to wear different underwear. They don't wear undershirts any longer.*

Oh, my heavens, Nancy says, and she knows her cheeks and ears are flushed. How could she not have thought of this? She's seen her developing, but since she stopped giving her baths and it's been the winter, with heavy sweaters and jackets, she simply hasn't given it a thought. Of course, there's still not much there, certainly not enough to warrant wearing a brassiere, but she knows what it's like with the other girls. Her own mother refused to buy her one. So she'd saved up her allowance and marched herself into Jordan's and bought her first bra, all by herself. *Yes,* she says now, *of course. They have a lovely lingerie department there.*

Thank you, Bea says, *I know I don't really need one, and I probably never will. My mother's flat as a pancake. Not me,* Nancy says, laughing, and they both look at her chest and then Bea looks away, and Nancy

161

can see she's embarrassed. Then there's that awkward space that often arises when Millie enters the conversation. Nancy can feel her there, listening and judging. She would have known to take Bea bra shopping months ago. She would have known how to help her with her grief. Nancy is used to boys. She was jealous of her friends and sisters when the children were little, with the dolls and the tea sets and the lovely books. But now that they're older? Well, she doesn't know the right thing to do. God knew what he was doing, she supposes.

But this whole conversation brings up something else that she hasn't had the nerve or the opportunity to discuss. She doesn't know whether Bea has started her menstrual period. What does she even know about it? Nancy had been planning to ask her sister's advice, as Sarah has four girls, all almost grown now, so she's gone through this already. Here, too, their own mother had done and said nothing. Sarah explained the basics to her, probably when she was just about Bea's age.

She steals a look at Bea, who's back to looking out the window. The Connecticut shore is beautiful, even in the mist, with the trees having a lovely haze of pale green on their branches. And the deeply blue Long

Island Sound, stretching away from the shore. She loves the start of spring, even welcomes a rainy day like this one. The early bulbs: the crocuses, the tulips, the daffodils. The hyacinths. Her favorite. *Dear,* she says, looking at the magazine in her lap, turning the pages. *Have you had your monthly visitor yet?*

Bea turns toward her. Lord, what a beautiful girl she has turned into. That dark complexion. The thick, almost black hair. The legs that go on and on. Nancy can see the adult she will become. She will look just like Millie. *No, I haven't,* she says quietly, glancing again over at the boys. *Lots of the girls have, though. Yes,* Nancy says, *I'm sure. But everyone's different.* There's a pause and they both look away. *I tell you what,* Nancy says. *I'll pick up some things for you when we get back. A belt, some pads. You can stash it away but then you'll have it when you need it.*

Bea nods in a way that makes Nancy understand she should have done this long ago. But she can't bring herself to say anything more. It's simply too awkward and if there's anything Nancy hates — and there's so little, really — it's being uncomfortable. She turns the pages of her magazine. *Oh, will you look at that,* she says. *Isn't* that a lovely sweater. I love the way the cables run down the length of each arm. That is nice, Bea says, taking a closer look, her hair falling into her face. I could make you something like that, Nancy says, tucking Bea's hair behind her ear. To have up in Maine this summer for the evenings. Would you like that, dear? Sure, Bea says. Or maybe I could make it, if you'll help me with the cables? Couldn't think of anything I'd rather do, Nancy says, squeezing Bea's hand, trying not to cry. Altman's has the nicest selection of wool. Let's be sure to get there, then, while we're in New York. She holds tight to Bea's hand, her fingers wrapped around Bea's, for longer than she should.

WILLIAM

On Friday, they take the IRT up the West Side and get out at 116th. William charges up the steps, leaving Bea and Gerald behind. *Here it is,* he calls back, *the entrance is right here.* They turn onto the campus of Columbia, budding trees lining a brick walkway. The campus opens up around them, buildings on every side. William spins in a circle, his arms out wide. This is where he wants to be. *Just look at this,* he says. *It's like an oasis in the middle of the city.* Students rush past them, on their way to class, bicycles carried up and down the great stone steps. It seems wonderfully crowded to William, even as he knows many are overseas. *That's the new library,* William says, pointing at the grand structure to the south. *Isn't it magnificent? Magnificent,* Bea says, with a tone in her voice. *My, what a vocabulary you have. What's happened to you, William Gregory?* William makes a face at her. The campus is even more beautiful than he had imagined. He has always loved New York. The museums. The people. The life.

But, Willie, you're going to Harvard, Gerald says. *That's where we go. That could be the stupidest thing you've ever said,* William replies. *But it's Harvard,* Gerald says. *Father went there. His father went there. All the men in Mother's family have gone there. It's practically our school.* William doesn't respond but instead runs up the steps of Low Library, taking two at a time, and turning around at the top to wave down at them. That litany that Gerald just spouted off, that legacy? That's exactly why he doesn't want to go there. He's desperate to break away, to start something new. Two more years of living at home. He can't wait to leave. If the war's still on, he's signing up on his birthday, August 20. If not, well, then he's going to start college. And certainly not at Harvard.

Let's look around back here, he says, calling down to them. *And then we'll go across the street and look at Barnard. You know, for Bea.* The other two run up the stairs and follow him down a path that cuts around the library, other tall buildings on the reverse side, manicured bushes lining the walk. *I'm not going to college,* Bea says to

166

him when she catches up. Mother had taken her to get her hair cut earlier in the week, and they curled it or something. He's not used to the way it looks yet. She looks older, somehow, more like the girls in his class at school.

What do you mean, he says, stopping short to face her. *Of course you're going to college. You're the smartest one of us all.* She laughs in his face. *No, I'm not. You do know this war is going to end, right? I'm going back to London when that happens.* We don't know *when that's going to be,* he says, realizing that he never thinks about that, he never thinks about her leaving. He did, at the beginning. *Couldn't you just stay for college, though? No,* she says. *My parents didn't go to university. That's not in my future. I'll go home, finish school, and then I'll get a job.*

Gerald's been standing to the side, listening to the two of them, his head cocked to one side. *I agree with William,* he says, *for probably the first and last time in my life. If anyone should go to college, it should be you. You're loads smarter than I am. Oh, G,* she says, *you're the sweetest but, really, you're both wrong. College isn't in the cards for me. The war will end. Then I'll go home to my mother.*

As they walk around campus, William knows that Bea is right. Somehow he hadn't truly understood that she would leave. He hadn't realized that leaving is something she's thinking about, perhaps even something she's looking forward to. This is all temporary to her. Years from now, she'll look back and this time will simply be a story to tell her children. When I was your age, she might say, I went and lived in America for a few years. I lived with this nice family outside Boston. Two boys, they had. One older and one younger. What will she say about him?

Later, they find a diner on the corner of 116th Street and Broadway. *Chock Full o'Nuts,* Gerald says, looking up at the sign. *William, they named the place after you.* They order date nut bread and cream cheese sandwiches, along with mugs of dark coffee. Gerald pours half the cream pitcher into his, along with three sugar cubes. *You're ruining it,* William says. He can see himself here, coming after class for a coffee, meeting a friend to study for an exam. He hadn't realized until today that he had assumed that friend would be Bea.

ETHAN

Ethan can't quite remember the last time he had the house to himself. It's been almost a full week without Nancy and the children. Blissfully quiet. He finished all his grading in the first few days so it wouldn't be hanging over his head all week. Then he did all sorts of things he knew Nancy would disapprove of: he left the bed unmade each morning; he piled dishes in the sink; he ate leftovers straight out of the icebox, spoon in hand. On the morning they left, she showed him the menu she'd drawn up for the week. Each dinner was made and labeled, stacks of glass containers piled on top of one another. She'd made a chocolate cake — his favorite — and a butterscotch pudding.

This morning — his last full day, as they'll return on the train this evening — he cuts a large piece of the cake and spoons out a generous helping of the pudding. He places the plate onto a tray, along with his cup of coffee, and carries it out to the back garden. It's a beautiful early spring day when it's hard to believe there's anything wrong in this world. That war is being fought on multiple continents. That boys he knows — boys he taught — are lying on battlefields, dying. Even with the rations in place, it's often hard to feel the war's effect here. But sometimes, when he stands in line at the post office or the bank, he looks around and realizes that he's the only man there. Too old for this war, too young for the one prior. It's a good thing, he supposes. He imagines that he would be a better soldier than he would like to be.

Some of the trees are just starting to bud. They're going to expand the vegetable garden this year, take over some of the lawn to grow more. A Victory Garden, they're calling it. Ethan leans back in his chair and stares up at the sky. There are times when he feels so parochial, so unworldly. The farthest away from Boston he's ever been is Chicago. He's never been to Canada. They were set to go to Paris and Rome on their honeymoon, but then Nan's father got sick and they went up to Maine instead. He assumes he will die here, in this house, when the time comes. In the same house where he was born.

It still amazes him that Nancy took a fancy to him back in college. They met at a Wellesley mixer. He hadn't much wanted to go but his friends insisted. And so he was sitting there, glumly, at a table, nursing a scotch, when this blonde sat down next to him. There was something about her, just the fact she would do that, he supposed, that she would just plop herself down next to him. *So tell me,* she said, *how tall are you?* She smiled at him. *Someone over there just told me that you're six and a half feet. Can that really be true?* He couldn't help but smile back. *Yes, ma'am,* he said. *Almost. I'm six-five. Wowzer,* she replied. *Well, sir, you're sixteen inches taller than I am.* And she placed her hand right next to his. *Will you look at the difference in the size of our hands. Here, hold your hand up. Let's compare.* He was smitten by her openness, by her comfort, by her big smile.

Funny how it's those things that now grate on his nerves. She tells everyone everything. He'll go to a faculty meeting, and someone will ask him something about the boys, and it's clear they know things that are private. She wants to be everyone's mother, including his. He misses the days when there was something between them, something that didn't include the children. And now, with Bea, it's overwhelming. She's trying too hard, all the time, to be a mother to this girl. The way that she told Bea about Reg's death, not waiting for him, telling him later she was the one who knew the right way to handle it. Time after time he has told her that Bea has a mother, to whom she will return, sooner rather than later. He's happy to have Bea here — happier than he thought he would be — but at least he understands it's just for now.

He spends the morning doing the dishes and cleaning up the kitchen. He makes the bed. He checks his lesson plans for the coming week. Finally, in the midafternoon, two hours before he must leave to pick up Nancy and the children at South Station, he sits down at his desk and pulls out the card he received ten days earlier. It was the game he and Reg had been playing before he died and he'd put it away, thinking that somehow the card had been found among his possessions, and someone had mailed it back to him. He hadn't wanted to look at it. Had Reg made another move before he died? Or was the card simply returned to him the way he sent it?

Instead, when he turns it over, he sees that a move has been made but in an unfamiliar handwriting. It's not smart, either. Check-mate two moves away. Down at the bottom of the card: *Forgive my poor effort. But I'm learning! All best to you and Nancy, Millie.* Millie! Who would have thought? He smiles and carefully considers his next move. Certainly not one that will lead toward victory. Still, it pains him to record such an ill-advised move. Most certainly Millie will see through this, will see that he's pandering to her. But he supposes that it's okay. Nancy always tells him that he's too competitive, that sometimes it's okay to do the right thing. And this, he thinks, this is the right thing to do. He looks back at the board. The king, he thinks. The king to f4.

BEA

The boys are leaving the island for three weeks: they're going to a camp in northern Maine. It came about suddenly. One day everything was just as it's always been and the next morning, this morning, Mrs. G announced at breakfast that they'll be leaving in four days, taking a bus from Portland. Bea's not sure what happened but she has a guess. She knows that William's been spending time with his friend Fred, who's already in college. Mrs. G rarely lets him come to the island so William's been staying on the mainland more and more. One night last week Bea heard him come back late, almost at midnight, and by the way he crashed through the house, she knew he was drunk. It's a miracle he was able to row the boat over and still be in one piece.

Both boys are furious about going. William, for obvious reasons. *It's my goddamn summer,* he said under his breath, and

Mr. G roared, in his quiet way, sending William to his room. And poor Gerald. He's never very comfortable in new situations. It's odd for such a generous soul. *Please, Mother,* he said, leaning across the table, *please don't make me go. I've already started organizing another scrap metal drive for next weekend. Oh, you'll have a grand time,* she said, waving her napkin in the air. *I hear it's such beautiful country up there. You'll get to sleep in the woods, just like you do here. Bea can handle the scrap metal, can't you, dear?* As Bea nods, she wonders what Mrs. G really thinks. Doesn't she know how hard this will be for him?

Bea doesn't quite know what to think herself. In one way, she sides with Mr. and Mrs. G, if this is, in part, about Fred and his friends. They frighten her. Once, in the market, one of them brushed past her while she was waiting to check out. *Hey, Chuck,* he called to his friend. *Here's that British girl we've heard so much about.* He gave her a look, up and down, and she hadn't known how to respond so she just stood there, dumb and mute. Later, on the boat ride home, she thought up a million smart responses. She should have stood up for herself in the moment. William dismissed her when she told him later. *He didn't mean anything by it,* he said. She didn't tell him how the boy looked at her. *What did you say about me?* she asked, and he shook his head. *Why would I talk about you to them,* he said, and it was just the way he would talk to Gerald.

William's always going on about wanting to go somewhere, to do something different. Now he has the chance to do just that. She'd love to go to northern Maine. To spend three weeks hiking and camping. But G, she feels for him. She knows how hard this is. She knocks on his door, in their code. *G,* she says, *let's row into town.* No response. *G,* she says again, a little louder. *Come on, let's go.* He opens the door, and he's been crying. *This stinks,* he says, lying back down on his bed, wrapping rubber bands around his ball. *Why do I have to do this just because they're mad at Willie? I know,* she says. *But it's only for a few weeks.* She walks over to his window and lifts the curtain. The air is so clear that she can practically see the clapboard on the houses in town. *You should be thinking about me,* she says, *stuck here with your parents.* She turns around then to see him smile, and she's reminded of that day on the dock, so long ago. How his smile had been the first thing that made her feel at home. *Come on,*

G, she says again. *Beat you to the boathouse!*

Later, they sit on the town dock, before heading home. *I was thinking earlier,* Bea says, *about the day I met you all. About how you came rushing up to say hello. William was being all proper but you were just you. You must have been scared to come here,* Gerald says. *I guess,* she says. *It's such a blur now. Is it horrible,* he asks, not looking at her, *to have your father gone?* Bea shrugs. *I think it'll be worse when I get home,* she says. *Here there's little difference, right?* She looks out toward the island. *I hadn't seen him in over two years. He hasn't been part of my daily life. So it's hard for it to feel real. Yeah,* he replies. *I get that.*

What I can't figure out, she says, *is where he is. I talk to him, G. Is that weird?* She wouldn't talk about this with William. She can tell Gerald anything and knows that he will understand. He never judges. *No,* he says, laughing. *I talk to myself. I think that's way weirder. I tell myself: you need to do this, you need to do that. It's like having Mother inside my head.* They both laugh. *Sometimes,* Bea says, *I feel as though my dad is right here, with me. That he helps me make decisions. I think that's great,* Gerald says. *I wish I had someone to help me.* Then he

177

turns to her. In the sunlight she can see flecks of green in his eyes. William's eyes are that same shade of green. *But what do you think happens when people die,* he says. *Do you believe in that stuff from church, about heaven and hell and all that? Or is it just over. Is your dad just gone?*

Bea has no idea. She's even asked her father the same questions when she talks to him late at night, or when she's out for a long swim or row. *I wish I knew, G. But I don't. So far I haven't seen all that much evidence of that benevolent God they talk about. It's hard for me to believe in the stuff at church, I guess. Yeah,* he says. *It's hard to figure out. I'd like to believe, though,* he continues, *I really would. I want you to see your father again after you die. I mean,* he says, waving his hands, pushing the air back, *I don't want you to die. But I want you to have the chance to be with your dad again.*

Oh, G, she says. *What a nice thought. Honestly, you're just the sweetest.* And Bea leans over and kisses him on the cheek. *I couldn't have asked for a better brother. I'm so lucky to have landed here, with you.* Gerald's cheeks are bright red and he doesn't look at her but stares out at the ocean. *I love Maine,* he says after a pause. *I want to keep coming here, summer after summer. I want to bring my family and my grandchildren. I want to die here and be buried on the island so I can be here forever. It's the best place in the world.* Bea agrees. To think that she could have lived her whole life and never seen this island. This place that feels like home. She loves the view from here, too, seeing the whole of the island, with the house hidden on the far side. A secret, of sorts, known only to a few.

MILLIE

On Reg's one-year anniversary, Millie takes the day off from work and goes to the cemetery. She pushes the leaves away from the grave and kneels on the cold earth. *I can't believe it's been a year,* she says, keeping her voice low even though there's no one else around. *I'm okay. I keep busy.* She tells him about work, about driving the ambulance, about the trip she took to the coast with Julia. *Just to get away,* she says, *a little holiday.* She doesn't mention the two chaps they met there, fighter pilots, and how she's meeting one at the weekend for a drink. She fills him in on the news from Beatrix, how well she seems to be doing. In the latest letter, Nancy had said that she had found a new group of girlfriends, that she wasn't spending as much time with William. *That boy,* Nancy wrote, *will be the death of me. Gerald, on the other hand, is so easy. With him, I never have to worry.*

180

Millie hasn't heard from Ethan in quite a while. The last postcard she received from him had his moves redacted. She asked around and learned that this was happening to other chess players. Apparently, officials believed that they might be coded messages. She didn't know what to do, so she sent him a short letter explaining what happened, carefully writing out all the moves they'd each made up until that point. But so far, he hasn't responded. She wonders whether the entire letter was redacted or perhaps destroyed. She could see how it could look like code to an untrained eye. Certainly, it would have looked like that to her less than six months earlier.

She takes in a breath and gazes around the cemetery. It's a beautiful spot, in every season, but in the fall the trees are ablaze with color. *So, Reg,* she says, *I've moved to a new flat. You were just in the old flat, somehow, all the time, and I needed a space that didn't contain you. Beatrix is not happy with me, I think, but I'm hopeful it will help her, too, once she comes home. To a different place and not one that's ringed with memories. It's closer to work, which is good, and only two flights up instead of four.*

Grief is a strange thing. It ebbs and flows, she's found. Some days she can think of him and be stalwart. On other days, though, someone will mention him, just in passing, and she'll get that tickle in her nose and know that she needs to turn away. The anger is mostly gone although that, too, seems to erupt at the most unexpected times. One night, a few drinks in, she wrote a letter to Beatrix telling her that Reg had been the one to send her away. She had wanted her to stay, she wrote, she had pleaded with him to change his mind. She couldn't send it, though. It seemed unfair to Reg and one day, hopefully soon, she can explain everything to Beatrix in person.

She stands up and kisses her fingers, then places them on the grave. *Bye, love,* she says. *I'll come back soon,* although she wonders whether that's true. It's easier to just forget. It's better to move on. She heads out of the cemetery. She and Julia are going to the clothes swap to find something a bit more fashionable to wear. A new scarf, perhaps, or a pair of flashy earrings.

BEA

The Emerys' house is lit up, with candles in every window, the yellow light reflecting onto the white snow. There was a huge blizzard the day after Christmas, and now, not even a week later, there is still over a foot of snow on the ground. Bea is worried about her new party shoes, which have blue velvet ribbons as ties and a bit of a heel. Mrs. G makes Mr. G drive, even though the Emerys live only a half mile away. Gerald has stayed home, and William's coming later, straight from a friend's house. This New Year's Eve party is all anyone has talked about forever.

The Emerys hired a swing band to play, and once Bea gets inside, and her coat is whisked away, and a drink is placed in her hand, Lucy's arm is wrapped tightly around her waist. *Come see the dance floor,* she says, and Bea is amazed to see they've removed all the furniture from the grand living room and rolled up the rugs. The band is set up in the far corner of the room, and people are already dancing. It's strange to see people from their class dancing alongside adults, to see her French teacher dancing with Gerald's science teacher. *Who would have thought,* Lucy whispers in her ear, *that Mr. Whitaker would have his hand on Mme. Broussard's ass. Oh, Lucy,* Bea says, *you're terrible,* and then Lucy pulls her away from the ballroom and into the library, which is crowded with everyone from their class. *Bea,* everyone shouts, and she curtsies and waves.

Finally, you're here, Nathan says in her ear, and she turns around to see him, all decked out in a tuxedo. Everyone is dressed up, but the boys look the most different, with their hair slicked back, their feet pinched into shiny shoes. Nathan is even wearing tuxedo shoes, which she knows about because Mr. G is wearing them, and she lightly taps one with her shoe. *Fancy,* she says, and he taps her foot back. *Same to you,* he says. He has that look on his face, and she wishes she felt something for him. She knows he's going to try to kiss her tonight. She likes him fine, but she doesn't want to date him. She doesn't want to date anyone. She pleaded with G to come, so she'd have someone to be with at midnight. *Don't let me be alone,* she said, *I don't want to kiss Nathan. Just go to the bathroom,* Gerald said. *That's what I do when I don't want anyone to find me. Keep an eye on the clock, that's all. I'll be Cinderella,* she said. *Don't want to turn into a pumpkin.*

Bea talks to Nathan for a bit, then escapes back to the ballroom, where she dances with Mr. G. *Nineteen forty-four,* Mr. G says as he swings her about, not quite to the beat of the music but with a joyousness that she finds remarkable. Mr. G, dancing up a storm. *Hard to believe,* he continues. *Every year goes faster than the one before.* Bea nods her head, as though to agree, but she doesn't. A year is a long time. It's been over a year since Daddy died and yet there are days when the sheer fact of it surprises her. She'll think of something to share with him — a book, a grade, the beauty of a Christmas blizzard — and be stunned that she can't. *Will this be the year the war ends?* she asks. *Wish I knew,* he says. *Let's hope, shall we? Although Mother's prayers are louder than our hopes.* They both smile. Mrs. G says the same prayer every evening at dinner: *Please God,* she says, *please make sure the war will end before William and Gerald turn eighteen.* It's a ridiculous plea, which William has made clear time after time. *Mother, if the war ends before I turn eighteen, it will most certainly be over before Gerald turns eighteen. Pshaw,* she replies every time. *I need to include both my boys when I ask God for a favor.*

Nathan comes up then and cuts in. Bea lets go of Mr. G reluctantly. *One dance,* she says. *I haven't eaten anything yet. Yes, of course,* he says, always obliging. *Wait until you see the desserts!* William calls him her golden retriever. *Just whistle and he'll be by your side,* he said last week, grinning. He's been dating some girl from a few towns over who goes to a rival school. Bea wonders whether he'll bring her to the Emerys'. She hasn't met her yet, but Lucy Emery told Bea she was blond and stacked. *Not surprising for William,* Lucy said, *because every girl he's ever dated has been built.* They all laughed, huddled together in the chilly cemetery, sharing a cigarette. Bea felt awkward and said nothing, as she always did when they talked about William. He's just William to her. It's as though they think he moves through the world in a different way from anyone else. Still, she looked down at her own flat chest and wondered whether what Lucy said was true.

She and Nathan head to the dining room, and she slips away from him in the crowd. Mrs. G waves her over from where she's sitting with her friends. *Isn't this a lovely party,* she says, smoothing out the folds in Bea's dress. *Just lovely. Have you seen William,* she asks. *It's just like him to set me worrying on New Year's Eve, when I want to relax and have a nice time with my friends.* He'll be here, Bea says, not sure at all. *Well, he better,* Mrs. G says. *Father will pop a gasket if he doesn't show up.*

At eleven thirty, Bea circles through the rooms again, trying to lose Nathan, trying to lose Lucy, trying to find refuge. She finds a window seat near the front door that's partially covered by a thick velvet curtain, and she sits down, pulling the curtain so that as much of her is covered as possible. She tucks her legs up under her dress and gazes out the window, adjusting her eyesight, wondering what her mother did this evening. Did she go to a party, too? She doesn't know whether her mother dates other men. Bea closes her eyes, not wanting to see it, a strange man with his arm around her mother, her mother kissing him on the lips.

A dark figure hurries down the icy path

toward the house, and Bea leans forward, squinting, trying to make out who it is. It doesn't look like William, and she's disappointed, although she's not really sure why. They've spent so little time together lately. She doesn't even much like him anymore. He's restless and jumpy. He almost always gets what he wants but even then, he's rarely satisfied. The band is playing one of her favorite songs, a Tommy Dorsey up-tempo number, and Bea starts humming along, tapping her toe. She loves these shoes. Lately she's started to wonder whether she'll be able to take her clothes home with her when she goes.

People walk by the window seat, and Bea pulls herself in even tighter. She knows Nathan is looking for her. She hears Lucy go by, chatting to someone else. *Everyone in the ballroom,* someone shouts. Bea closes her eyes and leans against the cold window. People are laughing and singing. A glass shatters. The band starts up a new song. She checks her watch. Ten minutes until midnight. She smiles to herself. She's almost made it.

Bea, a voice half whispers, half calls, and it's Gerald. *G,* she says, sitting up, surprised. *I'm in here.* He pokes his head in and then climbs in next to her. *What are you doing here,* she asks, smiling. *I thought you didn't want to come.* He shrugs. *Got bored at home. And I knew you would be looking for an exit right about now.* He looks around the window seat. *Looks like you did all right for yourself, though.*

How'd you know I was here? He sighs. *How long have we been playing hide-and-seek? You're pretty predictable, you know.* Bea sticks out her tongue at him. *You are,* he says, *but I also looked everywhere else. Mother, Father, and Willie are all in the ballroom.* Bea sits up straighter. *William's here?* Gerald nods. *He was with some girl. And Mother and Father were dancing.* Oh, Bea says, *that I want to see.*

Gerald scrunches his face. *Why would you want to,* he says, *they're just dancing.* Bea scrambles out of the window seat. *But they're never like that. They so rarely even touch each other. Come on, G, let's go watch. No,* he groans, *stay with me here, won't you?* Bea grabs his hand. *Come on, G.* They run together to the ballroom, just in time to join the crowd in counting down to midnight. They stay at the edge of the crowd, their backs against the wall. At midnight, everyone screams *Happy New Year!* The band begins to play "Auld Lang Syne." Bea turns

189

to Gerald and squeezes his hand. *Happy New Year, G,* she says. He squeezes her hand back. *You, too,* he says, and he gives her a quick hug.

Later, Bea ends up in William's car for the ride home. *What happened to your girl,* she asks as she climbs in front. *Don't you need to give her a ride home?* She agreed to another dance with Nathan, who found her right after midnight, and she saw William dancing with this blond girl, the two of them pressed so tightly together, she had to look away. *She went with her friends,* he says. *They all live in Wellesley.* They're both quiet as he pulls the car onto the street. *I looked for you earlier,* he says, his eyes on the road. *I thought maybe you'd left. No,* she says. *Just hiding from Nathan.* He smiles. *She's not my girl,* he says after a bit, *we just have a fun time together. I don't care one way or the other,* she says. *I know,* he replies. *I just wanted you to know.* She nods, and the rest of the ride is silent and dark.

In the warm kitchen, as they're hanging up their coats and hats, Bea takes her first real look at him. He looks quite elegant in his tux. He'll turn seventeen next summer; he's almost all grown-up. *You look nice,* she says, almost in spite of herself. *You, too,* he

190

says. *I wanted to tell you earlier but I didn't have a chance.* He's about to say something else when Mrs. G bursts in through the back door. *Oh, my Lord, it is freezing out there and those roads, well, they're just treacherous. We were spinning all over the place, and Father is a most wonderful driver on ice.* She turns to William, wagging her finger. *William Gregory, you left after us and here you two are, already home. You're driving too fast on these streets. And with such precious cargo.* William kisses her on the cheek. *Happy New Year to you as well, Mother.*

Later, as Bea's getting undressed, she catches a whiff of William on her shawl, and she presses the silk to her face before folding it up and placing it gently in her bureau drawer.

NANCY

This year, Nancy's the one who's not sure she wants to go to Maine. More and more of her time has been taken up with the war effort: making socks for the boys, canning vegetables and preserves, and now, in the spring, she's just gotten her Victory Garden going. If they leave for three months, her garden will be decimated. Sure, she could hire a local boy to come by and help out, but it won't be the same. It all seems too much. To use up all that gas just to sit in the sun and spend the summer enjoying themselves — it doesn't seem right.

I'm in awe of your mother, she says to Beatrix one afternoon in the kitchen as she's making the biscuits for dinner. Bea is at the table, working on her French homework. *Look at her,* Nancy says. *Working multiple jobs as well as driving the ambulance.* Bea raises her eyebrows. *I suppose,* she says. *But Mrs. G, she doesn't have a house to run like*

192

you do. You do so much: cooking and clean-
ing for us all, giving parties for the faculty.
Your ladies' group. The war effort. You're the
center of almost everything.

Oh, nonsense, she says, but she's pleased.
She suspects the boys never notice how hard
she works. *We women are always the ones in*
the middle, the caretakers. She lowers her
voice. *Not where I thought I'd end up, I'll just*
say that. Bea cocks her head in confusion. *I*
grew up in quite a fancy house, with maids
and butlers and all that, Nancy says. *Well,*
you see it, don't you, at Aunt Sarah's in New
York. Yes, Bea says, *they live quite differently*
than we do. That's how I was brought up, too,
Nancy says. *But when I married Father, well,*
that life was no longer possible. But this
house, Bea says. *This mess of a house?*
Nancy says, shaking her head. *It's practically*
falling down around us. It belongs to the
school, my dear. When we're all gone, some
other faculty family will live here. We're very
lucky. We're only living here because Father's
family lived here before us.

I had no idea, Bea says. *Well, why should*
you have had any idea? Nancy replies. *Now,*
Maine, that was built by my father. None of
my siblings wanted it so I took it after he died.
That was my entire inheritance, along with a

bit of jewelry. But, the island, well. She combines the dry ingredients with the wet. *Well, what,* Bea asks. Nancy has said too much. Should she tell the child that she and Ethan have talked about selling it? It's simply too much to maintain. She can't bear the thought of it, of course, and she just wants to muddle through, to somehow get to the end of this blasted war and have William and Gerald grow up and get jobs and then they can take it over. It can be theirs. Every night she asks God to make that happen. But Ethan has been calling her into the study to show her pages of numbers that she can't understand.

She knows that's partly why she doesn't want to go to Maine. It will break her heart to be there, to see the place she loves and may have to lose. *All my memories are there,* she said to Ethan one night. She was already in bed, and he was getting undressed. *That's my home. My true north. You'll still have your memories,* he replied. *No one is taking those away. Oh, for heaven's sake,* she said, throwing her book down on the bed so hard that the dog ran out of the room, *do you not have a heart? Do you not understand what the island means to me?*

I understand, he said in that calm voice that makes her want to scream. *But you need to understand that our expenses are taking over. And in a year, we'll have William's tuition for Harvard, on top of everything else.* She stared down at the blanket, smoothing the folds, unable to look up at him. She hates his rationality.

She turns to Bea now. *I'm just worrying about my poor island once William and Gerald take control. Can you imagine what that will be like? How will they possibly manage this together? You'll need to help mediate.* A pause hangs in the air. Bea looks down at her paper and finishes the sentence she was writing. That beautiful, assured handwriting. Will she receive letters from Bea after she goes home? Will they stay in touch? Or will Bea simply fade away? Nancy can't bear that thought. *Silly me,* she finally says as Bea continues with her homework, her head down. *Silly, silly me. Of course, you'll be back in England by then. But you'll come visit, won't you,* and Nancy turns back to her bowl, kneading the dough roughly, her head bent away from Bea. Then she reaches over, with her floured hand, turns up the radio, and begins singing along with the Andrews Sisters, as she rolls out the dough, as she uses a glass to cut the biscuits, as she washes out the bowl. When she turns back to the table, Bea is gone.

BEA

Bea is in the house alone. They're back from a short visit to Maine to celebrate their birthdays. Everyone's out of the house, doing this and that, and Bea wanders from room to room, with King at her side.

Ever since Mrs. G told her that the house doesn't belong to them, she's looked at it differently. She can't imagine another family living here, and wonders how that feels to Mr. G, who's lived his entire life here. What is it like to live in one place and one place only? She's already lived in two, and when she goes back, there will be a third, as her mother has moved to a new flat. She's described it in her letters. There are two bedrooms. Mummy found some new furniture for her room, and she's said that her window looks out on the street. *Only two flights up, sweetheart. So much easier to manage the groceries.* Bea can't picture it from the description, nor does she know the block, even though Mummy said they'd walked down it a million times.

For years now, she's clung to the image of their flat, of her father washing dishes, of her mother closing the curtains, of the smell of onions wafting up from the flat below. The crack in the living room ceiling that ran from one corner to another. The creak of the front door when Daddy came home. At night, she's lain in bed, remembering, trying to hold on to every detail. That was home. She drew a map of the flat a few years ago, which she keeps in her desk drawer, but the edges of her memory are starting to fray. Was there a chair in her room? What kind of wood was her dresser made from? She wonders what happened to all her belongings, everything that was in her closet. She had always thought she would return there, to the place where her father still lives in her mind.

Bea wanders the second floor with King. The twin beds in Mr. and Mrs. G's room are only a foot apart, with a small side table in between them, a lamp and books perched on top. She wonders whether they ever hold hands while they're lying in bed. Once, she asked Gerald about them not sleeping in the same bed. He was surprised she found it curious. *It's always been like that,* he said.

Don't all parents sleep in separate beds? Every time they were at someone's house together and Bea saw a bed for two adults, rather than one, she'd go find Gerald and show him. *This is normal,* she whispered when they were at Aunt Sarah's in New York. Gerald dismissed her, which he so rarely did. *You're wrong,* he said, his face flushing. *It's not right for parents to sleep together when there are children in the house.*

She can tell whose bed is whose by the books on the table: a romance on Mrs. G's side and a history book for Mr. G, along with a pair of half glasses. Bea sinks into Mrs. G's bed, which is soft and depressed where her body lies each night. Mr. G's bed smells just like he does and it's far stiffer. She imagines him lying on his back, his feet hanging slightly over the bottom edge. She reaches over to the other bed. *Good night, Nancy,* she imagines him saying in that voice of his, his teacher voice. Suddenly, it feels horribly intimate to be here, and she jumps up, smoothing out the bedspreads. *Let's go, King,* she says. *Don't say a word.*

Gerald's room is far more familiar. His bed, his mahogany desk. The always growing rubber band ball that he donates each month to the war effort, starting anew on the first of every month. A trunk with his grandfather's monogram in gold where he keeps his games and toys. How many times have they lain on this rug playing Monopoly? How many thousands of card games have they played? Recently, Gerald has been collecting little metal soldiers, spending most of his money on them, running down to the five-and-dime each Saturday morning to add more soldiers to his armies after Mr. G doles out their allowance. There's a battle in play right now on his window seat, the Allies versus the Germans. William makes fun of him for this, and Bea's noticed that he puts them all away, hiding them in his trunk, whenever anyone's over to play. He turned thirteen this summer and yet there are many ways in which he still seems the same boy he was when she arrived. There's an innocence to him, a guilelessness that she's never known in anyone else. It's this fragility that William pounces on, and it's the thing that Bea wants to protect, above all else.

She stands in William's doorway. The room is a mess. He hasn't unpacked from Maine, so suitcases and duffel bags are scattered across the floor. Baseball bats, mitts, and cards are piled up on his spare bed. *Oh, William,* Bea says to herself. Another way that the boys are different: Gerald's room is always neat, his desk chair pushed in, his bed made. Saturday morning he is the first to be done cleaning his room. William just throws everything in his closet. King has jumped up on William's bed, and she snuggles up next to him, her arm wrapped around his neck.

The pillow smells like William. She hugs King a little tighter and is drifting off when she hears footsteps on the stairs. William appears in the doorway. He must have been out at the batting cages with Bobby Nelson. Sweat has darkened the curls around his forehead. *What are you doing,* he asks, *why are you in my room?* His neck turns red. *Why are you on my bed?* Bea sits up, flustered. *I was walking by and I saw King here, so I came in to pet him. That's all. Certainly wouldn't want to be in your nasty bed. Can you get out of my room,* he says, and once again she feels as though he's talking to Gerald. *Jesus,* she says, *you're in a mood.* William sighs. *I wasn't expecting to come home to find some girl in my room. Some girl?* Bea asks, looking up into his face, her hands on her hips. *What the hell is wrong with you today?*

William walks over to the window and looks out at the garden. He grew almost four inches over the summer, and he's filled out, too. He blocks all the light that's coming in through the window. His back relaxes as he takes a deep breath before turning around. *Sorry,* he says. *I didn't mean to be an ass. I was just surprised, that's all.* Bea rolls her eyes. *Somehow I think you were saying what you really believe. What?* he says. *Never mind,* she says. *I'm talking about nothing. Come on, King.*

The dog obediently hops off the bed and follows her out of the room. She walks down the hall to her room, half expecting William to follow her. But instead, she hears his door shut firmly, and she goes into her room and does the same. She sits down at her desk. She feels edgy these days, impatient with everyone and everything. It's the limbo that's so frustrating. She doesn't know where she belongs. Some days, she wants to stay here forever. But on others, she wants to go home. She wants to see her mother. She's curious to be in London again, to see what the war has done to it, to see it with older eyes. Will it be at all familiar? Or will it be so changed that it will be new, a different place entirely?

Bea takes out a piece of airmail stationery. *Dear Mummy,* she writes, *I hope you are well.*

All is good here. She tells her about coming back from Maine and getting ready for the school year to begin. About the new haircut that she got the day before. About the fact that she must take Latin with the boys because she's the only girl in Latin 6. She closes the letter with a request. *Please,* she writes, *promise me that you'll send for me as soon as you're able, as soon as this dreadful war is over. I'm ready to come home.* She carries the letter with her for days, never managing to post it. Is she really ready to leave?

MILLIE

As Millie and Tommy leave the small chapel, Julia and the others throw rice and cheer. The wedding is small, with a small circle of friends and Tom's immediate family. Millie didn't tell her mother. And she hasn't told Beatrix, either.

She had been planning to wear an old dress, one that she bought in Paris with Reg years ago, but Julia made her go buy something new. They found a lovely cream-colored suit with satin trim at one of the clothes swaps. It looked as though it had never been worn. Julia found some hose on the black market that she gave her as a gift. *Seams and everything,* she said when she gave them to Millie. *With your legs, you need to show them off.*

The rain and wind earlier in the day had caused all the remaining leaves to fall off the trees, and they walk carefully through the wet, slippery streets as they head over to

Julia's flat for the reception. Millie makes the rounds, trying to talk to everyone. She wonders whether the guests are happier than she is. That's the thing about coming closer to the end of this war: everyone has been waiting for years to have some fun. The joys are that much more joyful.

As the party starts to wind down, Millie collapses into an armchair in the corner of the living room and kicks off her shoes. Tommy is across the way with his brother, their arms around each other, laughing at some joke or another. She likes him. She doesn't love him, she knows that, and she suspects he knows it, too, even though she's dutifully been telling him that she loves him for months now. But he's solid, she feels, someone who will be there. What she likes most of all is that everything is written on his face. She knows when he's upset or angry or happy. Nothing is ever hidden. In this respect, and in so many others, he's the opposite of Reg. Along with that, she knows, comes someone who is less intelligent, less complex, less interesting, perhaps. But she doesn't want that anymore. She wants to be protected. She likes how it feels when he wraps his arms around her.

She wonders how easy he will be, though. Tommy was a fighter pilot in the war and flew enough missions over Germany that he was discharged early. He loves telling stories about the war, and everyone always gathers round, just like they're doing now. She knows that they only hear the good stuff, the stories that entertain. He rarely talks about anything much darker, although it must be there. How can it not be? No physical scars, like Reg's brother in the first war, but she suspects there's a lot beneath the surface. A lot she'll probably never know.

He is handsome, though, and young. Very young. Nine years younger than she is. She brought him round to meet some of the girls from the old neighborhood, and she could read the disapproval in their eyes. Part of that, she is sure, is because he's not Reg, and they will never be able to see her with anyone but him. They had started dating when she was only fifteen. But still. Her friends from the ambulance corps have been supportive and jokey about it, wondering aloud about how great the sex must be with a younger man. Millie's laughed and covered her mouth. *Girls,* she's said, *really.*

But it is great. Now she understands what everyone has been talking about all these years. She had loved Reg, passionately and deeply, even as they argued, even as the relationship felt as though it was ripped beyond repair. But she'd never really cared about sex. She always just wanted it over with. With Beatrix right in the next room, it was easier not to do much of anything. But with Tommy, well, it is something else indeed. She disappears into the moment in a way she never did with Reg. He's so confident and assured. Afterward, he walks around the flat naked, and at first she was appalled and embarrassed, but now, after a drink or two, she does as well. She already knows his body more intimately than she ever knew Reg's body. She feels safe with such a physical man, someone so comfortable in his body. He knows hers as well, and sometimes he counts each small mole on her chest and stomach.

It all seems backward, somehow. Shouldn't great sex be partnered with deep love?

This is why she hasn't told Beatrix. Oh, she's written about Tommy, about how they've been dating, even shared some of the stories he tells about being a fighter pilot. Beatrix read that part of the letter aloud to the boys. *Now William wants to be a fighter pilot,* she wrote. *And they both loved the story about all the planes coming back on Christmas Eve, lit up like a Christmas tree.* But she hasn't told her that Tom is only thirty-one. She's sure that Beatrix, like those women from the neighborhood, will disapprove, will be uncomfortable. Why is it wrong for a woman to marry a man who is younger? Reg was almost ten years older and that was fine; Millie knows plenty of women who have married much older men. In her next letter, she'll tell Beatrix about the marriage. She'll tell her mother. But maybe she'll keep his age a secret for a little while longer.

Tommy looks over now and winks. She waves and lifts her glass of champagne. He lifts his, too, and kisses the air. She thinks of Reg, and she touches the pearl at her neck, rolling it around and around.

GERALD

Gerald sends King out to retrieve the morning paper. He's been carefully following the Battle of the Bulge, which began in December, and now, in mid-January, it appears the tables might be turning. He doesn't want to let hope have the upper hand, but the Allies do seem to be winning. An editorial in yesterday's paper even said that this could very well lead to the end of the war.

He loves mapping out what he reads, so he can see how it all works. He always understands things more clearly when he can see them. He's been carefully tracing the maps in his atlas and then using colored pencils to mark the progression of the different armies: the Allies in blue and the Germans in red. He likes studying the war in this way, looking at it from above, thinking about the strategy involved. This is the only way he could ever be involved in a war. He knows he never wants to fight. He can't kill an ant. How could he possibly kill a man?

Gerald hopes that this does indeed mean the end of the war. He wants to go to college, to study, to learn more about the world. He thinks about moving away from here, far away from here, to California, perhaps, although he's never mentioned this to anyone. He wants to be near the ocean, and he likes the look of Southern California, with its palm trees and miles of beaches. What must it be like to watch the sun set over the Pacific Ocean? But then he wonders about being so far away. Perhaps it's best to stay close by.

Mother comes into the kitchen and kisses the top of his head. *Good morning, sweetheart,* she says. *What do the papers say?* Gerald smiles at her. *They think this is the beginning of the end,* he says. He watches Mother as she wraps her apron around her waist. He has wanted to ask her something for days now and perhaps this is the right moment. *What does this mean for Bea,* he says. *Will she have to go back soon?*

Oh, we don't need to think about that yet, Mother says, cracking one egg after another into the big blue bowl. *The war's not over. Travel will be limited and even then, I'm not sure how it will work. They'll need to bring all* the boys home. *Even if the war in Europe ends, the war in the Pacific will likely go on. Not to worry, my dear.* Mother begins whipping the eggs with a fork, cradling the bowl in her arm, the fork banging against the bowl, again and again.

Gerald knows that she's trying to convince herself of this, trying to bury the fact of Bea leaving. He heard her on the phone with Aunt Sarah just last week. *Honestly, Sarah,* she said, *what am I going to do? Every time I think about her leaving I dissolve into a puddle of tears.* She dropped her voice. *I feel closer to her than I do to William. What does that say about me? What kind of mother even says that out loud?*

Gerald knows what she means. When they were younger, William would always pose moral questions at the dinner table: *If you were stranded on a desert island, what two items would you want to have? If you could pick one person and one person only to spend the rest of your life with, whom would you pick?* And so on. Gerald always hated these, as back then the answer was never clear to him. He didn't want to bring two items, he wanted to bring six. He couldn't choose one person, even though he knew that person would be William, but of course he would want to bring Mother and Father and some of the cousins and his friend from down the street.

This was all before Bea. Now he would probably choose Bea and Mother, and maybe even Bea over Mother, but he definitely wouldn't choose William. When William's in the room, everything feels uncertain and tense and ready to explode. Mostly he's not around. Gerald longs for the William he used to know. He knows Bea is often angry at William, but he guesses that she, too, simply misses him.

So when Bea leaves, he will truly be alone. He can't wish for the war not to end, as that's not right for the world or for all the men who need to come home, but secretly, in his prayers at night, he asks God to please let her stay.

WILLIAM

The warm letter of acceptance arrived from Harvard back in the fall, a personal note from the head of admissions welcoming him into the fold. But William also applied to other schools, using Bobby Nelson's address, and at morning assembly, Nelson passes a few envelopes down the row of desks, giving William a thumbs-up from across the room. William tucks the envelopes into his satchel and waits until the end of the day to open them. He doesn't want to be near anyone, so he heads into the cemetery, all the way to the back, where the trees are greening above their dark branches. He has a favorite maple tree, one that looks out over the pond, and he throws his satchel down, pressing his back up against the bark, and lights a cigarette before opening the envelopes.

It's hard for him to realize that he will be going to college in the fall. For so long, he's had the date of his eighteenth birthday in his head, with plans to march into Boston and enlist on the day. To head to basic and then off to Europe or the Pacific, wherever he is needed. But, instead, it now seems that the war in Europe, anyway, will end, and the number of new troops will diminish. The boys in Europe will be sent to the Pacific.

He slides his finger under the first envelope flap and pulls the letter out. A rejection from Columbia. The second: a rejection from Yale. He closes his eyes, and he can hear the birds flapping about above him in the tree. He doesn't want to go to Harvard. It's what everyone expects. He wants to explore something new. Now that he won't be going to war, he feels even more strongly that he doesn't want to go. But now he has no other options.

Before supper, he knocks on Bea's door with their special code, the one that Gerald created. *Come in,* she calls. *Hello,* he says, opening the door a crack. *Time for a chat?* Her face goes flat and she shrugs, not meeting his eyes. *I guess,* she says, *but I have a lot of homework. It won't take long,* he says, and he sits down in the desk chair that looks out over the backyard. *So lovely out today,* he says. *The sky looks like a Maine sky, doesn't it?* She closes one textbook and opens another; books and notebooks are strewn across her bed. *What do you want, William? I'm busy.*

He leans toward her. *I didn't get into Columbia,* he says, his voice low, and then she looks up in surprise. *You applied?* He nods. *But I didn't tell the folks. Didn't get into Yale either.* Bea shrugs. *Their loss,* she says, but her tone is unconvincing. *I thought I would,* he says, and he turns to look out her window so she can't see his tears.

I'm surprised, she says. *Always thought you could go anywhere. My grades are bad,* he says. *You know that.* He slides down to sit on her floor, his back against her closet door, and begins tossing one of her socks back and forth, from one hand to the other. *I don't know what to do. I don't want to go to Harvard. Well, that's just stupid,* she says, her voice hard, her ears turning red. *Ridiculous. You have an opportunity to go to one of the top universities and you're not going to go because you're a spoiled, petulant boy?*

Give me a break, he says, suddenly cross, refusing to look at her. *That's not why I don't want to go to Harvard. I want to do my own thing, for once. And what I'm asking you for, here, is how to talk to the folks about this.*

214

Don't twist this around because you're mad at me, too. He lies down on the floor and puts his feet up on her bed, his arms behind his head. He wants to go far away. *Don't you get it, Bea,* he says. *I'm ready for something new.*

She puts down her pen and looks hard at him, a searching look that reminds him of the old Bea, of how close they used to be. But she's different now. She's got a solid group of girlfriends, and she's always somehow in the center of that group. It's hard to catch her alone, and when he does, she's dismissive of him. She used to knock on his wall at night and they would check in with each other. But she hasn't done that in ages.

She sighs. *Okay, look. What do you want to do? You want to say no to Harvard?* He shrugs, then nods. *What would you do?* she asks. *I don't know,* he says. *Maybe travel? Maybe get a job somewhere else?* Bea shakes her head. *The men are all starting to come home,* she says. *All those jobs that we've been doing, that kids and women across the country have been doing, they're going to be gone. And travel? How are you going to do that? With what money?*

He shrugs again. *I have some money saved up,* he says. *I could figure something out.* She's not even trying to understand. She returns to looking at her books, turning the pages. *You're not being realistic,* she says without looking up. *You're just not. The kind of money that we save is not enough to live on.*

How do you know, he says, furious. *What do you know about all this?* He stands and walks to the door and as he's opening it, she speaks again. *Your parents are having a hard time this spring,* she says, still not looking at him. *I'm sure you haven't noticed. They're not going to want you to do anything other than what's already set. So do what you want but know that you may not get your way.* William doesn't acknowledge her words but slams the door behind him.

As he sits through dinner, not saying a word, he watches his parents, thinking about what Bea said about them. They seem the same to him, the same as always. Mother: too busy, too cheerful, too energetic. And Father? Who knows. William wrote down a list a few years ago of all the ways he would be a better parent. He remembers how once, in Maine, when he was little, he woke early in the morning and looked out the window, to see his parents standing on the shore, watching the sunrise. Mother turned to Father and curtsied and then he took her in his arms and danced her round and round, Mother laughing when he dipped her, right at the edge of the water. He remembers, too, how sometimes when he would come into the kitchen in this house, she would be sitting on his lap and stand up, all flustered, and start mixing batter or cutting up apples or cleaning a pot. Now he can't remember the last time he even saw Father in the kitchen.

After dinner he knocks again on Bea's door, opening it before she responds. *Jesus, William,* she says, *what now? I have a French exam tomorrow. I don't see you for a year and now you won't leave me alone.* He looks at the floor, his fingers deep in his pants pockets. *I miss you,* he says. And when she looks up at him, he knows he finally said the right thing.

Bea

In the woods behind the house, Bea has a favorite spot. There's an uprooted tree, covered with moss, that extends across the path, and now, in the late spring, it's completely out of sight of the house. She's taken to retreating here more and more. She lies back on the trunk and looks up, through the newly green leaves, to the blue sky beyond.

William fills her thoughts. During the last few weeks, as the spring days have begun to melt into summer, they have quietly left the house after everyone has gone to bed to lie in the hammock together, their arms and legs touching, a thick cotton blanket providing warmth. They don't talk much — they watch the clouds move slowly overhead, the stars suspended in the blue. Sometimes they fall asleep. She has wanted to kiss him, to do more than hold his hand, but she also feels as though everything is precarious, somehow on the edge, and to push beyond what they have may be asking for too much. She wants each moment to last and not to rush too quickly on to the next.

But last night, after they did the dishes, when everyone was elsewhere — Mr. G in his study, Mrs. G in her bedroom, Gerald upstairs as well — William grabbed her hand and pulled her into the pantry, where he kissed her long enough to make her want more. And then, this morning at breakfast, he slipped a note into her lap — asking her to meet him in the cemetery after baseball practice this afternoon — and when he left the table, when no one was looking, he bent down and kissed her neck, brushing her hair back with his hand. She knows they have now crossed a line, and she can think of little else.

But another letter has arrived from her mother. Bea never responded to the letter that came six weeks ago, the one that announced her marriage, and four letters have arrived since then. She knows she needs to write back but she is furious. She feels betrayed. She doesn't know what she's angrier about: that Mum got married or that she didn't tell Bea until after the wedding.

Darling, this letter begins, *Tommy has*

some connections and we've started the process of figuring out how to get you back home. Nothing definite yet, but the wheels are turning. The letter goes on to describe their new flat, and how there's not only a room for Beatrix, but also her own bath. It's in a part of London that Bea doesn't know at all. A posh part. She doubts her mother remembers the first letter from the Gregorys, which also spelled out that she would get her own bath. She hasn't looked at that letter in so long, but it's at the bottom of the pile of letters in her desk.

Hard to believe it's been almost five years since that letter. How different everything was then. And now, now that everyone is looking forward to the end, to having life return to normal, Bea is wishing that it wouldn't. She used to not know where she belonged. But now she doesn't want to go back, to her mother and her new husband — what kind of an adult man is called Tommy — or to move to a new flat and finish out her schooling at a new school. She wants to stay here, with her friends, and go to college. Lots of the girls are hoping to go to Wellesley or Radcliffe, so they can stay in the area. Keep shopping at Jordan's. Keep going to Fenway. Keep being with William. And yet, she knows it's not possible. This whole thing has been temporary. The war ends and she goes home. End of story.

There are tensions in the house. William has been fighting with the Gs for weeks about going to Harvard. Both Mr. and Mrs. G seem tense and out of sorts. And even Gerald, who has always been there for her, often disappears now into his causes, his maps, his other worlds. He seems angry with her, somehow, more distant than he has ever been.

Yesterday, she looked out of the library window to see Gerald walking across campus, alone, pinning up posters about this month's scrap drive. He's already filled one garage bay with scrap metal and rubber and is hoping to double it with donations on Saturday. One carrel over, she heard some of the boys in his class laughing. *Little Gregory,* one of them said. *Still collecting trash. Has anyone told him the war in Europe is over?* She marched over to the carrel and stood there with her arms folded. *Leave him alone,* she said, her voice hard, and they nodded, their eyes wide. *He's done more for the war effort than the lot of you, combined.* She felt sure an upper-class girl had never spoken to them like that before. Who would protect him once she was gone?

Bea reads the letter from her mother again. She folds it in half and tears it, the small pieces littering the ground, before grabbing her bookbag and running through the woods, a smile now on her face, knowing that William is waiting for her by the old maple tree.

MILLIE

As soon as it's feasible, Tommy talks to someone who talks to someone and suddenly it's set. Beatrix has a spot on a ship leaving New York on August 26, arriving in Southampton on August 31. Millie stares at the piece of paper Tommy brings home that lays out the dates in black ink. August 31. Less than three weeks from now she'll be waiting on a dock, and her little girl will come walking down the gangplank.

Tommy fixes martinis, and they settle into the chairs in the garden. *She's coming home,* Millie says. *She's actually going to come home.* Tommy smiles. *Can't wait to meet your girl. Who would have thought it, me with a beautiful wife and a beautiful daughter.* Millie turns from him and closes her eyes. In all the dreams over the years, all the ways she has imagined this moment, she has never once had Tom at her side. Reg, yes. Her mother, yes. Alone, yes. She realizes that's what she wants. Just her and Beatrix. She wants to introduce this new life to her slowly, not have Tommy there at all. It will ruin the homecoming she has dreamt of for so long.

You know, she says, not looking at him, trying to speak as lightly as she can, *maybe I'll head down to Southampton by myself. That's crazy,* Tommy says. *We're in this all together. The sooner we're a real family, the better.* She knows he means well but he's wrong. *I need to do this by myself,* she says, turning toward him. *You need to trust me here.* He makes a face and she knows what that means. Disgust. *Whatever you want,* he says, but he doesn't mean it, and as he stands she shrinks into her chair. He leaves his dirty, empty glass on the table and goes inside. Minutes later, she hears the front door slam and then the car start. What has she done? How will she ever make this house Beatrix's home?

ETHAN

Ethan picks up the phone on the second ring. *Telegram here,* Porter says. *Can someone stop by and pick it up? Will do,* Ethan says, and before he rows over, he tells Nan only that he has an errand in town. The sky is dark as he makes his way across the harbor. He doesn't read the telegram until he's back outside Western Union, where he leans against the outer wall, after saying hello, distractedly, to a few of Nancy's friends. BEATRIX'S PASSAGE IS SET STOP DEPARTURE NYC AUGUST 26 STOP DETAILS SOON STOP LOVE MILLIE. He closes his eyes. They knew this was coming, it's been in the works for weeks, if not months, but honestly, couldn't Millie have waited until September? They'll need to leave Maine early, maybe even tomorrow, to get home, to pack her up, to drive down to New York. August 26 is in six days. Less than a week away.

Ethan's nose drips as he heads back to the boat. Damn it all, he will miss the girl. He wipes furiously at his nose with the back of his hand, and he keeps his head down so as not to catch eyes with anyone he knows. As he rows back to the island, the telegram crumpled in his pants pocket, the rain never comes. Instead, the clouds make the evening sky come alive with shades of pink and purple. Ethan stops rowing and lets the boat drift, the current pulling him southeast, away from the island. He wishes he could let the water take him far away. He doesn't want to deliver this news. He wants to go to all those places he's never been. Instead, after a bit, he turns toward home.

NANCY

Oh, Lord, Nancy says when Ethan finds her on the porch. *August twenty-sixth, Ethan? That's next week. I know,* he says, *I know.* She flutters both hands in the air. *How can we possibly even make that ship? We'll have to leave tonight, that's all, we must leave right now. She needs to pack and say goodbye to her friends and I'll want to get her some new clothes for traveling and, really, she should get her hair cut and, oh my goodness, there's just too much to do.* Ethan reaches over and grabs Nancy's arm to stop her from pacing. *Sit,* he says, *sit down,* and she does, collapsing into the rocking chair.

She looks into his eyes, something she hasn't done in a long time, searching for an answer. *How will we tell her,* she says, *I don't think I can do that. How will we tell the boys? We'll manage, Nan,* Ethan says. *We all knew it could happen anytime. I know,* she says. *But you need to tell her, okay? I'll just be swim-*

ming in tears.

Yes, ma'am, he says, and he reaches out his arms and she moves over to sit in his lap, resting her head against his chest. She closes her eyes and listens to the rhythm of the waves, which seems to match the rhythm of his steady breath.

GERALD

Gerald doesn't want to let Bea out of his sight. If he can see her, she can't leave. *Monopoly,* he says at dinner, making his voice as cheery as he can, *what do you say? G,* she says, *I don't think we'll have time. I need to pack up everything here so we can get on the road first thing. Okay,* Gerald says, *but what if I help you pack? Then maybe you would have time? Maybe,* she says, laughing now, giving in. *Fine, you can help me.*

But he doesn't help her. He lies on her floor, watching. Even the way she packs seems perfect. She doesn't seem to be sad to be leaving, he realizes, but he's not really sure. He thought she'd at least be sad to leave William. *Do you want to go back,* he asks finally, not really wanting to hear the answer. *Are you ready to leave us? Oh, G,* she says, turning toward him but still folding her shirts. *I'll never be ready to leave you. But I don't have a choice, right? I expected this to happen a while back, so it's almost overdue. In that sense, it's a relief. No more waiting.* Gerald nods. That he understands. He hates being in a state of limbo, of not knowing what's happening next.

You'll come back to visit, won't you, he asks, telling himself not to cry. *Yes,* Bea says, *of course.* And then she sits down next him and rubs his back, and he puts his head down on the rug and closes his eyes. *But you need to write to me, G, okay? Tell me everything that's going on. And I promise I'll write back as soon as I receive every letter.* He nods. *I will,* he says. She stands to empty another drawer and he wipes his eyes when her back is to him and when she turns around, he points to a photograph in a frame on her bureau, one of the three of them on the shore from a couple of summers ago. Bea's standing in between him and William, her smile wide, her arms wrapped around each of their backs. *Can I have that,* he asks, and he can see her hesitate for just a moment. *Of course,* she says, *you keep it for now. But the next time I see you, let me have a turn at holding on to it, okay? We can trade it back and forth. That's the day I beat William swimming to the dock. I don't ever want to forget that.*

He nods and holds the frame in both hands. *I'll take good care of it,* he says, *don't you worry.* He's not sure he'll ever let it go.

WILLIAM

William turns the pages of the book that Bea made for him just a few weeks earlier. It's the story of her life. When she was born, where she lived, when she came to America. Photos from the last five years, but photos from before, too. Of her, in London, with her parents. He's studied them repeatedly. The way her smile hasn't changed. That look in her eyes. The small stuffed dog she held in her arms. He doesn't want to forget any of the photos, but he wants her to have the book when she leaves. It was her way of joining the two of them together, of blending the past with the present.

She's in her room, packing with Gerald. He can hear the rumble of their words. He'll meet her later in the woods, just as they've been meeting for the whole summer. She's already made him promise: no one can ever know. He wouldn't mind, but it's important to her. And as things have progressed, as they've become more comfortable with each other, Bea's become more adamant about their rules. *Don't you go touching me in front of your parents, William Gregory,* she said, and then she kissed him so hard that he tripped and fell backward onto the pine needles. *This is our secret, okay?* she said. *You can't be crying or touching me or doing anything on the day I leave, whenever that will be. Crying,* he said, pulling her down on top of him and twisting her thick hair in his hands. *Why would I be crying?*

In the spring, she convinced him to go to Harvard. She told him it was a gift he needed to accept. *Do it for me,* she said. She helped him choose his courses for the fall, and the other night he turned to her in the woods. *I'm really excited to start,* he said. *I hate to say that to you, when you won't be there with me, but I can't remember the last time I've been so ready to start something new.* She had smiled at him and kissed his cheek. *I can't wait to hear all about it,* she said. *You have to tell me everything.*

His stomach hurts. He feels physically attached to her, as though when she leaves there will be a part of him that will go as well. He can say things to her that he can't say to anyone else. He never has to perform. She is straight with him, honest, and he tries

233

to be the same with her. Mostly she quiets something in him, something deep inside. Last night, they lay on the rocks and watched the dark sky. Those are the moments he loves the best with her, being next to her, holding her hand, neither saying much at all.

BEA

After dinner, Bea stands on the deck of the ship and looks out at the black ocean. She knows there is no land to be seen. It's been three days since the ship slowly pulled out of New York Harbor, since she watched her family get smaller and smaller. For one brief moment, she had held them in her palms before they disappeared.

All she wants is to go back. For the ship to reverse its course. To stay in America. To go to college. To bake pies with Mrs. G. To play chess with Mr. G. To explore with Gerald. To kiss William. To marry William. To be in this family forever. But she knows that's not possible. The boat is churning forward, toward her mother, toward her new stepfather. The Gregorys are not her family. It's not the way the story is going to end. It never was.

On their last night together, in the woods, she told William to move on. *No,* he said, *I*

235

won't. We can write, I'll come to England, and she interrupted him. *No,* she said. *That's a dream, a moment out of time. I know about living across an ocean from people you love. It's worse if we try to stay connected, the way we are now. It's too hard. It's better for both of us if we cut it off cleanly. But,* he began, and she shook her head, laying her hand across his mouth. *I'm right,* she said, and he nodded then, quiet. She hadn't believed her own words, of course, but she knew it was the only way.

There is as much uncertainty now as there was five years earlier, when she'd made the crossing in the other direction. Still, she wishes she could go back and tell that little girl not to worry. That the life she would have in America would overshadow the life from before. That her family there — the one she only knew about from those early letters — would become her world. In her bunk, she pulls out the book that she made for William, the one that he slipped into her trunk when she wasn't looking. He'd turned it into a book about the two of them, not just about her. He extended the timeline to 1927, when he was born. He added photos from when he was little, matching the early photos of her. A photo of her in her crib, followed by one of him in a pram. She on the beach in Brighton, he on the rocky shore in Maine. One of each of them with a missing front tooth, smiling, their faces lined up as though they could see the other, as though they were both thinking the same thing. He also drew quirky little illustrations: a hospital bed when his tonsils were taken out. Pine trees for the island. A mug of coffee in New York. On the date they met, he drew a sun, a boat, and a dock.

The book blends them together, allowing them to share a single past. His childhood is her childhood. It's as if they were always together, as if there was no before.

■ ■ ■ ■

Part Two:
August 1951

■ ■ ■ ■

WILLIAM

That Sunday morning, William looked up from his book and gazed over the Parisian rooftops, the blue sky beginning to break through the haze. He and Nelson were planning to leave Paris in two days, heading to Rome, and they still had a list of museums to visit and sights to see. They had been moving at a fast pace, seeing as much as they could during each day, drinking long into each night.

In a little over a week, he would turn twenty-four. And here he was in an apartment in the sixth arrondissement. A little balcony overlooking the Luxembourg Gardens. The street noises floating up. The smell of burning leaves. William and Nelson there, together, the European trip that had been planned since they were young. Nelson was in between years at law school; William had accrued time off from the bank where he had worked since graduation. In the late mornings, before Nelson woke, William had taken to sitting out on the balcony, drinking a coffee and smoking a cigarette, one of the French unfiltered ones, the sun peering behind the ornate roofs. It was close to the Paris that he had often imagined. He didn't want the trip to end.

The phone rang, and William knocked over his coffee on the way inside but Nelson got to the phone before he did, answering in his perfect French. He listened, turning his face toward William and raising one eyebrow in that way he does. "Your mother," he mouthed. He nodded and held his finger up when William gestured for the phone. William knew something must be wrong. She would never call otherwise and certainly not so early in the morning. An aunt? Gerald?

Nelson handed the phone over.

"Mother," William said. "What is it?"

He turned his back on Nelson as he listened to her, once again looking at the Parisian skyline, and he knew before she said it that Father was dead. A heart attack, while he was out working in the garden. Mother was crying now, and he tried to understand what she was saying. He tried hard to be patient. "Mother, please," he finally said. "Just tell me the basic facts. I'll come home as soon as I can arrange it."

He kept nodding, trying to follow the broken conversation, but mostly he was ashamed at how angry he felt. Angry at Father for ruining this trip. He hadn't wanted him to go. The way he looked at him when he told him about it. It was as though he was twelve again.

He cut Mother off midsentence. "I'll send a telegram with my travel arrangements," he said. He hung up after saying goodbye and turned around to look at Nelson. "My father," he said. "Gone."

"Shit," Nelson said, and there were tears in his eyes. There were none in William's. Nelson had known him almost as long. William felt oddly numb. "What now?" Nelson asked.

"I need to head home," William said. "Mother's a mess."

He crossed the Channel on the night ferry. It took a bit of an argument, but he persuaded Nelson to go on to Rome as they had planned. "Look," he had said, "you don't need to be back until classes start up again. Go and enjoy. Who knows when we'll get here again?" He'd heard again from home, a telegram from Gerald, and the memorial service wasn't to be held until mid-September, to ensure that everyone at school could attend. He sounded in charge, Gerald did. He was the right one to be there, to help take care of Mother, to be the grieving face of the family. William knew he would only disappoint.

After he got off the train the following morning, he found his way to the ticket office in London and inquired about exchanging his passage for the earliest possible date.

"You're in luck, sir," the clerk said. "We've just had a cancellation. There's a place for you on the ship this Wednesday."

He handed over his ticket and his passport, and she wrote up the new ticket and handed everything back. This was why he had come to London; this was what he had hoped. He had two days until the ship was to sail. He wanted to be with Bea.

BEA

Bea was on the stairs, her arms full of groceries, when she heard the telephone ring. She ran up to her door, fumbling with the key in the lock.

"Sweetheart," a voice said. It was Mrs. G. How strange it was to hear her voice after all this time. She dropped the bags on the floor, and a few lemons rolled under the couch. This was her final week of summer holiday, before the fall term started up, and all the nursery school teachers were getting together Tuesday night for dinner. She was planning on making a lemon pudding cake.

"Yes," she said, trying to catch her breath, trying not to sound too winded. "Hello. Is everything all right?"

"It's Ethan," Mrs. G said, and Bea sat down. "It's Mr. G. I'm afraid he's had a heart attack."

"Is he in hospital, then," Bea asked, not understanding, not willing to hear past her words, forcing her to spell it out.

"No, dear," she said, the transatlantic pauses coming in between the words, stretching out the truth. "He's passed on."

Bea couldn't help herself then, and she placed a hand over her mouth to force any sounds to stay within. She shook her head, unable to speak. First Dad and then Mr. G.

"Dear," Mrs. G said, and how Bea wished she could wrap her arms around that wide waist. "Are you all right, dear? Are you still on the line?"

"Yes," Bea said, and she dug her fingernails into her palms. "I'm so sorry to hear."

"Yes," she replied. "We're all so very sad."

Bea nodded but was unable to respond.

"Both the boys are away," Mrs. G said. "But they'll be home soon. One sister is here. The others are on their way."

"That's good," Bea said. "Good to have everyone home."

"Indeed." There was a pause and then she could hear Mrs. G clearing her throat. "I best be off, dear. Just wanted you to know."

"Thank you so much, Mrs. G."

"Write soon, won't you? I want to hear what you're up to."

"I will," Bea said. "And, you too, okay? Thanks again."

The phone clicked off, and Bea could see

her, all those thousands of miles away, across the sea, sitting on the hard-backed chair in the front hall, next to the telephone stand. It's early in the day there, the sun flooding in through the windows. So strange to see her still and not moving. She's wearing the faded blue apron, and she slowly reattaches the earring she took off to make the call. Crossing Bea's name off a list, she looks at the rest of the names and sighs, then reaches down to pat King, who's lying by her side. She thinks about taking him out for a walk, now that the sun is up, now that the day has begun.

But of course that couldn't be, as King died a few years ago. They buried him in the back woods, and they were all there to say goodbye. Gerald had written to let her know. Now Mr. G was gone, and neither of the boys were at home. It's funny, she imagined that of course the boys would be there. She hates to think of Mrs. G having to make all these calls, telling everyone the news.

Whenever Bea thought of the family, she saw them in the house. Mrs. G bustling about, making bread or writing up a list. Gerald working on something — studying the paper, his war bonds collection, setting up a new scrap drive — at the kitchen table.

Mr. G in his study, reading, grading tests, playing chess. Bea could see the house as clearly now as when she lived there. The enormity of it. The light. The blue and white china in the corner cabinets. The pile of boots by the back door. The hallways that never end.

She always had a harder time placing William. Sometimes she sees him in a blur, running through the kitchen on the way to the back door. Sitting impatiently at the dinner table, looking at his watch, waiting for his mother to take her last bite of dessert. Or she hears him coming up the stairs, his heavy footfall. Memorizing irregular verbs by repeating them out loud. Slamming a drawer shut. Catching a baseball in his mitt, over and over.

She poured herself a glass of wine and sank into the couch, thumbing through the mail. Bills, a postcard from Mummy in Spain, a flyer advertising a sale at a clothes store downtown. *Having a wonderful time, love,* the postcard read at the start, and it didn't seem right that she should be having a nice vacation when Mr. G had just died. Bea added the postcard and the bills to the pile of mail already on the coffee table, to read later. When Mum was away, she always let everything go: dishes in the sink, an unmade bed, makeup littering the pedestal sink. It was her own pathetic way of asserting her independence. Her freedom. She called and canceled her plans for dinner on Tuesday, without giving a reason, simply saying she was beat from a long weekend. How could she explain the death of Mr. G to someone who wasn't there? How could she explain that she felt more attached to him than to her own father? She wished she lived in the States so she could go to the funeral. Eventually she fell asleep, a photo of Mr. G clutched in her hand.

WILLIAM

William found the nearest hotel and headed for the phone banks in the back of the lobby. Fifteen listings in London for "B. Thompson." He started at the top and began working his way down, hoping that the phone wasn't listed under Bea's mother's name, which he suspected was a possibility. He had no idea what her name was, though. She would have changed it, certainly, when she married. Mother had told him that she had recently divorced. What did women do then? He had no idea.

He hung up almost as soon as each person said hello, as he was searching for Bea's voice or, maybe, her mother's. He didn't know what he thought her mother would sound like, but it certainly wasn't the gruff, half-asleep voice at 2 Wellington Mews or the child's whisper at 14 Kelross Road. He crossed each name out, right in the phone book, as he worked his way through, getting more and more desperate. He reasoned he could call his mother and see whether she had an address for Bea, but he didn't want to do that. He didn't want Mother to know he was here.

And then there it was. "Hello?" she said, and it was Bea, it was her voice and he couldn't hang up. That voice. "Hello?" Bea said again, when she didn't receive a response, and he recognized that edge, that sliver of annoyance. "Is anyone there?" she asked, and it was Bea, although she sounded much more British, especially the more irritated she became. And then: "Oh, for Christ's sake. Don't call here again," and the phone was slammed down in his ear, and in spite of everything, William smiled.

He circled the entry and tore the page out of the phone book, but he had already memorized the address: 283 Liverpool Road, and as he opened the hinged door to the phone booth, he noticed the hotel gift shop to his right. Wouldn't be right to arrive at her doorstep without bringing something special, he could hear his mother saying, so he went in and looked about, thinking about this or that, wondering what Bea might like, and slowly realizing that he had no idea. She was certainly no longer the girl who left New York six years earlier. She had become someone else. Perhaps she had a boyfriend. Perhaps she was married. Perhaps he was a fool.

In the end, he left the hotel with directions from the hotel clerk, and no gift. But he passed a florist's shop on the way to the Underground, and he asked the fellow to put together a nice bouquet. Not too large a bouquet, as by now he had decided that Bea did, of course, have a steady boyfriend, and when he rang her doorbell, she would be there with him. They both would be on the couch, her bare legs stretched across his lap, and he would be massaging her feet. This fellow would be at home in her apartment. Did her mother like him? Probably. Bea rarely made decisions that others disapproved of.

But still. He wanted to get her flowers. He never bought her much of anything, really. Her very last night in Maine, the one when they didn't creep back into the house until the sun appeared at the edge of the sea, he picked her some wildflowers, and when they got back from taking her to New York, he found them in her room, the water evaporated, a yellow pollen-dust circle around the vase. He took them and pressed them into some book that meant something to a lovesick boy — *Romeo and Juliet,* maybe, or

Love's Labour's Lost — and then two years later, when he was taking a Shakespeare class, he turned the pages to find the flowers and he sat there, in Widener Library, with tears almost running down his cheeks.

But now, fresh flowers in hand, he found the right Tube station and descended into the bowels of the earth, it seemed, and then he ascended in another part of the city, somewhere else entirely, a neighborhood, with baby carriages and bicycles and a pub on every corner. Buildings covered in ivy. Flowers bursting out of window boxes. Her neighborhood. He couldn't quite believe that just yesterday he had been in Paris, looking out at that skyline. He walked the wrong way from the station but asked a fellow for help, and then he arrived at her building, and just before he was about to ring the bell that said Thompson, 3A, in black ink, a woman came rushing out, a kerchief covering her rollers, and she held the door without a smile and he walked inside and up the narrow, dark stairs. To her door.

BEA

At some point in the middle of that long, fretful night, Bea pulled out all the photos she had from America and spread them across the kitchen table. She hadn't looked at them in years. On the ship back to England, and for the first few months she was home, she had gone through them at least once a day, flipping through them like a pack of cards. The edges were cracked and limp, and some of the photos had begun to fade. A photo of her, William, and Gerald from the beginning: could it have been the first day of school? How young they were. How much time had passed. She'd now been back longer than she was gone.

In the morning, when she woke up and needed to remember all over again, she decided to put the photos in some sort of order, but there wasn't enough room on the table, so she put them on the floor, stretching from the front hall through the living room. And then she remembered that she had another stash of photos, ones that Mrs. G had sent over the years since she had been back, and so she added those to the originals, stretching the line into the kitchen.

Bea had never shown her mother any of those later photos and only some of the early ones. She knew the later photos would only annoy her. Her mother seemed to want to forget about the Gregorys, to erase the time in America. She wanted Bea to do so as well. Bea showed her one photo, early on, maybe the photo of William at his convocation, with William and Gerald and Mr. G in those ridiculous crimson bow ties, and Mrs. G in that maroon hat with the feathers, and Mum had sniffed. *Those people,* she said, and Bea felt those words as though she had been slapped. Those people were people she loved. People she missed. She learned it was better to stop talking about them, to keep them to herself.

She was on her knees crawling around the flat, getting each photo in the right place, when the buzzer rang. She wasn't dressed for company, and as she stood, she pulled her hair back into a loose ponytail. "Hello?" she said, somewhat softly, not wanting to answer the door, worried that it might be the annoying woman from downstairs who always wanted to borrow something. There was no answer, and so she crept to the door, hoping that whoever it was would just go away, but then there was an odd knock, a single knock and then another. It sort of sounded like the code, the series of knocks they had made up all those years ago, and she was right by the door, so she flung it open and there he was. William. He looked the same, of course, but all grown up. Exhausted and sad but there was joy there, too. Such a mixture of sorrow and happiness.

"Oh, William," she said. "It's you."

WILLIAM

He stood outside the door before ringing the buzzer, wondering, suddenly, whether he should even be here. They had been apart longer than they had been together. They had been children then. She would be a different person. And here he was, with a duffel bag swung over his shoulder, as though he was here for a long visit. But he pushed the button, and he heard a faint noise from inside but the door didn't open, so he knocked once, then again when he remembered that silly code that Gerald had made up. The door was quickly unlocked and swung open. There she was. It was almost as though she expected him to be there, in the dark hallway, waiting for her to open the door.

She was wearing a blue shirt with a striped skirt, and her feet were bare, her toenails painted a bright red. She was thin, her cheeks hollowed out, her shoulders pointy.

257

They didn't hug or kiss. They stared at each other. William didn't know what to say. He was worried he might begin to cry.

After a moment, she ushered him into the apartment, practically insisting that he sit down on the couch. It didn't seem right to touch her, even though that's what he wanted to do. But then, after he was seated, and she was still standing, she touched him on the shoulder and left her hand there for a long moment. "Your mother called."

"Yes," he said. "She told you, then?" He averted his eyes, looking around her place, relieved that he didn't have to tell her. He had been rehearsing what he would have to say and how she would react. Her apartment was less than half the size of his.

"I can't believe it," she said. "I never thought he would die. Certainly not yet."

"Yes," William said again, unsure of his ability to say anything else. Nothing about this seemed real. He couldn't risk looking at her face. She stood by his side, not moving, her hand on his shoulder, and all he really wanted to do was to wrap his arms around her waist. Instead, he remembered the flowers in his damp hand and handed them over to her. "Posies," he said. "For you."

"Beautiful," she said, and she smiled for

the first time, that familiar smile. "Simply beautiful. Let me get them in some water."

She disappeared into the kitchen, and he could hear the water running. "Coffee?" she called out, and he said yes. If he bent to the side, he could see her moving about. How odd it all was. To be there, with her. To feel so uncomfortable.

Suddenly she was in the doorway, her nose scrunched up in a question, just like always. Like no time had passed. "Cream? Black?"

"Cream and sugar, thanks." He spoke automatically while looking at her hair, which fell thickly down to her waist. Hadn't she just had it pulled back?

She shrugged. "I feel as though I should know but that's silly. Neither of us were drinking coffee then. When we were children." She disappeared again into the kitchen but then called back. "Oh, no, remember? Chock Full o'Nuts? In New York?"

He had forgotten. "Gerald," he said. "Indeed." He looked about the living room. Worn furniture. Stuff everywhere. A photo of Bea and her mother on the small table next to him. Oddly, there were photos on the floor in a circuitous line, leading from the front hallway, wrapping around a chair or two before disappearing into the kitchen.

Bea came out, holding a tray, and saw him looking at the floor. "Photos of you all," she said. "Just reminiscing after your mother called. And you know me, I like to put things in order." She looked around the apartment and laughed. "Well, certain things need to be in order."

She placed the tray down on the coffee table, pushing aside piles of mail. The bouquet of flowers in a glass vase. Two cups of coffee in white china cups, with saucers. A plate of cookies. Two pale pink linen napkins.

"Fancy," he said. "So grown up."

"I'm all grown up," she said with a smile. "I turned twenty-two last week. But Mummy's the one who made out with the wedding gifts." She sat on the other end of the sofa and handed him a cup and saucer. "Not so much with the wedding."

"I heard," he said. "Is she here?"

"Off for a holiday with her friends." She pointed at the mail on the coffee table. "I get postcards, almost every day. I think she's feeling guilty."

They smiled at each other then, for the first time.

"You," she said.

"You," he replied.

She looked away first, and when she

looked back, her eyes were dark. That's what he remembered from the beginning, from those first days. How scared she was. How it all showed in her eyes.

She didn't say anything for a moment. Her skin was paler than he remembered, a translucent ivory, set off by dark red lipstick. She hadn't worn lipstick then.

"I think he'd be happy to see us here together, don't you," she said.

He didn't know how to respond. She used to talk about her father like this, too, about what he could see, what he would think, as though he was hovering over her, as though he was in the room. He'd imagined, at the time, that it helped her to get through it. He'd hear her talking to her father, telling him about her day. It was almost as though his death didn't change their relationship.

They argued about it once. They were in the graveyard, sharing a cigarette between classes, and she's yelling at him for sitting on a gravestone. *They're dead,* he tells her, *it's just bones by this point. Bones and worms.* She makes a face at him. *You're disgusting, William Gregory. This is their final resting place. Have some respect.*

He flicks the cigarette butt into the pond. *I hear you talking to him,* he says, and he knows he shouldn't. He can feel it in his stomach as he utters the words. It's as if he's stepped over an invisible line, disturbing an intimacy that exists between her and her father. Her neck pulses as she picks up her bookbag. She doesn't respond but stares at him in that way she does, that way that she reserves only for him. *He's not there,* he goes on. *He's dead.* She turns then and walks away, without saying a word, leaving the graveyard by the back entrance, climbing over a fence, and later, at dinner, he noticed that her kilt was torn and that her tights had a run. They didn't talk for days, maybe weeks after that. And later, when they were together toward the end, they never mentioned it. He wanted to, but he couldn't think of what to say, of how to take it back.

William closed his eyes as he remembered this. He knew he was drawn to say or do the wrong thing. He had an impulse to hurt. His father had sat him down one afternoon in his office, after he'd mocked Gerald in morning assembly. *I know you think we're not alike,* he had said, *but this is one of the ways we're the same. My father was like this, too. We say what we think. Gerald and Mother are different, though, and you need to try to keep your thoughts to yourself.*

"Yes," he said now, at long last. "Mother

262

will be happy, too, when I get home and tell her I saw you."

Bea nodded. "She said you were away, but she didn't say you were *here*. Why didn't she tell me? Does she not know where you are?"

"Paris. With Nelson. We'd planned it for ages. But now I'm heading home."

She nodded, and he saw in her face the understanding that he hadn't planned to see her. That the trip was designed to avoid London. Nelson had asked, several times, but William had been emphatic. He hadn't wanted to see her. But then, when he learned of Father's death, he could think of nowhere else to go. Nowhere else he wanted to be. He told himself it was for her, that she would want the company, but he knew that wasn't true. He was the one who needed her. "Nelson," she said. "Bobby Nelson. I haven't thought about him in ages."

He told her about Nelson and the trip. The amazing things they had seen and done. They hadn't written to each other in a few years, so he caught her up about life at home, as best he could. His work at the bank. His friends. Finally, he told her about Rose. The baby that was due in February. And before that, just two months from now, the wedding in October. He could see the surprise and then the disappointment flashing across her face. He was surprised that Mother or Gerald hadn't told her. She tried to smile. "A baby," she said. "Wow." She disappeared into the kitchen to find a bottle of prosecco, and she poured the noisy bubbles into two slim glasses, barely meeting his eyes as they clinked their glasses together.

He asked about her life then, and she told him about her nursery school class, the friends she had from work, the complicated relationship she had with her mother. "I think she expected me to be a child when I came back," she said. "And Tommy didn't help matters." They talked about Father, briefly, neither of them quite ready to look at it head-on. To acknowledge its hard truth. Then there was a moment when it seemed as though there was nothing else to say. As though they were two strangers, somehow caught in an intimate moment. It was mid-afternoon by then. She stood to clear their glasses. He looked over at her, and again he was reminded of those early days, when she had been so lost, when he would wait for Gerald to do something silly, to watch her face transform.

They were silent. He stood, too, stretching his legs, and he walked down the line of photos, picking up one now and again to look at it more carefully. He carried the tray of coffee cups and flowers into the kitchen. There, he found newer photos, some that he had never seen. The very last photo was one of his father, grinning, holding up his postal chessboard and pointing at it. It looked recent. His hair was more gold than red, with gray around the temple, and William could see how thin he had become. How he had aged. In person, he hadn't noticed. He wondered when he'd last really looked at his father.

"What's this?" he asked. "Why is he pointing at the chessboard?"

Bea was standing in the doorway. "I beat him," she said. "Finally." And then she looked quizzically at him, her nose wrinkled. "You didn't know," she said in wonder, with a bit of a smile. "You didn't know we'd been playing for years?"

"Chess? You play chess? You played chess with him?"

"We started playing that summer you and Gerald went away to camp. Before I left America, he showed me how to annotate the moves, and we've played ever since." She started crying then, tears dripping down onto her shirt. "It's the one thing my mother approved about your family after I came home: playing chess with your father. Turns out both she and my father had played with him, too. I got a card back, actually, just the other day." She pulled it off the icebox to show him. "I've been thinking all day about what to do with this. It seems wrong not to play the next move. But I have no one to send it to."

He hugged her then. She felt different, much bonier, less comfortable somehow. He was used to Rose, the curve of her hips, the smell of her powder. And yet. It all felt so familiar. He didn't want to let go.

BEA

Bea went into her bedroom to change so they could go out for drinks and dinner. She closed the door, quietly, and sat down on her bed. William, here, in her home. She almost expected him to be gone when she reemerged, that he was just a mirage, that she had somehow conjured him up by spending all that time with the photographs. It was unreal. She had opened the door to the flat and there he was. How many times had she had this dream, that he would be here, in London. That he would be in her world. That they would be together again.

And yet, like with so many dreams, the reality flickered. The William in her dreams was not the one who was here. The one in her dreams was the one from six years earlier. Unpredictable. Angry. Sweet. Pushing at boundaries. Crashing into walls. This William was different. He seemed to have settled, to have taken on the mantle of a life that didn't quite fit. He had always been able to move easily through that world; she never thought that he'd end up living there. It was as though the fire within him had died back. She was reminded of that New Year's Eve dance, so long ago, when they were all dressed up. Acting like the adults they wanted to be. He looked beautiful that night, but he didn't look like the William she loved. This William, too, wasn't the person she had known.

The more she heard about his life, the sadder she became. What promise he had, what potential. She had convinced him to go to Harvard, to experience it for them both. And at the beginning, he had. His letters were full of the stuff of university, the excitement of it all. Then the letters began to come less frequently and when they did arrive, it was as though he didn't know what to write about anymore. She didn't want to hear about old friends or parties or new bars. In a way, she had been relieved when he stopped writing. Now he was about to get married, to have a baby. To be sure, this pregnant fiancée had a touch of the old William in it. How upset Mr. and Mrs. G must have been. She wasn't surprised that Mrs. G didn't mention it in her most recent letter.

She slipped on a dress and quickly braided

her hair, applying fresh lipstick. When she opened the door into the living room, William was on the sofa again, but he, too, had changed: a clean shirt, a new tie. He'd combed his hair, which was now cropped so close to his head. Not a curl remained. He stood up and bowed.

"M'lady," he said.

"Kind sir." She curtsied, holding her dress with both hands. "What's your fancy? A neighborhood pub? Or do you want to go down to the center of town, to see some of the sights?"

"Let's stay here," he said. "In your neighborhood."

Over dinner, they talked mostly about London, about the effects of the war. He'd seen it in Paris, too. He said that northern France — which he'd seen from the windows of the train — felt desolate. Few buildings from before. She told him how, when she first got back, she got lost again and again, even when she was in the old neighborhood. If she'd known to turn left at a church and then right at the market, she'd walk blocks longer than necessary because the markers were no longer there. There was so much unfamiliar sky.

"Well, that must have been beautiful," he said. "Remember how we'd lie on the grass in Maine and stare up at the sky?"

"This wasn't Maine sky. London sky. Mostly gray. Mostly not so beautiful."

He nodded and took a sip of wine, leaning his head back against the wall of the booth and closing his eyes. "I dream about Maine," he said. "The water. The sky. The sound of the seagulls. The smell of the pines. Just like it took you time to relearn this city, it's taken me quite a while to realize that the island is no longer ours. Funny how places become part of who we are."

"That news made me sad. Your mother must have been beside herself."

"I think they argued about it forever before doing it. They found my tuition money somewhere, mostly through scrimping and saving. But there wasn't enough for Gerald."

One day in the post Bea had received a large box from Mrs. G. In it were things from the Maine house: a berry pail, an enormous pine cone, the quilt from her bed. And a little note tucked inside. *I wanted you to have these things, dear. We needed to sell the house. I know you loved it just as we did. Savor these things. Hold your memories inside them. Much love, Mrs. G.* She wrote back to her immediately, with a million questions, but she never responded to what

Bea had asked. She rarely wrote about Maine again. Bea repacked the box and put it in the back of her closet. It was too hard for her to have those things in her life.

"I took Rose up there in July," William was saying. "I borrowed Mr. Lasky's boat and we rowed across, pulled ashore by the forest. Lasky told me the new people are from New York and only up in August. So we stayed in the house for a night, you know, so Rose could see it. So she could understand."

Finally, the William she knew. The William who would take a risk. "And," she said. "What did she think?"

"She hated it. She doesn't like doing the wrong thing — the sleeping in someone else's bed, the drinking of someone else's wine — and she didn't see it the way we do. I wanted her to love it, to share it, but that didn't happen."

"We know this," Bea said, conscious of drawing the two of them together in a shared understanding, one that excluded this Rose. "It's hard to understand someone else's past."

"Mostly she just found it cold and wet." He stopped talking and looked around the pub. "I've been trying to save money to buy it back," he said, not looking at her. "I want

271

it back. When she got pregnant, and I knew I was going to have a family, I wanted it even more. I want my child to have our childhood. She doesn't want that. She wants to buy a place on the Cape. I don't think we'll ever have the money for that. And I don't much want to be there."

Bea didn't know what to say. She had forgotten, for a moment, that he was about to have a child, that he was about to get married, that he was starting this new life, one that she wouldn't be a part of. She wanted to keep talking about Maine. Our childhood, he had said. As if they'd always been together. "Tell me your favorite memory from there," she said. "What is that moment from the island that stays with you?"

He smiled then, and the old William returned. Not so much in the way his face looked — how handsome he was now, movie-star looks, really — but in the way his body relaxed into the booth. "I can't choose just one. Here are the first ones that come to mind, though: Lying on the floating dock, spent, having beat you or Gerald or both of you, even better, feeling the sun on my face. Roasting marshmallows over the bonfire, the sparks rising in the night air. Watching Father bring his catch back from the boat, his glasses dotted with seawater." He paused. "And you. That final summer."

"Yes," she said. "Those are all good." And she looked at him and he looked at her and somehow, they were back there, on the island, their last night together. They sneak out, after everyone else has gone to sleep, and run along the path into the woods. He leads the way, his hand held back to grasp hers. They run to the shore, where she learned to swim, where the water is a bit warmer, and they drop their clothes onto the rocks and wade in. It's so cold and she has to put her hand over her mouth to stop from screaming, but she doesn't want him to see her body so she moves as quickly as she can into the deeper water. She walks out far enough for the water to rise to her chest and then she holds her breath and pinches her nose and ducks down, until she's completely under the water, and then she comes up laughing, her body shaking with cold. *Okay, we did it,* she says, barely able to speak her teeth are chattering so. *Now let's go,* and they move with the waves toward the shore, and she sneaks a look at his body, before they wrap towels around themselves and pick up their clothes, using the towels as cover as they dress.

On the way back to the house, in the

woods, she trips on a root, and they both fall to the ground, out of breath, laughing. He sits up and pulls her to him, and she climbs onto his lap so that they are facing each other. But it's dark there, the blanket of trees overhead. The fog is heavy. There's no moonlight and no stars, and she can't see his face. She doesn't know whether he's smiling, so she explores with her fingers. His cheekbones. His eyebrows. His chin. The surprising softness of the new hair on his face. The mole by his eye. His mouth. He is smiling. And then he's doing it back to her, with such a light touch. She wouldn't have thought he could be so gentle. One eyelid and then the other. One ear and then the other. Her nose. They kiss, and he tastes like salt, and then she wraps her arms around his neck and he wraps his arms around her waist and they sit like that, her cheek against his neck, his breath on her hair, not moving, feeling as though this is right, feeling as though this is what all these years together have been leading to. This one moment. This one glorious moment.

WILLIAM

He didn't go there, to London, to sleep with
Bea. He had wanted, only, to be with her.
But that's what happened. They stumbled
home from the pub, having drunk too much
wine, talked too much about the past,
shared too many memories. The present was
somehow washed away and forgotten. The
past loomed up and overtook them. Rose
didn't exist. His father was still alive. They
became who they were then. Teenagers,
eager to explore and be explored. He fum-
bled with her bra, she tugged impatiently at
the knot in his tie. He felt frantic, then,
desperate, wanting only to get inside her,
and then, when he was, he wanted to stay
there, to go to sleep on top of her. But Bea
kissed him on the cheek and wriggled out
from under him, squeezing his hand, an
apology of sorts. She fell asleep soon after,
and he lay there and watched her breathe,
the streetlights illuminating her naked body.

When he woke in the morning, her side of the bed was a mess of sheets, and it took him a moment to realize where he was. The bedroom was only large enough for the bed and a small dresser. The tiny window now let in bright, too bright, morning sun. He heard a noise and rolled over to see Bea standing in the doorway, dressed, with a piece of paper in her hand. She looked nervous, somehow, as though she was the one in a strange apartment.

"What's that," he asked, pulling the sheets up to cover his chest, suddenly feeling exposed. Had they actually had sex? Or did he just imagine it?

"Our plan for the day," she said. "I'm going to show you London. My London."

They had talked the night before about how difficult it is to know someone else's past. She had tried, back then, to tell him about her life in London but he'd never been able to see it, and over time, he knew, she had let her past slip away. She had, instead, become part of his world, of the Gregory world. And now, here he was, in her apartment, in her world. The roles had been reversed.

She'd already made coffee, and she poured him a cup before they went out. He watched her, sitting at the small table in the kitchen, as she got the cream and sugar, as she put a few slices of bread into the toaster, as she cut the buttered toast into triangles. He reached his arm out and grabbed her around the waist, squeezing him to her. She kissed the top of his head and then moved out of his arm before he was ready. She moved so lightly through the tiny space.

Outside, it was a cloudy Tuesday morning. The streets were busy with people heading to work and running errands, the men looking uncomfortable in their suits, their foreheads shiny with sweat. Children ran by, laughing. Women pushed enormous baby carriages. It must have rained hard at some point during the night, and puddles littered the streets and sidewalks.

Bea and her mother had moved back to the old neighborhood after the divorce, and she took William first to the site where her school had been. It was razed by a bomb not too long after she left, and a new school was now standing proudly in its place. On the wall facing the playground, she pointed out the bricks they had recovered from the original and used in the new building, a memorial of sorts. He remembered her story of the boys with their gas masks on, running around the playground, oinking.

They moved on to her local market, the

same one she'd been going to since she was a child, to pick up a bottle of wine. "Morning, Trixie," the woman behind the counter said with a smile, and with a long glance at William. "Where's that lovely mother of yours?"

Bea explained that she was off on holiday. "She'll be back at the end of the week," she said, her hand on his elbow, pushing him deeper into the store.

"Trixie," he said once they were surrounded by flour and sugar, the name uncomfortable in his mouth. "Trixie?"

She blushed, something he'd rarely seen her do. "That's what I'm called here. Mummy never liked the name Bea. A bee stings, she would say. Better not to be a Bea."

"But that's what we called you. All of us. Everyone."

"Not at the start. You all called me Beatrix and then it got shortened. I don't remember when or by whom. But I liked it. It felt right, somehow, to have a different name there. To be a different kind of person. But when I got back, everyone here knew me as Beatrix and then Trix was what they called me in school, and so here I am. Trixie."

"What do you want me to call you?" he

said. He was annoyed; he felt oddly deceived.

"Bea." She looked at him as if he was half-witted. "That's my name. To you. That's what you call me." She gestured toward the door. "You leave, okay, and wait for me on the street. I don't want to have to explain to the busybody up there who you are."

He shrugged and left, the ringing bell announcing his departure, and he lit a cigarette as he leaned his back against the building across the way, waiting for her to appear. He couldn't see into the shop; he could only see his reflection. Who was he? He could think of so many things for her to say to the clerk:

This is William, I lived with his family during the war.
Remember when I lived in America? The older boy I told you about? This is him!
For five years this boy was like my brother. And then, at the end, he was more.
Oh, and last night, I had sex with him.

Here they were, together for the first time in public. He wanted to hold her hand. He wanted the world to know they were together. Instead, she was treating him like a second-class citizen, a servant, someone to

279

wait on her in the street. When she finally emerged, running across the street to avoid a car, her smile disappeared when she saw his face.

"What," she said, walking briskly down the sidewalk, forcing him to catch up. "What is your problem?"

He waited until some people passed, walking the other direction. "You," he said. "You're the problem."

She rounded a corner and then stopped abruptly and turned to face him. He bumped into her. "What do you want me to do? Tell every nosy so-and-so my business? She knows my mother, William; she knew me as a child." The tops of her ears were bright red. He'd forgotten about that.

"I would have thought you could do more than just kick me out onto the street."

"What should I have said to her? This here is William and I lived with his family in America and, oh, we shagged last night."

He had no words with which to respond. She'd always been tough. It was one of the things he'd loved about her, how she stood up for herself. But there was an edge to her now that surprised him. It seemed ridiculous, but he wasn't sure he'd ever heard a girl speak like that. Even Rose, who was plenty rough around the edges, always said "making love," a phrase he hated. Sex, he would think. Just call it what it is. We're going to fuck. And while he was taken aback by Bea, it also excited him. He loved that she said exactly what he had been thinking. It had so often been like that with them, as though they shared their thoughts with each other without speaking. He'd never had that with anyone else. Not even with Rose. He pushed Bea against the wall and kissed her. Slow-like, not rushed. They were sober now, and all he wanted to do was kiss her. She struggled at first and then relented, kissing him back. "Yes, we did," he said in her ear. "And I hope we will again, tonight."

Bea

She was happy to find William still asleep when she woke early in the morning, the light just making its way into the room. She studied his face for a long time, memorizing it, trying to make this face the one she would recall in years to come. He was leaving the next morning, and she didn't know when she'd see him again. She held her hand over his face and outlined the contours of his lips, his eyes, his nose in the air. The lines that were beginning to form around his mouth and his eyes. He was even more beautiful now.

She didn't want to think about what had happened the night before. She'd thought about it happening for so long that she was too aware throughout. They hadn't had sex before she left. She'd slept with a few others over the years, sometimes thinking about him rather than them, feeling afterward as though she didn't quite understand the fuss.

It seemed wrong to be intimate with men whom she didn't know. They were messy, rushed encounters, having everything to do with want and nothing to do with need. But with William it was both, and she wanted it to feel right, to be with him. She thought they could become the people they once were. But it was wrong, in so many ways. He was engaged, for Christ's sake. He was going to have a baby with this Rose. And yet, it was William. Together, they would always be fifteen and seventeen, on the cusp of something. How sweet that moment is, that moment of before. When anticipation is everything. When everything is new. When there are no consequences, when there is no after.

She showered and dressed, and as she made coffee, she decided to keep him busy for the day. To keep his mind off his father, to avoid talking about the night before. She made a plan and then, when he got up, they set out. She showed him the neighborhood. Where her school had been. The building where she'd grown up. Their church. By midday it was drizzling, and he was dragging, so they sat down on a bench in the park to rest for a moment. She opened up her umbrella to shield them from the rain. He stretched his legs out and groaned as he lit a cigarette.

"You're tiring me out, Trixie," he said.

She frowned and shook her head at him. "What do you think," she said. "Is this what you imagined? Do you remember me telling you about all these places?"

"Yes, of course I remember," he said. "It's not what I saw, though. I never thought about how urban it all is. How different from home. How odd it must have been for you, to live the way we did."

"Yes," she said. "My memory of those first days, maybe the first year, is one of size. Everything was large, compared to what I was used to."

"What was it like on the other side, then? When you came back?"

"What you would expect. Dirty, compressed, gray. Everyone was thin and hungry. And yet there was joy here. Flowers springing up in the ruins. It was familiar, too, it was in my bones. As though this place is part of who I am. As though I was always meant to be here. As though I belong."

William nodded. "Just like what I was saying last night about Maine. I can't quite imagine living anywhere other than New England."

"Well," she said, looking away, disappointed in his lack of curiosity about the world. What happened to the boy who wanted to escape? "I guess we've both ended up in the right place, then. One old England and one New."

"Across the pond," he said. They were silent for a moment. A group arrived, a bit away from them, and began setting up to play cricket. "Where does that come from?" he asked, his eyes closed. "That phrase?"

"We learned about it in school," she said. "It's an old expression. It was originally 'across the herring pond.' It meant a trip, paid for by the king. A chance to be transported elsewhere. From before the American Revolution."

William nodded. "I like that, 'to be transported elsewhere.'"

"I remember thinking about it when I crossed the first time. The Atlantic seemed like it would never end. As though there would be no land on the other side. That we would just keep sailing and end up, one day, back in Britain." She didn't add that, when she crossed in '45, on the way back, she wished that they wouldn't be able to dock. That they'd be turned back. Then she'd hitchhike from New York back to Boston and walk right into that sunny kitchen. *I'm here,* she would say. *What's for dinner?* And they would all be there, and

285

rush at her, drawing her to them. She would be home. She wasn't sure she'd ever wanted something more, either before or after that moment.

"Such a typical Brit," she said finally, "thinking that the world begins and ends here."

"We're all like that, don't you think," William said. "Loyalists."

"Yes, well, easier for some than others."

"What does that mean?" He sounded annoyed, as though she was insulting him. It seemed so easy, now, to get under his skin. She didn't much like it.

"I don't mean you. I mean me." She gestured to the men playing cricket. "I don't know the rules."

"What? So what. Neither do I."

"My point exactly. My favorite team? The Red Sox. My favorite place? Maine. My favorite food? Your mother's muffins. And yet here I am. This is my home. My mother is here. I belong here and yet I'm in limbo, really, caught between two worlds. I can't seem to find where I fit."

William nodded but didn't respond. She wondered whether he could understand. She leaned over and kissed him on the cheek. He smiled.

She stood then and reached out her hand.

"Let's keep moving," she said. "There's so much more to see." He took hold of her hand and they set off, together, and yet not.

WILLIAM

What he remembered most from that day was watching Bea as she moved through her world. How kind and charming she was with everyone, from shop clerks to museum guards to children in the parks. This was a different Bea from the one he had known. She had always known the right thing to do — unlike him — but there was a self-assuredness now. A grace. And she was now the one to lead, the one to show him the way.

Outside the gates of Buckingham Palace, she chatted with some American tourists, who asked her question after question about what they should see, where they should go. She didn't introduce him or say that she'd lived in America. She became the Brit she was. At a tea shop, she asked the waitress about a necklace she was wearing and smiled at the busboy. And in the V&A Museum, they ran into one of the students in her nursery school class. The boy saw her from across the gallery and came running, full tilt, to wrap his arms around her hips, to rest his head on her stomach. She cradled the top of his head and smiled at his anxious parents before kneeling to look him in the eyes.

"Do you like your work?" William asked after they left the V&A and were walking back toward the Tube. "That boy certainly seemed to have a crush on you."

"Mostly I do," she said. "It's frustrating at times, to be sure. And I can hardly move when I get home. I lie down on the sofa and would go to sleep if Mummy didn't force me to eat supper. But it's wonderful to be a part of their lives."

"I wish you'd been able to go to college," he said. "Think about what you could be doing."

Her mouth straightened into a line. "Really, William? Is being a teacher not a worthy occupation? Not sure your father would approve." The old fury was there in her eyes.

"No, I didn't mean that," he said, feeling as though he was always one step behind, that he couldn't seem to say the right thing. "I just mean because you're so smart."

"Yeah, well." She marched ahead of him, and he was reminded of so many moments when she put him in his place. He both loved and hated this about her.

He grabbed her hand. "Slow down, will you? That was meant as a compliment. Jesus."

"You're doing so much with your Harvard education? Sounds like you sit in a cushy office, handing money to people." She was still angry.

"No," he said. "I'm not. It's a boring job. But it suits me. For now."

"Does it? What about what you wanted? To live in New York? To travel? The way your face lit up when you talked about Paris. I don't believe for one moment that you're happy to be in Boston. It's the story you've created, out of the bits and pieces. To make you feel as though you've made the right decisions. To make you feel as though you're heading in the right direction." She was facing him now, and people on the sidewalk were walking around them, averting their eyes. "These children, William, they have a chance to have a childhood. Something I never really had. It's my pleasure to be with them every day. That innocence. That wonder."

"I'm glad for you," he said. "Really I am. I'm being stupid. As always. I guess some things never change."

"You got that right," she said, and she was smiling now, but he felt as though he was widening the gap between them, that he was pushing her away with every word. Why were they spending the entire day arguing?

"Tell me about G," she said. "You've hardly said a word."

"He's good, I think," he said. "He seems content at Harvard, a solid group of friends."

"But now," Bea said, her voice trailing off. "Your mother will need him. She'll need you both, but he'll be the one."

He knew she was right. Even if not for the baby. Gerald would be there. Gerald would be the one she wanted.

They walked for a bit without talking. It was just as he would have expected London to be. Overcast, rainy, with a sun that rarely shone.

"What does he want to do, do you know?"

"No idea. Majoring in psychology, I think. He's talked a bit about graduate school, but don't know much for sure. He spends some time tutoring kids in the North End."

Beatrix smiled. "I can see that," she said. "He's got your mother's generous spirit. And her patience."

"I guess." He wished she would just come

out and say it, that she was disappointed in him.

"Anyway," she said, too brightly. "You're about to be a father. You're going to have your hands full. Your mother is going to love being a grandmother. I'm sure she's missed having children around. It'll give her something to do, now that your father is gone." She looked away then, blinking.

He didn't want to talk about Father. It was enough being here with her, knowing that she was also grieving, even as they argued and fought over this and that. This was their way, wasn't it? This was why he was here. By then he was tired of walking and playing the tourist. He wanted to be back in her flat, to have her to himself. His train would leave early the next morning, and they had such little time left.

BEA

It was odd, spending so much time with William. After all, they'd rarely been alone, just the two of them, for such a long period. Even the summers in Maine, when they worked together on the mainland, they had been busy. And at home, everyone else had always been there, too. There was an intensity about him — always challenging, always confronting — that was tiring. He exhausted her. There was also something undefinable, buried inside, a sadness of sorts, that had always been there, she realized, but it seemed more pronounced now. It wasn't simply his grief over losing his father. Having him there made her miss the others, too. Bea found herself looking for Gerald more than once that day.

In the morning, he would leave and go back to America and marry Rose and start his family. He was about to have a whole new life. She thought about how important it had been for her to understand their past. There were Gregory stories that she heard, again and again, that happened before her time and yet it was as though she had been there, too. She had tried, as best she could, to braid her life with theirs. She never thought then that their futures would diverge. That there would be two lines, heading in very different directions.

This certainly wasn't the way she had thought it would end. She was grieving for Mr. G but she was also grieving for William, as he stood right there beside her on the Tube platform, as they waited for the train to take them home. She missed the boy she knew. She had never stopped wanting him. If he hadn't come, she could have stayed inside her memory of him. The train rumbled in and she stepped aboard, putting her hand back to hold his, to pull him in beside her.

They passed the market on the way home, and he asked whether they ought to pick up anything for dinner. She was relieved; she didn't want to go out again. She had more than enough food, so she shook her head, and they rounded the last few blocks in silence, still hand in hand. She wanted to eat dinner and drink wine and crawl into bed with him. Maybe not in that order. Not to have sex, necessarily, but to hold him. To have him hold her. To recognize, without words, that this moment would be the last time they would be together in this way. The next time she would see him everything would have changed.

It was dusk by then, and she didn't look up to the flat's windows as she almost always did when she returned home. It was a reflex. But, for some reason, she didn't that evening, and so they climbed the stairs and she unlocked the door and they came through the doorway, flushed from the heat, laughing, and there was Mum, in the kitchen.

"What are you doing here?" Bea asked, dropping William's hand, pushing it away. "You're supposed to be in Spain."

Mum didn't respond to her but instead spoke to William as she dried her hands on her apron. "I'm Millie, Beatrix's mother."

William nodded his head and smiled at her. "So nice to meet you in person, Mrs. Thompson. Sorry, is that correct?"

"In person? Do I know you?"

"Mummy," Bea cut in, putting her hand on her mother's arm, "this is William. William Gregory. He was traveling through Europe and stopped by on his way home. He's to take the train to Southampton in the morning."

"William," Mummy said. "Well, my goodness." And then she looked at Bea and in her eyes Bea saw that she had seen the photographs lining the floor; the kitchen sink with the wineglasses and the coffee cups; and her bedroom with the unmade bed, the sheets in an unruly mess, the condom wrappers on the floor. "I wish I'd known! I could have made something a bit nicer for supper. I was just fixing some omelets, nothing special."

"That sounds fine, thank you," William said. "I'm not all that hungry. Tired, though. This daughter of yours took me on a whirlwind tour of London today. We went to, what, Trix, a museum, the Tower of London, Buckingham Palace." He sat down on the sofa, in the same place he'd sat the night before, his feet up on the footstool, pretending not to see Mum's frosty look. Bea knew he did, though, by the way he didn't call her Bea. He continued telling her all about their day. Mum nodded and smiled and he talked and all Bea wanted to do was disappear. She had never wanted Mum to meet William. It seemed wrong.

After she got back from America, sometime during that first year, she met a few other girls who'd been there, too. One in

Virginia and another in New York. Their mothers had found ways to visit them during the duration. For weeks, she wondered why Mummy had never mentioned this as a possibility. One night at supper, she asked her whether she had looked into visiting. *No,* she says in her direct way. *I never did. I know other parents went but it was difficult and it was expensive. Your father and I agreed.* She looks away. *Besides,* she continues, staring out the window, *I had no interest in seeing you there, in America. You belonged here, with me. I would have been on the outside there, looking in. I had no interest in that.*

Your mother, Tommy says, reaching across the table to hold her mother's hand, *sent you there to be safe. She's a terrific mother, a far better mother than that woman in America.* Bea glares at him but says nothing. *I thought she was looking down at us,* Mummy says. *She was quick to write when they taught you to swim or bought you fancy clothes. Those photos she used to send. Was that to show us how much more they had than we did?* Her mouth twisted. *We were in the middle of a war. She was sunbathing and making cookies.*

Bea pushes her chair back so hard it falls

297

back on the floor with a crash. *You know nothing,* she says. *You have this all wrong. She's wonderful. How dare you talk about my family in America that way. Your family?* Mummy says. *Your family?* She stands up and faces her. They stand eye to eye, fury to fury. *This is your family. This is your home. That was a place where you lived for a few years. That is all.* Bea runs out of the room and locks her door, spreading all the photographs across her bed and writing a letter to Mrs. G, asking whether she can come back, whether they will please have her. Her mother knocks on the door until Tommy drags her away. Later, Bea burns that letter, late one night in the courtyard, holding a match to her angry words.

Her two worlds, colliding. Smashing up against each other. She couldn't understand her mother's logic then: she took it personally, that she didn't want to see her. Her anger at and dismissal of the Gregorys was confusing. But standing there, in the flat, watching William and her mother dance around each other, neither being the person they truly were, it made more sense. Mrs. G used to say that she wanted the two families to go to Maine together when it was all over. About how the two families would magically become one. She had believed that then. The wonderful American optimism of Mrs. G. But Mummy was right. She would have been on the outside in America. Just like William was on the outside here. These two should have never met. They didn't belong together.

WILLIAM

Dinner that evening was a nightmare. Instead of what William had imagined — lying in bed, naked, eating bread and cheese, spilling wine onto the sheets — the three of them sat there, at that small kitchen table, struggling to meet one another's eyes. He had never seen Bea so stressed, seemingly every vein on her neck pulsing, her mouth in a severe, straight line. She barely said a word. He felt obliged to talk, to keep the conversation going, to skim over her discomfort. She had talked, the night before, about her strained relationship with her mother, but he hadn't understood the tension between them, or more accurately, he hadn't understood how her mother had tried to erase her time in America. He could see it in her mother's eyes, in the way she looked right through him. Those eyes that were so much like Bea's.

"How long have you been abroad?" Mrs.

Thompson asked. It was a table for two, and every time his knee knocked against Bea's, he shifted his legs. A rickety window fan noisily blew the air through the room.

"A few weeks. I'm cutting the trip short because" — and then he looked at Bea and she nodded, and so he continued — "because my father died. Unexpectedly."

"Oh, no," Mrs. Thompson said, and for the first time he had a sense of the woman beneath the veneer. He could see she really did care. "Oh, heavens, what happened?"

"Heart attack," he said.

She nodded, looking away. "Just like Reg," she said to herself. "What is it with these men and their hearts?" She looked back at him. "Just like Beatrix's father." She asked about the arrangements and how his mother was doing. Then she asked about his trip, so he told her about Paris. He told her about his job. He didn't talk about Rose or the baby. She didn't ask about Gerald. She seemed to be barely listening. Then they ran out of things to talk about. Sounds drifted up from the street below.

William knew he couldn't stay there the night. After dinner, he slipped into the bedroom to pack up his bag while Bea did the dishes. When he reemerged into the living room, Mrs. Thompson looked up at him from the sofa.

"It was a pleasure, William," she said. "Do come back sometime. Perhaps with better news." She didn't stand up but extended her hand for him to shake.

"Yes, I will," he said.

"Do tell your mother hello. I'm dreadfully sorry to hear about your father."

He nodded. "I'll do that, thank you."

Bea gestured to the door. "I'll walk him down," she said to her mother, without looking her in the face. "Be right back."

They didn't talk or touch as they walked down the narrow flights of stairs, his duffel banging into the corners as they turned onto each landing. He felt like a child who had been dismissed. Outside, the sun had set, and the air was chilly. Bea grabbed his hand and pulled him down the street, suddenly making a right into an alley.

"I'm sorry," she said, turning to face him. "This was not what I wanted."

He nodded, feeling helpless and frantic. "Can't you just come with me?" he said.

"William," Bea said. "You're getting married."

"I know that. I mean, for tonight."

She sighed. "No, I'll never hear the end of it. I can't."

"So, this is it? We say goodbye here?"

"I'll get away in the morning. I'll meet you at the train."

He nodded. It wasn't what he wanted but it would have to do.

"I'll meet you under the big clock at Victoria, by the entrance to the Grosvenor. What time is the train?"

"Nine thirty."

"Let's meet at seven thirty, then."

He nodded again. "It's a plan." He put down his bag and took her face in his hands.

"I love you, William Gregory," Bea said. "I just want you to know that."

"I love you, too, Beatrix Thompson."

They hugged each other tight and then they kissed but somehow everything had changed. It was a kiss between two old friends. Bea pulled away first. Back on the sidewalk she laid her hand on his chest before turning away, heading toward her building, and he walked in the opposite direction, toward the Underground. He didn't look back.

He returned to the hotel near the station and got a room for the night. He unlocked the door, kicked his duffel into the corner, and lay down on the hard bed. Staring at the bare ceiling bulb for quite some time, he finally sat up to open the bottle of wine they'd bought earlier in the day. He only slept for an hour or two. The bathroom was in the hall, and he could hear every time someone went in there to piss.

This was not the way he wanted this to end. He had wanted to spend more time with Bea, to ask her the questions he hadn't yet asked, to stretch every last moment of being together. He knew now that there was a finality to this moment. He would go home and marry Rose. He would stay at his boring job. He would support his family. Bea would stay here and teach and, one day, she, too, would marry and settle down. They were both doing what they were supposed to do. He had long ago understood that they were not meant to be together. That was why he had stopped writing to her. He had needed to let her go. It was why he didn't want to see her on this trip. He wanted to hold her in his memories. But there was no denying the way they felt about each other. He loved her in a singular way, in a way that was different from any other love he had known. But this weekend had shown him that Bea had moved on. She was no longer the girl from before.

As he lay there, he wondered what he should tell Rose. She knew that Bea existed, but that was about it. Some girl who'd lived in their house for five years. She'd been amazed at his parents' generosity in opening their house to her, something William had never questioned. *Who would do that, she says. I mean, it's nice and all, but, honestly, they could have taken in some child who carried diseases. Who would steal from you.* No, he says, curious to find himself to be the non-cynic, *these were children. Children in need. We would have done the same.* But he wasn't sure that was true.

He decided he wouldn't tell her much of anything. He certainly wasn't going to tell her that they'd slept together. There was no reason she needed to know. Just two friends, reliving old memories. He could tell her that he'd seen Bea, that he'd had a few days, so he'd rung her up and she'd shown him the town. What was it Nelson always said? The best lies are always half truths.

BEA

"If you would just read my postcards," Mummy said after she returned to the flat. "I told you right there. I told you we had to cut the trip short." She raised her eyebrows, finished drying the dishes, and unwrapped her apron, hanging it on its nail.

Nothing more was said about William or what her mother had found. Her bed had been made, the floor swept. Her clothes from the night before had been hung in the closet. The photographs had all been picked up and sat, in neat piles, on her bureau. Bea went through them again as she lay awake that night, angry at her mother for coming home early, but also confused about being with William. Perhaps she had made a terrible mistake. The present had disappeared under the weight of the past.

As soon as the sky lightened, she dressed and slipped out the front door. The streets were quiet and cool, an occasional rumble from a milkman's truck. She made it to the train station by seven, got a coffee, and waited by the clock. She knew William would be there on time and there he was, making his way through the early travelers. He took her hand and led her to a bench by the baggage claim. He sat down next to her and wrapped his arm around her shoulders, before kissing her on the cheek and pulling her close.

"Sleep well?" he asked, and they both tried to smile, knowing the answer was the same for them both. "Didn't you once tell me about that clock," he said, looking up at it. "There was something about a clock."

She nodded. "I think you're remembering the clock I told you about in Paddington. That's where I left from. I remember watching the hands on the clock, the light dimming from the windows above, as we all stood together, waiting for the train, not knowing where we were going."

They both looked up at the ceiling. The light fractured through the intricate ironwork far above.

"Such a mixture of light and heavy," William said. "The fanciful curves, the arch of the ceiling. The metal, the clunking of the trains."

"Those Victorians," Bea said. "The cathedrals of the Industrial Revolution."

"Yes," he said. "Almost as inspiring."

"You haven't told me," Bea said. "I'm guessing Rose is Catholic?"

"She is," he said. "Getting married in her church."

"That must be killing your mother."

"I suppose. She'll survive."

They looked at each other then, upset that they'd used those words. "Sorry," they both said at the same time, their words overlapping, then laughed.

"You're not converting, though, are you?"

"God, no. I'm a terrible Protestant, I'd be an even worse Catholic."

"But what do you believe?"

He held her hand tighter. "Oh, I don't know. I don't think about it much, it hurts my head. You? You used to believe more than I did."

"I've always wanted to believe there's a heaven. And your dad and mine are sitting there, together, meeting at last. Maybe they're playing chess."

William smiled. "That's a sight." Then he turned back to her. "Why didn't you tell me about that?"

"About the chess? I don't know. Didn't seem important."

"Why did you keep writing to Gerald?"

Bea was quiet for a moment. She wasn't sure he would ever be able to understand. "I was worried about him," she said finally. "Wanted to make sure he was okay."

"I should have kept writing to you. Because if we'd stayed in touch . . ." His voice trailed off, and he looked away.

"What, William, you wouldn't have met Rose? You wouldn't have become involved? She wouldn't have gotten pregnant? Come on. Life moved on. For us both. We were still children."

"How was your mother after I left?" William asked, looking around at the people walking by, refusing to be drawn into a fight.

"What you might expect," Bea said. "It was as though you were never there."

"Ouch," he said, and they both laughed, the tension released.

She'd been listening to the garbled announcements as best she could and then there it was: "Train to Southampton, Platform Ten." She stood and held out her hand. "We best get you to your train. Bound to be crowded, this time of year."

He stayed seated, looking up at her. "Don't make me go," he said. "Please."

"Don't be foolish," Bea said, but as she did, she tried to see the future that she thought he wanted. She could no longer imagine the two of them together. This thing she had thought about for so many years. This thing that she had wanted. They no longer belonged together. And she knew that he knew that, too.

"Stay with me now, then, won't you? I can board at the last moment if I have to."

She sat back down on the bench and he, again, pulled her close. It was comfortable to be with him, and she rested her head on his chest. There seemed to be nothing left to say.

WILLIAM

He'd never been good at goodbyes. He would always rather slip away. But there, in Victoria Station, he couldn't do that. Bea walked him down the platform and they had one last hug, then he climbed up the steps and onto the train. He found a seat, not at the window but on the aisle, next to an elderly woman with a hat, and Bea couldn't see him, even though he could see her. She was looking for him, but it was he who had the chance to gaze at her, to memorize the lines of her face, the way her hair framed her neck, the graceful way she moved her hands.

Then the train began to move and he leaned forward, over the woman next to him, and touched the glass with his palm, and she saw that and waved, and the train gathered speed as it pulled out of the station, as light filled the compartment, as they headed out of London. He lost sight of her, and he sat back in his seat and closed his eyes.

Later that day, the ship pulled out of the harbor so slowly at first that he didn't realize they were moving. He stood on the deck, looking at the faces on the dock below, people waving madly at their loved ones. He wished Bea had been there, so they could have replicated the moment that she left the States. It felt only right. Instead, he knew no one. He thought about waving, about pretending that there was someone there for him, too, but he couldn't do it. He knew he was alone.

Night fell and he wrapped himself in a deck blanket, looking up at the stars. This time in London, he decided, was to be a secret, one never to be shared. Not with anyone. He would keep it all to himself. He could be with Bea in that moment, for those days, for the rest of his life. Some secrets are weights to be borne. Others are gifts, little bits of warmth, to be revisited again and again. No one else ever needed to know. No one else had the right to know. It was theirs and theirs alone.

In the navy darkness he saluted to the east.

BEA

She watched the train carrying William away until it disappeared around the bend. She didn't want to go home, to deal with her mother and the disappointment that hung in the air, so she left the station and headed over to St. James's Park. It was a pleasant day, the sun occasionally peeking through the clouds, the rain held at bay.

Three days earlier, life was different. Mr. G was still alive. William was in America. Her mother was in Spain. Now, everything had shifted. The phone call. The knock on the door. She wasn't sorry to have seen William, and she wasn't sorry to have slept with him. It still felt like the right thing to do, the right way to close things out. It was hard to separate her grief from losing Mr. G and her grief at losing William. They seemed connected, and it felt final, as though the two things happening at the same moment were a necessity, a wall between the past and the present. As she sat there, watching the people as they hurried by, she saw this time as an inevitable moment in their story. They had to come together in order to move apart.

With her eyes closed, she could hear Mr. G singing that hymn that he so loved as he washed the dishes after dinner, his shirtsleeves rolled up, an apron tied around his middle. And Gerald, running down the stairs to ask her: *But are the mountains green? Are the pastures pleasant? What are the dark Satanic mills? Go away,* she says, laughing, but not really wanting him to leave, so they could be together in that moment with Mr. G, his marvelous tenor singing those beautiful notes. She joins in for the second verse, standing next to him at the sink, each of them holding a wet utensil in the air and singing as loudly as possible.

Bring me my bow of burning gold!
Bring me my arrows of desire!
Bring me my spear! O clouds unfold!
Bring me my chariot of fire!

He sings the final verse alone as she listens, conducting with a fork and a knife. Mrs. G — who always claims she can't sing but is the loudest of them all in chapel each

Sunday — is leaning against the door to the dining room, smiling, her arms wrapped around Gerald's shoulders. William's not there. Was he out of the house? Was he in his room, rolling his eyes?

She pulled the postal card out of her bag. She'd decided, finally, on a good move, one that would ensure the game would go on. No end in sight. She walked over to the Thames, as she had planned. She folded the card into a little boat, just as her father had taught her, and then she descended the stairs to the river. She'd come here once, late at night, with a man she'd met at a dance. He told her they could get access to the river, and she didn't believe him. This isn't Paris, she had said, and so he had to prove her wrong. They didn't stay long but they drank half a bottle of red, and she stumbled home, her clothes smelling of wine and river.

She bent down and placed the boat on the surface of the water. It was calm, without much wind, and it sat there, hardly moving, for a few moments, until it slowly started floating downstream. She called after the little boat, not caring who might hear her.

"Safe travels, Mr. G," she said. "You're heading for the North Sea. I thought you

315

might like to see it. Then you can choose where you want to go: France or Belgium. Holland. Or go north and visit Scotland, if you like. You always said you wanted to visit, to see where your ancestors came from." She stood and brushed out her dress as she lit a cigarette and watched the little boat meander through the water, utterly at the whim of the current. "Be safe," she called. "I will miss knowing you're in the world."

On the walk back to the Tube, she thought of when she first met Mr. G, on the dock that morning so long ago. She meets William first, and then Gerald, and then Mrs. G. Mr. G deals with that horrible paperwork woman and then he walks over to where they are all standing. He's tall and very thin, his pants belted high and tight. His hair is copper, just like Gerald's, and when he walks, it's with such purpose, his head down, his arms swinging at his sides. *Oh, Ethan,* Mrs. G says to him, her hand on his arm. *This lovely girl is Beatrix. The boys found her!* He nods his head at her, so formal, really, and then he extends his hand for her to shake. She hadn't shaken hands with anyone before that moment and so she extends her hand to his and, without even thinking, she curtsies just a little, bowing her head. *Lovely to meet you, sir,* she says.

Welcome to Boston, he replies. *We're mighty happy to have you with us.* He looks about the dock. *Your luggage?* Beatrix nods. *Just one small case. It's brown, it's right over there. William,* he says, pointing, *go grab Beatrix's case. We'll meet you at the car.* Mrs. G takes her arm and begins prattling on about this and that, about Maine and the traffic and getting ready for school and a box of toys from the cousins. Beatrix nods and smiles and says almost nothing. Then they arrive at the car, where William's waiting, and Mrs. G goes around to climb in the front seat, and William and Gerald climb in the back after they hoist the case into the boot. Mr. G opens the back seat door for her. *Beatrix,* he says, his voice low, right before she climbs in. *You'll get used to the chatter. Oh,* she says, *it's fine. You'll get used to it,* he repeats. *She has a heart of gold. Yes, sir,* she says. In the car, Gerald can't stop smiling at her.

Mr. G was dead. William was gone. It was time for her to move on, too. She thought back again to the knock on the door, just two days ago. The old code that Gerald had thought up. She could never keep the code straight. For the slightest of moments, she'd

317

been disappointed. She'd opened the door hoping to see Gerald.

■ ■ ■ ■

PART THREE:
1960–1965

■ ■ ■ ■

GERALD

How odd it is for Gerald to be back on the East Coast. When the headmaster called, saying that they were looking for someone to head up the new counseling and tutoring center and that they couldn't imagine a better person for the job, Gerald turned it down. He couldn't stop thinking about it, though, and then Mother called, having heard all about it. *Please,* she said. *Please come home.* He couldn't say no to her. The truth was that for the seven years he'd been out west — first graduate school and then working as a counselor — he'd felt as though something was missing. When he accepted the job, it was as though a weight had lifted. His friends at Berkeley couldn't understand. He was almost thirty — everyone else was getting married, having children, starting lives of their own. He'd tried to explain it by saying Mother was alone, and William's children — now eight and six

— were growing up without him. That was part of it, but, mostly, he simply longed for the comfort of home.

William had been dismayed, calling as soon as Mother had told him. *G,* he said, *don't do this. You got out. Don't come back.* Once Gerald had made it clear that his mind was made up, though, William let it go. Although the school had graciously told Mother she could stay in the house as long as she wanted, given how long Father's family had been associated with the school, Gerald didn't want to live there. He moved into a shared faculty house, the other side of campus from Mother, but he spent June and July fixing things around the house, eating dinner most nights with her. Stopping by one morning in late August, he finds Mother in the kitchen, putting together a shopping list. *The children are coming,* she says, smiling up at him. *William just called!*

Gerald pours a cup of coffee and sits down. William is forever dumping the kids and disappearing. It does make Mother happy — it gives her something to do, something to plan, something that ignites that old excitement — but Gerald already resents it. He had no idea this was happening on such a regular basis. He loves the children, too, and enjoys spending time with them, but he hates the way that William assumes. What if Mother had plans? But she rarely does, and when she does, she'll cancel or reschedule on a moment's notice. William knows that all too well.

Mother opens the fridge and begins moving things about. *I can never remember,* she says, her back to him. *Does Kathleen like raspberries and Jack blueberries? Or is it the other way around?* Gerald sighs. It's impossible not to get drawn in. How he loves those children. *Jack will only eat raspberries if they're whole,* Gerald says. *Raspberry pieces are not acceptable. That's it,* Mother says, *I knew you would remember.*

Later, after dinner, Gerald sits on Kathleen's bed, with Kathleen on one side and Jack on the other, bathed and in their pajamas, reading *Alice in Wonderland* to them. Kathleen loves it. *Oh, my,* she says. *Read that part again.* Jack leans forward to look at the illustrations, Alice stretched out long and thin. *It's like she's in a funhouse mirror,* he says. *Remember, Kat, when we went to the carnival with Daddy? I looked so thin and you looked so fat?* Kathleen sticks out her tongue at him. *Shut up, Jack,* she says. *Let Uncle Gerald read.*

Kathleen has taken Bea's room as her

own. After Bea left, Mother didn't change a thing. Gerald had found Mother in here quite often, early on, looking out the window or sitting in the desk chair. She'd always been flustered when he'd seen her, claiming to just be cleaning up, but he guessed that she was trying to stay close to Bea, too. On more than one occasion, especially after William left for Harvard, he'd snuck in here and slept in her bed, feeling her form in the mattress, wrapping his arms around a pillow as though it was Bea. Now Kathleen always takes this room, and Jack sleeps in William's old room. They are thrilled to have their own rooms; at home they share a small room, their beds only two feet apart. And when they stay over, Gerald usually does as well, the two of them waking him up in the morning, their eyes bright.

It is funny, sitting here now on Bea's bed, seeing what she saw when she went to sleep and when she woke. A beautiful view of the gardens, which are now in full late-summer glory. The walls are covered with a yellowing, peeling wallpaper dotted with tiny violets. Gerald has always loved this bed, so high off the floor it needs a footstool, and the children love it as well. As annoyed as he is with William, being here with Kathleen and Jack is a moment of pure bliss. This is why he came home. He can't understand why William spends so much time trying to get away.

ROSE

Rose told William that she and the girls were spending the weekend in New Hampshire, but right now she's in the front seat of Sheila's convertible, speeding down the highway toward the Cape. All four of them in the car — best friends since elementary school — are married and have school-age children. It's Sheila's birthday. A weekend away before the flurry of Labor Day and the start of school. They'd cooked up this scheme a month earlier. *I know where Rose wants to go,* Sheila said, casting a glance at her. Rose made a face. *Well, of course,* she said. *Who doesn't want to go to Hyannis in the summer?*

She knows her infatuation with the Kennedys is a little ridiculous. The girls tease her about it all the time. William refuses to talk with her about it. *But you know them,* she's pleaded more than once, *couldn't you arrange to meet for a drink? I don't know the senator,* William said. *I've told you that. I barely know Teddy. He was a year behind Gerald at Harvard. We're not friends.*

She'd held a party at their house during the convention, decorating the front porch with red, white, and blue streamers and balloons. When Jack won the nomination, Rose ran around and poured everyone more champagne. She stood in the back of the room during his entire speech, tears running down her face, as he discussed the obstacle of being a Catholic, as he defined the new frontier, and as he talked about what he would be asking each American to do for the country. *Give me your help, your hand, your voice, your vote,* he said. Rose loved that phrase and taught it to the children, adding it to their prayers each night.

She was disappointed when Jackie didn't join him onstage. Later, she learned that Jackie's pregnancy was difficult and that she was staying in Hyannis until the baby was born. *How lucky they are to be having another child.* A miscarriage in '55, in the same month that Rose had one, and the stillborn baby in '56. But then Caroline was born. Rose prays each night that this Kennedy pregnancy will be healthy and that Jackie will get to full term.

Rose knows that they won't meet or even see Jackie or Jack. But they just might run into some of the other Kennedys, out on the town at a bar or a restaurant. She looks around the car at her friends. They are thirty now, suddenly, with Sheila turning thirty-one this weekend. They all look good, having lost the baby weight — everyone else has been having babies every two years, like clockwork, but now they're done, or so they hope — and they're all nicely tanned from a summer outdoors. They have learned to cover up whatever disappointments they feel. She knows they'll turn heads when they walk, together, into a bar. She misses having eyes on her like that.

He's doing a bit better in the polls, Rose says now, shouting into the wind. *I'm hopeful.* Mary shakes her head. *Michael says there's no way he can win,* she shouts back. *No way this country will vote for a Catholic. I think he will win,* Rose says, tired of this argument that she's been having all summer. *I think we're not giving the rest of the country a chance.* Regardless of the pessimism, everyone they know is not only rooting for Jack but actively campaigning. Rose has been knocking on doors in Quincy all summer. *You're preaching to the con-*

verted, William has said, over and over, as she's headed out the door with her brochures and signs. *Of course every Irish Catholic in Boston is going to vote for him.*

Once in Hyannis, Rose tells Sheila where to go. *Just go straight and then slow way down when we get near the water. Oh, for the love of God,* Sheila says a few minutes later, all four of them gawking at the compound: the white picket fence, the enormous gray clapboard homes, the green lawn stretching to the sea. *What it must be like to live here,* Mary says, and Rose knows that they're each seeing their own small row houses, attached to the ones next door, with the leaky pipes and the narrow stairs, the arguments from one house spilling into the next. *I told you,* Rose replies. *I told all of you how gorgeous it is.*

She's been here multiple times. Early on in their marriage, when William was doing well at work, when Kathleen was still a toddler, they had talked about buying a place on the Cape. He was forever rambling on about that place up in Maine. He even forced her to go there one time. An island, for God's sake, with just one house on it. Who would want to live there? So they'd driven down to the Cape, and they'd looked at a few places nearby. She made sure to direct William to this part of town every time.

But now there's no extra money. They've moved three times since they've been married. Rose doesn't love being back in Quincy. It's nice to be near her parents and her old friends, but it all feels too familiar. To attend the church where she was baptized. To buy groceries where she once rode in the cart. It's like she never left. It's like she's still a child.

Maybe Jackie's sitting in one of those rooms right there, she says now. *Looking after little Caroline. Reading her favorite book to her. Please,* Sheila says. *They have people to do that for them. I wish I had people to do that for me,* Susan chimes in. *She probably stays in bed all day, eating chocolates and reading or doing whatever it is that rich people do in bed.* They all laugh. *I'd like to do what she gets to do in bed with Jack,* Sheila says. *Sheila,* Rose hisses. *That's disgusting. He's going to be the president.*

A car comes toward them, having backed out of one of the driveways. They crane their necks to see whether they might recognize the driver, but it's no one they know. *A flunky,* Mary says. *Probably off to run their er-*

rands. *Let's go, girls,* Sheila says, turning the car on. *Let's get checked into the motel and get changed. I want to be sitting outside on a patio, with a drink in one hand and a cigarette in the other, looking at the pink sky and the gorgeous men, within the hour.* Rose looks back through the side-view mirror as they drive away, holding tight to the scarf covering her hair as Sheila speeds toward the motel. That was the life she had dreamed of, the one now disappearing behind her.

MILLIE

Millie stands on a chair, wrapping blue crepe paper around the curtain rods. She is throwing a birthday party for herself tonight. Fifty-five. Impossibly old. She threw a fit when George included her age on the draft of the invitation. Most days, when she looks in the mirror, she thinks she could pass for fifty, especially when she holds her nose up in the air. She laughs with her friends that she doesn't need to lie about her own age, she needs to lie about Beatrix's age. She turned thirty-one over the summer. Thirty-one! By the time Millie was that age, Beatrix was already seven.

She hears the car pull up, and George stumbles through the front door, laden with packages. *Please tell me that's the booze,* Millie says. *I'm desperate for a drink.* He smiles at her. *Let me put them down and I'll pour you one,* he says. *But maybe we should get all the decorations up first? Don't want* them topsy-turvy! Almost done, she says. *Just want to crisscross the room. Spot me, will you?* She steps off the chair, twisting the roll of crepe paper, and then climbs up again in the middle of the room. George holds her waist as she affixes a piece of tape to the ceiling, standing on her tiptoes to reach. *Perfect,* George says. *Beautiful.* Millie places her hand lightly on his bald head and he lifts her up and places her gently on the floor. She drags the chair over to the far corner to affix the final piece, then cuts the paper and examines the room. *It'll have to do,* she says. *Better than that,* he replies. *Looks terrific. Fit for a queen.*

Beatrix's bringing some flowers over in a bit, and she's made a cake. Ooh, George says, patting his stomach. *I should have fasted. No,* Millie says, wrapping her arms around his middle, noting that her hands barely touch. *You look wonderful. No need to worry about your weight.* She walks to the front hallway to pick up some of the packages he brought in, hoisting one into each arm. Once in the kitchen, she empties the bags and begins to sort the vegetables for the hors d'oeuvres. She'll have Beatrix take the cake home after the party. No reason to keep temptations around.

He's a good man, she reminds herself, as she cuts up celery stalks into thin slices. A good man. A wonderful provider. Just then, Beatrix calls to her from outside, asking for her help. When Millie steps out the back door, Beatrix is coming from her car, her arms overflowing with flowers. *Oh, honestly, Beatrix,* Millie says. *This is too much. Nonsense,* Beatrix says. *You only turn fifty-five once.* Millie grabs as many flowers as she can hold from the back seat and follows Beatrix indoors. The kitchen is suddenly alive with flowers, a blaze of color. Millie sits down at the kitchen table and continues cutting up the vegetables while Beatrix arranges the flowers on the counter. *Where did you learn to do that?* Millie asks. *I've never been able to make them look so nice.* Beatrix is wearing a red skirt that stops just above the knee, with matching flats, along with that damn jacket of Reg's, the one with the leather patches, the one that she never seems to take off. Beatrix turns around to answer and catches Millie looking at her shoes. She points at Millie with her gardening shears. *Don't say it,* she says. *Don't say anything about my clothes. I brought something more acceptable for the party. I knew you would have a fit.*

No, no, Millie says. *It looks fine. You certainly have the figure for it.* And she does. She's tall and thin, and a skirt that short shows off her lovely, slender legs. *I know this is the new look.* Beatrix turns back without a word. They each work silently, Millie chopping the vegetables and Beatrix slicing the flower stems at an angle. *But no hose?* Millie asks after a minute, her head bent over the carrots. *Mummy,* Beatrix says, with an intentionally audible sigh, not turning around. *I just told you I brought a change of clothes.*

Is that the lovely Trix I hear? George calls from the front of the house, where he's been setting up the liquor table. *Indeed,* she calls back. *Just in here arguing with Mum.* George appears in the doorway and gives Beatrix a kiss on the forehead. They enjoy each other's company, Millie thinks. They truly seem to like each other. That's been a good thing. He acts as a bridge between them. *What are you two lovelies arguing about,* George says, not really asking. *Let's not do this today, shall we? Nothing important,* Beatrix says to him with a smile. *Just our usual, this and that.*

She finishes the flowers and begins carrying the vases out of the kitchen. *That beau* of yours joining us tonight, George asks her when she comes back in the room. *We would like him to be here. Oh, no,* Beatrix says, *not tonight. This is Mum's birthday, with her friends. Not the place for him. Why not?* Millie asks. *Why not have Sam come? We haven't had a chance to say more than hello to him, that one time we ran into the two of you on the street.* He was handsome, this man she's been seeing, but she seems to want to keep him far away, for some reason that Millie can't understand. Millie knows so few of her friends. She knows so little about her life. *Mummy,* Beatrix says now, that edge in her voice, waving her hand in the air, *George just asked us to behave. Don't start.*

Millie waits until Beatrix's back is turned and then she waves her hand in the air, in the same motion. George puts his finger on his lips. He pats Beatrix on the back. *Someday soon, then, eh?* he says. *Just want a chance to get to know the chap, that's all. Now, ladies, I need some fashion advice. Bow tie? Vest? Jacket on or off?*

Beatrix heads upstairs with George to help him pick out his clothes. She has become one of those people whom everyone relies upon. Millie wishes she could see her at work: she's the assistant director of her school now, and Millie is sure that she does that work effortlessly, as well. She is proud of her, but there's something else, too, a feeling that she had little to do with the woman Beatrix has become.

Millie finishes up the hors d'oeuvres and places the platter on the counter. She can't help but peek into the cake box. A lovely Madeira cake, with lemon frosting and white daisies scattered across the top. *Happy Birthday!* the cake says, in lovely script. Beatrix has become a wonderful baker. *Reg,* Millie whispers. *Our girl made me a birthday cake. Can you imagine. How the tables have turned.*

She thinks back to the birthday, the one before Beatrix left for the States, when she had to borrow sugar from a neighbor. She hadn't enough eggs. No frosting. The cake was almost inedible, and it looked horrible. She'd cried into Reg's neck that night. *This is how our girl will remember me,* she whispered. *The worst birthday party ever. Nonsense,* he replied. *You did your best. That's all that counts. And she knows it. Or she will, one day.*

Millie wonders about that. Here they are, all these years later, and she often feels farther from Beatrix than she was when Beatrix was in America. She knows she has made mistakes — marrying Tommy is probably at the top of that list — but she and Beatrix haven't yet found their way back to each other. She's not sure, now, that they ever will. She closes the cake box and undoes her apron. *Beatrix,* she calls up the stairs, *leave that man to his own devices. I'm the one who needs you.*

WILLIAM

William sits in the kitchen, dressed, nursing his fourth cup of coffee. The children were up before dawn, excited by Christmas, the stockings and the gifts opened and scattered by seven. The day feels too long already. Church, Christmas dinner with Rose's family, then to his mother's in the afternoon, where they'll stay for supper. He feels as though he can't see his way to the end of this day. He thinks about pouring a bit of whiskey into his coffee but it seems too early. There will be plenty of opportunities later.

Kathleen comes running down the stairs and bursts into the kitchen, the door swinging back and forth. *Daddy, I don't want to wear tights,* she says. *She's telling me I have to. They're so itchy and horrid.* She stands in the center of the small kitchen, her hands on her waist, her feet spread wide. When she gets mad, her entire face turns white, accentuating the freckles that explode across her nose and cheeks. He gestures for her to come close, and he puts his hands on her shoulders. *Lovebug,* he says, *it's twenty-five degrees outside. It's Christmas. You need to do what Mommy says. But, Daddy,* she wails. *Can't I just wear pants? Why doesn't Jack have to wear tights? You know why,* he says. *And besides, he has to wear a jacket and tie.* William takes his own tie and holds it up like a noose, his head lolling to one side and his tongue sticking out of his mouth. *Believe you me,* he says, *that's worse.*

A bit of a smile comes to her face. It almost always does. She looks so like Gerald at times that it takes his breath away. She's a Gregory. There's not a bit of Rose in her. Jack, though, is all Kelly: black hair, blue eyes, small frame. When the twelve grandchildren gather for a photo, Kathleen is the odd one out, with her red hair and towering height. She has to stand in the back row with the older kids, even though she's only eight. Rose is forever fussing about her weight. *She'll turn out like your mother if she's not careful,* she'll say when he tells her to back off. *And God forbid she gets as tall as your father.* Now he reaches into his jacket pocket and pulls out a foil-wrapped chocolate, presenting it to her on an open palm.

Don't tell Mommy, he says, holding his finger to his lips. *Eat it up quick. Then go put those tights on. It's almost time to go.*

He's seated next to Rose's father at dinner, the children and Rose down at the other end of the long table. This house has become another home. In some ways, it's the family he's always wanted. No one is ever disappointed in him. No one expects him to be more than he is. But like Kathleen, he knows he sticks out. They treat him differently than they do the other husbands. No one else graduated from Harvard. No one else works at a bank. Rose's dad is in commercial real estate. Her only brother is a priest, and her three sisters are married to men who work in more traditional jobs: one owns a bar, another a construction company, and the third is a fireman. They treat him with more respect than he deserves. He has told them repeatedly that they have better jobs than he does, but he knows they don't believe him.

Today, all the talk is about the incoming president. Michael, the fireman, calls down the table to him, asking him about Gerald. *He knows Teddy, right? Can he get us tickets to the inauguration?* William shrugs. *They were in school together,* he says. *But he doesn't really know him.* William doesn't mention that he met Jack a few times, back at Harvard, back when Kennedy was a state representative, making the rounds. Smart enough fellow, he supposed, but he didn't much like him. He was slick. Not to be trusted, William had thought at the time. He voted for him, of course, and he knows enough to keep his mouth shut at this table, where these men see themselves in Kennedy, believing now that anything is possible. The hope in this room is almost tangible.

Even Christopher, the priest, leads a toast to Kennedy. He's William's favorite in the family, a serious fellow who seems suited for the church. William enjoys their conversations, when they can get away from the others, when he can ask Chris questions about religion, about philosophy, about his beliefs. They've gone to the opera together, once or twice, and William can often interest Chris in heading to a museum. Rose used to be more interested in doing stuff like that. The last time he suggested getting a sitter on a Saturday so they could see the new exhibit at the Gardner, she had laughed in his face. *Are you crazy,* she said. *Kathleen has her ballet class on Saturday afternoon. Jack has a birthday party. And if I'm hiring a sitter, I want to go out at night, to dinner with friends, to have a good time, not to wander around some fake Italian palazzo in the middle of an afternoon. Never mind,* William said, wishing he had never suggested it, *I can go during my lunch break.*

The goodbyes take forever with this family but they're finally in the car again, heading to his mother's house. To home, that's the way he thinks of it, and yet he knows that's wrong. Rose would mock him if he said that out loud. Both children fall asleep almost immediately, Jack's head nodding on Kathleen's shoulder. Rose pulls her coat tightly around her shoulders. *So cold,* she says. *I wish this day was over. It won't be much warmer at your mother's. And how can we eat anything else? We have to,* William says. *They've been waiting all day for us. And you know she's cooked up a storm.* Rose sighs. *That's what I'm worried about,* she says. *I'm so tired. I just want to crawl into bed.* She turns her head toward the window and closes her eyes.

Kathleen wakes when they get there but Jack is still sound asleep, so William carries him inside and up the back stairs, waving at his mother and Gerald, to lay him down for a nap. Little has changed here over the years. His room still has two twin beds with white bedspreads, a needlepoint pillow with

343

a train adorning each. William's childhood is still here, too, on the bookshelves and on the bureau. Old, worn baseball gloves in various sizes. His varsity letters from high school. A box that he made in woodshop to hold his shoeshine kit. He sits down next to Jack and pulls the train blanket from the end of the bed up around him. Rose is right. It is freezing in this house.

Downstairs, he finds Gerald, Mother, and Kathleen in the kitchen. *Rose,* he says, and Mother points to the living room. *Went to lie down,* she says. *So tired, poor dear.* He knows she's happy that Rose is elsewhere, and he is, too. It's exhausting to watch the two of them pretend to like each other, saying one thing when they mean something else. He would have thought by this point they would just be honest with each other and with themselves. Now he understands that will never happen.

Sit, sit, Mother says, pointing to his chair. *Kathleen was just telling us about all her wonderful gifts from Santa.* Kathleen is on Gerald's lap, sprinkling red and green sugar onto a tray of unbaked star cookies. *I waited to bake them,* Mother says. *Kathleen can decorate cookies better than anyone else I know.* Kathleen smiles up at Mother, her face open and guileless. His chest feels full, and he collapses into his chair, averting his eyes, lighting a cigarette. *What a day,* he says. *It's not a day, Daddy,* Kathleen says, *it's Christmas! It's the best day of the year. That it is,* Gerald says, squeezing her around the middle. *And we're so very glad that we get to spend it with you!*

When Kathleen's done with the cookies, Mother takes her into the dining room to set the table. William puts his feet up on Father's chair and undoes his tie. *Honestly, G,* he says. *Why did no one tell me about the horrors of this day? It's got to be the longest day ever. G,* Gerald says, smiling. *No one calls me that anymore.*

Kathleen rushes back into the room. *Look what I found in the sideboard. Nana wants to know if you recognize them,* she says, putting a pile of cards on the table. *They're place cards,* Gerald says, looking through them. *They tell you where to sit at the table. I know what they are,* Kathleen says, frowning at him. *But Nana doesn't remember them.* William reaches across and picks them up, placing each one down on the table as he reads it out loud: *Mr. G, Mrs. G, William, Gerald, Bea.* Of course Mother knows Bea made these. He suspects she didn't want to explain to Kathleen who Bea is. *A girl made them,* William says. *A girl who lived here with us, when we were little.* He picks up Bea's card and shows it to Kathleen. *Her name was Bea.* Kathleen holds the card in her hand. *A girl lived here? With you and Uncle Gerald? Yes,* Gerald says. *She had to live here because there was a war where she came from. Oh, no,* Kathleen says, and once again William looks away. She's all heart. He worries she feels too much. *Is she okay now?* Kathleen asks.

William doesn't know. He hasn't heard from Bea in a long time. They had each written, a few times, after he came back from Europe. But then he got married and they had Kathleen and life got busy. He was the one, again, who stopped responding.

She's doing great, Gerald says, and William looks up in surprise. *She runs a nursery school in London. She what?* William asks. *You're in touch with her? You can see it, can't you,* Gerald replies, before pushing open the swinging door and disappearing into the hall. William turns to Kathleen. *She's like Principal Stevens,* he says. Kathleen smiles. *He's the nicest man,* she says. *But, Bea, she was here by herself? Yes,* Mother says, coming into the room, and William knows she was waiting on the other side of the door, listening, wanting to hear how the conversation would unfold. *She was most brave,* Mother went on. *She traveled here all by herself, can you imagine, Kathleen, taking a big ocean liner all by yourself? No!* Kathleen says, and then Gerald is back with a framed photograph in his hand. *This is Bea,* he says, handing it to Kathleen, *with your dad and me. This is the day she beat your dad at a swimming race. A girl beat Daddy?* Kathleen's eyes are wide and smiling, but then she hands the photo back to Gerald and she's off and scrounging in the table drawer.

I'll make new name cards, she announces. *For who we are now.* And she settles down at the table, creating a brand-new set of six. *Christmas card,* Gerald says, looking at William. *It's in the living room.* William nods. The conversation moves from this to that, William tracing the letters on the cards with his finger, that familiar handwriting, as Jack wakes up and comes downstairs, as Rose appears in the doorway, a blanket wrapped around her shoulders. When no one is looking, William drops the name cards into his jacket pocket. Later, he'll fold the one for Bea into his wallet, behind the photo of Kathleen and Jack.

BEATRIX

Beatrix is having a dinner party in her new flat. She moved, back in the summer, before school started, to a neighborhood far from school. She no longer wanted to run into students with her hair in a kerchief or wearing her denim jeans. And although it had not happened, she always worried that she'd run into a parent on her way home from a bar late at night or, God forbid, in the bar itself, a few drinks in. She is also now farther from her mother, which means she doesn't have to see Mum so frequently. At night, Beatrix often refuses to answer the telephone. She knows it's Mum calling to complain about George. It's only a matter of time before this marriage ends, too.

It has taken time to get used to the commute but it's worth it. A number of her friends live close by, and they regularly meet up for drinks or dinner. Once a month someone holds a potluck, and tonight is finally her turn. It's a cold, rainy Saturday in February, a perfect time to gather together. It will be a small group: her boyfriend, Sam, and two other couples. The flat has a nice, big kitchen, a fireplace, and there's a small garden in the back. It's her first apartment that truly feels like home.

She spends the morning vacuuming and cleaning. She sets the table, finishes as much prep work as she can, and then looks around the apartment with a critical eye. George had helped her hang a few pieces of artwork when she moved in, but they had belonged to Mum, and she has never much liked them. In the back of the front hall closet is a box sent by Mrs. G. When Beatrix moved, she'd sent out a change-of-address card, and the box had arrived a few weeks later. Beatrix hasn't been in touch as much as she feels she should — her life is busy, and there doesn't ever seem to be enough time. After Mr. G died, she wrote to Mrs. G on Sunday nights for almost a year. But over time she drifted away from that routine; Sunday nights were set aside to plan for the week, and as the school had grown and, along with it, her responsibilities, the letters became less frequent. Over the past few years she's sent Christmas cards and only an occasional letter.

Beatrix opened the box when it arrived to see that it contained framed paintings and to read the short letter. *Dearest Bea,* Mrs. G wrote, *Cleaning out the garage and thought you would like to have these. Enjoy, my dear. Hope everything is well.* Beatrix put the box away, wanting and yet not wanting to see what was inside. She's worked so hard to keep the Gregorys in the past. Now she pulls out two large paintings and recognizes both, Mr. G's signature carefully etched in the right-hand corners. They hung on the living room wall in Maine. One is a sunset view of the town from the island, the rocks and the forest framing the view. That orange rowboat is there, the rowboat that was owned by the man who ran the market, always moored right by the town dock. The boat is catching the final moments of the sun. It almost looks as if it's on fire.

In the other painting, the sun is high overhead, the sky a cloudless blue, and the floating dock is off to the left. She holds the painting up to the gray light by the front window to see the three bodies on the dock: one is lying down and two are sitting side by side, their legs in the water. And there's King, too, his head poking out of the sea. How often did they sit like this, she and Gerald, kicking their feet back and forth.

She hangs both paintings over the sofa in the living room but they look wrong there somehow. Her furniture is modern, her taste quite minimal. The colors are all wrong.

She retrieves the box to carry it to the trash and realizes there's a smaller painting hidden at the bottom of the box, under some crumpled newspaper. It's about the size of a book, and it's not familiar to her. A thin wooden frame surrounds the painting. She sits at the kitchen table and examines it more carefully. It's not watercolor but oil, and the rough swirls of the paint add to the richness of its color. The edges are sharper, too. It's a couple in a dance hall, twirling. The man is in a tux and the woman in a soft blue gown, the pleats opening as she spins, the man's hand on her back. Behind them a big band, the trumpets glinting gold. Beatrix can almost hear the music as she stares at the painting, as she wonders when Mr. G painted this. She guesses it's early, maybe even before William was born. Did they do this then, go out to clubs and dance? She looks more carefully at the couple. It can't be the Gregorys. They're too evenly matched. And yet it is them: the way the woman gazes up into the man's face, the way the man's head is gently turned toward hers. This one she quite likes, and she hangs it in the front vestibule, across from the mirror.

She's still getting ready when Sam arrives, his key softly turning the lock. *Hi, there,* she calls out. *Be ready in a sec.* When she comes into the living room, he's stacking the wood in the fireplace, and she leans down to give him a kiss. *What are those,* he asks, pointing above the sofa. *Have I seen them before?* She looks at the new paintings. *What do you think?* she says. *They're fine,* he says. *A bit amateur, maybe, but better than what was there before. Do you know anything about them?*

She shrugs. *Mrs. Gregory sent them,* she says. *You know, the family I lived with in America. I think I remember seeing them there, in their house.* She doesn't want to tell him anything else. She doesn't want to look at them, to talk about them, to think about what they represent. *You know what,* she says. *I don't like them. While I finish up in the kitchen, can you take them down and put the others back up? Sure thing,* Sam says.

The next day is bright and sunny. In the afternoon, Beatrix and Sam stop by an art gallery a few blocks away, one that is featuring the work of local photographers. They pick out two black-and-white prints, contemporary shots of London, and Sam insists on splitting the cost with her. *One day soon,* he says. *We'll have a place together.* Beatrix hangs them over the sofa. They look perfect. She writes Mrs. G to thank her for the paintings. She asks about the smaller painting, the one of the dancing couple. *Did Mr. G paint that long ago? Is that the two of you? I don't remember seeing it in the house.*

She waits for a response. Finally, a letter comes but there are no answers to her questions. Mrs. G writes about plans for her garden this year and includes a sentence or two about Gerald and William. She doesn't mention Rose or the children. But she does include her recipe for blueberry muffins. *Really the best, dear, with wild Maine blueberries. But you probably don't have those. Use the same quantity of regular blueberries, but just be prepared: they won't be what you remember.* And she is right, as always: Beatrix tries and tries, but her muffins never taste quite the same.

NANCY

In a month, Ethan will have been gone for ten years. It's hard for Nancy to believe. She visits him in the graveyard every day, no matter the weather. It's getting a little harder lately, but still, a day does not seem right unless she goes. It's the one saving grace of not going to Maine.

The boys don't like it. She knows they talk about it when she's not around. She hates them worrying over her, thinking they can care for her better than she can care for herself. Why did she ask Gerald to come home? Last winter, he blocked the door with his body one blizzardy morning when he'd come by to shovel the walk. *What are you doing, Mother?* he asked. *You can't go out in this. Oh, don't be ridiculous,* she said. *It's a little snow.* She pulled on her warmest hat. *We're made of tough New England stock.* (She did slip that day, rather badly, although she never told Gerald, nursing black-and-blue bruises up and down her left side for a good month. She lay in the snow where she fell, staring up at the flakes as they came down, as they covered her body and face.) She doesn't want Ethan to be lonely, that's all. He would want to know everything that's going on. He never got to see the boys as adults, never saw them making their way in the world.

Even now, the grief can paralyze her. Out of nowhere it comes, too, often on the cusp of something nice. In passing, at church on a Sunday, someone will say how they miss hearing him sing the hymns. Kathleen will ask a question about the grandfather she never met. Gerald will nod in that way, in that way that he and William and Ethan all nod, and she'll feel as sad as she did when she found him in the garden, his hand still grasping the trowel, his open eyes looking up at the sky, looking up at her but not seeing a thing.

She hasn't forgotten the way he could make her feel small and insignificant, the way that he always talked over her words. But she's not stupid. She watches her friends and their husbands, and she knows she had it pretty good. He was a gentle man who did his best. Who was as content as she was to have a small, quiet life. What more can you ask? She still catches herself looking into his study, expecting to see him there, grading tests, playing chess, reading. He looks up over the top of his glasses, his hair glinting in the lamplight. *All righty, then,* he says, and she smiles in return.

Today, though, she is taking Jack to the graveyard with her. He hasn't been yet, and she thinks it's time. He's seven and a half, a big boy, and he needs to know more about his grandfather. She suspects Rose says next to nothing. It's as though William and those children have been absorbed into the Kelly family, as though the Gregory name and the Gregory genes mean almost nothing. *Oh,* she says to her friends, waving her hand in the air, *I understand it, I do. I mean, it's just me here, rattling about in a big old house. And over there, in Quincy, there are cousins and aunts and uncles and all sorts of excitement. Kathleen has even ridden in a firetruck, for goodness' sake, with whichever one of her uncles is the fireman.* Nancy can't keep them straight. Those boys all look the same, and she gave up years ago trying to tell them apart. Except for Christopher. He's the priest.

But she wants Jack to know about his grandfather. Kathleen has more of a connection, she thinks, because Rose was already pregnant with her when Ethan died. She had asked her once whether Ethan had touched her before she was born. *Well, sweetheart,* Nancy said. *He couldn't have. You know you were born after he passed. No,* Kathleen insisted, *did Grandpa touch Mommy's stomach to feel me, to see if I was kicking. My word, child,* Nancy responded, turning around in the kitchen. *What a thing to ask! I should think not. Your grandfather was not the kind of man who would go around touching women's stomachs! Oh,* Kathleen said, her face confused. *Aunt Anna is pregnant, and PopPop is always patting her and talking to the baby.* Nancy had been appalled but tried not to show it. *To each his own, dear,* she said. *But the important thing is that your grandfather knew all about you and knew you were to be born. That's the thing to keep in mind.*

But she can't say that to Jack, born more than two years after Ethan's death. Today, Jack is here by himself because Kathleen is off at a sleepaway camp. Nancy packs a picnic lunch, having first checked with Gerald about what she should bring: peanut butter and jelly sandwiches and blondies. Once they're out the back door, she takes his hand to cross the street. In the cemetery,

Jack still holds her hand. It's unlike him. Usually he's the first to run off, no matter where they are. Nancy doesn't know what to talk to him about. She feels much closer to Kathleen. She's enjoyed having a girl around again. A shame, really, that she didn't have one of her own. She never knows whether she's allowed to count Bea.

They walk along silently for a few minutes, the road winding up and down small hills, the graves on either side. It's a beautiful July day, not too hot yet, not too humid. Lovely. The kind of day that would have been perfect in Maine. *Don't you find this a little scary,* Jack asks, finally. *You know, all these dead people? Oh, no, dear,* Nancy says, squeezing his hand just a little. *It's a place of rest. I find it quite peaceful, actually. But they're dead,* Jack hisses. *Dead people right here, right there, almost under our feet.*

Nancy turns to face her grandson. His dark blue eyes are troubled. She has wondered, occasionally, guiltily, whether Jack is even a Gregory. He's all Rose. *What do you think happens when someone dies?* she asks. *Their soul goes to heaven, hell, or purgatory,* Jack says. *Okay,* she says, resisting the temptation to tell him that purgatory doesn't exist, but making a mental note to talk to William about this later. Certainly, the traditional dogma can be adjusted to make room for rational thought.

So then what's left? she asks. *Their body?* Jack says. She nods and keeps walking. She wonders whether she'll get in trouble for what she's about to say. *Slowly,* she says, *slowly the body decomposes. Do you know what that means? Returns to the earth,* Jack says, and Nancy widens her eyes. *Okay,* she says, *yes. So most of these people aren't physically here anymore, right? For some of them, it's been over a hundred years. But you come here,* Jack says. *My dad said. He said you come here every day to talk to Grandpa. Yes, I do,* Nancy says. *But I'm talking to his spirit, not to his body. This is just a place where I know he'll be. I know where to find him. Okay,* Jack says, but his voice is unconvinced.

Go, she says, *go see if you can find Grandpa's grave. It's straight ahead there, by the pond and the willow tree. Ethan Putnam Gregory, it will say. Nineteen hundred to nineteen fifty-one.* Jack takes off down the hill, using his arms like wings, running in a haphazard line. *Give me your help, your hand, your voice, your vote,* he says again and again, his voice growing louder with each iteration. Nancy follows behind, her mood lightened. How wonderful it is to be a child. To be so troubled and then to have those cares lifted off a moment later. A magic trick of sorts.

She meets him at the grave, and she pulls out the blanket and the lunch. He seems content, eating his sandwich, asking her how many blondies he can have. Hello, Ethan, she says to herself. This is Jack, your grandson. It's high time the two of you met. *Your grandfather,* she begins, *was a most wonderful man. I wish you could have known him.* And darn it, here are those tears that come at the inopportune times, that render her speechless. Nancy brushes at her eyes with the back of her hand. *Tell you what,* she says. *Why don't you ask me questions about him? I'll tell you anything you want to know.*

I know all about Grandpa, Jack says. *Daddy tells us stories about him almost every night. About how he was a great fisherman. About how he liked to sing. About how he made him and Uncle Gerald really good in math.* Nancy smiles. She had no idea that William was passing the good parts of Ethan along to his children. Jack is looking at her with concern. These damn tears. *I'm all right, child,* she says. *No need to worry about me.* She's the caretaker. How she hates it when people want to take care of her.

WILLIAM

Twelve years in the workforce, and William has pretty much figured out how to make the most out of a deadening job. Early on, in the years after college, he let the boredom of the routine devour him. He felt shackled and imprisoned, reporting to supervisors who frustrated him with their incompetence. He got fired from his first two jobs by suggesting change, for letting on how he really felt. In this job he forced himself to stop caring, to distance himself from the work. He began doing less and less, spending more time out of the office than in. To his surprise, nobody really noticed. The benefit, he realized, of the blond hair and green eyes. Of the Harvard pedigree. It was simple, really: once you no longer cared, once you tossed ambition aside, everything was on a far more even keel.

Often, at lunch, he'll tell his secretary he has a lunch date and then he'll slip away for a few hours, to the MFA or to the Gardner. To sit on a bench and gaze into a painting, to escape into its world. Once, on a beautiful summer day, he took a tourist boat around Boston Harbor, just to be on the water. He felt odd, in his suit and tie, surrounded by teenagers in shorts and T-shirts, ignoring their parents, hardly looking at the ocean, sneaking smokes back by the engine. He wanted to shake them, to shake the boy he once was, lying on a floating dock off the coast of Maine. Enjoy this, he wanted to say. Try to stay in the moment. He wished he could be one of them, to still be in that place where everything seemed possible.

Tonight he's heading up to Revere, to the new Wonderland Ballroom, which opened earlier this year. It's right next to the water, much nicer than the ballrooms in the city. William has waited all week for this. He will sit at a table by the window, drink in hand, and take it all in. The trumpets blaring. The couples swirling and dipping. The music so loud and so brash that it fills every part of him. The last time he went, he could hear the rhythm of the waves when the band took a break, and when he walked to his car, he could see the entire expanse of the sky from the crescent beach. He stood there for almost an hour, looking east, the music still

363

throbbing within him.

But it's a hike from Quincy, and the last two times he had to leave before he was ready, before the night was over. He wishes they still lived on the north shore. Tonight, though, he can stay until they close, he can be the last man out the door. Maybe he'll even sleep in the car, looking out at the dark ocean, the car seat rolled back to horizontal. He pulls back into the driveway now, having dropped the kids off with Mother. A quick change and then he'll be on his way.

Rose is putting on her makeup at her dressing table. Photos of Jackie Kennedy are taped to the mirror. He has noticed her looking at them as she does her hair. She had bangs cut last month to mimic Jackie's most recent hairstyle. *Where you gals off to tonight?* he asks, sitting on his bed, pulling off his tie. *Sheila's,* she says, leaning in close to the mirror, putting on her mascara. *Maybe we'll go out for a drink from there.* She stands and faces him, a hand on her hip. She's wearing a tight-fitting red dress that stops just below the knee. They're definitely going out for that drink. *And you,* she says. *What are your plans?*

A few months ago, sitting across from each other at the kitchen table, both unhappier than they ever thought they could be, they agreed that every other Saturday night would be each of theirs to do whatever they chose. William had suggested it, and Rose reluctantly agreed. Their families share in taking care of the children: one Saturday for Rose's family, the next, two weeks later, for Mother. Everybody wins, William thinks. Their families don't know that they go their separate ways. They think it's so they can have a date night. And the funny thing is, they often do have sex on these nights, when William manages to make it back before the next morning, rolling in long after she's come home, half in the bag, climbing into her bed, naked. But she always rolls over to meet him, as though she was waiting, as though spending time apart was the only way for them to come together.

I don't know yet, he says now. *Maybe head over to Nelson's. Some of the guys from work are getting together downtown, so maybe that. Haven't decided.* Rose nods, and he knows she's not believing him either. Would it be easier if they just told each other the truth? Why can't he tell her where he goes? He wonders whether her truth is as innocent as his, but it's a casual thought, not anything he cares to think about for any length of time.

You look great, doll, he says, and she

365

smiles, checking her dress in the full-length mirror. He's not lying about that. She looks even better now than when they first met. All the guys tell him so. Partly, he knows, it's because she couldn't stay pregnant again after Jack. After the third miscarriage, they'd made her get her tubes tied. The other wives have gone on to have four children or more. Sheila and Michael have seven.

William watches her as she affixes her earrings. She'd been distraught then, the thought of no more children. He had been quietly relieved. He loves the two children they have. Why stretch even thinner? They can barely make do on his salary. He hated to see her so upset, though, month after month. Now she seems happier, although he suspects that he enjoys these Saturday nights more than she does. He wishes she would let loose a little. That she'd stop being so preoccupied with what others think. This is a gift he's given her. A release valve, he tells himself. A way for them both to still feel wanted and desired. Alive.

She spritzes Chanel No. 5 in the air and walks through it, back and forth, before slipping on her shoes. *I've got to dash,* she says, picking up her stole from her bed. *The girls are waiting.* She waves from the doorway. *I'll be back with the children by noon,* he says, and she waves again. He sits still, listening to her walk carefully down the stairs in her heels and then out the front door.

Less than a half hour later, he's on the road as well, heading north. The G-Clefs are playing tonight, and he doesn't want to miss a note.

GERALD

Mother spent the weekend before Thanksgiving making pies and now all three sit on the sideboard, slightly black and crispy around the edges, the fruit oozing out of small cracks. Kathleen and Jack stand close by, smelling and pointing, discussing which pie they want to eat first. *Blueberry,* Kathleen says. *Are you crazy?* Jack asks. *Pumpkin. Then apple. Blueberry is last.*

Linda laughs as she and Gerald watch them from the doorway. *Seems like siblings can't ever agree on anything,* she says. She smiles and squeezes him on the arm before slipping back into the kitchen to help Mother. William's in the living room, on the sofa by the fire, and Gerald joins him, sitting in Father's chair and putting his feet up on the old, embroidered footstool.

She's great, William says, raising his eyebrows, offering him the bottle of whiskey, which Gerald waves off. *Yes,* he says. *I know.*

What William is really saying, he suspects, is that Linda is not what he expected. Too pretty. Too blond. Too full of life. This is the first time William has met her, and Gerald knew he would be surprised. She also works at the school, teaching Latin and serving as a housemother in one of the girls' dorms. Gerald wouldn't admit it to William but he, too, is surprised, every day, that she wants to be with him.

William frowns. *You got to get yourself out of this town, G. How can you date someone when she lives in a dorm? Jesus Christ. We manage,* Gerald says, not wanting William to tell him what he already knows. *It's just that we want to keep it quiet. Well, that's impossible,* William says. *Those relationships never work out.*

William leans in close enough that Gerald can smell the booze on his breath. *A buddy of mine from Harvard is looking to rent out his place in Cambridge. I'll tell him you might be interested.* Gerald shakes his head. Why does William keep insisting that he knows how Gerald should live his life? He wants to say: Tell me about that job of yours, William, the job you can't even bear to discuss. Tell me about that wife of yours who's never around. Instead he says: *Thanks for thinking of me, but I'm pretty happy here. I'll get an apartment in town, eventually, but for now, the faculty housing is fine.*

Gerald readjusts the logs in the fireplace, and the fire flares up again. *So, where's Rose?* he asks William as he sits down again, raising his eyebrows. *She doesn't celebrate Thanksgiving anymore? Nothing to be thankful for? Her mother,* William says, so smoothly that Gerald knows it was rehearsed, knows that William is deliberately avoiding being drawn into a battle. *She's not doing well. Rose was needed over there. Too bad for us,* Gerald says. *I think she and Linda would really get on.*

They both say nothing for a few moments, staring into the flames. *I miss the old Thanksgivings,* William says, *with all the cousins.* Gerald nods. The wood cracks and snaps. *It was my favorite holiday when I was little,* he replies. *Even more than Christmas. The food is better. And this is fine and all, but I liked the messiness of those Thanksgivings. Mother running about, Father hiding in his study.* Messiness isn't quite the right word, but he doesn't know how to explain what he's feeling. An emptiness, a longing for something, but he's not sure what it is.

Don't you wish we could just go back, William says, almost as though he knows what Gerald is thinking. *To those days? When everything was so simple? No,* Gerald says, *I don't. I'm much happier now, as an adult. I know who I am, I know what's important to me.* And that really is the truth. William may have found himself inside a life that he doesn't care for, but Gerald hasn't. His life has barely begun.

Linda comes in from the kitchen with a platter of crackers and cheese. *More hors d'oeuvres,* she says brightly. *I think your mother is planning for a cast of thousands. Always does,* William says, sitting up a bit to face her. *We used to have a much fuller house than we do now. Gerald told me,* Linda says. *Sounds like it was a fun time. I never had much of a Thanksgiving growing up. It was just me and my parents. Kind of like any other day but with turkey and pie.*

Remember Bea on that first Thanksgiving, William says, leaning forward, looking at Gerald, and Gerald notices how drunk he's already become. *How she didn't know anything about it, really? How we had to explain about the Pilgrims at the table. How disgusted she was with the sweet potato casserole?* Gerald remembers nothing of this, but he nods. He wonders where this is heading.

William turns to Linda. *Gerald told you about Bea, right,* he says, glancing over at Gerald. *The girl,* Gerald says to Linda, *the British girl who lived with us. Right,* she says, *yes, he did. Such a lovely thing your parents did, taking someone in like that.*

What did he tell you about her, William asks, as if Gerald isn't in the room. Gerald leans back in Father's chair. Best to let this run its course. Linda shrugs. *Sounded like she was a wonderful addition to the family. Your mother told me about her as well. How she sees Bea in Kathleen.* Gerald suppresses a smile. So smart of Linda to turn the conversation back to William. That's the sort of thing he can never quite do in the moment. *Well,* William says, looking flustered. *I don't know about that. Kathleen is nothing like Bea. Oh, yes, she is,* Gerald says. *The look on her face when she's mad? The way she stands up for herself?* William shrugs, then leans toward Linda. *I'll tell you this, though. Our Gerald had quite a crush on her.* Linda laughs, and Gerald, in a rare moment of absolute rage, wants to slam William into the brick fireplace. Instead, he catches Linda's eye and shakes his head.

Dinner, Jack yells, and the three of them stand and head toward the dining room.

William pulls Gerald back and lets Linda walk on ahead, wrapping his arm around Gerald's shoulders. *I wish she was here,* he says. *Don't you?* Gerald is tired of thinking about the past. He shrugs the weight of William's arm away and catches up with Linda, his hand around her waist. She looks up at him with a smile, and he leans down to give her a kiss.

MILLIE

Mum, Beatrix says, in that warning tone. *Don't start. What,* Millie says. *I said nothing.* They're meeting for an early dinner. What with Beatrix's schedule and her living on the other side of the city, it's the only way Millie can see her. They're never very successful dinner dates: Beatrix is tired and cranky, always looking at her watch. Millie asks question after question. The gap between them continues to feel far too wide.

But at least they have this. For over a year, after Millie left George, they rarely saw each other. Beatrix always had an excuse, something else that needed to be done. Millie would lie to her friends, telling them elaborate tales about weekly dinners and mother-daughter holidays. She would call, the phone ringing and ringing, Millie knowing that Beatrix was there, refusing to answer, even if it meant missing a call from a friend. *All I'm saying,* Millie says, straightening the silverware on the table, *is that I don't want you to miss out. Look at all your friends who are already married, who already have children.* Millie takes a sip of wine and blots her lips with her napkin. She tries to cut back on the drinking when she's with Beatrix. Just one glass of wine. She crosses her legs and replaces the napkin on her lap but still doesn't look in Beatrix's eyes. *It's just that Sam seemed as though he was one of the good ones. I don't want you to wait too long.* She raises her eyes then and sees what she knew she would see, Beatrix's face dark and cold, closed off. That beautiful face. But she felt that she had to say something. She's trying to be more up-front with her, to say what she thinks. Well, she's always said what she thought. But she wants to have a more open relationship.

How difficult it is, though, with your own child. To change the patterns that have been set, to create a new way of being together. She thinks of the path that's been cut through the park near her flat, the grass slowly disappearing. A bootleg trail, she's heard it called. The best way of getting from here to there. Why can't she figure this out with her own daughter? She thinks of Julia's daughter, Louisa, now fourteen, and how much fun they have together. She loves taking Louisa shopping. Just last month Louisa had spent the weekend while Joe and Julia were out of town. How did she and Beatrix end up here, sitting across from each other, feeling worlds away? Strangers, almost. At least they're seeing each other again. But somehow that's made her feel even more desperate.

Millie leans across the table and grasps Beatrix's hand. *Sweetheart,* she says. *I missed so much of your childhood. I want to spend more time together. Can't you include me in your life? Jesus, Mum,* Beatrix says, pulling her hand away, running it through her hair. *You pretend this is about me but it's really all about you. As so much often is.* She picks up her menu and studies it, and after a moment Millie does the same. She always seems to say the wrong thing, even when it's what she most wants to say. They both study their menus for too long. The silence becomes unbearable.

So, tell me, Millie tries again. *Tell me about how work is going. It's fine,* Beatrix says, still not looking up. *Busy. We signed a deal to move into a new space, to have more room, to add another class. We'll move in this summer. Oh,* Millie says, nodding, *that's wonderful. Will you still have time for some vacation?*

She wants to go somewhere together, just the two of them.

Beatrix shrugs. *Not sure. Maybe.* She takes a sip of water. Millie doesn't really know why Beatrix is so angry with her. She knows she was furious that she left George. She stayed with him longer than she had wanted to, hoping, perhaps, that she could convince herself he was fine, that the marriage was worth sticking around for. And he was, he is, a nice man. But she wanted to be alone. She wanted to be on her own. Not like after Reg, when it hadn't been her choice. *Never again,* she told Beatrix when she helped her to move out. *I'm not getting married again. Three times is the charm.* The look on Beatrix's face had been full of so many things — disappointment, anger, disbelief — but she hadn't said a word.

Their dinners arrive. Millie pushes the food around her plate. *Do you ever hear from the Gregorys?* she asks when the silence has gone on for too long. Beatrix looks up from her food. *Rarely,* she says. *Christmas cards, mostly. What did the one this year say,* Millie asks. *What is happening with all of them?* There's a bit of a pause and then Beatrix replies, still holding her fork in her hand. *Mrs. Gregory is well, I think. Gerald's been*

377

back east for a few years — he works at the school. And William, Millie says, as lightly as she can. She has not mentioned his name since he left the flat all those years ago. *What has happened to him?* Beatrix looks around the restaurant and then back at Millie, before looking away again. *He's married, has two children.* Beatrix meets Millie's eyes. *What is it, Mummy?* she asks. *What's brought on this great interest in the Gregorys all of a sudden?*

Millie digs her nails into her palm. *Just wondering,* she says. *I know how important they are to you.* Beatrix shrugs. *They were,* she says. *Not so much anymore.* Silence falls again. *Nancy never remarried,* Millie says. *After Ethan died?* Beatrix shakes her head and almost smiles. *I can't imagine such a thing,* she says. *She would never. Isn't she lonely, though,* Millie asks, understanding as she does that loneliness is what has driven so many of the choices that she has made. *Isn't she terribly lonely? I don't know,* Beatrix says. *She's got Gerald close by, for company. And the grandchildren not far away.*

Beatrix puts her fork down and pushes her plate away. She's hardly eaten anything. *You know, Mummy,* she says. *Mrs. G thought the world of you. Of me?* Millie is genuinely surprised. *She didn't even know me. But she knew about you,* Beatrix says. *I talked to her about you all the time. I think she was even a little jealous of you. Of the way you held down a job, drove the ambulance, took care of Daddy. She felt horrible when Daddy died. For a whole month after, she brought cookies over to me at lunch. She'd come walking right into the lunchroom with these warm cookies, right out of the oven. Almost all the weekly allotment of sugar went into those cookies. I thought I might die of shame. I mean, everybody loved it, but, honestly, it made me feel like such a child.*

Millie doesn't know how to respond. This is more than Beatrix has said about the Gregorys in years. *Well, that's lovely,* she says. *I'm glad she took such good care of you.* Millie knows she would have dismissed this if she'd heard it at the time. How ridiculous to bring cookies over to the lunchroom, she would have thought, what is this woman trying to prove? Now she's able to see it for what it was: a genuine act of love. This woman loved her Beatrix as much as she does. She can see that now, in a way she never could before.

Beatrix is watching her closely. *How about,* Millie says, her head spinning with the idea, *how about we go to America, you and I, this summer? We could go to New York and then up to Boston. We could visit with the Gregorys. I've saved up to go on a trip like this with you.* Beatrix's face closes again, in that familiar way. *No,* she says, her neck tight, and Millie feels as though the door, which had opened just a bit, has once again been slammed in her face. *I mean,* Beatrix says, a bit more softly. *We can go to New York, Mum. I know you've never been. But I don't want to go to Boston. That's not my life anymore. My life is here.* Millie nods. She gestures for the check, her hand signing the air, hope blooming in her chest.

ROSE

Rose kisses Kathleen's cheek and rubs Jack's hair before turning to leave her mother's kitchen. The children run down the hall to the living room. Rose suspects they're happier here than they are at home. Her mother comes to the door with her and steps out onto the side porch. *You and William go and have a lovely Valentine's dinner,* she says. *We will,* Rose says, hating to lie to her mother but having no choice. *Don't let the children stay up too late. And please get them to school on time.* Her mother nods.

She passes one restaurant after another on the walk home, deciding, finally, to tell her mother that they had gone to the Chowder House for dinner. She could see from the window that the tablecloths had been switched from red to white and that each table sports a single red rose. Now she has enough details to make the story believable. The fish is always good there, and she'll say she skipped dessert, just going with a coffee, or maybe say they split a chocolate mousse.

Back home, she slips off her boots and changes into her slippers. She told William before he left this morning that she'd arranged for the children to stay over at her mother's. He had nodded but hadn't said much of anything in response. She has no idea whether he'll come home after work or just disappear. She doesn't know where he goes on these nights. When he returns and falls into bed, often late at night, sometimes so late that the room is no longer dark, he usually smells of whiskey and cigarettes.

Rose wishes she could hate him. It would make this all so much easier. She has every right to. He does almost nothing around the house. He's hardly had a raise in years. He doesn't do what he promises. They rarely talk anymore about anything other than the children. They adore him, though, and he is a wonderful father, when he shows up, when he doesn't disappoint. She longs for the days when he would look at her the way he looks at them. They had been in love once.

She tries to have fun on the Saturday nights. At the beginning it was a thrill, to get dressed up, to flirt with someone in a bar. To have a strange man run his hand down her spine. To hold her close while dancing. But she's not done anything more than kiss someone else. It's not right. And lately, after William leaves, she stays home. Tries out a new recipe. Takes a long bath with her magazines. Changes into a lacy nightgown. And waits for him to come home. He gets undressed in the almost morning light and she watches him, feeling herself almost fall for him all over again, even as she tells herself she shouldn't. Sometimes he's so drunk that he falls asleep on top of her and she rolls him off and then straddles him, resting her head on his chest, stretching her legs on top of his, listening to his heart slow its beat. When he appears the next morning, gray and stumbling for coffee, it's as though it never happened. She wonders whether he even knows they have sex. It's certainly not the way she thought marriage ought to be, and she wonders about all the other marriages she's ever known. Is this normal, what she and William have?

She has thought, occasionally, about leaving him. But she has seen what that looks like. Her friend Mary got divorced last year. She, too, would need to move back into her parents' house. Her father would be furious. Her mother would be ashamed. Even her brother, Chris, would be disappointed in her. She has read in her magazines that divorce isn't good for the children. And the worst of it all, perhaps, is that she can't quite seem to stop loving William even as she suspects that he stopped loving her long ago.

But tonight, tonight is all about Jackie. CBS will air her White House tour. Rose wanted the children out of the house so she could focus, so she could hear every word that Jackie utters, so she can take in everything that Jackie has done. So she could sit right up close to the TV and see it all. She hasn't been this excited for anything in a long time. She reheats the leftover stew from the evening before, pours herself a glass of red wine, and then settles into her armchair to watch Walter Cronkite, pulling her knees up to her chest and wrapping a blanket around her lap.

At seven fifteen, she hears noise on the front porch and turns around to look at the front door. It opens with a blast of cold air and William appears, his collar turned up against the wind, his hat pulled down over his forehead. She waves from her chair but quickly turns back to the television, annoyed. It's his house, but still. He knew she wanted to watch this program. Couldn't he have just left her alone? *Evening,* he says, and then he produces a bouquet of yellow roses from behind his back. Her favorite. How taken she had been with his ability to always know the right thing to do, the right way to make her forgive him again and again. But it doesn't work as well anymore. *Oh, William,* she says, *you shouldn't have,* and she wishes he hadn't. She needs to find a vase and put them in water and they do smell so heavenly and she should fix him dinner but what if she misses the start of the program?

I'll do it, he says, and he takes the flowers back, out of her arms. *Thanks,* she says, looking up at him, and he smiles. That goddamn smile. *Did you eat,* she calls to him in the kitchen when she hears the water running. *I can heat up some leftovers for you. I'm fine,* he says. *Got a bite after work.* He brings the flowers back in, along with a wineglass, and sets them on the side table, between her chair and the sofa. He sits on the sofa, undoes his tie, and takes off his shoes, resting his feet on the coffee table. Cronkite signs off, and Rose stands. *Don't yell at me,* she says, *but I'm going to sit on the floor. So I can see and hear everything as clearly as possible.*

385

William nods, and Rose blushes. She feels a fool. Why did he have to come home tonight? Tonight, of all nights. She sits right where Kathleen and Jack sit to watch *Mr. Ed,* her back to William. *I know you're laughing at me,* she says, not turning around, holding her back straight. *No,* he says, *I'm not.*

For the next hour, the only sound in the room is Jackie's soft voice, responding to Charles Collingwood's questions. She looks lovely, of course, and she knows so much about the history of the White House and the history of all the objects. At the end, the president talks for a few minutes, focusing on how Jackie's work is helping to bring alive the men who had inhabited the White House. Well, Rose thinks, and the women, too. The children. The White House is not only about the presidents. Then he says that if children see the White House as living history, they may want to come live here, too. Even the girls, he says, with his grin.

Afterward, Rose switches the television off and finishes her glass of wine, her back still to William. They haven't said a word to each other during the broadcast. *What did you think,* William says, and she can hear him stretching his legs out, his knees cracking.

Rose frowns. *I don't like that,* she says. *I don't like how dismissive he is of girls.* She turns around to face him. *Why shouldn't Kathleen think that she could be president one day? He makes it seem as though the only way she could get there would be as first lady. I told you,* William says. *He's always been some-what of an asshole. William,* Rose says. *He's the president.* She stands and picks up the empty wine bottle.

What's past is prologue, William says, clos-ing his eyes, repeating something the presi-dent had said. *What is that?* Rose asks. *It's familiar.* She looks at William, frowning. *Shakespeare,* he says, and she knew he would know. *The Tempest. Before two men decide to commit murder, one of them says it. What's led up to that point creates their destiny, in other words.* Rose nods. This is that free will, predestination stuff from church. She's never really understood it all. Be a good person, she tells the children, and all will work out. But she wonders: Is she being punished for choices she has made in the past? What does God think about her and William?

William leans back and yawns. *I'll be up in a bit,* he says as she picks up the empty wineglasses, and she knows that when she gets up in the morning, he'll be stretched out on the couch, fast asleep. Rose heads into the kitchen. *Thanks for the flowers,* she calls back. There had been a time, early on, when he'd brought flowers home every Friday night, the scent filling the small house. Somewhere she has journals filled with pressed flowers. She guesses the petals have turned to dust.

BEATRIX

Beatrix waits at the bar near her flat, a vodka tonic in her hand. She sees Robert at the door and waves. He pushes through the crowd and gives her a kiss on the cheek. *Evening,* he says, removing his hat and placing it on the bar, taking a long pull of the drink she ordered for him. Putting the glass back on the bar, he sighs and grins at her. *Nothing better than that first swallow,* he says. He's always tired by the end of the week; he works in ad sales for ITV. Beatrix doesn't really understand what he does but she knows he's good at it. There seem to be a lot of meetings and lunches.

She is exhausted, too. She just wants to move into the new building already. Architectural plans, electrical drawings, plumbing. Contractors and city officials. It's all important, she knows, but it bores her. She misses thinking about the children.

I got a letter from Mrs. Chisholm, Robert

says now. *Their plans are set for July. They'll be here for three days, right when you're in New York, so perfect timing.* Robert had been sent to America also, during the war. He'd lived outside New York with the Chisholms for a year and then he'd been sent to a boarding school in New Hampshire. *They sent you away?* she asked during their first date. *That seems unnecessary.* He shrugged. *It was fine, I liked the school. I didn't see them much anyway. Nannies and such. Gorgeous house, though. And at school, it was great fun being with boys, all day and all night.*

They'd been set up by a mutual friend who had been excited to match them. *Oh, Trixie,* she'd said. *He's perfect for you. Really. You have so much in common!* Beatrix generally shied away from meeting others who'd been sent away. The experiences were often so different, and she rarely wanted to revisit the past. At first, she assumed everyone had lived as she had. Robert's experience was more typical. He had been older. For him, it was something that had happened, a necessary thing, a few years that went differently than he had planned. That was it. A blip. He wasn't much interested in talking about it, though, which was fine with her, although he was looking forward to showing them around London this summer, taking them to his favorite restaurants.

Beatrix likes Robert. They've been together for almost a year now, and he's good fun. They go out to drink, to eat, to dance. They play tennis regularly — she hadn't picked up a racket since she came back from America — and she's started following baseball again, because of him. She's even trying to learn the rules of cricket. He's easy to be with, and he never pressures her about the future, not like Sam, who she heard is already married with a child on the way. Robert seems to live in the moment, and there's something refreshing about that. She has a hard time picturing them together forever, though. She wonders whether she's being unrealistic, whether she's searching for something that can't be found, whether she's trying so hard not to be her mother that she'll end up alone. Her friends tell her she's being too picky. She's not even sure what she's looking for. She only knows when it's not quite right.

Tea at Harrods, don't you think, he says now. *All the Americans love that.* Beatrix nods. *Maybe a show,* she suggests. *Something at the Aldwych? Yes, yes,* Robert says. *Of course. Right up their alley.* He pauses. *I keep thinking of them as they were,* he says, *isn't that funny? Frozen in time. As though they haven't aged. But of course they have. They must be at least seventy. Probably older.*

Beatrix thinks about Mrs. G. Gerald had written, out of the blue, to say that she'd fallen down the back stairs. For five hours she'd lain on the kitchen floor, unable to get to the telephone. *There she was,* he wrote, *lying on her back, reading one of her romance novels. It's a miracle that she only broke her ankle. And blind luck that I stopped by that afternoon.* Beatrix hadn't known how to respond. She hadn't really thought about him being there, taking care of her, and she wished he wasn't. Part of her wanted to tell him to run, to marry this teacher he'd been dating, to get the hell out. But she knew he would never do that. She could see Mrs. G, crying over her book, telling Gerald that it was nothing, she'd just had a little slip. Silly me, she would say. Silly, silly me.

They have changed, Beatrix says now, *it's forever ago, really. We're halfway through 1962 already. Twenty years since we were there.* And it's true: her memories of the time in America have grown a bit hazy. *I've been thinking about your trip,* Robert says, *and the Yankees are hitting it out of the park this year. Won't you go to a game when you're there, Trixie? Leave your mum and head up*

to the Bronx. *You could see Mickey Mantle!
You could catch a fly ball!*

Beatrix smiles. *Good idea,* she says. *That's
my girl,* Robert says. She would love to go
to a baseball game. She hadn't even considered the possibility.

WILLIAM

William stands by the kitchen sink, finishing his coffee, waiting for the children to get dressed. Rose is emptying the freezer to defrost it, piling the contents onto the counter, the ice melting and dripping onto the floor. He's heading up to Gloucester with the children to get some lunch, to spend the day on the ocean. He leans forward to catch a glimpse of the sky, just visible over the neighbor's house eight feet away. It looks to be a beautiful August day, the sky a brilliant blue.

Don't let Kathleen eat any ice cream, Rose says, throwing a few half-eaten pints into the garbage. *I swear she's put on ten pounds this summer.* William shrugs without turning around but doesn't respond.

Kathleen comes running downstairs in her nightgown and wraps her arms around his stomach, and he turns to hug her. He's hardly seen her this week. Her face is beautiful: a million freckles surrounding startlingly blue eyes, a generous mouth that signals her every mood. *Are we still going to Gloucester, Daddy?* she asks. He nods, feeling a tightness in his chest that she knows enough to ask, not to assume. He is the master of last-minute change. Jack hasn't learned that yet but he will, soon. *We are indeed, lovebug. Let's get some breakfast, get dressed, and we'll hit the road. Wear a long-sleeved shirt,* Rose says, her head still in the freezer. *I don't want you getting burned. Are you coming with us, Mommy?* Kathleen asks. Rose shakes her head. *You know how I feel about lobster,* she says. *That horrid smell.*

Kathleen grins. She dances around the kitchen table on her toes, her nightgown swirling around her ankles. *" 'Tis the voice of the lobster; I heard him declare,"* she says, reciting her favorite lines from *Alice in Wonderland.* William takes her hand and she twirls under his arm as he says, *"You have baked me too brown, I must sugar my hair."* Kathleen puts her heels together, her bare feet pointing outward, her eyes smiling. *"As a duck with its eyelids, so he with his nose, trims his belt and his buttons, and turns out his toes."* William flutters his arms, speaking in a breathy voice. *"When the sands are all dry, he is gay as a lark, and will talk in contemptuous tones of the Shark."* Kathleen crouches down and slowly comes to a stand, her voice getting softer as she speaks. *"But, when the tide rises and Sharks are around, his voice has a timid and tremulous sound!"*

She falls into him, and he hugs her. Rose is shaking her head. *You two,* she says. *You ought to take your act onto the stage. I think you missed your calling, William.* He knows she hates it when he fools around with the children. You get them all riled up, she always says. What's wrong with that, he wants to say, but never does. It's better than a father barricading himself in his study. *Go,* he says, softly slapping Kathleen on the bottom. *Go get dressed.*

Later, they visit the shops on Main Street and the harbor, paying a visit to the old fisherman cast out of bronze. *I love this statue,* Kathleen says. *Whenever I think of a fisherman, this is what I think of.* "They that go down to the sea in ships," Jack reads off the plaque. *It seems scary,* Kathleen says, *the way those words sound. It is,* William says. *It's a dangerous job. Many men have lost their lives.*

In the restaurant, Jack stands by the tank,

his nose pressed against the glass, watching the lobsters move through the murky water. William wonders whether Jack understands that the lobsters are just one step away from death, detained in a holding cell before getting submerged in the boiling water. He lights a cigarette and blows the smoke out in soft gray rings, watching them dissipate as they climb. *Daddy,* Jack calls out. *Look at this one! He's missing a front claw!* William nods from across the room where he and Kathleen are sitting in a dark wooden booth that looks out on the docks. The restaurant is empty, in that lazy stretch between lunch and dinner, all the windows open to let in the air.

Kathleen is busy building a house out of sugar packets. Her patience amazes him. The lightweight and fragile house has been knocked down, by her hand or a quick breeze off the water, over and over, and she gathers it all up and begins again. *Tell me about the house in Maine,* she says. *How many bedrooms on the second floor? I want to build this to be like that. Twenty-five,* he says, and she smiles, but she doesn't look up from her work. *Daddy,* she says, *come on. How many? Four,* he says, *four bedrooms upstairs.*

Their food is delivered, and Jack comes running over. The three of them attach their white plastic bibs and bend over the lobsters, now a beautiful bright red. They set to work cracking the shells open with their silver utensils, William helping Jack and Kathleen shrieking with delight as lobster juice comes flying out and lands all over William's face. *Did you have lobsters in Maine, Daddy,* Jack asks. *Of course,* William says. *They're even better there. Sometimes we'd buy them in town and then row back to the island.*

One time, he goes on, *one of them wasn't fastened well enough, and it crawled out of the bag. Nana just about had a fit. Did somebody have to pick it up,* Kathleen asks, her nose wrinkled. William nods. He can remember it as though it was yesterday: It was Bea who did it. She reached over, grabbed it by its middle, and held it in the air, the claws moving wildly. *I feel for them,* she said. *They must sense how close they are to the water. They just want to be back in the sea. Probably it was you,* Kathleen says. *Uncle Gerald wouldn't pick up a crawling lobster. It was me,* William says. *I held that lobster tight all the way back to the island.* He wipes his face with his napkin, the smell of the lobster

398

on his fingers, the image of Bea in the boat
all that he can see.

NANCY

Gerald is coming over for dinner tonight, and Nancy spent part of the morning pulling all the boxes out of the little closet off her room, the place where she's stashed all the family jewelry. She hasn't looked through these boxes in years. They split it up after her mother died, and Nancy hadn't cared much one way or the other about what she got, happy to let the others pick and choose. *You all live lives where you need such things,* she said. *Doesn't do me any good working in the garden.*

When William got engaged, he said that he didn't want to look at what she had; Rose wanted a new ring, and so he'd gone down to Long's on Summer Street and bought her this extravagant diamond. Nancy has always found it rather garish. She prefers the gemstones — the sapphires, the emeralds, the rubies — to the diamonds.

Nancy wonders what will happen to all

this jewelry. Gold chains, long dangling earrings, even a diamond tiara. She remembers some story about the earrings: that when her mother was little, their house had caught on fire, and a maid had thrown much of the jewelry out the window. The house had been ruined. Servants spent the following day, on their hands and knees, combing through the burnt grass, looking for jewelry, especially these earrings. One of few things to be salvaged.

Finally, she finds the emerald ring, nestled in a small, velvet-lined box. She tries to slip the ring onto her right-hand ring finger but it's too tight, so she puts it on her pinkie instead and holds her hand out, admiring the ring. A stunning oval, surrounded by tiny diamonds. Large enough to be noticed but not too ostentatious. Her own ring is a sapphire. Ethan had taken his grandmother's ring and had it redone. It's been with her for so long she can't imagine her hand without it. She can't even get it off. Her finger has grown around it. What a funny thing, an engagement ring, a wedding ring. Such a public way of announcing who you are. Ethan had always worn a wedding band, one that matched hers. Nancy was proud of that. So many of her friends' and sisters' husbands had never worn a ring.

At dinner, she pulls the ring box out of her apron pocket and places it on the table, sliding it toward Gerald with her index finger. *I thought you might want this,* she says. Gerald looks at the box but doesn't open it, doesn't even reach for it. *Mother,* he says, and she knows that tone. Both he and William use it. She never thought that she'd tire of hearing that word but how annoying it is said in that manner. *We're not,* he says, and then he stops talking and looks down at his food. Then he looks straight at her. How she loves that face. The older he gets, the more he looks like Ethan. He's even taken to wearing some of Ethan's bow ties. She worries that one day she'll slip and call him by the wrong name.

She's great, Mother, he says finally. *I love her, I do. I think she loves me, too. But I'm not ready for that yet. I don't know if she is either.* *But, Gerald,* Nancy says, willing her voice to stay steady, not to rise to a whine, *you're thirty-one. You need to move on. Don't you want to have a family?* He puts down his fork and wipes his mouth with his napkin. *Yes,* he says, *but not yet.*

Gerald takes another bite of chicken. Nancy sighs. It was all so easy when they were little. It was the part of motherhood she loved the best: making it all okay.

Somebody gets hurt and you make some chocolate chip cookies and everything's all right with the world. How things change when children grow up. *I just don't want you to miss out,* she says.

Mother, he says again in that tone. *Please stop. If I decide that I want to ask her to get married, I'll let you know, okay?* She opens her mouth and he leans across the table and places his finger in front of her mouth. *No more,* he says. *How about this. I'll take the ring and I'll hold on to it. When the time comes, I'll have it and be ready. How does that sound?* Well, it wasn't what she wanted, but it would have to do. She nods. *Don't you want to see it, though,* she says. *Make sure you like it?* He flips open the box. *Sure,* he says, *it's beautiful, I guess.*

Gerald snaps the box shut, ending the conversation, and they sit silently for a few minutes at the table, finishing their dinner. The wind blows outside and one of the shutters bangs against the house, again and again. *I need to fix that,* Gerald says. *And I need to empty all the gutters this weekend. We'll have our first snow before long.* Nancy smiles at him and pats his hand. How did she allow their relationship to become what it is? He shouldn't be taking care of her.

She needs to hire a handyman. She must let him live his own life. *I'm so lucky,* she says. *What would I do without you?*

BEATRIX

The first Christmas that Beatrix was back, the Christmas of '45, she'd bought presents for all the Gregorys and shipped off the box to America at the start of December, thinking that she sent it with plenty of time. Instead, Mrs. G wrote that the box arrived sometime in mid-February, looking as though it had traveled around the world. Half the gifts were gone, the box having been opened and resealed multiple times. By the time the next Christmas rolled around, Beatrix thought about it, even bought a few things, but ended up only sending a card.

This year, seventeen years later, she adds them to her Christmas shopping list. She hears from Gerald every few months now. Lately, he wrote that Mrs. G's ankle was still bothering her, after the fall, and she finds an antique cane in a shop, beautifully painted with wildflowers. For Gerald, a small chess set for his office at school. He started up a chess club, and he wants the boys to feel free to come into the area outside his office and play whenever they want.

William's gift is the one that she most wants to send and yet she's having trouble writing a note to go with it. When she was in New York with Mum in July, they had gone to a baseball game, the first game of a doubleheader. She had the travel agent look up the schedule months earlier, when Robert suggested it, not sure whether she really wanted to go to a Yankee game, but then, when she learned that the Red Sox were to be in town in late July and there was a day game, she planned the trip around it. She even persuaded Mum to go. It was a beautiful July day, too, and when they got there, when they emerged from the dark hallway, when the stadium light and noise opened up around them, the blue sky above it all, even Mum stayed quiet.

It wasn't an easy trip. Mum tried but she didn't like New York. She found it dirty and loud, the people pushy and hard to understand. Once they were inside somewhere — a museum, a theater, the hotel — it was mostly fine, but moving about and being outside was awful. And all Beatrix wanted to do was to be outside, to walk and walk and walk. She didn't want to be on the subway or in a taxi or on a bus. She wanted to walk until she became part of the city, until her feet simply gave out.

They found their seats in the upper deck and settled in. *Hot dog?* Beatrix asked, and Mum scrunched up her face. *Disgusting,* she said, but then ate half of Beatrix's. *Not bad,* she said grudgingly. The Red Sox beat the Yankees, much to the dismay of the crowd, but Beatrix cheered under her breath every time another ball was hit, another base reached, another run scored. They got to see Mantle hit a home run, which was something indeed, and Beatrix loved the new star on the Sox, who was playing in left field. She'd forgotten the feeling of sitting in the stands, the game unfolding below, the clouds shifting above. The sun, marking the movement of time, as they moved from shade to sun and back again. The smell of beer and mustard. The crowd. *What did you think,* she said to Mum on the subway ride back downtown, feeling lighter than she had in months. *Well,* Mum said, *it wasn't as long as I thought it might be.*

Later, without Mum, she stopped off in a gift shop in midtown and saw a Mantle doll, his head bobbing back and forth when touched. Beatrix laughed out loud and couldn't stop making him dance. She bought two: one for herself and one for William. A joke of sorts. She knew he would hate anything that was connected to the Yankees. But she also knew that he would love it. That he must secretly enjoy watching Mantle play. He had adored Bobby Doerr. His room was plastered with pictures of him, torn out of the newspapers and magazines. He would listen to the game on the radio, holding a bat in his hand, and when Doerr was up to bat, he'd swing at the same moment, copying his stance that he knew from photos and from games, turning his back foot in just the same way. *William Gregory,* Mrs. G would shriek when she saw him. *How many times do I have to tell you? No bats in the house.*

But how could she tell him that she'd been in the States and hadn't come to Boston? They stood in that big open space of Grand Central Terminal, the enormous clock suspended by the ticket window, and Beatrix heard the Boston train announced. *Big Ben,* Mum remarked. *Can't these Americans create anything by themselves?* Beatrix ignored her. A part of her wanted to run away from her mother, to jump onto that train, to watch the changing coast on the way north, to arrive at South Station, to burst into that kitchen in time for dinner. Just as she had wanted to do so many years before. *Let's go, Mum,* she said instead. *We have theater tickets tonight, and I want to change before we go.*

Dear William, she writes finally. *I couldn't resist. He's a marvel, isn't he. Mantle, I mean. I bought one for myself, too. I liked the thought of that: these two bobbleheaded Mantles, on either side of the Atlantic, nodding at each other across the pond. (Remember that?) So, yes, I was there, I was in New York. Don't hold it against me. You almost did the same. I miss you, my friend. Love to you and your family, and have a happy, happy Christmas, Bea*

She wraps up the gifts, carefully tying each with ribbon, and cradles each gift in scrunched-up pages from the newspaper. She has no address for William. So she puts all the gifts in one big box addressed to Mrs. G and takes it to the post office. *America,* the clerk says, running his index finger along the address. *You have family there? No,* she starts to say and then changes her mind. *Yes,* she says. *Yes, I do.*

GERALD

Gerald stops by the house, early on a snowy Sunday morning, to shovel the front walk so Mother can get out for church. The world is beautiful in its silence. This is part of what he missed in California, the stillness of a morning like this one, a sense of belonging to this place. He picks up the newspaper and brings it inside, leaving his wet boots on the mat and pulling on his old slippers that still sit by the back door. He makes a pot of coffee and separates out the sections of the paper. The order in which he reads the paper hasn't changed since he was in high school.

Such turmoil in the world. Linda is passionate about civil rights. Last summer, during their break, she'd gone home to Baltimore and spent her days working with some of the local politicians, out in the community. She asked him whether he wanted to come down as well, but he'd told her that he couldn't. He needed to stay in town, in case Mother needed him. She knew it wasn't the truth. He suspected she was disappointed in him, although she never said as much. It wasn't that he didn't care or didn't think what she was doing was important. He has learned so much from her. She has opened up his world. But reading and talking about it was one thing. Actually being there, out on the streets, was another.

But then, not even a month into the summer, he missed her more than he thought he would. The work she was doing sounded difficult and yet her letters were filled with an electricity that excited him. A passion. He wanted to be with her. He wanted to be by her side. So he cleared his calendar and took the train south. At the station in Baltimore, Linda's lips on his, her arms around his shoulders, he knew he had made the right choice.

The six weeks in Baltimore helped him to think more deeply about civil rights. It turned out he loved being out in the community, knocking on doors, talking to folks. He felt, at times, as though he'd walked into another world. And when they came back north, he started making plans for how to continue some of the work they had been doing at the school. There had been no colored students at the school when he was a student. Now there are a few and the summer made him realize how hard it must be for them. He is all too aware of how difficult it is to be different, to be anything other than the norm. Two of the boys travel to the school from Roxbury, and he wonders what is in their minds when they walk up the hill from the T, when they look out at the sea of white faces during morning assembly.

A car door slams in the driveway, and Gerald stands to look out the window. William. What is he doing here? The back door opens, and William steps inside, stamping his boots on the mat. *Morning,* Gerald says, saluting him. *Wasn't expecting you. Thought I'd swing by,* William says. *Didn't expect to see you here, either.* Gerald gestures to the coffeepot on the table and stands to get him a mug. William is dressed for a night out, his tie a bit askew, his hair uncombed. Gerald feels uncomfortable in his slippers. Why is it that William always makes him feel like a child?

Gerald sits back down and looks at William. *Looks like you never made it home last night,* he says. *Yeah, well,* William says. *Could be.* Gerald pushes on: *Too early to go home? Too late?* William shrugs. *I'm heading home,* he says, *but I was passing by.* He takes a sip of coffee. *Why are you here?* he says. *Don't you have your own home?* They sit in silence for a few moments, Gerald trying unsuccessfully to read the paper, William blowing on his coffee before swallowing. *It's not that hot,* Gerald says finally. *Jesus.*

William puts his feet up on the chair, leans his head back, and closes his eyes. *Hard to be in this kitchen without thinking about Bea,* he says. *You heard from her?* he asks. *You know, since the Christmas gifts?* Gerald looks at him for a long moment before responding. William's still in love with her, he realizes. All these years later. He'd always suspected something had happened in London, after Father died. *No, I haven't,* he says. *You?* William shakes his head. *Hey,* Gerald says. *I've always wondered: when you were in Europe, way back when, did you see her?* William makes a face, looking at his hands. *What? No, didn't think of it, actually,* he says. He has a sip of coffee. *You two were always closer. You should go see her sometime. She'd probably like that.*

Gerald begins to laugh. *You think me a fool, William? The two of you, out canoodling*

413

in the woods in Maine? He's held on to this for years. *What are you talking about?* William says as he stands and goes to look out the window. Gerald shakes his head. *Maybe Father and Mother didn't know, but I sure did.* He wants to smile at William's discomfort, at the rigid line of his back. How could he possibly think that Gerald didn't know? The two of them, running down the hall late at night, here and in Maine. And that last night in Maine, when Gerald was unable to sleep, because he was so distraught at the thought of Bea's departure, he followed them into the woods. He watched them swimming in the ocean, naked, saw them kiss and touch and cry. He'd stayed in the woods, after they had gone back into the house, until the sun had fully risen, unsure of what to do with the anger and loss lodged in his chest. It's never really gone away.

I don't know what you're talking about, William says. *I mean, I think she might have had a crush on me, or something, but nothing ever happened between us. You were the one who had a crush on her.* Gerald laughs even as he wants to cry, but it's a mean laugh. Maybe he is a Gregory after all. *You can't even tell the truth about her,* he says. He knows William saw Bea in London. He was cagey when he got back, vague with answers to questions. There were missing days.

Mother appears in the doorway, and William turns to smile at her, giving her a kiss on the cheek. She kisses the top of Gerald's head, leaving her hands on his shoulders. *To what do we owe this wonderful surprise?* she asks. *Not one but both of my lovely boys!* William shrugs. *Passing through,* he says. *Just like I told Gerald. Well,* she says, taking a Kleenex out of her cuff to blow her nose. *That's lovely.*

Her hands tighten on Gerald's shoulders. *As long as you're here, William,* she says. *I have a request. Sure thing,* he says. Always so slick, so obliging, Gerald thinks. Don't agree until you know what she wants. *I want to go to church with my boys,* she says, and Gerald can hear the joy in her voice. *Please. Most weeks I go alone. Sometimes* — and she pats Gerald on the shoulders — *sometimes, I can persuade this one to go with me. But to go with the two of you. Well, we haven't done that since your father's funeral, I don't think. And that was eleven and a half years ago.*

To Gerald's surprise, William says he'd be happy to go. They drive over to the chapel in William's car, Mother chatting away up front, Gerald silent in the back seat. Once inside, they make their way down the center aisle, Gerald leading the way. Mother moves slowly, waving and saying hello to person after person, Gerald acknowledging people but not having any extended conversations. He can feel the students' eyes on him. He doesn't come to chapel very often. They know Mother of course, but William is new to them. He'll have questions to answer at school tomorrow. Gerald turns into the fourth pew on the left, where they always used to sit, Sunday after Sunday. Mother sits down next to him, with William on her far side. *My boys,* she says, her voice low. *I can't remember when I've been so happy.* She brushes away tears with her Kleenex.

Gerald's become friendly with the new minister, and he's impressed with the way he leads the service, talking about things that should be meaningful to the students. Although he wonders how much they listen when they're here. He didn't when he was their age. His mind was always off somewhere else: setting up the next tin drive, mapping the armies through Belgium. He watches the pew in front of them: one boy is turning each of the pages of his hymnal inward to form a fan of sorts; another is asleep; and a third — one of his chess students — is passing a note, torn out of the hymnal, to the pew in front, by using his shoe to propel it forward. He thinks of the night he came here with Bea and William after her father died. He thinks about Father's funeral, and the Sundays that followed, when he would look up from his hymnal, shocked to find that Father wasn't there.

Everyone stands to sing the final hymn. Gerald looks up at the board and then finds the hymn in the book. "Jerusalem." It was Bea's favorite. Father's, too. The organ starts to play, and the words dance on the page. Mother is singing loudly, as always, just a little off-key. Gerald looks over at William, on Mother's other side. He can't hear his voice, but he sees him moving his lips, singing the words. There's no need to look at the hymnal. They all have it memorized. William catches Gerald's eye and smiles, not his usual grin, but a smile so sad that it makes Gerald look away. Gerald reaches his arm behind Mother to put his hand on William's shoulder. William lifts his right hand up to grasp Gerald's. They stand like that, singing, all three of their voices gaining strength as the song builds to its final sweet notes.

MILLIE

Millie recognizes the handwriting on the letter, even though she hasn't seen it in almost twenty years. It's Nancy's round script, which sits somewhere between block letters and true, angular cursive. She turns the letter over and over in her hand, not wanting to open it. She's not sure what she's so worried about. That Nancy will be somewhat cold, having not heard from Millie in all these years? She knows that won't be the case. That woman would be kind, truly kind, to her worst enemy, or at least that's Millie's suspicion.

She slices the envelope with her letter opener and pulls out the letter, written on stationery with Nancy's name and that familiar address printed on the top. *Dearest Millie,* the letter begins, and Millie shuts her eyes for a moment before reading on. What must it be like, she wonders, to have a heart so full? She reads on. The letter is mostly about Gerald and William and William's children. Some updates on Nancy's foot — apparently she broke her ankle a while back — and a report on her garden. *But, dear Millie,* Nancy writes, *I want to know more about what you're doing. I'm such a bore. Do write back and fill me in. And thank you so much for breaking the ice after all these years.*

Millie hadn't been able to stop thinking about Nancy since she and Beatrix got back from New York. There was something about being there, in America, that made Nancy come alive to Millie in a way she never had before. Her openness was a classic American trait, one that Millie had never quite believed. And yet here they were, all these Americans, being loud and friendly and willing to talk to you about almost anything. They'd gone to the theater one night, and the woman next to Beatrix talked to her the whole time. They exchanged addresses and phone numbers before the evening was over. Millie couldn't imagine such a thing happening in London. Before, she'd dismissed this quality about Americans. But then she wondered. She suspected you had to be that way to open your home to a stranger. To love someone else's child as your own. Millie understands now, in a way that she never did before, that had the tables been turned, she would not have done the same.

She tried writing Nancy a few times, but the letter always felt wrong so she threw each version out. Once she even affixed a stamp before tossing it in the garbage. Then one night, unable to sleep, she put on her robe and slippers, went to her desk, and wrote the letter in one go. No editing, no considering. All she really wanted to do was to open the line of communication.

Later, she meets Beatrix at the park halfway between their flats to take a walk around the pond. They started doing this when the days got longer this year, and it's worked out well. There's something to be said for talking while walking. You don't have to look at the person. You can keep your eyes on the path, on your shoes, on the landscape. And somehow that means that more gets said.

I got a letter from Nancy today, Millie says when they're about halfway round, when a pause presents itself. *Nancy,* Beatrix says, stretching the name out. *My Nancy? Mrs. G? Yes,* Millie says, and nods, thinking of a time when Beatrix saying "My Nancy" would have set her off. *I wrote to her a while back. After we came back from New York. And,* Beatrix says, in that tone that Millie recognizes. It's a tone she uses as well. A

420

way of pretending you're not interested when, in fact, you care so awfully much. *She's well and so are the boys. I guess she broke her ankle? Yes,* Beatrix says. *Quite a while ago. I didn't know it was still bothering her.*

And they talk, back and forth, about Nancy and about Gerald and about William, even. Millie tells Beatrix that the children were over for the Memorial Day weekend, that Kathleen had helped plant some of the later lettuces. *They have a large vegetable garden then,* Millie asks, and Beatrix bursts out laughing. *Mummy,* she says, *it's practically the size of this park. They had one when I got there, but every year she added to it. And then with the war and Victory Gardens becoming a thing, well, it just took over. I wouldn't be at all surprised if they have no more lawn. If it's just all vegetables. Well, and flowers. She loves flowers, too.*

They walk in silence for a bit. *Tell me,* Millie says, her eyes on the footpath, *tell me a memory from there. To help me see it all a bit better.* Beatrix is quiet for a moment. *Back behind the garden,* she says, *there's a path that takes you into the woods. When you're back there, amid the trees, it feels so far away from everything. It's hard to believe you're just seconds away from the house or from school or from the cemetery. I used to go there in all seasons. There was a tree that had fallen across the path and that's where I used to sit. I'd read your letters there, Mummy. I'd go out in the snow, following the tracks of the dog or maybe a rabbit. I'd go in fall, when the leaves were turning, a bright, bright yellow against the bluest sky. In summer, it was cool there, when it was hot everywhere else. And in spring, well, that was my favorite. Day by day I could see things changing, the leaves unfurling, the plants pushing themselves up out of the dirt.*

She stops talking, and they're almost back at the start of the path. This is more than she's said to Millie in years. Beatrix keeps talking, her face turned away from Millie. *The best thing about it, Mum, and I feel bad about saying this, was that I could forget about the war there. I could forget about you and Daddy. I could forget that Daddy was dead and that you were so far away. It was just me and the woods. The island was like that, too.*

I have to tell you something, Millie says, and she puts her hands on Beatrix's shoulders, turning Beatrix toward her. *I wasn't the one who sent you away,* she says. *Your father insisted.* Beatrix starts to say something, and Millie puts her hand up. *I'm not blaming him. I'm saying he was right. You were safe there. You were happy. What more could we have wanted?* Those five years were a lifeline. That place formed who Beatrix is now. That's the piece that she's never really understood. *The whole point was for you to forget.* They turn and head out of the park, Millie's hand tucked into Beatrix's elbow. She's looking forward to writing Nancy back.

ROSE

The doorbell rings, early on a Sunday morning, and by the time Rose gets downstairs, Kathleen has already opened the front door. She turns around to look at Rose, her face worried, and Rose sees the cop uniform before she sees that it's Jimmy Maguire, one of the boys she grew up with who's now on the force. *Upstairs,* she says to Kathleen, pointing, *go back upstairs and keep Jack up there, too.* Kathleen nods and disappears as Rose steps out onto the narrow porch, closing the door behind her.

What, Rose says to Jimmy. *What is it?* His face is a mess, and he takes off his cap, holding it to his chest. She remembers when he was six or seven he trampled on her mother's daffodils in the front yard and he was forced to apologize, standing on their front porch, looking so much like he does now. *Rosie,* he says, *I'm so sorry. What is it,* she repeats, even though as she does, she knows.

424

William's bed was empty, still freshly made. *It's William, isn't it?* she asks. *What's happened to William. Just tell me, Jimmy.* He raises his head to look her in the eyes. *Car accident,* he says. *Car flipped going around a turn. Over at the beach. He almost made it home, Rosie. Where is he?* she asks. *The hospital,* he says. *But, he's gone. I know,* she says. *I know that.* For a moment neither of them speak. *Your brother,* Jimmy says. *You want me to get Chris over here? Yes, please,* she says. *But don't tell anyone else.*

Inside, Rose closes the door and leans against it. All those late nights that turned into early mornings. William driving back from some ballroom on the North Shore. *I go to hear the music,* he told her, sitting at the kitchen table one recent Sunday morning, still a bit drunk. *To watch the dancers. The grace in their steps. The sound of the surf when the music fades away.*

She will wait for Chris to tell the children. He will know best how to do this. He will help her to make a plan. She slides her back down the door to sit on the floor. She should have known that Patrick Kennedy's death two weeks earlier was a bad omen. His tiny lungs were incapable of giving life. He only lived for thirty-nine hours. She had cried and cried when she'd heard. Now, sitting here in the dirty front hall, the children's flip-flops and sneakers scattered about, she feels oddly calm. There are no tears. As though she had always known this is how it would end.

It is still early and quiet. Then she hears the faint sound of the newspaper boy making his way down the street, the wheels of his bike splashing through the puddles, and the Sunday paper landing with a dull thud on one porch after another.

GERALD

Gerald is outside, packing Mother's car, when an unfamiliar car turns in the driveway. He's borrowing the car to head down to DC for the week with Linda, to meet up with some friends from Berkeley, to attend the March on Washington on Wednesday. To march in the March. He hardly slept last night. He tossed and turned just the way he always did the night before Thanksgiving.

He pulls his head out of the trunk to look at the car as it comes closer. Rose's brother, the clergyman. The priest. Chris gets out of the car and walks toward Gerald, extending his hand. No, Gerald thinks, no. Please, God, no. He wills himself to stand where he is, not to move a foot, not to run in the opposite direction. He meets Chris's eyes as he shakes his hand, Chris's other hand coming on top to cradle Gerald's. *Yes,* Chris says, nodding, understanding. *A car accident. All of them,* Gerald says, his stomach

427

suddenly empty. *No,* Chris says, quickly, shaking his head, clasping his hand more tightly. *No, Rose and the children were at home.* *Thank God,* Gerald says, and is ashamed by his relief. *Thank the Lord.* He looks at the ground, then up at Chris. *Quickly, do you think?* Chris nods. *I do,* he says, *I don't think he suffered for long. Where?* Gerald asks. *Quincy Shore,* Chris says. By the ocean, Gerald thinks. By the place they all love best.

I appreciate you coming out here, he says, staring down at the driveway, then out at the garden. *How's Rose?* he asks. *She's okay,* Chris replies. *You know Rose. She's made of tough stuff. And, as we both know, this is the easy part. It's the weeks and months and years down the road.* Gerald nods. He knows this to be true. *And the children? As you would expect,* Chris says. *It'll take time.* Gerald can't think about them, can't allow himself to see Kathleen's mouth or Jack's dark eyes. Chris looks up at the sky. *What a beautiful day,* he says. *I can never decide. Is it better or worse when the world looks like this? Does it mitigate the loss when the world is so insistent on being beautiful?*

Gerald stays outside until Chris's car disappears. How is he going to go into the

428

house and tell Mother? He stands, facing the parked car, for as long as he can bear to. There's so much to do. He must tell Mother; he must tell Linda; he must re-schedule his plans; they need to figure out the arrangements. He needs to call friends and family. He turns around, finally, to face the house, and Mother is in the kitchen window. He waves at her, and by the way that she waves back, he knows that she already knows.

Later, they make phone calls, pushing the phone back and forth across the kitchen table as they take turns sharing the news. Gerald makes Mother a cup of tea, and as he sets it down next to her elbow, she looks up at him, her eyes bloodshot and tired. *We need to tell Bea,* she says. *And we need to do it soon, given that it's almost the end of her day.* He nods. *But please, Gerald, can you call? I don't think I can tell one more person.* So, an hour later, when she falls asleep on the couch, he closes the swinging door to the kitchen and finds Bea's name in her ad-dress book. Mother has always used pencil for address book entries, and he can see that she's erased and replaced Bea's addresses and numbers again and again.

He received a letter from her, just the week before, after he wrote to tell her about the March. She was excited for him to go and asked him to write to tell her all about it. He dials the number, and after a few rings, her voice, that familiar voice, is on the line. *Hello,* she says, and Gerald is surprised to feel his pulse in his throat. *Hi, Bea,* he says, the words uncomfortable in his mouth, *it's G.*

BEATRIX

Beatrix hangs up the phone with Gerald and goes out back to her small garden. She's planted some vegetables and herbs this year, along with flowers, and she holds a golden cherry tomato in her hand before pulling it off the vine, the smell exploding in the air, and then pops it into her mouth. It's warm from the sun. She rubs her thumb and forefinger on a basil leaf and lifts them to her nose. Mrs. G always had basil in her gardens. Sitting down on the lawn chair, she stares up at the sky. A beautiful blue sky, on the cusp of dusk, before it turns violet. A Maine sky, William would have said.

William, dead. She was shocked but somehow not surprised when Gerald called. She and William had exchanged a few letters over the past months, ever since she'd sent that silly bobblehead. He never said anything, specifically, but under and between the words, she could feel his uneasiness. Not unhappiness, per se, but a feeling that nothing was quite aligned. That the life he'd wanted, the one he'd expected, had failed to appear. It was as though that fire that had once been in his belly — his desire to be in the world — had somehow been extinguished. She wondered whether he'd ever been truly happy. A malcontent, she once called him to his face. With the children he seemed to have found something, though. She knows he loved them. She knows they gave him joy.

She doesn't want to think about the last hours of his life, and yet she can't not see him in the car. By the ocean, Gerald said. Of course. The car flipped and somehow, Gerald wasn't sure how, they found him a ways from the car, lying on his back. Sunbathing on the moonlit beach, the sun just peeking from the edge of the sea. She hopes that he wasn't in physical pain, she hopes it was quick. *I just wanted — we all just wanted — you to be happy,* she says out loud, talking up to the blue sky. Why is that difficult for so many people to achieve?

How strange it was to hear Gerald's voice after all these years. Still so earnest and forthright. His voice cracking just slightly when he told her the news. But then, later, a laugh over something — she can't remember what — and suddenly an image of him bloomed in her head, Gerald on the dock at the very beginning, his excitement, his lopsided grin. She sat in her kitchen chair, the phone between her shoulder and ear, and smiled back.

NANCY

All day, Nancy sits with Gerald and Linda in the living room to watch news coverage of the March on Washington. She can't concentrate on the television; she can't stop weeping. The humidity makes her upper lip sweat, and she blots at it again and again. The fan does little to move the air through the house. She can tell by the way that Gerald is leaning forward, gazing at the television, not really responding to her, that he wishes he were there. Should she have urged him to go?

She has tried to support him in his interest in civil rights. Ever since he was little, he has worked for one cause after another, always believing in the good of others. When he was little she was proud of his generosity, his openness, his optimism. Now she finds herself envious of the passion that he and Linda share, their conviction that they can help to make this world a better place.

What had she and Ethan done? Ethan, at least, was a teacher and a role model. She raised two boys, one of whom was now gone. Dead. Never again will he appear unannounced at the back door, dropping the children off for the weekend. Never again will he flirt with her, bending down to kiss her on the cheek. Never again will she see that beautiful face. It is a fresh wound, one that opens again and again. She forgets that he is gone and must remember all over again.

Last night, at dinner with Linda, they told stories about William and, after dessert, they flipped through some of the photo albums. Gerald told Linda that when he was little he'd been jealous that William was said to be like his father. *But now,* he said, glancing at Nancy, *now I'm glad I'm more like Mother.* Nancy nodded, patting him on the knee. What a sweet man he is. *We are alike, aren't we,* she said. *You and me.* She turned the pages in the album, looking for one she remembered of William and Ethan together, both looking solemnly into the camera. *A melancholy,* she said. *They shared that, for sure.*

Dr. King is speaking now. How quickly everything changes. What would her mother make of this new world? Nancy closes her eyes and leans back into the couch. She knows that whatever arrangements Rose is putting together for the funeral are not what she would do. All that Catholic nonsense. She wants to have the funeral in the chapel, just like Ethan's. She wants William buried in the cemetery, right by the house, right next to Ethan, so she can visit him every day. So they can be together. *No*, Gerald said earlier. *This is for Rose to decide. It's not your decision to make. You have to let it go.* And she knows that Gerald is right. Nancy reaches into her apron pocket to retrieve Ethan's handkerchief and wipes the sweat and tears from her face.

MILLIE

Millie pushes a thick envelope across the kitchen table. *It's a funny story,* she says, lighting her cigarette, blowing the smoke toward the ceiling, longing to wrap her hands around a cool drink. *My mother gave this to me, a million years ago. She wanted me to go see you when you were in America.* Beatrix looks at her, puzzled. Millie wonders whether she has slept since she got the news. *But you told me,* Beatrix says. *You told me you never considered it. We agreed we wouldn't go,* Millie says, not really responding. *Dad didn't think it was safe. For you to come home early or for me to visit you there.* Beatrix is frowning but says nothing more. Millie knows that at any other time she would be pushing back, asking questions, demanding to know more. But not today. She's not sure she's ever seen Beatrix so sad.

But, anyway, she continues. *That's water*

under the bridge. Now is now. I tucked this envelope away then for a rainy day. And I've added to it over the years. Mad money, don't they call it? Clearly, it's been waiting for the perfect moment. And this is it. She pushes the envelope closer to Beatrix. *More than enough money in there for a plane ticket there and back.* Millie feels flooded with pleasure.

I can't go, Mum, Beatrix says dully, staring at the envelope, not opening it. *School is starting in two weeks. It's Thursday, and the funeral is Saturday. It's impossible. Nothing is impossible,* Millie says. *Nothing. I want you to take the money and go to the travel agent and buy a ticket to get on a plane tomorrow. Someone can cover for you at school. You're important, my dear, but you can disappear for a bit. You need to disappear for a bit.*

Millie can see Beatrix hesitate. She knows she wants to go. Millie regrets much that has happened between them, even though she tries hard not to. She shouldn't have married Tommy before Beatrix came home. She should have tried harder with George. She shouldn't have been negative about the Gregorys. She will not take no for an answer here. *What can I do to persuade you,* she says. *This is important.*

Beatrix looks away. *I hate to admit it,* she says as she looks round the kitchen, *but I*

438

think you're right. Millie could almost cry with relief. *I need to go,* Beatrix says. She picks up the envelope and looks inside. *Jesus Christ, Mum, there are hundreds of pounds here. Thousands?* Millie smiles. *I haven't counted it in forever,* she says. *I just kept putting money in whenever I had some extra. So, go. Buy yourself a lovely dress or two. Take some extra time there, as long as you go all that long way. Give yourself a chance to say goodbye to William. It will help you down the road.*

Thanks for this, Beatrix says. And she half smiles at Millie. *Now, out of here,* Millie says. *You have much to do. Go. And tell me everything when you get back.* Finally, Millie thinks. Finally, she has done the right thing.

BEA

Beatrix asked for a window seat so she could see the ocean, but of course it is hidden beneath layers of clouds. Up here, the sky is always blue, the horizon in sight. That original trip, the one that took two long weeks, is now reduced to a day on the plane. It's amazing, really. Tomorrow she will see Gerald and Mrs. G. She will say goodbye to William.

She wishes now that she had told Mrs. G or Gerald that she was coming. Gerald telephoned with the details at the start of the week before she decided to go. Before Mummy made it possible for her to go. Before the assistant director at school was more than understanding. *Absolutely,* Susan said. *You haven't taken time off in years. A week,* Beatrix said, *I'll be back in a week. School won't even have started,* Susan replied. *Don't even think about us. Take more time if you need it.* Her plan is to stay at a hotel near the airport tonight and then take a cab out to Quincy in the morning. The service starts at ten. But she'll need to call the house tonight, to tell them she'll be there. She can't just arrive. This can't be about her.

As they descend, the clouds fade away, and the blue sea lies far below. Bea rests her forehead on the cold glass. Land comes into view, the gold of the beach marking the transition between the sea and what's beyond. The place where William died. *Goodbye,* Bea whispers. *Goodbye.* The plane banks to the right, and all she can see is sky.

NANCY

Gerald knocks as Nancy is trying on the last of her black dresses, each of them fitting less well than the one before. *Oh, Gerald,* she says, almost in tears, *what am I going to do? What am I going to wear?* He pushes open the door and looks at her critically. *It's fine, Mother,* he says, *really. I can't zip it all the way up,* she says frantically, her voice rising. *I can't go to my son's funeral with an unzipped dress!* He motions for her to lift her arm. *It's hardly noticeable,* he says. *Don't you have a cardigan or something that can cover it up?* She turns back to the mirror and holds her arm firmly down at her side, covering the zipper. *I suppose,* she says. *But just my luck, the whole thing will split wide open, right there in that garish church.*

Gerald starts to laugh, wiping tears from his eyes as he sits on her bed. *Oh, Mother,* he says. *You need to let this go. I know,* she says. *I'm just getting it all out of my system* now. *So I can behave tomorrow. When they start swinging that ridiculous incense. Good for you,* he says. Then he looks her in the face, and he's happy and she can't understand it. Something's coming, although she doesn't know what, so she sits down next to him on the bed, the dress tightening around her middle. She reaches over and unzips it all the way. *The phone,* he says. *I just got off the phone.* He's grinning. *You won't believe who's going to be here tomorrow. Who just arrived in Boston. Who?* Nancy asks, running through her sisters and their husbands and their children in her head. Everyone has been accounted for.

Bea, he says simply. Bea, she thinks, and she remembers that morning, so long ago, Beatrix standing alone on the dock, in that red dress with the white collar, her thin little legs poking into heavy black boots. *Will we recognize her?* she asks, and Gerald laughs. How she loves that sound. *Mother,* he says, *of course. How could we not?* She supposes he's right. She sees that dear face in her dreams.

ROSE

Back at her parents' house, after the service, Rose collapses into a chair in the crowded kitchen. Her sisters are running around, putting food on the table, pouring drinks. Kathleen and Jack are downstairs in the rec room with the cousins. Rose knows she needs to go out to the living room, but just for a moment she sits. *You doing okay,* Chris asks, his hand on her shoulder. She nods. *Take your time,* he says. *Nothing is expected of you.*

The service is a gray haze. Gerald, Bobby Nelson, and Chris spoke. Kathleen and Jack read an excerpt from *Alice in Wonderland.* Sheila slipped her a few Librium before they left the house, and she managed to get through it all with only a few tears. The worst part was walking out of the church behind William's casket, looking at all those faces, hearing Gerald sob as he helped to lift the casket into the hearse. At the cemetery, they each tossed a handful of sand into the grave, instead of dirt. Nancy insisted on this. *Send him along with a little bit of Maine,* she said, although of course her sisters' husbands had dug up the sand from Wollaston Beach. A basket of small seashells was passed around. Some people took a shell home with them, others placed them gently on top of the casket before it was lowered down.

Jack comes running into the kitchen and tugs at Rose's hand. *Come see all the food,* he says. *There's so much to eat!* Rose smiles. Her sisters have outdone themselves. She allows Jack to pull her out of her chair and into the dining room. She makes a plate for Jack and then wanders through the familiar rooms, trying to smile, stopping to talk at each small group. The two families have separated as she knew they would: her family in the living room and the Gregorys in the den. Gerald catches her eye and waves her over, giving her a kiss on the cheek. *Lovely service,* he says. *Yes,* she replies, *and your eulogy was perfect. Just perfect. He would have loved that.* And it's true: Gerald told story after story about William as the perfect older brother, followed everywhere by his goofy younger sidekick. Gerald nods. *Your mother,* she says, seeing her across the room with Linda. *How is she doing? How is she handling it all? She's okay,* Gerald says. *Remarkably okay. But this* — and he waves his hand in the air — *is her kind of thing. She loves being surrounded by family and friends. Unlike me,* he says, his voice lowered. *All I want to do is go home.*

Rose smiles and leans into his familiar body. For a moment she thinks he's William. *It's just the kindness that makes me crazy,* she whispers. A woman appears at Gerald's side, her shoulder brushing his arm. Rose doesn't recognize her. *Oh, Rose,* Gerald says, straightening up, pulling away from her, *have you met Beatrix? Beatrix Thompson? No,* Rose says, extending her hand. *I'm Rose Gregory. Nice to meet you,* the woman says in a clipped British accent. This must be that girl, Rose realizes with a start. The girl from when they were little. *Are you the one?* she asks. *The one who lived with the Gregorys during the war? Yes,* Beatrix says, smiling, *I did. A very long time ago.* She's quite beautiful, her thick, dark hair parted on the side and pulled up into a French twist. Dark eyes. A stunning long-sleeved black dress with lace around the neck. Tall and very thin. *I'm so very sorry for your loss,* Beatrix says. *Thank you,* Rose

446

says, and then blurts out: *You came all the way from England for this? For William's funeral?*

Beatrix nods. *I wasn't able to come to their father's funeral.* Rose isn't sure how that's an answer to her question. She sees Kathleen across the room and motions her over, giving her a kiss on the cheek. Rose wonders when Kathleen became so tall. *Kat,* Gerald says, and oh, how Rose hates that nickname. *Kat, have you met Miss Thompson?*

Kathleen looks at Beatrix. *No,* she says, and Rose sees a flash of the woman she will become. Direct, straightforward, honest. *Nice to meet you,* Kathleen says. *You, too,* Beatrix says, nodding at her. *I've heard lots about you.* Kathleen looks perplexed. *Really?* she says. *From whom? Oh,* Beatrix says lightly, and in that tone, in that one word, Rose knows that William told her about Kathleen. Did they talk on the telephone? Did he write her letters? Was there something between them? *From your grandmother,* Beatrix says. *She's very proud of you. From Nana?* Kathleen asks, and Beatrix nods her head. *Oh, Mom,* Kathleen says, turning to her, and Rose knows that she's already moved on, she's already forgotten about this woman. *Nana brought lemon squares. May I*

447

have one?

Rose smiles at her and runs her hand through Kathleen's unruly hair. They had a hell of a time finding a dress that fit. But the girl should have a treat. *Let's go do that,* she says, and she turns back to Gerald and Beatrix before they head to the dining room. *Such a pleasure to meet you,* she says to Beatrix, making her voice silky smooth, feeling removed from her body, not meaning a word of what she is saying. As she walks with Kathleen across the room, to the dining table overflowing with food, she finds herself looking for William, sure to find him sitting in the corner with Chris, a beer in one hand and a cigarette in the other.

GERALD

Back at home, in the kitchen, Gerald can't keep his eyes off Bea. All day, since he first saw her outside the church, he has been waiting for this moment. For everyone else to disappear. For Linda to go home. To have Bea all to himself. And here she is, sitting in her seat, her slender fingers wrapped around a cup of tea. It's as though she never left. And yet. He feels at a loss for words. He's having trouble looking her in the face. So familiar and yet so different. Mother, though, can't stop touching her. *It's you,* Mother says, and Bea smiles. *It's me, Mrs. G. I'm here. I'm back. You must stay the night,* Mother insists. *Please don't go back to that hotel. We can pick up your things tomorrow. Your room is just as you left it. Kathleen sleeps there, but it's all just the same.*

She looks like you, G, Bea says. *I couldn't believe it. I saw her walking down the aisle, and I knew, instantly, who she was. Jack,* though, he looks more like Rose. They're nice children, Mother says. Maybe you can spend some time with them while you're here. Get to know them a bit. She squeezes Bea's hand. William was a good father, she says. I wasn't sure, you know, how that would all turn out. I always knew this one — and she nods her head toward Gerald — would be — will be! — a wonderful father. I wasn't sure about William. But how he loved those children.

Bea nods. I'm not surprised, she says. They're quiet for a moment and then Bea yawns, covering her mouth with her hand, and shakes her head. I'm sorry, she says, I'm past exhausted. Tomorrow? We can talk more tomorrow. She stands and puts her hands on Mother's shoulders. I'll take you up on your kind offer, she says, for tonight at least. Mother walks with her toward the door, her hand tucked into Bea's elbow. Let's find you something to change into, she says, and at the door, Bea turns and waves. Night, G, she says. See you in the morning.

Gerald sits and listens to the two of them head up the stairs. The floorboards creak as they move above his head. He knows he should go back to his own house. Linda is waiting. But Bea is here, and William is gone. He turns off the light and stays in the quiet, dark warmth of the kitchen, his stocking feet resting on William's chair.

BEA

Bea is up early, and she slips out the back door, trying to be quiet, remembering too late that the screen door will slam behind her. So many things have flooded back. The field between the house and the school is ablaze with wildflowers. The path they took to school each day is no longer there. Back in the woods, the canopy is thick overhead, and she wanders the still familiar trails before crossing the street into the cemetery.

She has a rough idea where Mr. G's grave is: toward the back, by the pond and a willow tree. It never occurred to her, back when they would sneak in here for a cigarette, that it was such a beautiful place. The rolling hills. Flowers planted where the lanes diverge. Stately old trees protecting the graves underneath. Bea finds Mr. G's grave and lays the wildflowers she picked in the field on top of the gravestone. The grave site is well tended; both Gerald and William wrote to her that Mrs. G comes here regularly.

Beatrix understands that need. She sits down on the grass, close enough to trace the letters on his gravestone. She tells him about the funeral and what it's like to be back. What it was like to sit in that kitchen last night, with Gerald and Mrs. G. The odd comfort of sleeping in her old bed. Glancing in his study as she walked by, expecting him to look up from his papers, to wave in that way he waved, all his fingers moving as one, his thumb stuck out to the side. Listening for William's step on the stair, hoping to see William rushing through the kitchen, flashing a smile.

She had been frightened to look in the mirror in the bathroom, half expecting the girl she had been to be there still. Bea doesn't tell Mr. G, but she was shocked by the look of Mrs. G. She's no longer dyeing her hair, and she moves slowly, her back hunched over. All that energy seems to have flown away. Gerald is different, too, but with him, it's a wonderful transformation. He's steadier and calmer, more self-assured. *I expected a boy,* she says to Mr. G. *What was I thinking?* She wonders what Gerald and Mrs. G think of her. How has she changed since she left?

Bea hears footsteps and turns around to see Gerald approaching, saluting her as William always did. *How'd you know I'd be here,* she asks, and he smiles, sitting down beside her. *Hide-and-seek,* he says. *You were always easy to find.* Bea nods. *A beautiful spot for Father,* he says, rolling a blade of grass between his fingers. He's dreadfully tall now, almost as tall as Mr. G. *Were you taller than William,* she asks, apropos of nothing, and he grins, just the way William used to. *I think we were pretty close,* he says, *although William never thought so. I think it depended on who was standing up the straightest.*

When was the last time you saw him, Bea asks, not looking at him, but watching how the boughs of the willow tree bend toward the earth, lean toward Mr. G's grave. *He brought the children over two weekends ago,* Gerald says. *It seems like a lifetime ago, though.* He sighs. *I just keep seeing him driving that night. He was probably drunk and tired and couldn't see where the road goes around that curve.* Gerald pulls a handful of grass out of the ground and lets it scatter through his fingers. *It's the children that worry me. I'll get beyond this, and you will, and Mother will. Rose, too. But will Kathleen and Jack? I know how hard it was for me with*

Father, and I was much older.

Bea is surprised to hear that he struggled after Mr. G's death. She had no idea; she'd never thought they were particularly close. *It was hard for you, then,* she says, feeling that she should have known. He nods. *Partly why I went to Berkeley,* he says. *I mean, I finished up at Harvard and was here for Mother during those two years. But then I wanted nothing more than to get far away. I was looking for him everywhere.* Bea nods. *I get it,* she says. *But I wouldn't worry about the children. Sometimes I think children handle death better than adults.*

Gerald shakes his head. *I'm such an ass,* he says. *Here I am, wallowing about, and I'm not even remembering that you lost your dad when you were just a little older than Kathleen. Is that right?* Bea nods. *And look at me,* she says. *I'm doing okay. But mostly because I had all of you. William's children will be fine,* she says again, almost as an afterthought, almost to herself. *They'll be just fine.*

They sit in silence for a few minutes. How easy it is to do that with Gerald. She's never had to pretend. *I have a painting from Maine,* she says finally, *with the three of us on the dock. Do you remember that? I think so,* Gerald says. *It was in the living room?* Bea nods. *I love it,* she says. *William lying there, his hands behind his head, staring up at the sky. That's the way I want to remember him.*

He started painting, Gerald says. *Did you know that?* Bea shakes her head. *I can't imagine it,* she says. *I can't imagine he'd have the patience. The children changed him,* Gerald says. *I think he learned patience from them. He took all of Father's old painting stuff — easels, paints, brushes, everything — and brought it over to his house, set it up in his garage. I never really saw much of what he produced. He showed Mother some things. But I don't know what Rose is going to do with it all. I was thinking I might bring it back here.*

Don't you think, Bea? Gerald asks, turning toward her finally. This is the Gerald she knows: the earnestness, the quiet honesty. *Don't you think it belongs back here? I'm worried she might throw it out. Yes,* she says, *I agree. I think you should do that.* Bring it all home, she thinks. Keep him as close as you can. Gerald lays his hands on the grass, and she's startled by how familiar they are to her. That scar on his index finger. The freckles. She looks up into his face and smiles.

NANCY

Nancy sits at the kitchen table, making a list for the grocer. She wishes she could remember some of Bea's favorite foods, but she can't, not really. But she feels sure that she likes apple pie. Doesn't everyone? She'll make that for dessert, with some of the Granny Smiths from the trees in the garden. And perhaps a nice meatloaf and mashed potatoes for supper.

She saw Bea out in the garden earlier and then, a bit later, she heard the door close again and saw Gerald cross the field toward the woods. Good, she thought. They need some time together, to get reacquainted. It must be strange for them both. To not only be together again but to be together without William. Those summers in Maine, those few sweet summers when the three of them were thick as thieves. Those days that passed by far too quickly and that she can only remember snippets of now. The three of them, racing out to the dock, King following behind. Picking blueberries in the hills. Camping out in the woods. Late at night, the world quiet around them, the lights from the house reflecting in the dark sea. Oh, why can't time be stopped in those moments. Why is it so hard to understand how fleeting it all is?

Nancy feels desperate now, in the same way that she did after Ethan died. A need to scramble back in time, to pull up old memories, to regret words, to re-create moments. Gerald told her that the last time they had seen William was two weeks ago. What did she talk to him about? Did she remember to kiss him goodbye? Did she scold him about something? She tries to remember. The children came running into the kitchen, as always. She'd made the dough for the pie crust, had it all ready for Jack to roll out, for Kathleen to place into the pie pan. Kathleen was talking about some book she was reading, and Jack was telling Gerald about the baseball game he'd just played. That's right, he was still in his uniform, because she'd washed it that evening, scrubbing hard to get the dirt stains out of the knees.

But William. Why can't she remember him on that day? Did he not come into the house? Nancy hits the side of her head. Stupid, stupid memory. Back when she was young, she was the one everyone in her family turned to when they wanted to remember something. She knew it all. She recalled names and places, could recount the smallest of details. But now, well, now it's as though things are there only in the moment. She has a dickens of a time coming up with names or specific memories of more recent events. Stuff from her childhood is still there, though, clearer than ever. Recipes. The layout of the garden. It doesn't seem right that she can't remember the last conversation she had with her son, but that she can recall the words to a silly song they sang in primary school.

Bea and Gerald come in the back door and she can tell, by the looks on their faces, that they're having a nice time together. She pours them each a cup of coffee, and they sit together at the kitchen table. Bea puts her hand over Nancy's. *I went and saw Mr. G,* she says. *It was nice to talk to him. Oh, good,* Nancy says, *I'm so glad.* She hasn't been going as regularly anymore. She tells Gerald it's because it's harder to get there, with her ankle and all, but that's not the truth. It's that she ran out of things to talk to him about. It seemed silly, after a while, to tell him everything that was going on. Not all that much was happening. It also occurred to her that maybe he saw everything, so there was little point in recounting it all for him. Oh, she goes to share with him the big things. She went over after they learned about William. But she no longer goes every day.

How did you find him? she asks, and Bea's face pales just a little. *He seemed fine,* she says finally, and Nancy laughs. *Oh, no, dear,* she says. *I meant, how did you find the grave? Did you remember where the plot was? Did Gerald show you?* Bea smiles. Her face has changed, become more angular and yet softer at the same time. The fear is gone, replaced by a sort of elegant grace. *Ah,* Bea says, *I understand. William had told me. He drew me a little picture of the cemetery, with the willow tree and the pond, and that's how I knew. Then Gerald met me there, so we walked back together.*

Wonderful, Nancy says. *So lovely to see the two of you together, to hear you laughing. I have missed that,* she goes on. *Gerald and I do all right when he stops by for dinner or for tea, but we don't laugh as much as we should. We need to do better, Gerald, you and me. Yes, Mother,* he says, and she knows by his tone that he is appeasing her. *We will try to laugh more,* he says. *But I'm not all that funny, really. Maybe we should just watch more television. We could watch television while we eat dinner, even.* He grins at her.

Nancy wants to glare back but she can't. How he looks like William when he teases her. This was a fight she'd had with William, again and again. The children always want to eat dinner in the living room, for goodness' sake, so they can watch some program or other. We always do at home, they say, and Nancy refuses. Dinnertime is for having a nice conversation, she says to them, for spending time with your family. Not for watching some silly show on television! Over and over she had talked to William about this, but then they'd come back and it would start all over again.

I do that, Bea says. *I got myself one of those TV trays. But,* she says quickly, *I live alone. That's a different sort of a thing. Indeed,* Nancy says, *that's just right.* And she won't admit it, but she does the same. *Now,* she says, *where is that list I was making? I wanted to make a special dinner tonight, just for you, Bea. You will be staying with us a bit longer, won't you?* She looks at the calendar on the wall. *My goodness,* she says, *it's September*

461

already. September 1963. How did that hap-pen?

Bea smiles at her. *My flight is on Wednes-day*, she says. *So, if it's all right, I'll stay here until then.* Gerald looks at Bea and raises his eyebrows. *Shall we*, he asks, standing. *We're going to go over to Quincy*, he says to Nancy. *So Bea can see the children. Oh, wonderful,* Nancy says. *I'm so glad to hear that.* Those poor, dear children. She wonders whether she'll ever forget the look on Kathleen's face in the church. They'll need to keep the spirit of William alive, for the children. And for all of them as well.

ROSE

Rose hears the car doors slam and pulls the curtains aside to see Gerald and the British woman heading toward the house. She runs her fingers through her hair and pinches her cheeks. She knows she looks a fright but it's just Gerald, after all. *Kids,* she calls up the stairs, *looks like Uncle Gerald is here for a visit.* Jack runs down the steps, two at a time, with Kathleen right behind, and they pull open the door, just as Gerald is about to ring the buzzer. They step out onto the porch to hug him, and he swings both into the air before setting them down.

Morning, Rose says to the British woman, hoping that Gerald will say her name. *Nice to see you again. You as well,* she replies. She does not look a fright. Her hair is still in that French twist. Does she do that every morning? And today she's wearing a pale blue dress that ends above her knees. *Bea and I thought we'd take the kids up to the*

North Shore, Gerald says. *If that's okay with you.* Rose could hug him. He always knows the right thing to do. *That would be lovely, Gerald,* she says. *Thank you.* Bea smiles at her. *Will you come with us?*

Gerald laughs. *Not really Rose's thing,* he says. *Happy to take them off your hands for a few hours. Actually,* Rose says, *I'd like to tag along. If you don't mind.* In the car she sits in the back seat, on the hump, one child on either side, holding tight to their hands. She wonders whether she'll ever be ready to let them go.

BEA

In Gloucester, Bea and Gerald walk together down Main Street, heading for the water, the sun melting their ice cream cones faster than they would like, Kathleen and Jack up ahead with Rose. *I like her,* Bea says. *I didn't think I would. But there's something of William in her, isn't there? A fire, an intensity?*

Gerald nods. *She's very passionate about the things she's interested in, that's for sure.* He grins, and Bea has to look away. There are moments now when he looks quite a bit like William. *She has a thing about the Kennedys,* he says. *It drove William crazy. But she campaigned for JFK tirelessly. She's not just some silly housewife. I'll be interested to see what she does now. You know, in terms of work. It's wonderful, isn't it,* Bea says, *how all these women are entering the workforce.*

It's a beautiful early fall day, the ocean a deep velvet blue, the whitecaps skimming across the surface. Bea takes a deep breath in. *I rarely get to the sea,* she says. *This isn't Maine, but it's pretty close.* Gerald nods. *William brought the children up here all the time,* he says. *I think he felt it was as close as he could get.*

The children have run ahead to a statue of a fisherman, and Rose waits for Bea and Gerald to catch up. *We were just talking about Maine,* Gerald says to Rose. *I think he came here as a stand-in, of sorts. He loved that place,* Rose says. *There were times I thought that he felt that loss almost more than the loss of your father.*

Did he ever take you there? Bea asks, knowing the answer but curious to hear how she responds. *Once,* Rose says, *a long time ago. We stole a boat and broke into the house, for God's sake, drank the people's whiskey. Ate some ice cream that was in the freezer. Slept in their beds!* Gerald laughs. *Such a William thing to do,* he says. *Jesus. I'm glad he never told my mother about that. Still, I'm jealous you were there. I'm starting to forget it. I'll wake up, late at night, and I can't remember how the living room looked or which path to take through the forest.*

Rose made a face. *I didn't much like it, Gerald, and you know me, I made sure William knew that. He wanted to buy it back, and*

I told him that was a stupid idea. But, who knows? She turns and faces Gerald, ignoring Bea completely. *Would that have made him a happier person, do you think? If he still had Maine?* There's a raggedness to her voice, a desperation. Bea wants to tell her no, that William was just one of those people who can't ever quite find happiness, no matter what. But she waits for Gerald to answer, curious to hear what he'll say.

Gerald puts his hands on Rose's shoulders and looks her straight in the face. *Rose,* he says quietly. *William was always searching for the next thing, you know that. Maine wouldn't have helped. The children did, though. They helped to keep him in the present. You can't take this on. You mustn't. He had a good life.* Rose nods. *I know that,* she says, *but it's hard not to wonder.*

She turns to Bea. *When did you last see him?* she asks, and Bea can tell that she's been wanting to ask that, that she's been wanting to know who she was to William. *When you left after the war?* Bea feels the blush rising through her throat. She steals a look at Gerald, not sure what he knows either.

No, she says quickly, knowing that she'll lie if she gives herself a moment. *I saw Wil-*

liam in London, just after their father died. Gerald shakes his head, his mouth a thin straight line, and, looking at the ground, kicks a cigarette butt into the street with a fierceness that surprises Bea. *I knew it,* he says, and his voice is cold. *I asked William, later, and he said he didn't see you, but I knew he did. I knew he couldn't go to Europe and not see you. Yes,* Bea says. *But he didn't plan on it — in fact he planned most definitely* not *to see me — but then your father died and he had a few days before the ship sailed and so he came to London.* She can see Rose thinking and remembering.

I was pregnant with Kathleen then, Rose says, and Bea nods. *Yes,* she says. *He told me. He told me all about you. About how excited he was to get married. About how nervous he was to be a father.* She gestures to Kathleen and Jack, who are waiting for them by the statue. *And it looks to me,* she says, *as though he — as if the two of you — ended up doing a great job.*

All three of them wave at the children, and they start to walk toward them. Rose grabs Bea's upper arm. *But since then?* she asks. *Did you see him after that?* Again, Bea feels her desperation. *No,* she says. *We wrote a few letters over the years. I heard more often from Gerald and Mrs. G.*

Later, back at William's house, Gerald, Rose, and Bea go into the small garage to pack up all the painting supplies and canvases and load them into Gerald's car. Bea doesn't want to look at the paintings, so she focuses on boxing up the supplies. Under a bag of oil tubes, she finds a sketch of a man and a woman dancing and realizes it's the same man and woman in her painting at home. The unsigned canvas Mrs. G had sent a few years earlier. Of course it wasn't painted by Mr. G. And she finds another drawing of a clock in a train station, realizing with a start that it's Victoria Station, the last place she saw William. *I'm happy to have a garage again,* Rose says. *But if you find any drawings with the kids, you'll bring those back, yes? Those I would like to keep. But painting after painting of a blue sea is something I can do without.*

Before they leave, Kathleen leads Bea upstairs to show her their room. *This is my bed,* she says, *and Jack sleeps here.* In between their beds is a small rag rug in shades of red and blue. *Do you two talk to each other at night?* Bea asks. *Do you tell each other stories? Sometimes,* Kathleen says. *Sometimes I have to throw things at him to make him stop snoring.* She laughs. Her openness is so like Gerald's. *But the best nights were when Daddy would come in, late at night, after we had been asleep forever, and kiss us each good night on the forehead. I'd always pretend I was asleep until he kissed me. Then he'd lie down on the floor right here between the beds and tell us a story and then he'd go to sleep, too. I'd give him my extra pillow.*

Bea nods, not trusting herself to speak. She looks around the room. On the dresser stands the Mickey Mantle bobblehead doll. *Oh,* she says, startled. *It's Mickey Mantle!* Then she turns to Kathleen, her eyebrows raised. *Where did that come from? Is that allowed in a Red Sox house?* Kathleen grins. That Gregory grin. *Daddy gave it to Jack. He said we have to learn to love our enemies. Your father,* Bea says, not looking at Kathleen, *was a very wise man.* She touches the bobblehead just enough to make him wobble, the head moving back and forth.

GERALD

Gerald insists on driving Bea to the airport. He wants time alone with her. She hasn't said much of anything about her life. They've talked about being educators — how funny that they've both ended up working with children — and she told him a little about her mother, but he doesn't feel that he's learned much of anything about how she lives, about who her friends are. About who she is now. Mother beat around the bush last night at dinner, but Bea just kept changing the topic. She's good at that, Gerald realizes. How deftly she handled Rose when Rose was asking about when she had seen William. He knew that they saw each other that summer and again he feels the weight resting in his chest. He wonders what happened between them. Bea won't say, he knows that. It's not even worth asking.

Bea climbs into the car, holding a round

471

tin container in her arms. *Cookies,* she says. *What am I to do with three dozen cookies.* She's laughing and crying all at the same moment and then Mother is knocking on the window. Bea rolls it down. *The recipe,* Mother says, handing her a tattered note card littered with butter stains. *But you won't have it then,* Bea says, wiping the tears from her face. *Oh, child,* Mother says. *It's all in my head. Everything is in there. I don't need the words anymore.* Mother kisses her fingers and blows toward Bea. *Safe travels, my dear. Please come back soon.*

Neither Bea nor Gerald speak until they've pulled out of the driveway and are on the avenue heading for the highway. *I hate saying goodbye,* Bea says finally, looking out the side window. *I would rather just disappear. An Irish goodbye,* Gerald says. *Wouldn't we all. William was the master of that,* Bea says. *I learned it from him.* Gerald knows that William is never far from his thoughts. It's clear that it's the same for Bea. Never more than a breath away.

Bea turns to face Gerald. *You mustn't come into the airport, all right? Just drop me at the curb. It'll be much easier. For us both.* He nods. *Your wish,* he says. *Your wish is always my command.* As it always has been.

He heads onto the ramp and accelerates as he merges onto the highway, heading north. *Tell me, Gerald,* Bea says. *Tell me more about Linda. She seems like someone I'd like to know.*

Gerald doesn't want to talk about Linda. When she met Bea, after the funeral, there had been a cool look in Linda's eyes that filled him with a surprising fury. He'd kept them apart in the days after that. He didn't want them to share the same space. He wanted to keep Bea to himself. *She's terrific,* he says, his voice trailing off. *Is she the one, then,* Bea asks. He takes his eyes off the road for a moment. He wishes he could say yes. *I don't know,* he says. *How do you know?* Bea shrugs. *I wish I knew, G,* she says. She looks out the window at the water. *And you?* he asks, not wanting to pry but desperately wanting to know.

Well, she says. *I was dating a man named Robert for a while but we broke it off a few months ago. He was fine, but not my Prince Charming. And I wasn't his Cinderella.* She says nothing for a long time, and he wishes he wasn't driving sixty miles an hour, so that he could turn and look at her face. Her beautiful face. *I loved William,* she says finally. *You know that.*

Later, Gerald drives home the long way,

taking Quincy Shore Drive, the road hugging the curves of the coast. At the airport, he gave Bea the framed photo of the three of them that he'd had all these years. *I promised you,* he said. *I told you I'd give this back to you the next time we were together.* Bea kissed him on the cheek, unable to speak, and he hugged her, his eyes closed, not wanting to let go. Now he pulls over at the spot where they found William's car and his body, and he takes off his shoes, rolling up his pants, and walks across the hard, damp sand to stare at the sea. Of course he knew how Bea felt about William. He just hadn't expected her to say it out loud.

MILLIE

Millie hasn't heard much about the trip to the States. Beatrix has been quiet and withdrawn since she returned. But Millie hasn't asked any questions. She understands now how private Beatrix is, how much she hates the way Millie wants to be a part of her life, especially her life with the Gregorys. Millie was concerned enough, though, to suggest a weekend holiday to Scotland, without even mentioning that they go together, even though that's really what she wanted. Beatrix had gone, alone, and had reported back that it was a lovely spot. Millie hasn't seen her since she got back. But then last night, Beatrix called and asked Millie to go Christmas shopping with her. *I want to get gifts for William's children,* she said, and Millie was thrilled to be asked.

They decide on a few of the Paddington Bear books for the boy and a needlepoint kit for the girl. *Nothing for the others,* Millie asks, trying to be off-handed. *I don't think so,* Beatrix says. *I wouldn't know what to get.* Then she looks up at Millie with tears in her eyes. *There's too much sorrow, Mum. I don't think anyone's in the mood for gifts.* Millie nods. *I understand,* she says. *The first Christmas after your father died I was furious at all the joy.*

Later, as they're walking through the crowded streets, Bea tells her about Rose and her infatuation with the Kennedys. *When I heard about the assassination,* she says, *I immediately wondered how Rose was handling it. You had a thing for Princess Margaret,* Millie says. *Do you remember that?* Beatrix smiles. *Of course. The first year I was in America, Mrs. G took me to buy a party dress. And all I wanted was the one that looked just like a dress Princess Margaret wore the year before.*

Did you enjoy spending time with Gerald while you were there, Millie asks, knowing as she does that she's breaking her own rule, but she can't help herself. *I did,* Beatrix says. *I feel as though I have a new friend. A new old friend. And I have you to thank for that, Mum. Going to William's funeral was the right thing to do. I didn't understand how important it would be.*

Millie smiles, turning her head away so Beatrix can't see. She can't retrace her steps, she can't redo the things she regrets, but maybe, just maybe, she and Beatrix can come out all right.

Millie, mother turning her head away so
Hattie can't see. She can't look. Nor
can she turn into the sickroom, so she
hurries downstairs. Go and look, they say.
She won't look.

GERALD

Once the weather gets warm enough in the
spring, Gerald decides to go up to Maine,
telling Mother and Linda that he's visiting
friends in Connecticut. He's never been
back, not since they sold the place, and he
hasn't been able to stop seeing Rose and
William there. He's angry that William
never told him.

In all those years, all those trips, he always
sat in the back seat. He misses gazing out
the window at the sea on the right side,
noticing the gas stations and the church
steeples and the lobster shacks along the
way. In town he parks the car and heads
toward the market. *Mrs. Lasky,* he says to
the familiar woman at the counter, who
looks thin and surprisingly old, and she
looks at him with no recognition. *Sorry,* she
says, *do I know you? Yes, I'm Gerald Gregory,*
he says, pulling himself up to his full height.
Oh, my goodness, she says, putting her

hands to her cheeks. *Yes, of course, it's you. All grown up! Yes,* he says. *All grown up.*

We sure do miss you folks, she says. *How long has it been now? Seventeen years,* he says. *We sold in '47, right after the war.* He smiles at her. *I'd love to go out to see the place. Think I might be able to borrow a boat? Well, I should think so,* she says. *Nobody out there now. John does the caretaking, so he can give you a key and you can look around. Marvelous,* Gerald says. *That sounds perfect.* A key, he thinks. They never had a key. What would be the point?

Mr. Lasky walks him down to the dock. *Just prepped the boats for this year,* he says. *Your father always liked the color of this one.* Gerald looks at the boats moored nearby, and there's the orange rowboat, the one that Father painted again and again. He has one of Father's paintings in his room, a painting that he looks at every morning as he's putting on his tie. *Wonderful,* Gerald says. *Nice to see how little has changed.* Lasky hands him the key. *You could stay out there the night,* he says, *but it'll get pretty near freezing. You might want to come back into town.* Gerald nods and shakes his hand before climbing into the boat.

He hasn't rowed in a long time, and it

takes a minute before his arms find the rhythm. Halfway out to the island, he lets the oars go slack and lets the boat drift, the current pulling him south. It is a bit overcast and windy now, the clouds moving at a quick pace. He turns the boat toward the island and moves it as quickly as he can. Pulling ashore on the beach, Gerald heads into the forest. The trails they made and followed so long ago are still there. Desire lines, his father called them. The quickest way from here to there. The leaves are beginning to unfurl. Spring comes later here. The forest looks empty, somehow, without the new growth. And yet it almost seems as though it's coming to life as he walks through it. As though if he stopped to watch, he could see the plants pushing themselves out of the ground, searching for the sun.

The house appears around a bend, and Gerald quickens his pace. It looks remarkably the same. Brown shingles, faded gray paint on the steps and the porch. He walks round the porch and sits down in a chair. He can see Father here, a glass of whiskey in one hand, his pipe in the other. Waiting for the sun to set. Looking out at the sea.

He doesn't want to go inside. Here, the view is the same, and he knows, when he steps inside, things will be different. There will be different mugs on the pegs. Their collections of rocks and shells and feathers will be gone. The array of pine cones, from smallest to largest, which ran across the windowsills in the living room, will have been replaced by something else. Still. This is what he's come for, isn't it? To be in the house again? To smell it, to touch the banister, to lie down on the floor by the picture window? To remember the boy he was, to try to understand the way that boy is connected to the man he is now.

By the time he's ready, the sun has dipped low in the sky. He unlocks the door and steps inside, closing his eyes and inhaling the stale cottage smell. When he opens his eyes, it does look different, brighter somehow. But there's the old icebox, with the pull handle, and the box on top. The window seat, with the same faded floral cushions. The bookshelves lining the far wall. He wanders upstairs and pokes into each bedroom. He's glad the owners haven't changed much and yet it feels different. It no longer feels like home.

He knows this all needs to be behind him now. He returns to the porch and waits for the sun to set. He could never understand Father's need to do this each evening, to just sit and wait. He didn't have the patience then. He can see the sun moving closer to the dark mainland, he can actually gauge its movement in the sky. The dark clouds from earlier have blown out to sea. The sky is clear and blue. As the sun disappears, the sky turns shades of pink and purple, for as far as he can see, the colors changing and growing in intensity. He sits, without moving, and takes it all in.

NANCY

For almost a year now, Nancy has planned to clean out William's room. She should have done it years ago, and she has emptied closets and drawers. But she wants this to be Jack's room, for Jack to feel that he has a home here. He shouldn't have to live in his father's shadow.

She still can't bear to throw out William's things, though, so she heads up to his room with spare boxes from the liquor store. At some point, she thinks, Kat and Jack will want to know more about their father, and all these things from his childhood will still be here for them to discover. Photos in frames, baseball gloves. A school pennant. His diplomas. An old wooden bat.

Gerald pops his head in the doorway. He and Linda are leaving in the morning to go south, first to Baltimore for a week and then to Mississippi for the month of July. Nancy insisted that they take her new car, with its roomy trunk and that fancy air-conditioning. Nancy had thought they would be working with others to help integrate the schools. Instead, they'll be teaching in a summer school. *I thought you were interested in education policy,* she said last night at dinner. *If you want to teach, why not do that here? I am interested in policy,* Gerald said. *But this is a way we can actually be helpful. By working in the classroom, with children who need help. Teaching them things like their constitutional rights.* Nancy frowned. She doesn't like the idea of him in a strange classroom. Will all the children be colored, she wanted to ask, but didn't. She's never been to Mississippi. She can't imagine it, really, except that it will be hot. *Will you be safe,* she said finally, turning to Linda, and they both laughed. *Will you, Mother?* Gerald said. *Don't worry about us.*

But she does. She looks at him critically, trying to see him as he is now. How difficult that is to do with your own child, to not always see him as the boy he once was. His hair is darkening a bit, she has noticed lately, and he does hunch over, just like Ethan, but how well he looks! He's been outside since school got out, helping to build some new structures around campus.

There's a vigor to him now. Linda has been a wonderful addition to his life, although, honestly, do they need to go all the way to Mississippi to create change? She's going to miss him terribly. And she's not happy that they're traveling together like this and not married. She told all her friends that he's going alone. Honestly, what is the boy waiting for?

In the morning, she packs up a picnic basket for them, and when he's not looking, she puts three tins of cookies and muffins in the trunk, whispering to Linda so she knows where they are. It's a long drive. Gerald and Linda come out the back door together, their arms piled with books and blankets, already sweating but with wide grins. He opens the car door for Linda and bows, holding his arm to the side, after she gets in. What a gentleman he is. It should make her content to see him like this, so grown up, such a confident man, and it does, but it also, inexplicably, makes her want to cry. Instead, she stands on her tiptoes to kiss him goodbye. Moving to the shade by the back door, she waves until they are out of sight.

As she pulls on her gloves to do the breakfast dishes, she wonders again about why they haven't gotten married. She knew right away that Ethan was the one for her. Oh, they had their ups and downs, and he could be such a pill, but she's never even thought about anyone else. She'd known it, too, when she saw him at that dance, all those years ago, sitting at the table. When she'd held her palm up against his, skin touching skin.

Bea

Every Sunday afternoon in July, Bea has sat down at her desk to write to Gerald. He's been sending her long letters from Mississippi, once a week since he's been there, filling her in on everything he's doing. She has loved reading them. His descriptions of his classroom, the children, and the other volunteers are alive with excitement and passion. Freedom School, it's called. She's glad that he seems safer than those who are working on voter registration. Bea was worried when she learned of the men who had been killed, but Gerald promised her that he was in no danger. *Everything I've learned and experienced,* he wrote in his most recent letter, *means that I will be a better counselor. I can't wait to bring all I've learned back to school.*

Bea reads each letter several times and has kept them all in her desk, in order. It's almost the end of the month, and he'll be heading home soon. The letter she's writing today will be the last one she sends to Mississippi. She has struggled with writing him back because her life seems so tame. All she wants to do is ask questions, to learn more about what he's doing. Who would have thought, she thinks again and again, that Gerald would be the one to live the exciting life. William, for all his talk, would never have done something like this. She wonders whether Gerald would have done this if William was still alive. She understands now that death has a way of providing freedom.

Dear G, she writes, *I'm sad to think that your time there is coming to an end. I have so enjoyed reading these letters. I feel as though I'm there. What an amazing opportunity this has been for you.* She remembers writing to her parents all those years ago, deciding what she could write about and what she couldn't. What might make them happy and what might make them sad. Constructing a life out of the raw pieces. She wonders what Gerald is leaving out, what he is not telling her. There is rarely news about Linda, even though she knows Linda is there, too. Are they living together? Has he proposed to her? Picking up the framed photograph on her desk, the one that Gerald gave her when she went over for the funeral, she smiles at the three young faces. How safe she felt then, with them on either side.

ROSE

Rose pulls the car into the Gregorys' driveway. For the past two weeks she's been coming over every afternoon, with or without the kids. Nancy has been distraught. Kathleen told Rose that when they stayed with her for a visit, Nancy put the radio on first thing in the morning and didn't turn it off until she went to bed. The paper was read every morning and night, the articles cut out and pasted into a scrapbook. She even allowed dinner to be eaten in the living room so she could watch the evening news.

After the children returned from that weekend, Jack said that he didn't want to visit again until Gerald was home. Kathleen is also reluctant, but there's a bit of her, Rose thinks, that understands. That empathizes. She has always been like this, able to be in someone else's body, to understand their pain. William had worried about it. *She feels too much,* he said. *We need to*

490

*toughen her up. She's going to turn into Ger-
ald.* Rose smiles as she shuts the car door.
If William could see Gerald now. She
doesn't know whether he'd be shocked or
proud. Probably a little of both. One more
week and Gerald will be home.

But for now she wants to keep tabs on
Nancy, so dropping by for a late-afternoon
visit has become part of her daily schedule.
It hasn't been so bad, actually. There is
something calming about this house, even
amid Nancy's fear. Nancy waves at her from
the kitchen window, and Rose steps into the
surprisingly cool house. It's been a hot summer.

Did you see, Nancy says, not even bothering to say hello. *More riots. More police dogs.
More tear gas. He's fine,* Rose says, pouring
herself a cup of coffee and sitting down at
the table. *Gerald can take care of himself.
He'll be home soon. I know,* Nancy says. *I'm
being silly.* She looks at the door. *Did you
bring the children?* Rose shakes her head.
Not today. Maybe tomorrow. Nancy is wearing the same dress she wore the day before.
She hasn't been to the hairdresser in weeks.

How about a walk, Rose says. *Why don't we
take a walk in the cemetery? Maybe visit
Ethan's grave?* Nancy makes a face. *Isn't it*

491

awfully hot out? she says. *Seems like too much right now. Nancy,* Rose says. *It's not that far of a walk. You used to go every single day, without fail. I know,* Nancy says, sighing. *I know.* Rose stands up and holds out her hand. *So let's go.*

It is a lovely graveyard. Rose had forgotten. There was a tussle, when William died, about where he was to be buried. Nancy wanted him to be with Ethan, had insisted that they use the spot reserved for her. Rose's father asked that they use their family plot, so that when Rose died, they could all be together. Rose hadn't known what to do, hadn't known what William would have wanted. She wasn't sure he wanted to be with her for eternity. She wasn't sure he wanted to be with anyone for that long. He probably would have wanted to be cremated, to have his ashes sprinkled up in Maine or at least in the sea. As they walk through this graveyard, though, she wonders whether she made a mistake. This feels more like where he belongs.

There it is, Nancy says, pointing down the hill. *There's Ethan. It's funny,* Rose says. *I didn't get to know him very well, you know. I was only with him a handful of times. But I feel that I did because of all the stories I heard from William. And now from the children. It's like he's still with us. Isn't that marvelous,* Nancy says, smiling, and for the first time in weeks, Rose feels that she's forgotten Gerald for at least a moment. They walk in silence toward the grave.

I hope, Nancy says, *that we can do the same for William. But it's harder, isn't it, when someone dies so young.* Rose shrugs. *I don't know,* she says. *I try with the children, as much as I can. Talking about him, telling them stories to keep him with them. Oh, I know you do,* Nancy says. *And I'm so appreciative. But still. Less of a life. Fewer moments to remember.*

They sit down on the bench that's near Ethan's grave. *I do love this bench,* Nancy says. *Really, what a stroke of luck that someone decided to put a bench here!* Rose looks away so Nancy can't see her smiling. Gerald had it installed a few years back when he realized that she was going to the cemetery less, and he thought it was, perhaps, because it was harder for her to sit on the ground. Gerald refused to tell Nancy he'd done that. *She doesn't like it when I take care of her,* he explained to Rose. *So I try to keep my distance. Do my caretaking undercover.*

Rose turns and looks at Nancy. *I should have buried William here,* she says. *I'm sorry.*

That was a mistake. Nancy waves her hand in the air. *Nonsense,* she says. *Nonsense. He loved your family, felt a part of it maybe even more than he felt a part of his own family. Ancient history, as they say.* She looks at her watch. *Let's get going, shall we?* she says. *I don't want to miss the evening news.* They walk back through the cemetery along the winding paths, the occasional breeze blowing only the highest branches of the trees.

MILLIE

Millie met Alan through mutual friends and when, after six dates, he asks her to marry him, she tells him to bugger off. *You don't want to marry me,* she says, swirling the wine in her glass. *I've done this three times already. My batting average is not good. Or at least that's what my daughter — who was partially raised in America — tells me. Oh, but I do want to do this,* he says, reaching his hand across the table to grasp hers. He's a lovely man, a little older than she is, just turned sixty-five this month. Her sixtieth is next year. *I want to spend the rest of my life with you, Mil. We can travel, we can sit by the fire, we can walk down the street arm in arm until we're old and gray. That's what I want. It's the only thing I want. Please say yes.*

She tells him she'll think about it, and when she goes back to her flat that night, she wanders around, a cup of tea in hand, and wonders why the hell not. They have a nice time together. He's good company. He's loaded. He's not dashing like Tommy. Or solid like George. And he's not Reg. No one will be Reg. But now, at least, she knows that. He's Alan. *Why not?* she says out loud to the walls. *Why not?* she asks the photo of Beatrix, a recent shot taken at a friend's wedding, Beatrix laughing, her hair gorgeously pinned up. *Why not?* she asks Reg, living within the frame by her bed. *He seems like a good find. I think we'll be happy together. Isn't that enough? Isn't that what we all want?* She has never thought of herself as an optimist, but she's grown to understand that she is one, at least when it comes to love.

GERALD

Dinners at Gerald's house rarely start on time. They have a schedule pinned to the kitchen wall — who's to cook, who's to clean — but they often all find themselves in the living room at well past the time set for dinner, arguing about politics or gossiping about the goings-on at school, the coffee table littered with wine bottles and full ashtrays, their stocking feet up on the coffee table. Four men and two gals live here. There's Stephen and Joy, who have been dating for several years: Gerald hears them slipping in and out of each other's rooms at night. Ben is in the history department, and Mike is the drama teacher. Then there's Annie. She's new this year, a few years out of college, here to teach French, and Gerald wishes he had paid a bit more attention in French class. Only present tense remains, and she teases him about it. They've flirted a bit, even made out once at the end of a long, drunken night, Gerald waking up on the couch in the living room, his arms wrapped around her waist. But he's not yet ready to move on.

He misses Linda. She took a job, suddenly, at a school in Baltimore. He hadn't expected she'd be the one to leave. She interviewed for the position on their way down to Mississippi and received the offer while they were there. When she looked up at him, the letter in her hand, he knew what he was supposed to do: tell her not to take the job, to marry him, to stay with him forever. But he couldn't do it. He didn't even try. He had never felt they were equals, somehow; she was always a step ahead and above. They'd stayed together for the month, sleeping together even, but they both knew it was over. There were few words to be said. When he dropped her off, on the way back, she touched his face before turning away, and he felt deeply ashamed. He's spent his life doing the right thing.

He told Mother but then stayed away as much as possible. He knows the news was an enormous disappointment to her, and he didn't want to have to see that on a daily basis. She and Linda had become quite close. It turned out, though, that giving her space had been the perfect solution. *What an idiot I've been,* he wrote to Bea. It's as though his absence has turned back the clock, has allowed her to blossom. *I should have done this years ago.* When he occasionally stops by, he finds her gone, out to lunch with her friends or in town running errands. The other day he wandered all through the house only to find her on her knees in the garden, digging out the last of the potatoes, her cheeks bright from the cold.

Tonight, though, she's coming over for dinner for the first time in a long time, and he stands at the front window, waiting. Finally he sees her, coming down the sidewalk. She's no longer using the cane, and he realizes she's lost weight. He opens the door wide. *Welcome,* he calls. *Welcome to our humble abode.* Everyone gathers round to say hello. Stephen and Joy are making dinner tonight, and they wave from the kitchen. *Got started a little late,* Joy calls, *but make yourself comfortable. We'll whip something together as quick as we can.*

Mother sits in the armchair by the fireplace and happily accepts a glass of wine. *Well, isn't this lovely,* she says, even though Gerald knows it's not. The house is furnished with a hodgepodge of items that were handed down or found at local garage sales. Still, it's comfortable. Many a night, after supper, they all sit in the living room, grading, working on lesson plans for the next day. More than once he's had to try to wipe away stains from his wineglass that ended up on a memo or on a student's report.

Annie sits down next to Mother. *Tell us Gerald stories. We're dying to hear them.* Gerald closes his eyes. Jesus. Having Mother to dinner was a bad idea. What embarrassing story is she going to tell them? His toy soldiers? His stamp collection? He wants to talk about the upcoming election, which looks as though Johnson's going to win in a landslide. Anything, really, would be better than this. Mother looks over at him, and he's relieved to see that she understands. *He was a lovely boy,* she says quietly, *just as he is now. He has been my rock, since my husband died, since my son — his brother — died as well. But as a child,* Annie says, pushing, and Gerald decides that he is no longer interested in her. *We want to know what he was like as a child. Full of energy,* Mother says. *Loved to play games. He and Bea would play Monopoly for hours on end.*

Bea? Annie asks, looking at Gerald. *Was that your live-in help?* Gerald looks at Mother, and they both laugh. *No,* Gerald says. *Bea was a girl who lived with us during the war. From London. They were so close,* Mother says. *I'd say they were closer than Gerald was to his own brother. Wouldn't you agree?* she asks, looking at Gerald. He nods but says nothing. *What happened to her?* Annie asks. *Are you still in touch?*

Oh, yes, Mother says. *She lives in London, and she came over for William's funeral. It was lovely to see her again. What a strange thing,* Ben says. *A sibling but not really a sibling. Part of the family and then not. You keep up with her, too?* he asks Gerald, and Gerald doesn't know what to say. *I'd say he does,* Annie says, and Gerald looks at her with surprise. *I see those letters from London. I wondered what that was all about.* Gerald blushes, and they all laugh. *Dinner,* Joy calls. *Can't wait to hear what's so funny.*

Later, after Gerald has walked Mother home and returned, after he's taken off his shoes and pulled out his planner, Joy comes and sits down beside him, tucking her feet under a blanket. He likes her. She and Stephen came to William's funeral, and she's been here for him ever since.

Joy touches his arm now to get his attention. *She seems well, Gerald,* she says. *A new leaf, perhaps.* He smiles at her. *I know,* he says. *If I didn't know better,* Joy says, *I'd think she was getting younger.* She squeezes his arm. *Must have been hard on you,* she says, *to lose your father and then your brother. But you'd never know, my friend,* she says. *You're the most stable of us all.* He gives her a hug. He's not sure about that. How he longs for what she and Stephen have found.

BEA

Bea pushes the letter into the postbox before she can rethink her decision. She's asked Gerald to come to London for her mother's wedding in December. She's thought about asking him for weeks. She wants to see him. They've spent so much time together now through their letters, over these past months, writing each other back and forth. Nothing makes her happier than coming home from work to open her front door and find a letter from him on the floor, having fallen gently there through the mail slot. She changes her clothes, eats some dinner, and then curls up on the sofa, his letter in hand. His round script, his well-developed thoughts, his honesty. His openness has allowed her to respond in kind. She always writes back the same evening.

She wishes she could go to America but she doesn't have the money to travel. So she asked Mum whether she could invite him to the wedding. The thought of being there alone, without a date, is crushing. She knows she'll feel the odd man out. She's tired of feeling like that. It's as if she's been standing still and everyone else has rushed by, gotten to a new destination. Her friends not only have babies, they have little girls who are going to school and having tea parties and even starting to think about boys. They don't even try to fix her up anymore. She is a lost cause. *Oh,* but her friends say, *you have your marvelous career, Trix. You run a school, for God's sake. That's an enormous accomplishment!* And she knows that's true. She does. But at night, sitting in her flat, looking round at her books and her paintings and her pots and pans, she wonders what it's all for. This is not where she thought she would be in her life by now.

She and Mum, though, are in a far better place. They talk almost every day, and they have apologized to each other for many of their past mistakes. It took Bea years to realize that she was at fault, too. For years she blamed her mother for so much, and she now understands how that created so much unnecessary pain. The wall has slowly started to come down. They still have their moments, of course. There was a row in a restaurant when Mum told her she was getting married again. But when they left the restaurant that night, before they went their separate ways, they hugged each other and for the first time Bea can remember, she didn't want to let go.

On Sunday evening, the phone rings as it so often does. One teacher or another has come down sick, won't be able to make it in Monday morning. *Trix here,* Bea says into the receiver. There's a pause. *Bea?* Gerald says. *Is that you?* That voice. That sweet, familiar voice. *Gerald,* she says. *Sorry. Thought you were someone from work. Didn't expect you to call. Is everything all right? Your mother?*

Yes, yes, he says. *We're all fine. It's just.* He stops. *I got your letter,* he says, starting again. *And, well, I'd love to come. How wonderful,* Bea says in a rush. *You know, I've never been abroad,* Gerald says. *We'll fit in more than the wedding, then,* Bea replies. *Whatever you want to see or do.* She doesn't want to sound too eager. *Mum will be thrilled,* she says. *She'll send you a proper invite, I'm sure. Is this the one for her, do you think,* Gerald asks, and Bea laughs. *Please, God,* she says. *Don't think I have another wedding left in me.* After she hangs up, she stands to look at William's painting above her bureau, at the two bodies moving to the music, moving as one.

NANCY

Nancy waves the envelope in the air when Gerald comes in the back door, stamping his boots on the doormat. She'd called him and asked him to stop by. She hadn't been able to get all the storm windows in place, and temperatures would be well below freezing tomorrow night. It's still early November; this could be a difficult winter.

What is that? Gerald asks as he unwraps the scarf from around his neck. His nose is bright red from the cold. *Let me get you some tea,* Nancy says. *And help yourself to some cookies.* She turns around at the stove after she's turned the burner on and set the water to boil. *It's a wedding invitation,* she says with wonder. *From Millie. She's getting married again!* Gerald smiles. *Yes,* he says, *I heard. But she invited you, Mother? That's awfully nice! I know,* Nancy says, and it's true, she's been on cloud nine since she received it earlier in the day. Silly to feel that way. Of course she can't go, but still. What a lovely gesture.

Gerald sits down at the table as she sets his teacup before him, along with a plate of cookies. He picks up the invitation and opens it. *December twentieth,* Nancy says. So close to Christmas. *You're going to go, aren't you?* Gerald says. *Oh, heavens, no. To go all that way for a little wedding. For some-one I barely know. Doesn't make sense.* She's hardly traveled since Ethan died, a trip now and again down to New York to see Sarah. She hasn't been abroad since before they were married. She's never been on a plane. But London, in December, all dressed up for Christmas. How lovely it must be. *Mother,* Gerald says, and there's that tone again. *She invited you. That's something special. You've never met her. You can spend time with Bea.*

I couldn't, she says, as she's wondering what she could wear. *It's all too much. The plane ticket alone.* But the money from the Maine house has been nicely accruing after all these years, or at least that's what the nice Mr. O'Connor down at the bank tells her. Perhaps she could even buy a new dress. Or have one of her old ones taken in by the tailor. What should one wear to a late-afternoon wedding, anyway? A fancy London wedding, at that? *You could stay with Bea,* Gerald says, *or we could get hotel rooms nearby. How happy she'll be to show us around!*

Well, Nancy says, and then she looks up. *We?* she says. *Us? Were you invited as well?* Gerald smiles. *I was,* he says. *Got my invitation yesterday. Oh, my,* Nancy says. That settles it, then. A trip to London with her son. *Aren't we just a couple of world travelers? Jetsetters,* Gerald says. *That's what they call people who travel all the time.*

Nancy lifts her teacup and they clink them together. *To us,* she says.

Later, in her room, all her nice dresses spread across her bed, she wonders at this life they've cobbled together. Certainly not the place she would have guessed she'd be if someone had asked years ago. To lose Ethan, to lose William. And yet here they are, she and Gerald, on the other side. They've made it through. Why shouldn't they have some fun? She slips on the crimson velvet dress, bought decades earlier for some Harvard party. The zipper slides up easily, and she smiles at her reflection in the mirror before twirling around the room, her arms caught up in Ethan's.

ROSE

The second Christmas without William is almost over, and Rose is relieved. Holidays, she knows, make the past present in unexpected ways and she was worried, in particular, about Kathleen. She knows she feels William's absence keenly. She hears her crying in the shower, sees the sadness in her mouth. She's been struggling in school. But today has been pleasant. Just the three of them for the morning, then her family in the afternoon and now William's family for a late supper. Just like always.

Nancy brought back gifts from London for the children, including a jigsaw puzzle of Big Ben, which the children poured out onto the kitchen table and are now working on, trying to get the outside edges complete before they have to leave. Nancy brought Rose some beautiful Liberty fabric. *So, tell me,* Rose says, unfolding the fabric on the cleared dining room table, wondering what to make out of it. A skirt, perhaps? Something for Kathleen? *Tell me about this wedding.*

It was simply lovely, Nancy says. *I wasn't sure what to expect, of course, and I've never met the woman, you know, but really, it was. I do hope the marriage lasts.* Rose nods. Before Nancy had gone, she'd talked on and on about the foolishness of this woman marrying yet again. She seems to be seeing it differently now. *What was she like?* Rose asks. *Was she what you expected?*

Nancy considers this. *Yes,* she says, *and no. It's odd to meet someone in person after knowing them only through their words. She was nice, but tough. Tougher than I would have thought. A little rough around the edges, perhaps.* Gerald laughs. *What did you expect,* he says. *Didn't you live here with Bea all those years? Where do you think that came from? Well, I know,* Nancy says. *But Bea is more sophisticated, I think. Smarter. All those years,* Gerald says again. *Must be your influence.* Rose laughs, and Nancy sticks out her tongue at Gerald. *Now stop that,* she says. *It's not nice to tease an old lady.*

Did it make you think you might get married again? Gerald asks his mother, glancing at Rose with a smile in his eyes. *Oh, heavens,*

Gerald, what a thought, Nancy says. *Of course not.* Rose knows that's true. She can't imagine Nancy remarrying. She has a hard enough time thinking of it for herself, although that's all her friends and family seem to think about. They've fixed her up over and over again, to no avail. She's not interested. It seems too complicated, with the children and all.

And you? Rose asks, turning to Gerald. *Nice time? Yes,* he says, his eyes on the table, his neck turning red. *The wedding was lovely.* And then he looks Rose in the eyes, and she knows. He's in love with this Bea. *Next it'll be your turn,* Nancy says, oblivious to what's transpiring between Rose and Gerald. *Oh,* Rose replies, *I don't think so,* then realizes that Nancy's talking about traveling. *I've never been anywhere, really. Maybe when the children get older. I would like to go to Paris someday. William loved it there.*

How's the job? Gerald asks, and she can tell he's desperate to talk about anything else. *I like it,* Rose says, and she does. She's working in the offices of a state senator. It's close to home and to the children's school. She worried, at first, that she wouldn't be able to handle it all. What if the children got sick? What if she needed to pick them up early? The first few weeks were stressful. Often dinner ended with all three of them in tears. But since then, it's gotten easier. It's fast-paced work, and now that she's got the hang of it, she feels good about it. People depend on her there. They know she'll get the job done. Senator McIntyre even patted her on the shoulder the other day, telling her she was doing a great job. A great job! She caught herself smiling on the walk home.

I want to hear more about your trip, she says. *Did you leave London at all? No,* Nancy says. *We just stayed put. I liked all the pomp and circumstance, the Changing of the Guard and all that. But Gerald and Bea walked and walked and walked. And what was that museum you liked so much, Gerald? The war museum?* Gerald nods. *The Imperial War Museum,* he says. *Just fascinating.*

Rose laughs. *That's such a Gerald thing to like,* she says. *Really. Can you imagine how much fun William would be making of you right now if he heard that?* Gerald's face closes in slightly, and Rose cringes inside but then Gerald laughs, leaning back in his chair. *Yes,* he says. *He would be merciless about it. Wouldn't understand why I wouldn't spend all my time in the Tate, the V&A. Different strokes,*

Nancy says. *The two of you were oil and water. I knew that if one of you liked something, the other would hate it. It was so predictable.*

I often wonder what would have happened, Gerald says, *if we'd been able to get old together. Would we have found a common ground? Or would we have fought until the bitter end? People don't really change,* Nancy says, and though Rose disagrees, she says nothing. Of course people change. Back when she was a teenager, she could not have imagined this life for herself. Even after William died, she wouldn't have foreseen that she'd still be this close to his family a few years down the road. Or be holding down a real job. And yet here she is. When you look back, it's so easy to see the path that you've traveled. But looking forward, there are only dreams and fears.

She looks up to see Gerald wiping some tears from his eyes. *Even with the ribbing,* he says, *I do miss him. I wish he was here. Me, too,* Rose says, standing to give him a hug. *Me, too.* So many things she would have done differently. Regret, she has found, is the loud thing that's left.

MILLIE

Millie and Alan are meeting Beatrix at a restaurant downtown for dinner. They do this regularly now, once or twice a month. *Tell me what you've heard from Nancy and Gerald,* Millie says. What a pleasure it had been to meet them, to have them at the wedding. *What a nice boy,* Millie said to Beatrix when Beatrix was helping her with her dress on the afternoon of the wedding. *Really. He reminds me of Nancy, the way he's so open about everything, so friendly. That's Gerald,* Beatrix said, buttoning each small button that ran up Millie's back. *Mrs. G has always said that he was the one cut in her mold. I think it was truer then, frankly, when we were children. There are moments when I see Mr. G now, in the way he'll look up when he's reading, for example, or the way he waits to respond, to gather his thoughts.*

Millie wonders about this newly rekindled friendship. It grew out of Beatrix's trip to

515

the States back when William died. When Beatrix told her that she wanted to invite Gerald to the wedding, Millie was curious. Beatrix explained it away by saying there was no way that Nancy would come without Gerald, but Millie knew that wasn't the reason. It was that Beatrix wanted to see him.

They seemed, though, more like good friends, like siblings. She's always imagined that's what they are. William had been the one. But then, at the wedding, Millie reconsidered. They were dancing together, and Beatrix leaned her head on his shoulder. He looked down at her in a way that reminded her of Reg, of the way that she and Reg used to be together, of the way Reg looked at her. There was a comfort there, a tenderness, that made Millie's eyes fill unexpectedly with tears.

All is well, Beatrix says now at the restaurant. *Same old, I suppose. But . . .* And her voice fades away. *But what,* Millie says. *Spit it out. It's silly,* Beatrix says, playing with her napkin, *but they've invited me over for Easter. We have our spring holiday then, so technically I could go. But the airfare's awfully expensive. Nonsense,* Alan says. *What's a little money when you want to spend time with friends? Consider it an early birthday present from the two of us.* He laughs and pats Beatrix's hand. *Just remind me when your birthday is again, dear?* Dear Alan, what a treasure he is. Millie grabs his hand under the table and gives it a squeeze.

Later, in the ladies' room, Millie catches Beatrix's eye in the mirror. *You will take him up on it, won't you?* she asks. *Yes, Mum,* Beatrix says. *I'd be a fool not to.* Then Beatrix smiles at her. *I think you might have actually hit the jackpot with this one. About time,* Millie says. She turns to face Beatrix, looking straight into her eyes. *We love people for all sorts of different reasons and in all sorts of different ways,* she says. *Remember that. And it only gets better, the older you get. Young love isn't necessarily the best love.* Beatrix nods, and Millie knows they're both thinking back to the same night all those years ago, the wineglasses in the sink, the unmade bed. It's time for her to let William go. She puts on a new coat of lipstick and blots her lips with a tissue before smiling at Beatrix in the mirror.

BEA

It's Opening Day, and Bea is sitting in a grandstand seat at Fenway. It's a little chilly, but it feels wonderful to be back. Bea remembers her final spring in America, when a group of them went to Opening Day. It was a Friday, she remembers, a bit foggy and drizzly but quite warm. They snuck out of their afternoon classes and ran down the hill to the trolley. She can't recall now who else was there, or anything about the game, really, but she remembers the smell of spring. The feeling of freedom. The rare joy of doing something illicit. She'd been a good girl for so long.

Gerald comes back to their seats with hot dogs and beers, and she bites down into the hot dog, wiping the mustard off her top lip with the napkin. *Nothing like this at home,* she says. *I'm so glad I decided to come. Me, too,* Gerald says. *Twenty years,* Bea says. *Twenty years since the last time I was at*

Fenway. Were you here, too, that day? Gerald shrugs. *I don't know,* he says. *I don't think so. Didn't you say you cut school to come? That wasn't really my thing.* Bea laughs. *Agreed,* she says. *It wasn't mine, either, the only time I ever did, but it was fun. I can't remember if we got into trouble for going. Probably your father talked to me sternly about the importance of rules.* They both smile and cheer on the runner headed for first.

William was probably here, Gerald says. *Maybe,* Bea says, *but I don't really remember.* She knows he was. Gerald nods. *That was a tough spring for him,* he says. *All those fights about college.* Bea nods but doesn't respond.

What happened with the two of you, Gerald says after a pause, not looking at her but squinting out at the field. *What happened in London?* Bea knows he's wanted to ask this. He almost did ask, again and again, when he was in London for the wedding. She could feel him trying to get there, trying to find the right words. And she's considered, over and over, how to respond. What the right answer really is. *What do you mean,* she says, stalling. *He had a few days, he was upset about your father, he came to see me. Bea,* Gerald says. *It's me. Not your mother, not my mother, and certainly not Rose. Me. What happened? This is important.*

Now he turns and looks at her. Freckles are still sprinkled on his nose. His honest gaze is still the same. *Nothing,* she says. *Nothing happened.* Gerald looks back at the field. *You told me you loved him, back when you were here for the funeral,* he says, cheers erupting around him as the Sox even up the score. *I did love him,* she says, *I do love him. He was my first love, Gerald, you know that. But, in London, in 1951, we were different people, even though only six years had passed. He was getting married. Rose was pregnant. We were no longer teenagers. There was no way we could have been together, even if we had wanted to.* She pauses, taking a sip of beer, looking out at the field. She can't tell him the truth. To hold on to that moment is the only way for her to hold on to William. She doesn't want to share him with anyone else, even with Gerald. *By the time he got to London,* she says, *the moment had passed.*

Really? he asks, turning toward her again, and he looks like the Gerald from those early days, so earnest and open. *Really, nothing happened?* Bea shakes her head, forcing herself to meet his eyes. *Honestly, G? We spent most of the time fighting. You know what he was like.* She watches Gerald try to smile. *We had a nice time together,* she says, *we did. When we weren't fighting. But he was sad and I was sad and we also had to deal with my mother.*

Wait, Gerald says. *Your mother was there?* Bea nods. *She'd been somewhere on vacation. Italy? Spain? With some friends. But she came home early, same time William showed up. So, we all spent the time together. I didn't know that,* Gerald says. *Somehow, I thought it was just the two of you. We had this awkward dinner in the kitchen,* Bea says. *She didn't make it easy for him. And then he left?* Gerald asks. Bea nods. *He took the train to Southampton. We said goodbye at the door of the flat. And that was it. Hard to believe that was almost fourteen years ago.*

Bea watches Gerald's jaw relax. Not telling him doesn't have anything to do with the way she feels about him. It's simply a way to protect what she and William had. And then they're both on their feet. A run is scored and the tie is broken and they're winning at last.

GERALD

After Rose and the children leave, and the dishes are done, Mother tidies up before heading to bed. *I know it's still light out,* she says. *But I'm beat. What a lovely day this was. It was indeed,* Bea says, holding up her arms to give Mother a hug from where she sits at the kitchen table. *And what a delicious lemon meringue pie. You outdid yourself. Thank you, my dear,* Mother says, and she lays a hand on each of Gerald's shoulders and kisses the top of his head. *I'll see you in the morning,* she says to Bea, *and Gerald, you'll come over to get Bea to the airport? Absolutely,* Gerald says. *I'll be here.*

Let's go sit in the living room, Bea says. Gerald nods and grabs two beers from the fridge before following her down the hall. The dark is just beginning to fall, and from the pair of armchairs by the tall windows, the highest branches of the trees are set in relief against the sky. *I love this view,* Bea says, settling into her chair, tucking her legs up under her. *It hasn't changed. All this land. I love my garden at home, but it's not this. It doesn't have this feeling of expansiveness.* She turns to Gerald. *I wish you'd seen my garden in bloom. I've become somewhat obsessed. Maybe you can come over this summer?*

I'd love to, he says, *although I'm planning to go to Mississippi again. So wonderful,* Bea says. *Really. Your father would be proud. Would he, though?* Gerald asks. *I don't know for sure. He's like Mother. A different generation. I think she believes this is just a phase, and by next year I'll take up golf or something, and move along. I don't think you give her enough credit,* Bea says. *Look where she came from. Look at how well she's doing. This is not the life she thought she would have. But she's managed, she's adjusted, she's figured it out. Did you see her dancing with Kat after dinner?*

They both smile. *That Kathleen,* Bea continues, *she has your father's brain. We've been playing postal chess, did I tell you? Her moves are something else — so similar to the kind of moves he used to make. But she looks and acts like you. Jack, though, reminds me of William. I told Rose this afternoon that she's going to have her hands full in a few years.* Gerald smiles. *How did she respond?* he asks. *She laughed and said she knew. That she already did.*

They each take a sip of beer. Bea wraps her sweater around her shoulders and yawns. *Do you want to call it a night?* Gerald asks, and Bea shakes her head. *I want to stay up as long as possible,* she says. *I don't want to miss a minute.* Gerald nods. *Who do you think you're like?* he asks after a minute. *Which of your parents? I don't know,* Bea says. *I really don't. It's not that clear for me. It's way muddier.*

Why? Gerald asks. *What do you mean? I had four parents,* she says. *I think a little of each of them is in me, in some way or another. It's a nice thought, though, isn't it,* she says, turning toward him and away from the darkening sky. *Dead or alive, we carry these people with us. Your father is always with me. That's lovely,* Gerald says. *That makes me happy.*

Bea is quiet for a moment. *This is the place that feels like my home,* she says, *no matter what I try to tell myself, no matter how hard I work to be at home there. I became who I am here. And I'm so happy to be able to come back. I'm sorry that it took William's death to allow this to happen, but there you have it.*

Gerald turns toward her and wants to hold her dear, familiar face in his hands. They hadn't switched on the lamps, and it's dark enough now that they are both covered in shadows. He can't quite see the contours of her face. He pulls the ring box out of his pocket, the one Mother gave him a few years back, having carried it around with him since the night before, never able to find the right words. He cups it in his hands, one hand under, the other over, not quite ready to open it up. *Bea,* he says, feeling his cheeks turn red — but knowing this must be the moment, that he needs to do this now if he's going to do this at all — *could you see your way clear to staying here? To truly making this your home?* She leans toward him, and now he can see, in the gaze of the moon, her cheekbones, her wide smile. She stands and holds out her hand, and he takes it, his palm touching hers. *Let's take a walk,* she says. *Let's take a walk together.*

■ ■ ■ ■

EPILOGUE:
AUGUST 1977

■ ■ ■ ■

GERALD

Today, the ocean is calm. From where Gerald sits, on the porch of the house in Maine, he can watch the few puffy clouds make their slow way out to sea. He sits here almost every afternoon, watching the water and the sky, smelling the air. It's been a warm summer and yet, there is always a breeze. He still can't quite believe they're back, that the house belongs to them once more.

They bought it in the spring, after learning from the Laskys that it was for sale. Mrs. Lasky called, and the next day Gerald drove up to put in an offer and to pay the deposit. It was like it was meant to be. There's a lot to do to get it back to the way it exists in his memories. And without Father, without William, it will never quite get there. But what a joy it is to be here, to sit on the porch, to hear the water on the rocks. He thinks of Father as he sits in his chair, the way he would so patiently wait for the sun to set, for the day to end. It is odd to think that he is now older than Father was back then.

Today is William's fiftieth birthday. A half century gone since he was born. He looms large in this place. On their first day back, when Lasky rowed them across, Gerald stared at the approaching island, the cluster of trees becoming more defined the closer they came. As he helped Lasky pull the boat up onto the rocky beach, he half expected William to be there, waiting, hiding behind a tree. *Race you to the house,* he would call, getting a head start, looking back with that half smile, and Gerald would follow. As he almost always did. But now Gerald is the one who is forging the way. He is the one who remains. He left the school ten years ago to start up a tutoring and counseling center in Dorchester, and now he manages seven sites and a team of young, energetic employees. His work is difficult and frustrating and exhausting — and he loves it.

Mother is in the kitchen, making a raspberry tart for dessert. He can smell the butter and sugar as the crust bakes. She is singing as she putters about. How happy she is to be back. Planning meals, gardening, sitting in the sun, her bathing suit straps pulled down off her shoulders. She wants to winterize the house so she can live here year-round. *Home,* she said on that first boat ride back, so softly that Gerald could barely hear her, her hands gripping the side of the boat. *Home.*

Early this morning, he went out to catch a bluefish for dinner. The water was calm then, too, a cool sheet of gray. It didn't take him long to find the one he wanted. On his way back in, the rising sun lit up the house and he rowed quickly, wanting more than anything to be back inside, to feel the warmth of the sun through the glazed windows. After putting the fish on ice and spritzing his hands with lemon, he checked on Nell, then crawled back into bed, wrapping his arms around Bea's familiar body. Home, indeed.

BEA

Bea waves at Gerald from her spot in a chair on the beach, a towel wrapped around her middle, as they both watch Nell swim out to the floating dock. She'll be eleven next week, born just a year after she and Gerald were married. She's a Gregory, with that copper hair and those freckles, that big, open smile. She has already made this her home. The past is more present here, and she's beginning to ask about those who are gone, interested now in the stories from before.

Returning to Maine was a dream, one of few that William and Gerald shared. After they got married and after Bea began running the Lower School, they started putting away money each month in the hopes that one day it could be theirs. It seemed almost too much to hope for. Now that they're here, now that they're back, Bea understands that they bought the place for themselves but also for those who are gone. There is a way in which they are now all here together. William, in particular, is never far from her thoughts. He is with her as she swims each morning, as she rows to town, as she wanders through the forest. Mr. G is here as well. And so, in his own way, is her father. But it's not just peopled with the past. Being back on the island allows the old to blend with the new.

Rose and Frank came up for a weekend earlier in the summer. They're living in Back Bay, walking to work at the State House. *Why didn't I know I was a career girl,* she asked Bea late one night. She's become a good friend. Bea often wonders, with a smile, what William thinks of that. Rose was pleased to be here, content to spend time in a place that means so much to them all. A place where William lives on. She brought a sign as a housewarming gift, a line from Shakespeare: WHAT'S PAST IS PROLOGUE. She said William would understand. It's now hanging over the front door to welcome everyone who visits. Bea hopes that next year she can persuade Mum to come over with Alan.

Kathleen and Jack are coming up later today, in part to celebrate William's birthday. They've never been here, of course, but they know all the stories. Kathleen told Bea on the phone the other night that she feels as though she, too, will be coming home. Jack is looking forward to swimming round the island, to beating Kathleen. They're both in New York, living three blocks away from each other on the Upper West Side. How did they know to go there? Bea wonders whether they understand that they are living one of William's dreams.

Nell is waving from the dock and Bea calls back, her words lost to the wind. Tomorrow, Kathleen will be out on the dock with Nell, the two of them lying on the hot wood in their bikinis, trading secrets, laughing, their hair wet and tangled. They look like sisters. Fourteen years apart and yet the best of friends. Nell waves again and then dives off the dock. Bea watches her as she swims to shore, her stroke steady and sure, and Bea will be there, as she always is, to cover her wet shoulders with the large, striped towel. Then they will climb the stairs to the second floor, and Bea will run her a bath in the old claw-foot tub. She will hold her hand under the stream of water until it is the right temperature. Nell will step into the water and lie back, closing her eyes. The little bathroom will fill with warm steam and the smell of lemon soap. Bea will sit there with her, on the worn wooden stool, as they make plans for Kathleen and Jack's visit, as they talk about all that is to come.

ACKNOWLEDGMENTS

Enormous thanks to Gail Hochman, my agent; Deb Futter, my editor; and Randi Kramer, my assistant editor, for loving this book, giving it a home, and helping to make it the best it could be. Rachel Chou, Jennifer Jackson, Sandra Moore, Christine Mykityshyn, Jaime Noven, Rebecca Ritchey, and Karen Xia — thank you for tirelessly championing my work. Anne Twomey and Erin Cahill — thank you for creating such a beautiful cover. And thanks to Morgan Mitchell and everyone else who took such care of all my words. Thanks as well to everyone at Brandt & Hochman and Celadon Books for their dedication, hard work, and enthusiasm.

My journey as a writer took off at the *One Story* conference in 2013. Will Allison and Hannah Tinti — I wouldn't be here without you. Jon Durbin — I'm so glad we've been on this path together. To Maribeth Batcha,

Kerry Cullen, Ann Napolitano, Patrick Ryan, Lena Valencia, and everyone else at *One Story,* past and present — thank you for publishing my first story and for all the love and support. It is a joy to be part of your family. I can't wait to be a Deb.

Rutgers–Newark was a marvelous place to get my MFA. Many thanks to the faculty there, including Jayne Anne Phillips, Rigoberto González, James Goodman, A. Van Jordan, John Keene, Akhil Sharma, and Brenda Shaughnessy. Extra thanks and hugs to Alice Elliott Dark, my beloved teacher and thesis adviser. Special thanks to Megan Cummins, Michelle Hart, Leslie Jones, Mel King, Aarti Monteiro, Anisa Rahim, Evan Gill Smith, Laura Villareal, Matt B. Weir, and Angela Workoff for their friendship and writerly love.

This novel would never have been completed without the help of the yearlong Novel Generator class at Catapult. Thank you to Julie Buntin for creating the class and to Lynn Steger Strong for being all that you are. Thanks to my wonderful classmates for their support and encouragement. Meghan Daniels and Rebecca Flint Marx — you are the best. I feel so lucky to share work with you.

I owe much to the many teachers I've

been fortunate to learn from over the years, including Robin Black, Andrea Chapin, Elizabeth Gaffney, Lauren Groff, Bret Anthony Johnston, Meghan Kenny, Ada Limón, Claire Messud, Ann Packer, Jim Shepard, Claire Vaye Watkins, and Meg Wolitzer. Thank you to the writers who inspire me, including Jamel Brinkley, Claire Keegan, Jhumpa Lahiri, Yiyun Li, Susan Minot, Elizabeth Strout, Colm Tóibín, and William Trevor.

Michael Henderson's memoir, *See You After the Duration,* is a wonderful account of his experience as a British evacuee in the United States during the war and provided the initial spark for this novel. The Imperial War Museum in London and the BBC's story archive were treasure troves of details and inspiration.

Thank you to the organizations who provided financial support and a place to write and learn: Rutgers University–Newark, Catapult, Kimmel Harding Nelson Center for the Arts, Sewanee Writers' Conference, Virginia Center for the Creative Arts, and VQR Writers' Conference. Thank you to the journals who published my work: *One Story, New England Review, Crazyhorse,* and the *Ploughshares* blog.

To all the writers I've been in workshop

with over the years — it was a joy to read your work, and your feedback was invaluable. Thanks, also, to my students, from whom I have learned so much. To all my friends and family — your belief and support has been lovely. Thanks to the Sunday afternoon Zoom fam for listening to the step-by-step birth of this book. And special thanks to Lorna Strassler for being my biggest cheerleader. I know her spirit was in the room when Gail read the novel for the first time.

My parents, Mary and Donald Spence, died before my writing journey truly began. How I wish I could have shared this part of my life with them. How I long to hand them a copy of this book: to hear my mother's cries of joy upon seeing the cover; to see my father smile, nod, and begin to read. This novel is both for them and of them: they are on every page.

To Hannah and Nate — you are my world. To Adam — thank you for over forty years of unending support and love.

And to you, dear reader: thank you, thank you, thank you.

ABOUT THE AUTHOR

Laura Spence-Ash's fiction has appeared in *One Story, New England Review, Crazyhorse,* and elsewhere. Her critical essays and book reviews appear regularly on the *Ploughshares* blog. She received her MFA in fiction from Rutgers University–Newark, and she lives in New Jersey.